"John English's son came here to talk."

Olivia was stunned by Darcy's news. "Sloan came *there?* I'm surprised. I thought he'd been sick."

"He *is* sick," said Darcy. "He passed out in the foyer. An ambulance had to come and take him away. He wasn't in any condition to be checking out his father's love life."

"Oh, dear. Do make sure Sloan's as comfortable as possible. He *is* our guest."

"He's *not* our guest. He just descended on us. He—"

"Now, there is absolutely no sense in you younger people having this Montague-Capulet mentality about our relationship."

"Mother," Darcy said with suspicion in her voice, "if you're comparing John English and yourself to Romeo and Juliet—"

"True love *can* happen quite fast. I used to think it was a myth—but it's not. Maybe you'll find out yourself someday."

"I might point out that Romeo and Juliet were kids who got into a lot of trouble by rushing into things. Utter disaster, in fact."

Dear Reader,

This is a story about old-fashioned romantic things: flirting,
love letters and courtship. But sometimes old-fashioned
romance takes surprising, newfangled turns.

If Cupid loves mischief (and he does), he must adore
e-mail. It gives him zingy new darts that are far-ranging,
super-speedy and very, *very* potent.

Darcy, the heroine, is shocked when her beautiful mother
falls in love with a man she's met on the Internet. She's even
more stunned when that man's son shows up on her own
doorstep.

He's determined to find out the truth about this unexpected
love affair. So is she. The last thing they expect is a love
affair of their own.

I hope you enjoy *P.S. Love You Madly,* and that it will bring
you a smile or two.

Happy reading!

Bethany Campbell

Books by Bethany Campbell

HARLEQUIN SUPERROMANCE
837—THE GUARDIAN

P.S. LOVE YOU MADLY
Bethany Campbell

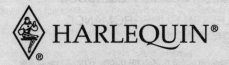

HARLEQUIN®

TORONTO • NEW YORK • LONDON
AMSTERDAM • PARIS • SYDNEY • HAMBURG
STOCKHOLM • ATHENS • TOKYO • MILAN • MADRID
PRAGUE • WARSAW • BUDAPEST • AUCKLAND

ISBN 0-373-70931-5

P.S. LOVE YOU MADLY

Copyright © 2000 by Bethany Campbell.

This edition published by arrangement with Harlequin Books S.A.

® and TM are trademarks of the publisher. Trademarks indicated with
® are registered in the United States Patent and Trademark Office, the
Canadian Trade Marks Office and in other countries.

Visit us at www.eHarlequin.com

Printed in U.S.A.

To My Roommate at Bentley's

CHAPTER ONE

IT WAS A SATURDAY MORNING in May, and the Texas Hill Country was in bloom. Wild roses clambered up the fences, violets blossomed along the creeks, and the bluebonnets blanketed the fields so thickly, it was as if they were turning the earth into a second sky.

The Hill Country was celebrating spring, and at its heart, the city of Austin celebrated, too. It was the time of the yearly Old Pecan Street festival.

But on his long drive here, Sloan English had paid no mind to the beauty of the countryside. Now in the festival's midst, he cared nothing for the city's revels. He wanted simpler things: to get back to Tulsa, find some sorely needed peace, and start putting his life back together.

Instead, he had come to Austin against his will to track down a woman he didn't want to meet. And she was not where she was supposed to be—right at the festival's center. She had vanished.

Not only had she disappeared, so had her shop. At the address where it should have been was a candy kitchen. It advertised, among other things, The Best Little Horehounds in Texas.

Sloan went in, glad to escape the insanely churning crowd outside. There was no one else within except an attendant behind the counter, a chubby woman with an eager-to-please air. She wore a white apron spotted with colored sugar sprinkles, and a name tag that said Velda.

She told him she hadn't lived long in Austin and had but an imperfect memory of the shop called The Prickly Poppy.

"They lost their lease or something," she said. "They been gone a couple months. You want to try the gumdrop of the day? It's jalapeño flavored."

He didn't want the gumdrop she offered, which was neon green and shaped like a chili pepper.

He shook his head. "You said 'they.' There was more than one person involved?"

She nodded, which made her multiple chins bob. "They were a cooperative or something. All women." She offered him a sample tray of nuts. "You want a spiced pecan? They just came out of the oven."

He didn't want a pecan. "These women—they were all artists?"

She took one herself and chewed it thoughtfully. "I guess. One made jewelry, and one did paintings, and one blew glass, and the other one—I don't know what they call what she did."

He narrowed his eyes, which were as green as a cat's. "What would *you* call it?"

Velda gave an expressive shrug. "She made weird things. Scarecrows. Kites. These sort of *doll* things."

"You mean like toys? For kids?"

She shrugged again. "Some of 'em was, some of 'em wasn't. She sort of did her own thing, you might say."

I'll bet she did, he thought. He said, "You know where she went?"

Velda helped herself to another pecan. "I don't know where any of 'em went. They've scattered. Like to the four winds."

He was tired, he felt feverish, and the too-rich scent of chocolate made his stomach squirm queasily. He set his jaw and said, "Who might know where she is?"

Velda licked her upper lip thoughtfully. "They might know at one of the galleries. These artist types, they come and go. She might even be out on the street—it's festival. Lots of booths and vendors. Just ask around. Somebody'll know. You want to try a honky-tonk surprise? They got tequila filling."

The last thing he wanted was a honky-tonk surprise. The pain was tripping in his temple like a tiny hammer. He thanked Velda and went back outside into the glare and the noise.

Sixth Street, with its bars and galleries and shops and restaurants, was considered the heartbeat of Austin, and today the heartbeat had gone mad with spring.

The arts festival was in full swing. The streets were roped off and bursting with tents that were cornucopia-full of Texas food and Texas merchandise. The scent of tacos and chili floated on the sun-warmed air. Young couples drinking champagne mimosas strolled the sidewalks, looking at the paintings, the pottery, the jewelry, the T-shirts.

The onslaught of the sun magnified the pain drilling at Sloan's skull, and he slitted his eyes against the brightness. His eardrums danced with the street's din. There were Native American dancers and lively Tex-Mex *cajuno* bands, country fiddlers, and even a harpist in medieval robes. A clown on tall stilts walked down the street with the swaying grace of a giraffe.

Fortune-tellers told fortunes. A face painter, crowned with flowers, painted the faces of children. Jugglers juggled. A large man with a bald head walked a pair of albino ferrets on a leash.

From a truck, a yellow dog wearing sunglasses watched the street with kingly indifference. Slowly, it turned its face toward Sloan, as if recognizing a fellow spirit. Its aloof expression seemed to say, *Lord, what fools these mortals be.*

Sloan thought, *You've sure as hell got that right, dog.*

But he set off on his own foolish errand, which was to find the woman.

The dog, looking more superior than before, stared after him a moment, then turned his attention back to the human carnival around him.

IN HER MAKESHIFT STUDIO beside the river, Darcy Parker worked alone. She had a deadline, and that meant she was spending her afternoon with a worm.

He was a bookworm, a comical soft sculpture that she had been commissioned to make for the children's section of the main library. He was four feet long, his flexible body composed of cuddly green-and-yellow globes.

He had a yellow head with a benevolently mad smile. He wore red spectacles and sported twelve pliable lavender legs. He was not exactly a handsome worm, but he was a winsome one, and Darcy was pleased with him.

This morning she had finally got his antennae right. Now she experimented, trying him in different poses. Worm—reading studiously in an armchair. Worm—standing on a library stool, reaching for a book on an upper shelf. Worm—stretched out on his belly on the floor, his head cocked over the Sunday comic papers.

You look good, Worm, she thought. *You just might be a star.*

She took snapshots for her files. Around her, the room was crammed with her other projects: stuffed toys, quilts, puppets, experimental clothing, fabrics she had dyed and silk-screened by hand. It was a happy hodgepodge that probably made sense to no one but her. But there was method in her madness—a great deal of method, in fact.

In Darcy Parker's nature was an equal mix of whimsy and practicality. She was successful at what she did, although she could not explain exactly what her profession was. Sometimes she was an artist, sometimes a craftswoman, sometimes a seamstress. She had a questing curiosity, and she followed where it led.

She was a whip-slender woman with a quick mind, lively eyes and clever hands. She was thirty years old. From her father she had inherited the midnight darkness of her hair; from her mother, her quick-silver smile and fair skin. Unlike her mother, she didn't hide from the sun, so she had a dapple of freckles sprinkling her nose and high cheekbones.

Her studio was makeshift, temporarily set up in the guest

cottage of her mother's weekend house on Lake Travis. She hadn't wished to impose on her mother. But when the lease in downtown Austin was lost, she'd had no choice.

The lake property was for sale, so Darcy didn't want to grow overly fond of the little house. It was airy and full of brightness, and she loved the sweeping view of the lake and the looming limestone cliffs.

There were no neighbors. She lived in splendid isolation. On Saturdays, Rose Alice, the housekeeper in town, drove out to vacuum and dust the lake house. She was a tough-looking woman with tattoos on both biceps, but she was hell on every sort of dirt. Her spanking white pickup was parked in the service driveway today.

Rose Alice didn't touch the guest house; it was Darcy's responsibility as long as she stayed. Besides, she didn't like anyone disturbing the disorderly seeming order of her studio, and Rose Alice attacked clutter with the energy and ferocity of a pit bull.

Rose Alice had taken one look at the studio room after Darcy moved in, winced, and shook her head. "No offense, kid," she said. "I love ya. But I don't think I ought to look in here again until you're gone. I got delicate sensibilities."

Before Rose Alice left the main house today, she would telephone Darcy and invite her over for coffee. She had known the family for almost twenty years, and, in her rough-spoken way, was fond of them.

"In the meantime, it's you and me," Darcy told the worm. "Want to curl up with a good book?" She wound him into a coil and put an oversize picture book in his grasp.

Darcy was kneeling to snap his picture, when her phone rang. It was Rose Alice.

"Hey, Darcy," she said in her sandpapery voice, "storm warning. The kid just drove up. She don't look happy. Something's wrong."

Darcy stiffened in apprehension. She loved her sister, but Rose Alice's tone was full of foreboding. "Oh," said Darcy. "Thanks."

"Batten down the hatches," said Rose Alice, and hung up.

With a sigh, Darcy set down the receiver and put aside her camera. There'd be no work done if Emerald was having a crisis. It had seemed lately to Darcy that perhaps both her sister and mother were calming down, getting their lives in order at last. Nothing could please her more. But Rose Alice's message was clear: it wouldn't happen today.

She heard Emerald stamping across the concrete service drive toward the guest house. *Curtain going up,* thought Darcy. *Let the drama begin.*

Emerald didn't knock. She burst through the door, clanking. She wore a good deal of chain mail and a buckler and sword. Her short hair was tousled by the spring wind, and her cheeks were red as flame.

She had been at the Pecan Street Festival with her fellow members of the Medieval Society. The Medieval Society usually turned out for the event in full costume, as knights or damsels or wizards or monks or warlocks. Emerald was presently in her warrior maiden phase, which she had described as "sort of Joan of Arc without the religion or politics."

Darcy crossed her arms and allowed herself the smallest of smiles. "This is unexpected. Why aren't you at the fair, jousting or minnesinging or whatever you do?"

"Somebody stepped on my lute, the clod," Emerald said with passion. "I had to go home for my other one."

"Hmm, sounds serious. When a man breaks your lute, doesn't that mean you're engaged—or should be?"

Emerald flashed her a resentful look. "You always want to make a joke out of everything. This is serious."

Darcy shrugged. "I'm sorry. Can it be restored to its former virginal state? Do you need a lute-repair loan?"

Emerald put her gloved hands on her hips. "This isn't about the lute, Darcy. This is about Mama. I'm *very* worried about her."

Darcy gave her sister a skeptical look. "Mama's fine," she said. "She just had her physical. The doctor said she's in wonderful shape."

"Mom's in *fabulous* shape," Emerald said, tossing her head. "That's never been the problem—has it?"

"No," Darcy admitted, but she thought, *It hasn't been much of a solution, either.*

Their mother, Olivia, had been a great beauty in her day. She was still stunning, tall and shapely, with platinum-blond hair she wore in a sleek chignon.

Emerald was small and wiry and brown-haired, like her father, and she had inherited their mother's blue eyes. Darcy had her mother's height, but she was dark-eyed and slim like her father.

Olivia had married three times. Now she was a widow, and if she was not exactly merry, she seemed content with her lot. She'd lived in Austin for the past twenty years, but had grown up Portland, Maine. When her third husband had died last autumn, she'd waited a decent interval, then bought a vacation condo back in Maine.

She wanted to spend her summers on the seacoast she'd loved as a girl. For the past month she'd been in Portland, working on the condo with a decorator.

"Oh, God," Emerald said in exasperation. She threw herself down in the studio's one armchair. This caused more clanking, and her sword stuck out at an awkward angle. "I don't even know how to tell you this."

"Would you take off that sword? You're going to run it through either my cushion or yourself."

Emerald ignored her. She threw back her head and stared at the ceiling dramatically. She sighed.

"I mean," Darcy said, brushing back a dark strand of hair, "if you went home, why didn't you take off the sword? Why didn't you change clothes? You didn't have to come stomping in here sounding like a bag of hubcaps."

"I was too *upset*," Emerald said, and scowled harder at the ceiling.

"Upset why?" Darcy demanded. "You said it's about Mother. What is it?"

"I'm trying to tell you," Emerald said righteously. She put her gloved hand over her mailed heart. "Oh, Gad."

Darcy cleared the scraps of Velcro from the corner of her worktable and sat on its edge. "Yes?" she prodded.

"I don't know where to start," Emerald said. Her voice quivered.

Darcy wanted to snap *just start, dammit!* But she knew this tactic never worked. Instead, she mustered her best semblance of kindly patience. "Well—why don't you just begin?"

Emerald slumped more deeply into the chair and gazed more fiercely at the ceiling. "Do you know that laptop computer you bought Mama?" she asked. She gave the word *computer* a sinister fillip.

"I should," said Darcy. "I'm the one making the payments."

She had bought the computer so their mother could e-mail them from Maine. It was cheaper than ordinary mail and than phoning, and Darcy, who was new to the computer world and excited about it, had thought it an inspired idea.

"Well," said Emerald, "you know how she said she had a phobia about it?"

Darcy waved away the thought dismissively. "Once she gets used to it, she'll wonder how she lived without it. That phobia'll fly out the window."

"It *has* flown out the window," Emerald said ominously. "And guess what's flown in?"

Darcy lifted one brow. "I can't guess. Just tell me."

"A man," wailed Emerald, sitting up straight again. "She's got herself a gigolo! This—this e-mail Don Juan. She's head over heels. She's gaga—she sounds like a teen-ager—our *mother!*"

Darcy looked at her sister and shook her head. "No," she said with certainty. "Not Mother. Not Olivia."

"She *has*," Emerald said, her cheeks flaming even more hotly.

"She's only had the computer six weeks," Darcy argued. "I don't think she's ever turned it on."

"She took it to Maine," Emerald said accusingly.

"Only because I nagged her. She hasn't sent a single message yet."

"Maybe not to you, she hasn't," Emerald said, her eyes suddenly glittering with tears. "But to *him* she's sent plenty. I've got proof—she sent me one by mistake. It's this—this steamy love note."

"What?"

Darcy did not want to believe this improbable news. Yet Emerald's tears were disturbingly real, and despite her sense of drama, she truly hated for anyone to see her cry.

Emerald got to her feet and began to forage in her scabbard. "Damn!" she said. She stripped off her black leather gloves and threw them to the floor. She groped in the scabbard again. "I've got the letter," she said. "I'll show you."

"You could," Darcy said dryly, "carry a purse, like other women."

"Joke all you want," Emerald retorted. "You won't think it's so funny when you read *this*."

She thrust a folded paper at Darcy, then angrily dashed the tears from her eyes. "Mama's too old for this kind of thing," she said bitterly.

The paper crackled as Darcy unfolded it—it clearly *was* an e-mail printout—but she told herself that Emerald had to be exaggerating; she always did.

But as Darcy read the message, she felt the blood drain from her face and her brain dance dizzily.

SUBJECT: I Saw You in My Dreams
From: Olivia@USAserve.com
To: BanditKing@USAserve.com
Copy To: MaidOfOrleans@USAserve.com

Hello, you big sexy thing—just a little mid-morning hello (and a hug and a kiss and a squeeze and another hug and another kiss…I could go on and on!!)

Last weekend was too fabulous; you're too fabulous.

I dreamed of you again last night, of your green eyes, your slow hands, your deep chest, and your divine Etcetera.

I had a thought for your free week—what do you say to coming here? I got the brochures you sent on lower Florida. You're right; it looks like an excellent buy.

Oh, darling, I've got to figure out when to tell my girls about this, but I think it's way too soon. They don't even know I'm online yet. You're so-o-o brave to tell your family.

But I will try to drop Em a short note today. I worry about her. I know she's twenty-one, and it's time for me to let her fly on her own, but it's hard for a mama to let go. You know, darling—you're a parent yourself.
Love to you (and your Etcetera)
Olivia, whose mouth waters for another taste of her BanditKing.

P.S. Thanks again for the anniversary roses. Who could believe we met only three weeks ago? Blessed be the name of the Chat Room. Oh, darling, we *do* live in an age of miracles!!

Darcy stared at the message in bewilderment. "Ye gods."

"Well," demanded Emerald. "Still think it's funny?"

"Maybe we're reading too much into this," said Darcy. "Maybe we're—misconstruing it." But the explanation struck her as pathetically weak, even as she said it.

Emerald snatched back the paper. "How do you misconstrue something like this—? Her 'mouth waters for another taste of her BanditKing'?"

"Maybe he's a chef," Darcy said lamely. "Maybe he cooked for her."

"Something's cooking, all right," Emerald retorted. "Mama's libido. She's spent the weekend with this man. She's going to do it again. And she barely knows him—it's here in black and white." She rattled the paper under Darcy's nose for emphasis. "Three weeks—and she's having an affair. She met him in a *chat room.* God—a seventh-grader would be more careful."

"Let me think," said Darcy. She raked her hand through her hair and tried to control her wildly spinning thoughts.

None of Olivia's marriages had been happy—certainly not the ones to Darcy's father or to Emerald's father. But the third and last, to Gus Ferrar, had at least been tolerable—some of the time.

Gus had been good-hearted, but oversexed and quarrelsome and brash. He had clearly adored Olivia, but just as much, he loved bickering with her. He had honed complaint into an art form, and the older he got, the more he demanded to be the center of Olivia's universe.

After Gus's death last year, a well-meaning friend had told Olivia that she was still young and attractive, that someday "someone else will come along."

"I'm through with marriage," Olivia had said with cynical conviction. "I'm through with *men.* I'm going to get a Pekingese. A Pekingese doesn't argue, it doesn't nag you about how much you spend, and you can make it sleep in a separate room."

Olivia had been true to her word. Because she was beautiful and well-off, eligible men tried to court her. She'd rebuffed them all.

"In my golden years, I'm going to be as chaste as a nun," she'd told Darcy. "Besides," she'd added thoughtfully, "sex has never been as much fun as shopping. Not really."

Olivia bought the Pekingese, got it neutered, and named it Mr. Right. Mr. Right was spoiled rotten and had an engraved collar of silver links and ate from a silver dog dish. But he made her sneeze, so she gave him to Rose Alice, saying that apparently she was allergic to all things male.

"Mama said she was through with men," Emerald fumed. She began to pace. "I don't want another stepfather. One was enough."

More than enough, thought Darcy, who had lived through

two. But someone had to be calm, she thought with wry resignation. It wouldn't be Emerald—she'd spent too many years competing with Gus for attention; his tempestuous ways had rubbed off on her.

"She's not going to marry anybody," Darcy said, almost certain it was true. "She's having a little fling, that's all. This thing will run its course, and she'll snap out of it. She's not a stupid woman. Or a naive one."

Emerald stopped pacing and drew herself up to her full height of five feet one inch. "She *is* naive. She knows nothing about the Internet or these chat room Casanovas. She's like a little child—a total innocent."

Darcy crossed her arms again. "Emerald, that letter was hardly written by a 'total innocent.'"

Emerald threw out her arms in despair. "But don't you see? She's at a terrible disadvantage here. She's only had experience with *real* men."

Darcy frowned, trying to digest this logic.

"This man is a fantasy," Emerald persisted. "He can pretend to be anything she wants. *That's* what she doesn't understand. I grew up with the Internet. But she has no idea what it's about—do you?"

Darcy felt an uncomfortable sense of disadvantage. She could use the computer for basic things, but she knew only a fraction of what Emerald did. Emerald had spent most of her teenage years cloistered in her room, communing with cyberspace.

"Well, *do* you?" challenged Emerald.

Darcy looked down at the library's bookworm, curled up at her feet. She thought about books and research and computers and networks of knowledge.

Defensively she said, "It's about communicating. And information. It's about accessing vast reserves of—"

"No, no," Emerald said with emotion. "The Internet is about *lying*."

Darcy gave her a skeptical look. "That can't be true. Al Gore wouldn't like it so much."

"It is—it's about lying," Emerald repeated emphatically. "You get in these chat rooms. You write messages to people you don't know. You can't see them and they can't see you—so what does everybody do? They *lie*."

Darcy shook her head stubbornly. "That's an exaggeration."

"It's not," Emerald tossed back. "Suppose I'm wandering around the Internet, and I meet a guy who seems interesting. Do I tell him I'm short, that I have a thirty-one-inch bust? That I'm blind as a bat without my contacts? That I've been on Prozac for four years? Of course not!"

"Well—" Darcy said. "Withholding a few facts at the start isn't lying...exactly."

"Right," Emerald replied sarcastically. "So this guy doesn't tell *me* that he weighs four hundred pounds and has the social skills of a clam. Or that he's a fourteen-year-old horny geek. Or worse, a horny old married man. Either way, he's horny. Because, first the Internet's about lying. And second, it's about sex."

Darcy blinked in displeasure. "Maybe that's true for some people. But Mama's an adult—"

Emerald narrowed her eyes. "Mama's a babe in the cyberwoods. *And* she's a rich widow. You think there aren't men out there waiting to pounce on women like her? Oh, they'll sweet-talk you, these guys. They'll make themselves sound like God's gift to women. Darcy, I've *been* there."

Darcy's confidence took an unsteady stagger. She realized that she had entered a realm where, for once, Emerald was far worldlier than she was. Emerald might be dressed as a creature of fantasy, but her words had the ring of cold reality.

"He's talking to her about investing," Emerald said ominously. "In Florida—swampland, probably. He's already sweet-talked his way into her bed. Next it'll be her bank account."

Darcy's muscles tightened. Olivia wasn't exactly conservative with money. To protect her, Gus had left her a generous monthly allowance dispensed from a trust fund, as well as a large sum to tide her over. But Olivia had already spent almost a third of the ready money on the property in Maine.

The rest of her inheritance was tied up in bonds and real estate. But not so tightly that a clever and determined man might not untie it—the lake house was already for sale.

The nickname of Olivia's new paramour echoed in her mind like an evil prophecy: *BanditKing*. Darcy thought, *My God! He could be a con man. He could ruin her. Take everything she's got.*

Emerald said, "Mama's never had much luck with men. This could be, like, the final insult. He could take all her money and destroy her pride."

The two women looked at each other, and Darcy knew they were thinking of the same thing: Gus's will.

To each of my stepdaughters, Gus had decreed, *I leave the sum of $10,000 in cash and the solemn charge to watch over the welfare of their mother. She's a wonderful woman, but stubborn, and frankly, sometimes she doesn't know her ass from a muffin.*

Only Gus would have slipped such a phrase in as staid and somber a document as a will—but there it was. Olivia, of course, had been furious, and the girls had only shrugged and smiled sadly.

Neither of them had expected to exert any control over Olivia, or to even have to. The purchase of the house in Maine was inevitable. She had talked about it for years. Gus, of course, had hated Maine. "It's cold, it's spooky, it's full of bears. Stephen King lives there. What does that tell you?"

Emerald squared her shoulders and put her hand on the hilt of her sword. "We were given a solemn charge to watch over mother. It's a matter of honor. You'll have to do something— right now."

"Me?" Darcy said, startled. "Do what?"

"You figure it out," said Emerald, raising her chin. "You're the oldest. Call her. Talk some sense into her. Call her now. Do you know her number?"

"I can't jump into it just like that," Darcy said. "I'm going to have to think of a way to do this tactfully. If that's possible. Good grief, the situation *couldn't* be worse—''

The phone rang again.

''What now?'' Darcy sighed and plucked up the receiver. ''Yes?''

Rose Alice's voice was rich with suspicion. ''There was this man just drove up, come to the front door. He wanted you. He wouldn't identify himself. He's on his way around there now. I said to him, 'Hold it, buster,' but he wouldn't stop. Gus's rifles are still in the gun cabinet. You want me to load up, come over there, show this guy the way out?''

Darcy struggled not to flinch. Rose Alice had once been imprisoned for shooting off a man's ear. ''No, no,'' she said. ''I'll handle it. Don't worry.''

''I'll keep my eye on him,'' Rose Alice promised. ''Don't you worry, honey. Rose Alice is right here.''

The line went dead. Darcy heard footsteps stalking up the front walk to the cottage. She and Emerald both turned toward the living room door.

There was a furious knock, so forceful that the very air of the studio seemed to shake.

''Who is it?'' Darcy demanded.

There was no answer except another hail of knocking, even more earsplitting.

''All right, all right,'' Darcy called, anger rising. ''Don't bang the door down.''

''What is this?'' Emerald asked apprehensively.

''I don't know,'' Darcy said, stalking to the door. ''Rose Alice says it's some man.''

She flung open the door.

A tall man stood there. He was expensively dressed, but his black tie was askew and his suit coat was off. His white shirt looked crumpled, and its sleeves were rolled up unevenly on his forearms.

With a jolt, she realized he was an extraordinarily handsome man—or would be, if he were not so lean that he was almost gaunt. His thick brown hair was unruly, and the forelock fallen over his brow gave him a dangerous air. His lips were unsmiling. His brows were dark and stern. His eyes were a feline green.

He looked at Darcy, then Emerald behind her, then at the bookworm curled on the floor. "Which one of you is Darcy Parker?" he demanded.

"I am," Darcy said. Her eyes locked with his. His gaze glittered with a frightening intensity. "Who are *you?*"

"My name is Sloan English. I've come from Tulsa. Your mother and my father are…acquainted. They seem to have met on the Internet. I think you and I had better talk."

A kaleidoscope of disjointed impressions reeled through her mind.

This man is hostile—
His father? My mother?
What does he mean?
This man is wild—

Emerald stepped to her side and took a militant stance. She gripped the hilt of her sword more fiercely. "Zounds!" she said between her teeth. "It's the son of that cur, the Bandit-King."

CHAPTER TWO

SLOAN BLINKED. The light was playing tricks—or he was sicker than he thought.

Another woman had appeared beside Darcy Parker, a woman who was little more than a girl. Yet she was dressed as a knight in a black leather doublet and breeches. She wore a jerkin of chain mail and ornate metal guards protecting her shins, shoulders and elbows.

Her hair was cropped short like a boy's. She was a delicate little thing, but anger flashed from her eyes. Around her waist was buckled a scabbard, and she gripped the silver hilt of a sword as if she were about to draw it and run him through.

He knew she had said something to him, but it was so extraordinary, so preposterous, it did not register. Perhaps he had dreamed it. Yet she seemed completely real.

"Churl," she snarled. "Varlet."

"What?" he asked, frowning.

The girl glared and started to say something more, but the Parker woman clapped a hand over her mouth. "Emerald—hush!" she commanded with such authority that whoever or whatever Emerald was, she hushed. But she kept her grip on the sword's hilt.

With effort, Sloan turned his attention back to Darcy Parker. The effort, he realized hazily, was worth it.

She wore faded blue jeans and a dark red T-shirt with a batik design of armadillos. She was half a head taller than the girl, slender but nicely curved. She had a mane of jet-dark hair pulled back in a ponytail, but strands of it had escaped and framed her face like waving wisps of smoke.

Her face was not one of classic beauty. It was sprinkled with freckles, and the jaw was too square, the nose too snub. But her eyes were so liquidly dark, he had the dizzying feeling he could fall into them and keep falling until he disappeared in their depths. His chest tightened, and it burned to draw breath.

Darcy dropped her hand from the girl's mouth, at the same time drilling her with a warning look. The girl stepped backward, as if forced by the other's sheer will. Darcy looked at Sloan again. One of her dark brows cocked in what seemed a combination of curiosity and suspicion.

"Mr. Sloan is it?" she said. "I think you'd better state *exactly* what your business is."

"English," he said, his chest growing tighter. "Sloan English." He offered her one of his business cards, holding it up to the screen door so she could see it before she took it.

It said Sloan J. English, Vice President, Development, PetroCorp Oil Company. It was an expensively printed card, meant to be impressive. She read it and looked as unimpressed as possible.

She didn't open the door to accept it. "Thanks," she said, "but we don't need any oil."

This straight-faced flippancy irked him. He stuck the card back into the breast pocket of his shirt. *Okay,* he thought. *That's the way you want it? Let's go straight for the jugular.*

He said, "Your mother is Olivia Ferrar?"

She folded her arms. There was neither anger nor shyness in the movement; it seemed coolly casual. "Yes. What about it?"

"My father is John English," Sloan said. "He and your mother seem to have met on the Internet."

"Our mother's met *someone,*" said the girl in the chain mail. "We don't know who. But he'd better watch his step."

Darcy's head whipped about, and once more she silenced the girl with a look. Then she faced Sloan again, her gaze measuring him with absolute self-possession.

Can she really be this calm? he wondered. *Or is she bluff-*

ing? He himself was not at his best, and he knew it. His head ached, his temples banged, and a small man with a drill seemed to be trying to make an excavation in the center of his forehead.

"Tell me what you want," said Darcy Parker.

Behind her, through the screen door, he saw a hallucinogenic welter of objects: kites, dolls, puppets, quilts. They made the background dance crazily.

He touched his fingertips to his forehead, then drew them away. He shook his head to clear it. "I'm sorry," he said. "This is—perhaps too sudden. I shouldn't have barged in here without warning."

She tilted her head to one side. "Right. You shouldn't have."

"My aunt's concerned," he said. "My father's sister. She—reacted strongly. She gets...overdramatic about things."

Darcy's mouth quirked slightly and a dimple played in her cheek. It was as if she were saying, *Okay. I can sympathize with that.*

What she actually said was, "What's that got to do with my mother or us?"

His temples banged more clamorously. He found himself putting out a hand to lean against the door frame. He realized that the underarms of his shirt were soaked with sweat, and his knees felt as if they belonged to someone else.

He struggled to give a sensible answer. "My father," he said, "and your mother are...involved. After a short time. An exceedingly short time. The Internet—they met there. My aunt was surprised. Shocked, actually. Perhaps this is also a surprise to you."

"Not—completely," Darcy Parker said. "You haven't caught me off guard. Not at all." Her smooth brow furrowed. "Are you all *right?*" she asked.

He ignored this question, trying to stay focused on the previous one. "As I said, my aunt reacted strongly. She told my father this relationship is—hurtling along too fast."

"Ha!" said the girl in the knight's suit. "See? I told you so."

"Emerald, hush," said Darcy over her shoulder. "You said you wanted me to handle this." She peered more closely at Sloan. "Mr. English, you don't look well. I asked if you were all right."

He realized he was far from all right. But he felt compelled to finish what he'd started. "The two of them quarreled," he said from between his teeth. "My aunt and my father. Now he refuses to talk to any of us about it. So I've been sent— as an emissary to your family. To see if you can…enlighten us about what's happening."

Her exotically dark eyes looked him up and down.

He hated himself for saying it, but he asked, "Would it be all right if I stepped inside, sat down a moment?"

"Don't let him in," said the girl dressed like a knight. "It might be a trick—like the Trojan Horse."

Darcy's face grew sterner. "Mr. English, I don't let strangers in my house. Not under any circumstance. I'm sorry."

He swallowed, suppressed a shudder. Her stare seemed to go through him like an ebony skewer, so he dropped his gaze to the bricks of her porch, which seemed to writhe and weave about in a most unnatural fashion.

"I understand perfectly," he said as civilly as he could. "I shouldn't have asked."

"That's right," she said.

He watched the bricks squirm and wriggle. He squared his shoulders and said, "Perhaps we can set up an appointment. Meet somewhere that you'd be comfortable. I don't think I have your current phone number. I couldn't find it. If you'd be so kind—I could call you, set up something."

She was silent a long moment, as he watched the bricks slither drunkenly beneath his feet. His feet, it occurred to him, suddenly seemed a great distance from the rest of his body, and his pulse clanged like cymbals in his head.

She said, "I had to change the number. I've just had some new cards made up. I'll give you one."

"That would be excellent," he said. *Alice in Wonderland,* he thought. *Didn't she get a long way from her feet? A very reckless thing for her to do... How could a person explain such a thing?*

"A mosquito," he said. The statement made perfect sense to him.

"Excuse me?" said the woman's voice. It was low and soft, but it echoed. *Excuse me, excuse me, excuse me.*

"A mosquito," he repeated. "In Kuala Lumpur."

"What?" said the woman, and her lovely voice echoed the word again and again, as if his mind had turned into a cave.

"A mosquito in Kuala Lumpur," he said with great effort. "I picked up some sort of fever. Not contagious. You needn't be concerned. It's not catching. I—I'll phone you."

The bricks were doing an interesting sort of polka now, way down there in the distance, whirling around his feet.

"I haven't given you my number yet," she said in her multiple voices. "Here—take it. Then I think you'd better go."

She opened the door. On rubbery legs, he stepped back to allow it. The edges of his vision darkened and kept darkening until only she was left at the center of his sight. She seemed to glow like a flame.

She held a card toward him. He reached for it.

"You're very beautiful," he said. She had become luminous, and the words seemed so truthful that they were mystical. They liberated him.

He tried to take the card, but it fell, fluttering to the bricks. She looked at it, then at him, her dark eyes widening.

He looked into those eyes and began falling. He felt he was falling down into something without end.

DARCY WATCHED IN HORROR as he took one step, then another, and began to collapse.

He would have pitched face forward onto the marble of the entryway if she hadn't broken his fall. He was a big man, but she managed to catch him in her arms.

She stumbled backward with the awkward burden of him. For a few seconds they were caught in a frightening dance in which gravity led.

She staggered, still desperately embracing him, and tumbled to her knees. But she did not relinquish him, and she kept his head from striking the marble. Clumsily she managed to turn him as she let his body ease to the floor.

"My God," she breathed. She had felt the heat of his body; it had been as if the man had a fire in him.

Now he lay at her knees like one dead. She put her hand on his forehead. It burned and was moist with fine sweat. His breath was shallow.

"What's wrong with him?" Emerald asked in a tremulous voice. "Did he have a fit?"

"He's got a fever," Darcy said. "Get me something to put under his head—now—quick."

With apprehension, she put her hand over his heart. Its beat beneath her fingers was strong and regular. But the white shirt was damp to the touch, and through it she could feel the hotness of his flesh.

She studied his face in bewilderment. The high cheekbones had hollows beneath them, and she saw that his tan was recent and not deep, as if he wore it as a mere illusion of health.

She wondered if he was having a fever dream, for there was a frown line between the dark brows. He had long lashes for a man, and they gave minute jerks as his eyelids twitched. The corner of his mouth twitched, too, as though some tormented impulse in him fought to speak.

She resisted the urge to touch that restless mouth, to try to sooth it. It was sensually shaped, yet the lines that bracketed it seemed to have been engraved by years of discipline.

He was handsome, but too thin. She remembered the feel of his ribs jutting beneath his shirt when she had held him for those few moments.

Almost guiltily, she smoothed his hair from his forehead.

Emerald, clanking, came to her side, dragging something. "Lift up his head," she said.

Darcy gritted her teeth and slid her hand beneath the man's neck and up to the back of his skull. His brown hair felt moist at the roots. She lowered his head to rest against the cushion Emerald had brought—before she realized it was the bookworm.

"Not *that,*" Darcy rebuked, and threw Emerald a sharp glance.

"You said to get something for his head," Emerald said defensively.

Oh, what the hell, thought Darcy.

"Should I call an ambulance?" Emerald asked.

"Yes," Darcy said. She touched his brow again. "He's burning up."

Emerald arose with the clinking of chain mail. Darcy bent over the man to loosen his tie and undo his top shirt buttons.

Rose Alice burst through the front door. "I saw the whole thing," she thundered. "I called 9-1-1. Don't touch him, Darcy. Get back. I've got him covered."

With a shock, Darcy saw that Rose Alice had one of Gus's golf clubs and was brandishing it at the fallen man.

"Rose Alice," she cried. "Put that down. He's *unconscious.* He's ill—this is a sick man."

"Probably drugged to the gills—" Rose Alice sneered "—I *thought* he had a funny gleam in his eyes. Never should have let him come over here. Get back, Darcy. I'll teach him to mess with my girls."

Emerald, halfway to the phone, had stopped dead and now stared fearfully at Rose Alice.

The man stirred. He gave a small groan, and a muscle played fitfully in his jaw. His head rolled back and forth against the bookworm.

"Stand back," commanded Rose Alice, her grip tightening. "He's coming to. If he tries anything, I'll knock his butt to kingdom come."

"Rose Alice," Darcy said in her most menacing tone, "put that *down,* dammit. Right now."

She put her arms around the man so that her body shielded

his, and she glowered furiously at Rose Alice. "I mean it," she said. "We're fine. *He's* the one in trouble. He's got some sort of fever."

Reluctantly, Rose Alice lowered the golf club. "I would have got a gun," she said. "But I couldn't find any bullets."

"Thank God," Darcy said. "Emerald—call. Make sure an ambulance is coming."

Emerald went to the phone, dialed and began to talk excitedly.

The man moved again. The frown line between his brows deepened. The dark lashes flickered restlessly.

Suddenly, his hand rose and clamped hotly on her forearm. His grip was surprisingly strong, and she stifled a gasp of surprise. Instinctively she tried to pull away, but he held her fast.

She found herself staring into a pair of green eyes that were narrowed in pain. He raised his head so that his face was close to hers.

"How'd I get on the floor?" he demanded. His voice was a harsh whisper.

"You fell," she said.

He sank back against the bookworm. "Sorry about that," he said. "Give me a minute. Then I'll get out of here."

He didn't relax his hold on her, but she hardly noticed. With her free hand, she smoothed back his hair. "No," she objected. "You've got a fever, a bad one. We've called an ambulance."

He groaned. "I don't want an ambulance. I'll be fine. Just let me rest a minute." His eyes squeezed shut, and he grimaced.

"You need to take it easy," she cautioned.

He opened his eyes and studied her face with perplexity. "You're the Parker woman, right?"

She nodded. She had a strange, swooping sensation in the pit of her stomach. "Right."

He put his free hand to his forehead. "And I showed up

on your doorstep demanding we talk about our parents, right?''

"Right," she breathed. His hair had fallen over his brow again, but this time she fought down the impulse to stroke it back into place.

He made a sound of disgust. "I shouldn't have come. This thing—it sneaked back up on me. I wasn't in my right mind. I'm probably not in my right mind *now*."

He swore and pressed her hand against his chest, and once again she felt the surging beat of his heart.

"Take your mitts off her," ordered Rose Alice.

He raised his head and looked at her in pained disbelief. Rose Alice was a large, stocky woman with peroxided blond hair. She wore ragged shorts and a T-shirt with the sleeves torn off. She did not pull the golf club back in a threat to swing, but she gripped it more tightly, and her arm muscles tensed. The movement made the tattoos on her biceps ripple.

"Who's *that?*" he demanded.

"My mother's housekeeper," Darcy said. "Please—lie back down."

Rose Alice said, "He shouldn't be hanging on you that way. It's too damn familiar."

"I'm sorry," he said, but he kept her hand pressed against his heart. "You keep the room from spinning round."

"I don't mind it," Darcy told Rose Alice. "Please," she said, turning back to Sloan English, "don't exert yourself."

"I think I hear sirens," said Emerald. "Hark." She stalked to the door with a jingle and metallic clatter.

Sloan gave her a puzzled scowl. "And who's *that?*"

"My sister," she said, trying to coax him to lean back again. "You said something about Kuala Lumpur. Is that where you caught this fever?"

"Yes," he said, sinking back. "And it's a devil. But you won't catch it. Humans don't pass it to humans."

Rose Alice curled her lip. "Says you. How do we know you're not running around spreading your cooties?"

"It's only transmitted by mosquitoes," he said.

"Girls," said Rose Alice combatively, "when he's gone, *spray*. Darcy, I wouldn't touch him."

"Rose Alice!" Darcy said, offended. "He just said it wasn't contagious."

"What's he know?" Rose Alice sniffed. "Him staggerin' around like Typhoid Mary, flingin' his germs this way and that."

"It's sirens, all right," said Emerald, staring out the door with interest. "It sounds like a lot of them."

Sloan English let go of Darcy's wrist. He struggled to rise. "I don't need an ambulance. I'll leave. I'm just causing trouble here—"

He heaved himself up enough to prop his weight on his elbows. Even that exertion made him gasp, and his chest rose and fell alarmingly. Darcy saw a vein in his temple banging like a small blue hammer.

"Please," she begged, grasping his shoulder to restrain him, "don't... Please."

His flesh was hard beneath her hand, the muscles lively. But his skin was still unnaturally hot and his shirt damp with perspiration. He struggled to a sitting position, and she could not stop him; for a sick man, he showed an astonishing amount of strength.

But then his strength failed him. He tried to pull himself to his feet, but instead toppled like a marionette whose strings have betrayed it. He would have struck the marble, but once again Darcy caught him.

He fell back, his head in her lap, his eyes clenched shut in frustration and pain. "Sorry," he rasped, "sorry."

The vein in his temple beat more violently. Darcy cradled his head helplessly. The sirens' whine grew higher, louder. "Help's coming," she whispered. "Just stay still."

His eyes opened tiredly. His head turned, and he stared into the grinning face of the bookworm. "My God," he breathed hoarsely. "What's that?"

"It's only a bookworm," she soothed, pushing it away.

"Shouldn't I be protecting *you* from it?" he asked, and tried to smile. Instead he shuddered, as if racked by a chill.

"It's harmless," she said. He squeezed shut his eyes, frowning, and shuddered again. She used the hem of her T-shirt to wipe the mist of sweat from his forehead, his upper lip. "Shh. Easy."

Sloan's hand fumbled to find hers again, then closed over it.

"Room's spinning again," he said through his teeth. "Anchor me."

She laced her fingers through his, held on tight.

The skirling of the sirens became unbearable, overwhelming. They filled the air, they beat on Darcy's eardrums, they sounded like all the hounds of hell about to close in.

Then came a moment of miraculous silence, so absolute she thought she'd gone deaf.

"They're here," Emerald said with excitement.

A flurry of sounds—metallic doors slamming, people's voices, hurried footsteps. Darcy thought she could hear a police radio in the background.

"Here!" yelled Rose Alice, opening the screen door. "He's in here! He's declared germ warfare on us! Hurry!"

Dammit, Rose Alice, lighten up. Anger flashed through Darcy, but vanished almost instantly, swallowed up by the chaos spilling into the house.

Paramedics swarmed inside. They pushed her away, they hovered over Sloan English, poking and prodding him. They barked terse, incomprehensible orders to one another. Darcy rose to her feet to watch them, but she felt limp and spent. Rose Alice and Emerald stood on the porch, talking animatedly to a tall policeman.

Attendants were strapping Sloan to a gurney and unfolding a blanket to cover him. "What'd he say he had?" asked a boyish paramedic with a shock of blond hair.

"Malay fever," said a stocky Hispanic woman, stowing a blood pressure cuff in a black bag. "It's an ugly bastard. It can come back on you."

"Ugh," said the youth, cringing. "Can we get it?"

"No way," she answered. She turned to Darcy. Her brown eyes were coolly professional, yet not unkind. "He said he'd been in the tropics. That right?"

"I think so," said Darcy. "He mentioned Kuala Lumpur."

"How long ago did he get this fever? Doesn't look like he really recovered from his first bout with it."

"I—I have no idea," Darcy stammered. She looked at Sloan, strapped to the gurney, covered now, his blanket like a shroud. His head rolled back and forth as if the fever were riding him into a land of nightmare.

"Will he be all right?" Darcy asked, touching the woman's arm.

"Should be," the woman said shortly. "Needs rest. Here—" she said. "He seemed to want you to have this." She handed Darcy the card she'd refused before. Numbly she took it.

The two male attendants began wheeling the gurney toward the door. Darcy quickly moved to Sloan's side. "Sloan—Mr. English—can you hear me?"

"Stay back, lady," the blond boy said. "You can't come."

"Sloan?" she begged.

His dark lashes flicked. He turned his head toward the sound of her voice. The green eyes opened. "I'll make this up to you," he said in a thick voice.

"It's all right," she said.

"We still have to talk," he said, then sucked in his breath sharply.

"Yes," she assured him. "We do."

"I—I never got your phone number," he said. "I dropped your card."

They were nearly to the ambulance now. She looked back at the porch. She saw her card lying at the policeman's feet. "I'll get it for you," she promised.

She turned and sprinted back to the porch, then snatched up the card. But by the time she ran back to the ambulance, Sloan's gurney had been loaded. They were shutting the doors.

"Please—please," she begged, thrusting the card at the woman. "Give this to him. It's important."

The woman looked at her, her expression unreadable, but reached out and took the card.

"Step back," said the ambulance driver. Darcy found herself pushed backward. The doors clanged shut. She watched as the driver climbed inside. He fired up the engine, turned on the hellish siren. He pulled away and left her standing there.

She watched it go, until it disappeared around the curve of the long drive. She looked down at the card in her hand.

It bore Sloan English's name and corporate title. It told her his business address and phone number, gave her a company e-mail address, but nothing else. It told her nothing of the man himself.

SUBJECT: WHAT HAVE I DONE?
From: Olivia@USAserve.com
To: BanditKing@USAserve.com

Oh, Lord, darling, what have I *done?* I hit the wrong button and accidentally sent a copy of the message I wrote you this morning to Emerald OF ALL PEOPLE!!!

She'll have kittens—medieval ones. She'll run to Darcy and carry on and make it sound as if I'm the scarlet woman of the Apocalypse.

Bloody computer. I could kick it around the block. Oh, hell—I could kick *myself* around the block. How could I pull such a fumble-fingered stunt?

I can only hope my girls will be as understanding as your family. Otherwise they'll think the little men in white coats should come and lock me up. Oh, sweetheart, I feel like such an utter fool. I hope with all my heart that this doesn't make any trouble.

Love and many desperate kisses,
Your Repentant Olivia,
Who now wishes she'd met you via carrier pigeon

SUBJECT: Calm Down, My Lovely
From: BanditKing@USAserve.com
To: Olivia@USAserve.com

My Dearest Olivia—
Not so much wailing and lamentation, dear heart. This
e-mail is a new sort of magic loosed on the world, and
like all magic, it can backfire as we try to master it. You
are like the Sorcerer's Apprentice, my dear, only far
lovelier.

My love, no one should be allowed to wrest from us
this sweet and delicate thing we have been fortunate
enough to find. Not your family, no matter how beloved
they are, and not mine.

But, most treasured Olivia, I have a confession. My
family did not take the news as well as I had hoped. We
had, in fact, a bit of a set-to about it.

I did not mean to deceive you, dearest, but neither did
I wish to burden you. As the Bard says, the course of
true love never did run smooth.

We must take these challenges as they come, and
calmly.
A thousand kisses,
Your Devoted John
P.S. What are medieval kittens?

SUBJECT: THE DARK AGES, OR SULKING AS A
MILITARY ART
From: Olivia@USAserve.com
To: BanditKing@USAserve.com

Medieval kittens don't just throw a fit; they set it on fire
and catapult it across the moat. Trust me on this, I've
been in the castle when it's under siege.

Darling, you say the wisest and most tender things,
but *exactly* what do you mean—your family didn't take
the news the way you'd hoped? That there was "a bit
of a set-to"?

My sweet, handsome, sexy John, *please* don't with-
hold things from me. You promised you never would.
What, *precisely,* are your sister and son saying to you
about this?
Concerned But Trying To Be Calm,
Your Own Olivia,
Who Loves You Truly, Madly, Deeply

CHAPTER THREE

"You have to phone Mother," Emerald said. "Right *now*. This has gone too far. Rose Alice nearly hit that man with a golf club."

Darcy turned to a mirror and tried to smooth her tumbled hair. Her heart still knocked unaccountably hard against her ribs, and the mirror showed her that her face was pale, but her cheeks bright pink.

"Da-ar-cee," Emerald said with something close to a whine. "I mean it. You've got to call Mama."

"Give me a minute," said Darcy, fastening her silver barrette. She took a deep breath to calm herself.

The studio was quiet again. Rose Alice, still in high dudgeon, had stalked back to the house, obviously feeling unappreciated. The ambulance had left; the police cars were gone.

Sloan English's BMW still stood in the driveway, and Darcy supposed someone would be sent for it. It was the only sign the man had been there—except for his business card. It lay on the bookcase between a vase of fantastic silk flowers and a sock monkey.

The card was nothing, she told herself—a scrap of paper with fancy engraving, a boring corporate ID signifying nothing. *Wrong,* said something deep and unexpected within her. *It signifies him. Why does that make my heart rattle like a trapped thing shaking the bars of a cage?*

She shook her head to clear it, but his image wouldn't go away.

Emerald sat in the armchair watching her closely. "You

certainly fussed over him," she accused. "Was it because he's handsome?"

Darcy turned from the mirror with an innocent air. "Handsome? Was he? I didn't notice."

"Ha," sneered Emerald, polishing the studs on her gloves. "He's handsome and you noticed. But you'd better remember—he's the enemy."

"He's not 'the enemy.' Don't be melodramatic."

"I don't have to," Emerald said with a superior look. "He was melodramatic enough for everybody. He roars up to the door like a fire-breathing dragon. He rants. He raves. And then he falls over."

"He wasn't himself," Darcy said defensively. "He was ill. I don't think he knew how sick he was. His fever affected his judgment."

"It was kind of cool how he keeled over that way," Emerald said, pulling on her leather glove and admiring it. "Like he had the plague or something. I wonder if that's how they did it during the Black Death."

"Oh, really," said Darcy, turning from her in irritation.

She picked the bookworm up from the floor. She set him on the worktable and adjusted his antennae.

"Anyway, you *have* to call Mother," nagged Emerald. "That man's in the hospital—somebody's got to tell his family. She's the only one who knows anybody, so you've got to. Unless you want his people to just get a cold, soulless call from the police."

"I thought you considered them the enemy," countered Darcy. "Why all this tender concern?"

"Well—" Emerald shrugged "—I *have* taken a vow of chivalry and courtesy and all that. Besides, it sounds like some of them might be on our side."

Our side. Their side. Darcy fought not to flinch. She didn't want her mother hurt by a frivolous and possibly dangerous romance, but neither did she want battle lines drawn.

Nor did she relish being the bearer of bad news. When she

called her mother, she would deliver bad news not once, but three times over.

First, she and Emerald had learned of Olivia's headlong affair, something Olivia had obviously wished kept secret, at least for now. Second, BanditKing's family was also upset about the romance, sufficiently so to send Sloan English. And third, Sloan had been carried off to the hospital—and who knew how sick he was?

"Of course," said Emerald, "I could ask Rose Alice to call. She wouldn't be scared. She doesn't mince words."

Darcy wheeled to face her sister. "I'm *not* scared. It's just that this is—a delicate matter. I have to think how to do it."

"Just spit it out the way you usually do," Emerald said. "You've always been mother's daughter in *that*."

"All right, fine," Darcy grumbled, hooking her thumbs in the back pockets of her jeans. "I'll call. But I want some privacy. Go take a walk by the lake or something."

"She's my mother, too," Emerald said, her chin high. "I have a right to stay and listen."

Darcy drilled her with a look that would have made Attila the Hun obey. "Out," she ordered.

With a resentful expression, Emerald went.

Darcy watched her leave. Then she gritted her teeth in uneasy anticipation and reached for the receiver.

OLIVIA FERRAR was a tall woman, slender and straight-backed, with her hair swept back in a chignon. Her face was still lovely, though not unmarked by time. Laugh lines crinkled the corners of her blue eyes and bracketed her mouth.

The mouth itself was usually set at an amused angle, and the eyes had a cool, irreverent twinkle. She was dressed in a cream-colored caftan that emphasized her graceful carriage, and the diamonds in her ears and on her fingers were tastefully understated.

Her condo overlooked a craggy strip of dark shore and a foaming sea. Spread on its rented sofa were wallpaper samples, fabric swatches and paint chips.

The smell of fresh paint hung heavily in the air. The old carpeting had just been, as her decorator said, "terminated with extreme hostility." Olivia felt as if she were living in a five-room war zone.

But she had created a fragile island of peace in the front bedroom. She headed for it now, leaving the disordered living room. She was unusually pensive this afternoon, wondering how long she had before she heard from her daughters.

For she would hear from them. Of this there was no doubt.

They had been fine when dealing with a mother who had forsworn men. She doubted they'd be nearly so accepting now that she was having a passionate affair. Emerald, especially, would not.

For weeks now Olivia had come into the refuge of the bedroom with pleasure and excitement. It was where she usually communicated with her darling John.

She'd put a simple TV table next to the windows overlooking the harbor. On the table she'd set up the new computer, as if she were placing it on a shrine.

She did not, of course, think of the computer as a god. But it was as if she had miraculously been given a servant with magical powers—a benevolent troll, for instance. It existed to do her bidding, and at any time of the day or night, it fetched and sent love letters with breathtaking speed.

But today for the first time, the troll had whipped off its friendly mask and shown its ugly side. Its benevolence vanished in a twinkling—and it gave Olivia a frightening glimpse of its infinite capacity for mischief.

Olivia stared at the shiny little box squatting so proudly on her table. "Trickster," she muttered. "Electronic toad. Traitor."

She sighed and turned away, knowing the computer hadn't betrayed her secret to her family. The fault was hers. Yet how was a woman to know that a machine so small would have so many confusing features? And that a simple tap of the keys could accidentally send one's most private thoughts zipping around the stratosphere?

What made her feel worst was her fear of how the wayward e-mail message would upset her daughters. She loved her girls deeply and worried about them more than they knew. The last thing she wished to do was to worry them in return—especially Emerald.

Emerald had always needed the safety of her family, and until recently she'd needed it too much. The only friends she had were those in the Medieval Society, and the only time she seemed comfortable was playing a role. A senior at the University of Texas, she'd been offered dozens of scholarships, some quite wonderful. But Olivia knew Emerald would probably reject the best; the thought of going very far from Austin filled the girl with anxiety. For all her flamboyance, she was secretly shy.

Darcy, in contrast, was independent to a fault. She was talented, she was successful—but she seemed not to care a bit for money. She waved away fat contracts and sweetheart deals, determined to follow her own, often peculiar, interests.

Darcy was self-sufficient in other, more disturbing ways, as well. Men were interested in her, but she was seldom interested in return, at least not deeply or for long. She claimed she would never encumber herself with a husband. Lately Olivia had been beset by a nagging wish for grandchildren, but she was beginning to fear she would never have them. Perhaps both her daughters were too unconventional for marriage.

The phone rang, and she knew who it would be. Not John, who would be at work at this time of day. No. It would be her offspring, demanding to know if she'd lost her marbles.

The phone rang again, and Olivia squared her shoulders. She did not like confrontation, but after twenty years with Gus, she certainly didn't fear it. She sighed, ran her hand over the perfect smoothness of her hair, and picked up the receiver.

''Mother, it's me,'' said Darcy.

Olivia was relieved to hear Darcy's voice. Darcy certainly

had her eccentricities, but she was a rock of stability compared to Emerald.

"Darling," Olivia said with admirable calm, "I've been *expecting* to hear from you."

"You have?" Darcy's tone was cautious.

"Yes," said Olivia. She looked out the window and watched the gray sea froth against the dark shore. "Did Emerald ask you to call?"

"Well, yes, actually, she did." Darcy paused. "Do you know what this is about?"

Olivia drew in a calming breath. "I accidentally sent her a copy of a letter meant for someone else. The blasted keyboard has too many keys. I keep hitting things I don't mean to hit. I suppose she went and read it."

"Yes," said Darcy. "She did."

"And I suppose she came running with it to you."

"Yes. She did."

"And I suppose *you* read it."

"Yes. I did."

Olivia believed the best defense was a good offense. "In my day," she said loftily, "we wouldn't dream of reading another person's letters. It would be considered the vilest form of snooping. The mail was *sacred*. Privacy was *respected*."

"E-mail isn't real mail, Mother. No law protects it. It's about as private as a billboard. You shouldn't say anything in it you wouldn't want the world to know. I could take that letter and copy it a hundred times and tape it to every telephone pole in town."

Olivia frowned. "That's shocking violation of rights," she said. "I will write my congressman."

"You do that," Darcy said. "It won't change a thing. In the meantime, Emerald's concerned over your involvement with this—this BanditKing person. I'm a bit concerned myself."

"Do I intrude on your love life?" Olivia challenged. "No,

I do not. Not since you were fourteen and came home with that dreadful hoodlum with the green hair and the nose ring.''

"He grew up to be an accountant," Darcy said. "He belongs to the Conservative Voters League and the Rotary Club."

"Obviously not your type, either way," said Olivia. "Not that I'm a meddler. And I'll thank you not to meddle, either."

Ha—take that, Olivia thought. Darcy loved her freedom too much to be comfortable interfering with someone else's.

"I don't want to meddle," Darcy said, and to her credit, she sounded as if she meant it. "But Emerald's worried. She says you have to be extremely careful about getting involved with someone on the Internet. She knows her way around it better than you and me put together."

"Emerald sat in her room talking to boys who pretended they were wizards and Vikings. She only knows about the *fantastic,* not the real."

"Isn't this romance moving awfully fast?"

"Fiddle-dee-dee," Olivia said with blitheness she did not really feel. "I am an adult and, if I do say so myself, a woman of some sophistication and experience. I can handle my own business, thank you very much."

Olivia bit her lower lip and waited for Darcy's reply. In truth, she was herself amazed by how quickly she had fallen in love with John English. She felt she knew him better and more deeply than she had ever known another human being. And, miraculously, he felt the same about her.

Olivia had spent her adult life hiding her emotions behind an aloofly flippant attitude. But somehow John English saw through the facade to the vulnerability she had never let another person glimpse.

"Mother," Darcy said carefully, "this is so *unlike* you."

"No, it's just unlike my marriages. No man's ever treated me this way before," Olivia said, and it was the truth. "He's kind and affectionate and understanding. I can talk to him about anything, and he's always interested. I truly did not know the male of the species could be so sensitive and caring. It's a new experience.''

"But you haven't really—" Darcy sounded uncomfortable "—you don't really know each other that well."

Olivia smiled and thought, *You've got no idea, darling.*

The letters between Olivia and John had opened into intimacy with amazing swiftness. It was as if, cut loose from earthly bonds, the letters let them explore each other's mind and soul in supernatural detail. Such mingling of thoughts and emotion quickly led them to question if sex could have the same, almost perfect, intensity. It did.

"Mother," Darcy said in the same uneasy tone, "this isn't easy to ask. But this man—"

"John," corrected Olivia. "He's not 'this man.' John English. Of Key West, Florida."

"Fine. Whatever. John English," said Darcy. "Do you have any idea how *his* family feels about this?"

This question came as an unpleasant surprise to Olivia. She realized that although her closeness to John seemed absolute, he had been hesitant about discussing the *exact* nature of his recent trouble with his family.

"His kin have been good enough to spare me their opinions," Olivia said.

"Unfortunately, they haven't spared *me,*" Darcy said. "John English's son came here to talk."

Olivia was stunned, horrified. "He came *there?*"

"Yes," said Darcy. "To the guest house. Emerald was here—she'd just gotten your letter. Then *he* showed up. Sloan English."

Olivia felt as if the wind had been knocked out of her. "Oh," she said. "Yes. Well. Sloan. We've never met. But— I'm surprised. He just got back to the States. I thought he'd been sick."

"He *is* sick," said Darcy. "He passed out in the foyer. An ambulance had to come and take him away. He's in the hospital."

"The hospital! My God," said Olivia. "Is he going to be all right?"

"I have no idea," answered Darcy. "But you'd better tell your Mr. English. We had quite a scene here."

"A scene?" Olivia asked, feeling suddenly queasy.

"Rose Alice wanted to hit him with a golf club. She couldn't find the bullets for the guns."

Olivia put her hand to her forehead.

"And Emerald was in full knight rig, ready to run him through—but nobody stabbed him, nobody shot him."

"Dear heaven. He'll think we're all insane."

"Mother, he wasn't quite in his right mind himself. He had a fever of a hundred and four. He wasn't in any condition to be checking out his father's love life."

"Oh, damn, oh, dear," Olivia said, flummoxed. "It doesn't sound like what I've heard about him at all—just the opposite. Well, he shouldn't have done it. It's an invasion of your privacy, and it's a threat to his health. He's been a very sick man. I'll have to tell John. What a shock. Which hospital?"

Darcy told her. "What exactly *is* wrong with this man, Mother? He said he had a fever he caught abroad, but—"

"Malay fever," Olivia said. "There's no cure for it but rest. He was supposed to be convalescing. Oh, John will be *so* upset. Do make sure Sloan's as comfortable as possible. Please. He's our guest—in a way."

"*Me?* Make him comfortable?" Darcy was obviously appalled. "He's *not* our guest. He wasn't invited. He just—just descended on us. Now I know he wasn't himself, so it may not be completely his fault, but—"

"No buts about it," Olivia said. "He's the son of my very dear friend. There is absolutely no sense in you younger people having this Montague-Capulet mentality about our relationship."

"Mother," Darcy said with suspicion in her voice, "if you're comparing John English and yourself to Romeo and Juliet—"

"True love *can* happen quite fast," Olivia said with authority. "I used to think it was a myth. It's not. You may find out yourself someday."

"I might point out that Romeo and Juliet were kids and got in a lot of trouble by rushing into things. Utter disaster, in fact."

"Only because their families wouldn't act civilized," Olivia retorted.

"Wait, wait, wait," Darcy begged. "You're turning everything around."

"I'm in love with John," Olivia said. "I hope to remain in love with him for the rest of my life. And I hope all of our children can learn to coexist like mature adults."

"And I'm sure we all hope that our parents will act like mature adults," Darcy said with unpleasant sharpness.

"A member of John's family is ill in Austin," Olivia said loftily. "My family lives in Austin. A member can look in on him and see to his well being. It is, Darcy, nothing more than simple courtesy."

"Mother, it's anything but simple."

"It's plain old-fashioned good manners," Olivia returned. "And it is *not,* I think, too much to ask. Goodbye now, darling. I need to call John immediately. Love to you and Emerald, too."

"Mother—"

"Kisses for you both," she said, and hung up.

Olivia stared out at the ocean, the white surf breaking on the rocky coast. She rebuked herself for her cowardice. But she had meant to reveal things to the girls at her own pace, little by little. Darcy was strong, but Emerald was a different matter. Olivia feared springing things on Emerald.

So Olivia had said nothing about the brand-new engagement ring on her left hand. And she did not yet intend to.

She picked up the phone and dialed John's number. "Oh, sweetheart," she said apologetically. "I hate to call you at work. But this really *is* an emergency…"

SLOAN FELT LIKE A JACKASS.

He'd been wheeled into the emergency room with as much melodrama as if he'd been spurting blood from a dozen gunshot wounds. He'd been poked, prodded, squeezed, palpated, stripped, sponged and medicated.

Now he was trapped in a hospital room with a small, withered nun with cold hands. She had a thermometer in his mouth and was feeling the glands in his throat with her icy fingers. Her touch gave him an attack of the chills so severe that he feared he would bite the thermometer in two and die of mercury poisoning.

The phone beside his bed rang, but when he reached for it, she slapped his hand back. She picked up the receiver herself. "This is Mr. English's room," she said in a voice so brisk it crackled. "Sister Mary Frances Foley speaking. Mr. English can't talk right now."

"Yes, I can," said Sloan around the thermometer.

The little woman glared at him. "No, you can't," she snapped. She addressed the caller again. "May I take a message?"

She listened, then covered the receiver and stared at him through her wire-framed bifocals. She had pale eyes that seemed to look directly into his brain and see all the sins he had ever committed and all that he would commit. "It's a woman," she said disapprovingly. "A Darcy Parker."

Sloan felt his face flush, his shudder of cold replaced by a surge of heat. He didn't know if it was due to his fever or to the mention of the Parker woman. If the woman caused it, he didn't know exactly *why*.

Was it shame over how foolishly he had gone to her door, his judgment warped by fever? He supposed it was. Yet the memory of her dark eyes and slender curves stirred a warmth in him that he suspected had nothing to do with Kuala Lumpur and its mosquitoes.

"Miss Parker has a question, but—" The nun paused dramatically, then held up her hand like a traffic cop. "*I do not want you to speak.* I will give you a notebook. On it, you will write down your answer. Answer clearly, write neatly, and don't ramble.''

Sloan gave her a stare that told her he was not pleased with her high-handedness. She gave him one that told him she did not care.

She withdrew a notebook from the folds of her black gown and set it down smartly on his bedside tray. It had a black pencil attached.

She said, ''Miss Parker says your car is at her house. You left it open with the keys in it. She wants to know if you need anything from it. Or if you want the car taken some-where.''

Sloan scowled and wrote *There's an overnight bag in the trunk. Tell her to put it in a cab. I'll pay for it. I'll send someone for the car later.*

He paused and thought again of raven hair and a quirking, voluptuous mouth. He gripped the pen more tightly and added *Thank her for her kindness.*

The nun related his message, then listened again. ''No, he's doing well,'' she said. ''He's having his temperature taken, that's all. And he needs his rest. Goodbye.''

She hung up, glanced at her watch and took the thermom-eter from his mouth. She gazed upon it without emotion. ''You've gone down a degree.''

''What did she say?'' Sloan demanded. ''Miss Parker.''

The nun marked his chart with painstaking care. ''She said that she'll bring your bag herself.''

''She doesn't have to do that. I told her to send it by cab.''

''I wouldn't object to a kindness,'' the sister said primly. ''There's little enough of it in the world.''

''I mean, she doesn't have to go to the trouble.'' He hes-itated, then tried to sound nonchalant. ''She, uh, asked how I was?''

''I thought that was obvious from my end of the conver-sation.'' Neatly she shut the notebook, restored it to the folds of her black garment, and turned away. She left the room so silently that it was as if she weren't walking, but levitating just above the surface of the floor.

He looked after her, half wondering if she had been a hallucination. Why did half the women he'd talked to today seem as if they'd come from fever dreams?

There had been Velda with her jalapeño gumdrops, the girl dressed in chain mail, and the large woman who'd been built like a World Federation wrestler and who had brandished a golf club at him. It was tempting to dismiss them as creatures of a delirium.

On the other hand, there was Darcy Parker, just as unexpected and not at all easy to dismiss. He thought, *I was lying in her lap. Her arms were around me. I was foolish and weak, but she tried to give me comfort. Her breast touched my cheek...*

"Oh, hell," he muttered, trying to thrust away the image.

He was a man used to being in control. She'd seen him when he wasn't. He didn't relish her seeing him again in circumstances just as pathetic—stuck in a hospital bed wearing a stupid hospital gown, having nuns and nurses descend upon him.

He opened the drawer of his bedside table, fumbled in his wallet for her card and found it. He would call her, tell her not to come. He reached toward the receiver. He would wait to see her until he was his old self, back to normal and once again in charge of his destiny.

But before he could touch the phone, it rang. He frowned and picked it up. "Hello?"

"This is your father," said John English's voice. "I don't know what to ask first. How the hell are you? Or what the hell are you doing in Austin?"

Sloan gritted his teeth and fell back hard against the pillow. "Hello, Dad," he said with resignation.

The last time they'd talked, his father had hung up on him. That, in a way, had triggered the entire circus of fever and folly in which he now found himself.

"I talked to the doctor who admitted you," John English

said gruffly. "He said that damn fever's recurred. That you'll be fine—if you'll rest."

"Yeah, yeah," Sloan said. He glanced around the barren hospital room. It looked as amusing as the inside of an empty eggshell. "I'm resting right now. I'll be fine."

"You were *supposed* to be resting in Tulsa—what happened?" John demanded. "This is how you got so sick in the first place. You wouldn't slow down. Oh, no. Not you, the iron man."

Sloan shrugged irritably. "It crept up on me. I didn't realize it, that's all. It's no big deal."

"You're in the hospital, but it's no big deal. I see."

"I lost consciousness for a few seconds," Sloan said, sneering at the absurdity of it. "They put you in the hospital for that these days—for observation. People overreact."

"You weren't supposed to be running all over creation," John accused. "You were supposed to be *recuperating*."

"I felt fine. I felt great." It was the truth. He'd jogged the day before—five miles, like the old days. His body had sung like a finely tuned string. He'd felt like himself again.

But then he'd gone back to his apartment, and his aunt had called, and she, who for years had manipulated his emotions, had wept and begged.

Now he put his hand to his forehead, which was still hot. Remembering Trina made his temples throb again. He squeezed his eyes shut against this energetic new onslaught of pain.

"So you took off for Austin," John said suspiciously. "And you went to see—to *confront*—the daughter of the woman I love. May I ask why?"

It seemed like a good idea at the time, Sloan thought, his head aching harder. "I was passing through," he lied. "I thought it might be good to meet."

"Ha," snorted John. "Why? Because Trina's 'worried'? She put you up to this, didn't she? Her and her goddamn emotional blackmail."

Sloan massaged his eyebrows. The old man was plenty

sharp in his way. Yes, Sloan had come to Austin half to placate Trina, half to appease his own demons. Trina had helped create those demons, and for years she had nurtured them.

He'd been a fool to come here. But she'd pleaded, and her pleading worked partly because he owed her. So, for that matter, did his father. Promises had been made. An honorable man kept them.

"Olivia's a wonderful person," John said. "Trina's jealous, it's that simple."

"Dad," he said wearily, "why'd you even *tell* her about this woman?"

"Because it's the truth," John shot back. "Hell's bells. I get sick of pussyfooting around with Trina. She's fifty-eight years old. Every time something doesn't go her way, she pulls her martyr act. Think about it, boy."

I can't. A mosquito just pinned me, two falls out of three. Sloan touched his aching head. Lord, he was too tired to think anything, let alone of the complexities that Trina had created in his life—and in everyone else's. Someday when he was old and gray, he would hobble off to a hermitage and meditate until he figured it out. In the meantime, he simply wanted his head to stop thudding.

"Trina asked me straight out if I was seeing a woman," John said defensively. "I don't know how she knows these things. Maybe she has flying monkeys that report to her, I don't know. But I thought, Why should I lie? I told her the truth. She kept asking. I kept telling. Until she said, 'God have mercy on your deluded soul' and hung up on me. Me— her own brother. Her own flesh and blood."

"Um," Sloan said, massaging his brows again. "So when I called, you hung up on me. Your own flesh and blood. Why? Payback time?"

"Hell, you *said* you'd just talked to her. I knew she put you up to it. I refuse to play her games anymore. If you were smart, you wouldn't let her catch you up in these things."

Sloan grimaced. His father was right; he shouldn't have let

Trina pull his strings. If he'd been well, it never would have happened. Yet, for all her carrying on, Trina had a point. John should not plunge into another marriage. He had bad luck picking women.

His father's tone changed to one of concern. "I told you we'd talk when everybody was calmer. That time is probably not now. You sound worn out. I'll call again—later."

"Dad," he said, "my main concern is that you and Trina have an *understanding* about certain things. For instance, there's—"

"Later, son," John said with surprising gentleness. "Don't worry about Trina. Take care of yourself."

"Dad—"

"Goodbye for now. Get some rest."

The line hummed meaninglessly in his ear. He opened his eyes long enough to hang up the receiver, then sank back against the pillow.

Oh, hell, he thought bleakly. *That's another bloody thing. I need to call Trina—or she'll worry.*

But for a moment he needed to lie there, his eyes shut against the erratic ebb and flow of the pain in his skull. He told himself he would choose his words carefully for Trina, rehearse them to perfection.

But he did not. Exhaustion covered him like a dark blanket. He slept.

DARCY GOT OUT of the hospital elevator lugging Sloan's leather overnighter in one hand. In the other she carried a bunch of wildflowers, a gesture she now supposed was ridiculous.

She'd made a card with a foolish cartoon face on it and had tied it with a ribbon to the clay vase. She'd pondered fretfully over the message and finally settled on the highly unoriginal but dependable Wishing You a Speedy Recovery.

She had brushed her hair and let it hang loose. She had changed her T-shirt for a white silk shirt and a vest she'd made of interesting silk scraps. But otherwise, she hadn't dressed up. Whether he found her attractive was of no concern to her, she told herself. None at all.

Yet she was nervous as she approached his room. It was an odd, silly kind of nervousness that she connected with very young girls who have just discovered the opposite sex. She hadn't felt it in years, and it unsettled her to feel it now.

Maybe he won't be in his room, she thought with edgy hope. *Maybe they'll have him off somewhere immunizing his blood or x-raying his head.*

His room was number 1437, and its door was open only a few inches. She raised the hand with the flowers to give the door frame a hesitant knock, but the door itself opened. She found herself staring into the eyes of a tiny, wizened little nun.

"Oh," she breathed, startled.

The nun looked her up and down without emotion.

"Mr. English," Darcy said in a hospital whisper. "I've brought his overnight case and some—" she gestured self-consciously "—flowers. Is it all right to go in?"

"He's sleeping," said the nun. "He shouldn't be disturbed."

"Oh," Darcy repeated. She felt both relief and a strange disappointment. Behind the little nun, she could see the hospital room, and it looked so bland and joyless that she was glad she'd brought the flowers.

In the bed, she saw Sloan English's long form stretched out beneath a sheet and thin blanket. His face was turned away from her. His brown hair seemed dark against the stark whiteness of the pillowcase.

"I'll take these things," the little nun said firmly. She commandeered the flowers and tried to take possession of the suitcase.

"No, no," protested Darcy, "it's too heavy. Let me."

For a moment, the nun's cold fingers rested next to hers on the case's handle. She studied Darcy's face as if it were a book with large print, and she could read everything in it with no difficulty whatsoever.

"As you wish," she said without emotion. Silently she turned and placed the vase of flowers on the bedside tray. She nodded at the bureau, and her meaning was clear: Put the case down there. *Quietly.*

Darcy obeyed. Carefully she set down the overnight bag so it would make no noise. Then she turned to leave.

On the bed, Sloan stirred, and his head turned. She could see his face, and although illness had whittled it too lean, there was still beauty in the strong, fine bones of it. The cheekbones were high and sharp, the jawline strong, the chin stubborn and marked by a deep cleft. His nose had an aquiline curve that reminded her of a Roman prince.

The face was almost in repose, but even in sleep the dark brows drew together as if trying to frown. His lashes were thick and black, like blades of jet.

Her heart seemed to spin out of her body, as if it were trying to hurl itself into some higher, more intense world. She took in a sharp but soundless breath. She lost herself in staring at him.

She was an artist, and she knew comeliness when she saw it, but she saw more than just handsomeness in his sleeping face. There was a solitariness about this man that was both touching and disturbing.

Then the nun motioned toward the door, and Darcy understood. She should go. She stole one last glance at Sloan, then ducked her head and left, feeling guilty.

The nun followed, easing the door shut behind them. She looked up at Darcy.

Darcy's heart had come home to her, but it felt changed. "Will he—will he be all right?" she asked.

"If we can tie him down and make him rest," said the woman.

"I never heard of Malay fever before," said Darcy. "Is it bad?"

"He obviously had a bad case. It could have killed him," said the little nun, looking her up and down again. "This relapse should be a lesson to him. Make sure he pays attention. He needs to learn to stop and smell the flowers. I'd take good care of him, if I were you.''

Darcy gave a small, embarrassed laugh. ''He's not mine.''

The woman gave her a look that told her not to argue. ''You brought the flowers, didn't you? Maybe you're supposed to teach the lesson, too.''

She turned and glided off, leaving Darcy standing alone.

The faintest scent of wildflowers still hovered in the antiseptic air.

CHAPTER FOUR

SLOAN AWOKE to a fragile, foreign perfume that he couldn't identify. It was so delicate that he at first thought he was having some sort of rare hallucination of the nose.

It would go away, he thought; all he had to do was open his eyes.

A hard job, but he was the man for it.

Yet when he forced his heavy lids to raise, the scent did not fade, and his vision was filled by an unexpected kaleidoscope of color.

Flowers. He frowned. Someone had brought him flowers. But not from a florist. This was no formal and formulaic bouquet, its design picked from a catalog and its flowers arranged by rote.

No, the flowers were a wild profusion of untamed color— brilliant scarlets, vivid yellows, and blues as profoundly deep as the spring sky.

They spilled out of a strange clay vase painted with a bright design that wasn't quite like anything he'd ever seen. It was not elaborate—just the opposite. But it was the perfect complement for its rich cache of blossoms.

A rainbow-striped ribbon had been tied around the vase. From the ribbon hung a card with a charming cartoon face. He groaned, raising himself on one elbow. Merrily colored letters spelled out Wishing You a Speedy Recovery. It was signed with the initials *D.P.*

The card was made by hand, but the hand had an expert and impish touch. *D.P.*—Darcy Parker. He thought of the tall woman with the offbeat beauty and the tousled dark hair.

He looked at the bureau. His overnighter rested there. She'd been in his room. She'd left this unlikely bouquet as if it were some sort of souvenir of a Midsummer Night's Fever Dream.

He fell back to the pillow, squeezing his eyes shut against the blaze of color. He'd have to thank her. He'd have to apologize to her. How? He didn't want to think about it, and he was momentarily saved from the task—his telephone rang.

He groaned and hoisted himself back up. His head still ached, and his joints still throbbed, but neither pain was as epic as before.

He lifted the receiver. "Hello?"

"Hello, you stupid horse's neck," said a familiar male voice. "Who in hell told you to drive clear to Austin?"

Sloan sank back against the pillows with a harsh sigh. The voice, which had a permanently mocking edge, belonged to Tom Caspian. Tom, a former fraternity brother, was now his doctor in Tulsa.

"I felt fine," Sloan said. "For the first three hundred miles."

"Dammit, there shouldn't have been a first three hundred miles," Tom chided. "I told you to take it easy for at least another six weeks. Malay fever's tricky. You take care of yourself, or the angels'll be scattering posies on your grave."

One already has, Sloan thought, opening an eye and regarding the bouquet of wildflowers.

"Where'd you get the bright idea of a trip?" Tom persisted. "I told you to stay put."

"I was tired of staying put," Sloan grumbled.

"Follow doctor's orders, buddy. Or you'll be staying put under a tombstone."

"I'm sick of hearing about it," Sloan said with distaste. And he was. He'd convalesced two endless months in Southeast Asia. When they'd finally let him come back to the States, he'd been given the impossible command to rest and mend for another three. He was a man built for action, not relaxing. Physical idleness was hellish.

"You been running?" Tom asked, his tone accusatory. "I told you to take it easy on the running. Jog a mile a day, at most. Have you been holding it down to that?"

Sloan thought of the five miles he had done the day before. His body had felt whole again, a strong, efficient machine, all pistons pumping and powerful as ever. "I did a little more," he admitted.

"Hell, Sloan," Tom said in disgust. "Have you got a death wish?"

"No. A life wish," retorted Sloan. "I used to have a life, and I want it back, dammit."

"It won't happen overnight, Superman. Lord, Sloan, you've always pushed yourself harder than anybody I know. That's not how you beat this fever. You've got to respect it. The Angel of Death passed you over once, buddy. Don't give him the chance to make a U-turn."

Sloan put his hand to his forehead, which was hot and sweaty and had started to bang again. "All right, all right," he said impatiently. "How'd you find me, anyway? Did you implant a microchip in my ass last time you gave me a shot?"

"I ought to, you knothead. No. The hospital down there tracked you through your insurance card. I've talked to the admitting physician. He's referred your case to a specialist in tropical diseases from the university."

"I don't want a specialist in tropical diseases from the university. I'll stick with you. You play bad tennis and have good scotch. What more could a man want?"

"Listen, pal, you've already got a specialist. The name is Dr. Nightwine, and we've talked. You'll get a visit by late this afternoon."

"I want to be *out* of here this afternoon."

"No way. You're under observation."

"Observation, hell. Come on, Tommy. Make them release me. I'll come straight home. I'll get in bed and pull the covers up to my chin. I'll watch soap operas all day and take up knitting. Just get me out, will you?"

"You don't travel until Nightwine says you can."

Sloan swore, but Tommy was adamant. "Nightwine'll keep you around a couple of days at most, it's for the best. Another thing—I know you don't want to hear this, but I've put off saying it long enough. I don't think you should keep taking these extreme assignments. You get in these dangerous environments and—"

"It's what I do," Sloan said, cutting him off. "Changing is not an option. Don't even mention it."

There was a moment of awkward silence. Tom cleared his throat. "If you don't mind my asking—exactly what made you take off for Austin like a bat out of hell?" He laughed. "A woman?"

Sloan looked at the vivid wildflowers in their odd yet perfect vase. *A woman,* he thought. He said only, "Family matters. That's all."

He said goodbye; he hung up. But in his mind hovered the image of Darcy Parker, her pert face and her cloud of dark hair.

What, in the name of all that was holy, was he going to say to her?

SUBJECT: Notes on a Prodigal Son
From: BanditKing@USAserve.com
To: Olivia@USAserve.com

Olivia, Beloved—
It was so good to hear your dear voice.

But you *must* stop apologizing about your housekeeper. If a strange man invaded my premises, I might brandish a golf club myself. It is altogether understandable behavior.

As for my son's actions, I can only repeat, my sister has always tried to manipulate him, and this time she obviously caught him with his resistance down—both physical and mental.

I've talked to him just now for a second time. He still regrets the whole, embarrassing incident (and he damn well should).

Physically, he's on the upswing, thank God. He's seen a specialist, a Dr. Nightwine. With luck, he'll be out of the hospital tomorrow, but he's not to travel for a few days. Dr. Nightwine wants to do some blood work and to monitor a new medication.

I offered to go and keep him company, but he'll have none of it. He says he'll be fine, and the situation's embarrassing enough without having his old man flying in to hold his hand.

Ah, would that I were closer to you to hold yours, my love, to take you in my arms, to kiss your deliciously kissable lips (and every other part of you, for you are infinitely kissable and delicious). I recall the sweet taste of you and feel as if I have savored the wine of the gods.

My dear, my own incomparable Olivia, I love you endlessly.

Devotedly,
John

P.S.—You were really only joking about your house-keeper once shooting a man—right?

SUBJECT: Arrangements, Winchesters, Etcetera
From: Olivia@USAserve.com
To: BanditKing@USAserve.com

To the darling bandit of my heart—
So glad to hear your son is better. And don't apologize for him—it's not his fault. That wretched mosquito made him do it.

Hope he's out of the hospital as soon as possible. I've been in that very one. There used to be the tiniest little nun there with the coldest hands—even the memory chills me—brrr. Wish you were here to warm me, my sweetheart. You do light my fires, you know. (Yes, you know, you sexy devil.)

Oh, dear, I must watch what I say. This is how I got us in trouble in the first place.

So—explain to me about Sloan. If he's released but has to stay in Austin, *where* will he stay? Does he have friends there?

Kisses and Caresses from
Your Own Olivia

P.S. No, I was not joking about Rose Alice. She shot off a man's ear with a Winchester rifle. She's never told me why, exactly, but apparently he irritated the very *hell* out of her.

SUBJECT: Hotel Rooms are Wonderful Places
From: BanditKing@USAserve.com
To: Oliva@USAserve.com

Darling Girl—
Just a note before I'm off for the evening's work.

Your housekeeper is beginning to sound rather fearsome. Don't you think your household might be more peaceful if you hired someone a little more, well, mellow? And without a felony conviction? Just a thought, sweet girl. I don't mean to interfere.

Sloan says he'll check into a hotel near the university. Don't worry about him. Hotel rooms can be wonderful places—as you have proved to me beyond the shadow of a doubt.

I can't wait until we can be together again. I will gladly come to Maine. Shall I tell you in minutest detail, the tender and pleasurable things I want to do with you?
Missing you body and soul—
John

SUBJECT: The Most Marvelous Idea!
From: Olivia@USAserve.com
To: BanditKing@USAserve.com

Dearest, most marvelous man—
You in Maine—how wonderful! I've got a new four-poster bed with a mattress soft as clouds. Would you like to play in a cloud?

As for Rose Alice, she's mellowed considerably since her gun-slinging days. I'm sorry that when she backslid, your son was the target. I've already spoken to her about *that*.

And darling, about your Sloan—I have the most marvelous idea. I'll call Darcy right away...

DARCY CLUTCHED THE PHONE so tightly that her fingernails paled. *"What?"* she asked in alarm and dismay. *"What* did you say?"

"I don't want Sloan stuck in some impersonal hotel room," Olivia said firmly. "I want him to stay at the lake house."

Darcy was appalled. "But *I* live here," she said.

"No, you don't," Olivia corrected. *"You* live in the guest house. Nobody's in the big house. It's just sitting there, going to waste. He'd be so much more comfortable there—he could spread out, read, listen to music, use the hot tub, the pool."

Darcy pictured Sloan English's nearly bare body sweating in the hot tub, glistening in the pool. Her nerves skittered to a higher level of anxiety.

"He'll have a nice view," Olivia went on. "He can take the boat on the lake if he wants, walk in the garden, get some nice, fresh, healthy air..."

Emerald came into the room from the kitchen. She had taken off her chain mail and sword and boots. She had a peanut butter sandwich in her hand and a curious look on her face. "Who's on the phone?"

Darcy didn't answer her. "You can't just give a stranger the run of your house," she told Olivia.

"He might not be a stranger long," Olivia said. "He might be your stepbrother."

"Stepbrother?" Darcy asked, stunned. "Mother, surely you're not thinking of getting married—you hardly know this man."

Emerald's face went white and her mouth dropped open, forming an *O*. The peanut butter sandwich fell to the floor. She clutched the edge of Darcy's worktable as if she needed support.

"I know John intimately," Olivia said. "I know him better than I've ever known any other human being. And yes, we've talked about getting married. It's like that 'September Song.' Our days are dwindling down to a precious few, and we want to spend them together."

"Mother," Darcy said desperately, "don't do anything rash—please. If you're going to get engaged, at least make it a *long* engagement. Be sure that he's right for you—"

"He's perfect for me," said Olivia. "And I want his son to stay at the lake. It's a sort of peace offering from our family to his."

"The lake house," Darcy said tonelessly. "Our future stepbrother in the lake house."

Emerald looked even more stunned. She reeled away from the table and flung herself into the easy chair. She bent her head and covered her face with her hands to hide the tears glinting in her eyes.

"Why should *our* family make a peace offering?" Darcy demanded. "He owes us an apology, not the other way around."

"Darcy, he's deeply sorry. I'm going to tell him I insist. I won't have it any other way. If he really wants my forgiveness, then he can prove it by accepting my offer."

Oh, Lord, Darcy thought, her stomach twisting sickly. She knew that tone in Olivia's voice. Her mother had made up her mind, and nothing, nothing, nothing on earth could change it.

Darcy felt overwhelmed. Olivia was about to rush into a

foolish marriage, Emerald was distraught and Sloan English was moving in practically on top of her. The thought of having him so near was unsettling, even somehow menacing.

"I'm e-mailing you a list," Olivia said with her same blithe air of certainty. "I want you to stock the refrigerator for him. He needs nice, healthy foods to build his strength back."

Emerald hunched in the chair, eyes still covered, her shoulders heaving with silent sobs.

Darcy shook her head in frustration. "Mother, I'm not going to play nursemaid to this man. I'm not going to get all chummy with him just because you're—you're under the delusion that you're in love—"

"Darcy, it's my house, and he's my guest. As are you, I might point out. When you lost the lease on your studio, I was glad to let you use the guest house."

Darcy ground her teeth. It was true. Olivia was generous to a fault. She would accept no rent from Darcy, not a cent.

"Now," Olivia said, "I'm asking you a simple favor, that's all. He's a sick young man in a strange town. How can it be wrong to offer him food and shelter?"

Damn! Now Olivia was making her feel guilty. Darcy raked her hand through her hair in exasperation.

"I'm asking you," Olivia said, "for very little. Create a hospitable setting for him. Be polite. Get to know him as well or as little as you like. But remember, he's going to be my stepson. In all probability, that is."

Darcy winced. She had a horrid premonition that there was no "probability" involved. That Olivia *would* become Sloan English's stepmother.

"Can I count on you?" Olivia asked.

Darcy pressed her hand against her midsection, which was suddenly queasy. She looked at her weeping sister. "Yes," she said unhappily. "You can count on me."

"Give him a chance, darling," Olivia said. "You might actually like him."

Right, Darcy thought bleakly. *I'll love him like a brother.*

She hung up and turned to her sister. "Emerald," she said as kindly as she could, "don't cry—please."

Emerald, who hated to be seen crying, stared at Darcy with swollen, brimming eyes. "She's going to do it, isn't she?" she said bitterly. "She's going to marry that man—isn't she?"

Darcy tried to keep her expression composed. She nodded. "It sounds like it."

"It'll be terrible," Emerald said, and burst into a new freshet of tears. "It'll be a disaster. He's probably just after her money, and he'll spend it all and make a fool of her—" Emerald gave a strangled little wail and hid her face in her hands again.

Stay calm, Darcy cautioned herself. *Somebody around here has to.* She went to Emerald and knelt beside her. She put her hand on her sister's slender arm. "It may not happen. This thing may end as quickly as it started. These intense romances are like that. I've seen it happen before."

Emerald straightened, dug a tissue from her waistband and wiped it across her nose with an angry gesture. "And that man—that churl who passed out on the floor—Mama wants him to come live in the lake house?"

Darcy shrugged as if it didn't matter. "For just a few days. You don't even have to see him. It's all right."

Emerald rolled her teary eyes heavenward. "I can't believe it. His family's *already* moving in and mooching off her. He'll probably go through all her closets and drawers and steal the silverware—"

Darcy took Emerald's chin between her thumb and forefinger. "Em, look at me. Calm down."

"I don't want to calm down," Emerald shot back. "I don't want a stepbrother. I don't want a step*father.* I don't want a step anything. Why can't we just have Mama to ourselves? Why does she have to get mixed up with *him?* She can't really know him. He could be a gigolo. Or a bigamist. Or one of those lonely hearts killers. Or—"

"Shh," Darcy said, and laid her finger across her sister's

lips. "Listen. We don't know anything about him—good or bad. But if the son comes here, we can find out. This is an *opportunity.*"

"Some opportunity," Emerald said disdainfully.

"No. I mean it. I can find out things, feel him out."

"He'll probably feel you *up,*" Emerald retorted. "He's probably a wolf like his father."

"Whatever he is, I can handle him."

"Ha! You don't know that," Emerald scoffed. "You don't know a thing about him."

"He may be just as suspicious of us as we are of him," Darcy reasoned. "But I'll gain his trust, win his confidence. Bit by bit, I'll draw him out, and then we'll know—"

"We won't know anything," Emerald argued. "He could lie his head off. I've got a better idea. Let's *not* be nice to him. Let's make him hate us. *That'll* stop them."

Darcy squeezed her sister's arm. "No. Mama'd be appalled. We can't—"

"We can't let her go through with it, *that's* what we can't do," Emerald said passionately. "I say that we break it up. Whatever it takes, we do."

"You'll do no such thing," Darcy warned. "My way's best."

Emerald narrowed her eyes. With a fierce gesture, she scrubbed away the last of her tears. "We'll see whose way is best."

Then she stood and walked to the fallen peanut butter sandwich. She picked it up, dropped it into the wastebasket, turned and left the room. She came back, almost immediately, wearing her boots. She carried her armor, her sword in its scabbard. Her back straight, she walked out the front door.

Darcy followed her as far as the porch. She put one hand on her hip and watched her sister stalk to her car.

"Emerald, where are you going?" she demanded. "What are you going to do?"

"I'm going home," Emerald said sulkily. "I've got to think."

Once again, foreboding filled Darcy. "Then think over what I said. We have a great deal to gain from being nice to this Sloan person, and nothing to lose—"

"Except the silverware," Emerald said sarcastically. "And, of course, Mama."

SLOAN HAD STUDIED Darcy's business card as diligently as a fortune-teller studying a tarot card for the answer to an impenetrable mystery.

The mystery, of course, was what he would say to her.

Roses are red.
Violets are blue.
I behaved like a jackass—
Now what do I do?

Three times he had picked up the receiver to call her. Three times, he had set it down again, suddenly convinced the words he'd rehearsed were inadequate, utter tripe.

The clay pot of wildflowers sat on his bedside tray like a perfectly constructed rebuke to his foolishness. He had burst in on her rudely, full of suspicion and self-righteousness. In return, she had given him courtesy and a gift of beauty he did not deserve.

He stared at her card and eyed the flowers. He wondered how she had put such simple elements together in a way that was so striking and original—just as she seemed to be.

He was usually an articulate man, but he found himself tongue-tied. He was normally confident, but now he brimmed with indecision. He hated it, and, irrationally, he resented Darcy Parker for reducing him to this state.

A pretty Hispanic nurse looked in on him. She had raven black hair, which made him remember Darcy even more keenly. She had dark, bright eyes that had the same effect. She tilted her head and gave him a smile.

"Can I get you anything?" she asked.

An eraser that rubs out the whole day, he thought.

It occurred to him that he had a small electric notebook in his suitcase. It was powered by batteries and had Internet capability.

He could write Darcy, not phone her. It would be far less complicated. He could send her an e-mail—short, succinct and highly polished. He wouldn't have to take the chance of bumbling and stuttering on the phone like an awkward schoolboy.

"Yeah," he said with a feigned easiness. "In my over-nighter, there's a little computer in a leather case. One of the super-compact ones. Could I use it to send some e-mail?"

"Sure," she said without hesitation. "At least I think so. They wouldn't allow one in Intensive Care—it could interfere with the machines. But here? I don't see why not."

He started to rise, gripping the IV stand so he could roll it with him. Gently she pushed him back. "I'll get it for you. Relax."

She brought it to him. "I never saw one like that," she said with delight. "It's so little, so *cute*—like a toy."

He nodded, but the thing was no toy; it was a five-thousand-dollar PowerBook, upgraded to the max.

"I hope you're not going to work," she joked. "You're here to rest, you know." She adjusted the IV dripping chemicals into his bloodstream.

"I'd rest better if they'd unhook this thing. It's like being caught in a spiderweb."

"Soon," she said soothingly. "Another couple hours or so. Then we'll have you up in no time."

He nodded grimly, but thanked her. She left, and he switched on the computer. He typed in his password and pulled up his e-mail service. He hit the command to write, then stared at the blank screen. He drew a long breath from between clenched teeth. He began to type.

He tried to choose his words with such precision that it made his head ache again. He discovered his forehead was damp with sweat and his body taut with tension. He rearranged sentences, changed words, added phrases, deleted them, put them back.

He wrote and rewrote until the words danced like drunken elves in his brain. They chittered, idiot-like, and made no sense. Finally, in despair and fatigue, he gave in. Imperfect as the message was, he sent it. He switched off the computer and put it in the drawer beneath the bedside tray.

He lay back and closed his eyes. His head banged a doleful cadence like a funereal drum. He saw a silent fireworks show on the backs of his eyelids. For the thousandth time, he cursed Malay fever and every mosquito that had ever sipped blood.

His phone rang, and the noise was like a nail being driven into his skull. He winced and opened one eye. He picked up the receiver.

A perfectly charming voice spoke in his ear. "Hello, Sloan. My name is Olivia Ferrar. Your father's friend. I'm so sorry to hear you're ill."

Oh, my God, thought Sloan. "Ms. Ferrar," he said miserably, "I'm sorry I interfered in your personal business. I wasn't myself, but that's no excuse. Please accept my deepest apolo—"

"My dear, are you *truly* sorry?" she asked. The question took him aback.

"Absolutely," he said with conviction. "If there were anything I could do to—"

She interrupted, but her voice was so warm and honeyed, he hardly noticed. "If there were anything you could do to make up for it, you'd do it?"

"Absolutely," he repeated. "I'd do anything that—"

"Anything at all?" she cooed.

"Yes. Certainly. Anything," he babbled. "Your wish is my—"

"Command?" She laughed. It was a bewitching laugh, low and genuine. "Is that what you were going to say?"

"Precisely." He stifled a groan, closed his eyes and watched the fever fireworks. A particularly lovely cascade of dots exploded across the darkness. He watched them fall and die away.

"Your father says you have to stay in town a few days," she said in her nectar-like voice. "My wish is that you stay at my house by the lake. As my guest. If you grant that wish, then I'll know your apology is sincere."

Sloan's eyes snapped open, and he sat up in bed so fast it dizzied him. "Ms. Ferrar, I can't—"

"Olivia," she corrected. "And you must. If you won't accept my invitation, you'll simply break my heart, that's what—"

"I can't—" he tried again to say it. She wouldn't let it be said.

"It wouldn't be—" he tried to explain. She wouldn't let it be explained.

She reasoned and teased, she begged and beguiled, she turned logic on its head and argued so sweetly and relentlessly, he ended up saying, "Yes," in spite of himself.

"You're a darling man," she crooned in his ringing ear. "You sound just like your father."

When she at last said goodbye, he fell back against the pillow, exhausted. She'd rolled right over him like a freight train full of charm.

His father, he realized, had never had any chance of resisting this woman.

Neither had he. A man could fight Malay fever and he could fight Olivia Ferrar—but he couldn't fight both at once.

He closed his eyes and wearily thought, *Let the fireworks begin.*

They did, a whole rainbow of them, colorful as Texas wildflowers.

CHAPTER FIVE

RESIGNED, DARCY SAT at her desk and switched on her computer.

She typed in her password to open her electronic mailbox so she could read Olivia's instructions. It was galling, really, to be expected to fetch and carry for Sloan English, as if she were the lowest scullery maid.

"I am my brother's keeper," she grumbled to herself. "My *step*brother's keeper."

Then she read her list of new mail and blinked in astonishment. There was a message from *him*—the dreaded stepbrother-to-be.

SUBJECT: All in the Family
From: SloanJEnglish@PetroCorp.com
To: DesignByDarcy@USAserve.com

Dear Darcy Parker:

My father is a good man, but he sired a fool. Your mother is obviously an extraordinary woman; she raised a daughter who is lovely, cool-headed and kind.

I brought only anger and sickness to your door. In return, you gave me compassion. I was intolerable, but you tolerated me; I was insufferable, yet you suffered me.

From the bottom of my heart, I apologize. And for the way you received my folly and gave me only good in return, I can but sincerely echo Shakespeare's words, "Thanks, and thanks and ever thanks."

Sincerely yours,
Sloan English
P.S. Can you forgive me? We may, after all, become family. If so, I would do all in my power to make it a happy one.
P.S. 2 Tell the bookworm, "Hello." Right now I feel like a worm myself, although a lower form...

"Oh, damn!" Darcy whispered in frustration. He sounded...decent. He sounded reasonable. And he sounded sincerely repentant. How much easier it would be if he remained a toad and didn't turn into a prince.

What should she say in reply? What *could* she say? She gnawed at her lower lip, her heart knocking uncommonly hard at her ribs.

The beauty of e-mail, of course, was that you could take your time in answering. It wasn't like a conversation or a phone call. There was no pressure to make an immediate reply. He'd sent the message over two hours ago. He had no way of knowing if she'd even read it yet.

She hit the button that would save the message and keep it in her mailbox. She would respond later—if, after careful thinking, she chose to respond at all.

He had said nothing about staying in the lake house. Why? Perhaps Olivia hadn't yet asked him. Perhaps she had, but he had been a gentleman and refused. If he were truly sorry, he would refuse, wouldn't he? Of course, he would.

She saw that she indeed had the expected message from Olivia. It had been e-mailed shortly after Sloan sent his. With apprehension, she hit the command that opened Olivia's note.

SUBJECT: Company's Coming—Tra-la!
From: Olivia@USAserve.com
To: DesignByDarcy@USAserve.com

Good news, my dear Darcy-Duck—Sloan's agreed to use the lake house.

He tried to protest, but I caught him at a moment when he was both groggy and guilt-ridden. Ha-ha! I prevailed.

Everything at the house should be in order, provided Rose Alice isn't lurking behind the portieres, brandishing a five iron. I am phoning her to tell her to stay out of his way, or there'll be the devil (i.e., me) to pay.

All you need to do is make sure there's plenty of food and drink, fresh flowers, and a nice supply of masculine toiletries. To help organize your shopping, here's a little list—

The "little list" was approximately as long as the Austin telephone book. Olivia was a gracious, even an extravagant, hostess. She wanted Sloan pampered as if he were visiting royalty.

Champagne, Darcy read, shaking her head in disapproval. *Imported beer. Smoked salmon. Barbecue from the Ironworks. Chili from Guero's Taco Bar. Lasagna from the Spaghetti Warehouse. Chocolates from The Confectionery.*

Flowers for the living room, dining room, master bedroom, master bath and kitchen table. A nice selection of guest soaps and shampoos and aftershaves. Everything that was presently on hand, Olivia had declared, was "too froufrou" for a man.

Good grief, Darcy thought in exasperation. *He'll think that Mother's filthy rich. Or a hopeless spendthrift. I can't make this huge a show—I wouldn't do it for the Prince of Wales.*

She shook her head. Olivia obviously wanted to make a good impression on Sloan English—it was almost touching, this eagerness to please the son of her beloved.

But it was ill advised, Darcy was certain. Olivia's liberality as a hostess had always grated on Gus, who had been tight-fisted and held her in check. Now she was indulging her generous nature to the utmost—or trying to.

"No," Darcy said to herself in determination. Sloan English would be treated as any other guest—no worse, and no better. She would put in a sensible supply of food and drink.

The man had been sick, for God's sake—what would he want with chocolates and smoked oysters?

And she wasn't spending Olivia's money on a florist. She could pick flowers for free. If she had to provide Sloan English with soap and shampoo, he would get the same kind used by ordinary mortals—and that was *that*.

Darcy knew better than to argue with her mother. She did not want to deceive Olivia, but neither did she want to openly fling down the gauntlet and defy her.

Olivia was so giddy with love that she needed to be protected from herself. Emerald was right about that, but wrong about the means, which must be discreet.

Darcy reread the end of her mother's message.

—I don't know when they'll release him from the hospital, but I'll let you know.

It would be a lovely gesture if you went to pick him up and brought him to the lake house yourself. I would appreciate it so much—and so would John. If Sloan is anything like John, dear, you're just going to *love* him.
Your ever fond and grateful
Mama

P.S. It would probably be best to keep Emerald out of this, for the time being. She'll want to mount a crusade against him or something. You're the one I'm depending on, Darcy-Duck.

Darcy sighed and blew a wayward strand of hair from her eyes. She squared her shoulders, ready to type her reply. She would not lie to Olivia, but she would not tell the whole truth.

Dear Mama—
Don't worry a bit about Sloan English. I'm looking forward to getting to know him.

I'll pick him up at the hospital when he's ready, and

I give you my solemn promise that I'll take care of him.
All my love—Darcy

She hesitated. The message was duplicitous, and she knew
it. She intended to win Sloan's trust, to get to know him better
than he wanted to be known.

If there were family secrets, she would ferret them out. If
there were skeletons in the closet, she would pounce upon
them and drag them, rattling, into the light. She would dis-
cover all she could about John Sloan and his entire gene
pool—for better or worse.

Darcy's finger hovered above the send button. It was not
her nature to be devious. But it was her duty.

Her finger descended. The message was sent.

Then she retrieved Sloan's e-mail note and reread it to the
end.

P.S. 2 Tell the bookworm, "Hello." Right now I feel
like a worm myself, although a lower form…

Darcy turned and looked at the bookworm. She had sat
him down in the armchair, holding an open volume of fairy
tales. He grinned at her as if in innocent conspiracy.

"Our 'brother' says, hello," she told him.

A wayward May breeze came through the open window.
The bookworm's green antennae bobbled, and he seemed to
return the greeting.

"I said I'd take care of the man," Darcy told the worm.
"And I will. I most certainly will."

The bookworm kept his manic grin. His antennae nodded
with even more verve, as if he read her thoughts and gleefully
approved them.

SLOAN SLEPT DEEPLY. The IV dripped its curatives into his
system, and when he awoke, he felt strangely restored.

He no longer burned with fever or shuddered with chills.

By turns, heat and cold took to rippling through his long body, but only feebly now, with the mere ghost of their former power.

The nurse came, took his temperature and consulted with a doctor. They removed the IV. Food was brought to him. It was bland and unappetizing, but he ate ravenously.

"You look like a new man," the nurse said, her head cocked in marvel.

He smiled and, with his fork, speared a piece of something that might possibly have been a potato. "It's a crazy fever," he said. "It recurs in different cycles. They can last twenty-four hours or thirty-six or forty-eight."

"This one," she said, "you think is twenty-four?"

He glanced at his watch and nodded. He'd started feeling fuzzy-headed and irritable about this time last night—just when Trina had gotten weepy and begged him to go to Austin. Fever had made a fool of him; he'd agreed to what she wanted—anything to stop her carrying on.

But the longer he'd driven, the worse he'd felt, and the more reluctant he had been to admit the depressing truth. Malay fever hadn't died in his system, after all. It had only been sleeping. When it awakened, it had sucker-punched him so hard, he couldn't think straight.

"If it's only twenty-four hours, you're a lucky man," said the nurse.

"Yeah," he said without conviction. "Lucky."

Yet she was right. Malay fever could kill a man or weaken him for life. A bad relapse could be crippling. He had beaten the fever once and gotten cocky. Now it had come back to shake him to his marrow, and humble him.

He looked at the flaring brightness of Darcy's bouquet, and winced, remembering the scene at her house. No. He had been more than humbled. He had been humiliated.

His wolfish appetite vanished. He pushed aside the tray.

"You don't want your tapioca?" the nurse asked with concern.

He gazed at it dubiously. It looked like library paste with warts.

"I think I'm through," he said.

He sank back against the pillow to consider how low pride and fever had brought him. It was abysmal. He remembered writing an e-mail of apology to Darcy Parker. He didn't quite remember what he'd said; he didn't want to.

It was bad enough that he'd made a fool of himself in front of a stranger. That the stranger happened to be a talented and beautiful woman made it too shameful to contemplate.

Then another recollection smote him, and he groaned. He'd had a phone call from Olivia Ferrar, the object of his father's affection and his aunt's concern. She'd called just when he was getting pummeled in another round against the fever. Somehow she had beguiled him into agreeing to stay at her lake house.

Return to the scene of his crime? Was he *crazy?* Some of the wildflowers in the eccentric pot were round and cheery yellow. They reminded him of Happy Faces smirking at his asininity.

Strange emotions warred in his chest. If he didn't go to the lake, he might never again see Darcy. This would be a most excellent thing.

If he did go, he most certainly would see her. Paradoxically, this also seemed most excellent. He never wanted to lay eyes on her again. Yet he itched with the desire to do so.

The Happy Face flowers seemed to dance before his eyes, and his head began to bang again.

"Are you all right?" asked the little nurse. "You look pale again, all of a sudden."

"This fever—it takes it out of a guy," he said.

"I'll leave you alone," she said, taking his tray. "You need rest. It is the best cure of all."

"Right," he said. A chill, surprisingly strong, stole over him, made him clench his teeth. She left. The chill struck more deeply into his bones, and his fist tightened, wringing the sheet.

Oh, hell, he thought, Darcy Parker was a no-win proposition. He found her indescribably lovely—but her mother?

Her mother was clearly a siren, a Lorelei of the highest power. She'd sung her song, and John English had fallen under its spell. He thought he loved her; he thought he wanted to marry her.

And if Sloan was sure of anything on God's green earth, it was that his father had no business getting married again.

Sloan swore wearily. With luck, the infatuation between John and Olivia would burn itself out. Without luck—well, what was one more stepmother in the scheme of things?

Except this one came with daughters—and *what* daughters. He suddenly wondered if Darcy had read his e-mail. Even more intensely, he wondered if she'd answered it.

He took his computer notebook from the drawer, switched it on and typed in his password. When he checked his mail, his heart took an uncertain leap. He had mail from his father, from Tom Caspian, and—he tensed his jaw—his aunt Trina.

But what caught his attention and held it in uneasy thrall was that he had a return message from Darcy Parker.

He drew a deep breath and summoned her message to the screen. Would she tell him to go to hell? She had every right to do so.

SUBJECT: Reply to All in the Family
From: DesignByDarcy@USAserve.com
To: SloanJEnglish@PetroCorp.com

Dear Sloan English—
I know that you weren't yourself when you came to my house, and it was your illness that spoke, not you.

Your apology is accepted. A wise man once said that whoever cannot forgive others breaks the bridge over which he must pass himself, for every one has need to be forgiven.

So—let's put the incident behind us. As for our parents, perhaps we should try to live and let live, don't you think?

My mother said you agreed to spend some time at the lake house—I can't tell you how happy you've made her. Her greatest wish is to be in harmony with your father and those he loves.

I'll be there at the hospital to pick you up when you're released. Please don't object—Mama wouldn't have it any other way.

If there's anything I can do to make your stay more comfortable, *please* don't hesitate to ask.

Cordially,

Darcy Parker

P.S.—The bookworm sends his best wishes for a speedy recovery. He says if you need any health food, he can recommend a perfectly delicious first aid manual.

Sloan's mouth went dry, his pulses hammered in his temples. *Damn,* he thought, she was too good to be true. *Damn, damn, damn.*

A fine sweat filmed his forehead. Wait a minute, he told himself sternly. That was exactly it: she *was* too good to be true. Why were these women, mother and daughter, practically killing him with kindness?

Could they really be that forgiving and gracious? Or did they have some hidden motive?

His father, after all, had property. It was valuable, but exactly how valuable Sloan didn't know. Olivia's late husband had left her seemingly well off. Did she think John was a suitably moneyed replacement, a new source of income?

Hell, he told himself disgustedly, it wasn't his business. Darcy was right. Live and let live. But he didn't know how to reply to her. He'd have to think on it.

He read his father's e-mail message. It was a short, stern note, advising him to accept Olivia's hospitality.

"If you really want her forgiveness," wrote John, "do as she asks. You're being given a chance to wipe out the first impression you made—use it wisely. And remember—these women are going to be our family for the rest of our lives."

Sloan clenched his jaw. Could John really believe that this late in the game, the two families would join as one, an adult version of the Brady Bunch? Lord, he couldn't be that naive, could he?

He steeled himself and pulled up the e-mail he wanted to read the least, the one from Trina.

SUBJECT: Please Tell Me, What is Happening?
From: TrinaK@SuperNet.com
To: SloanJEnglish@PetroCorp.com

Sloan—What is happening? You haven't answered your cell phone. Why? Are you all right? You know I am already worried sick about your father. Do you know anything more about this woman he's picked up?

Please answer soon. Arthur senses my dismay, and it is upsetting him too.

It is so hard feeling as helpless as I do. I can't rest until I know the truth about this woman.

Your loving aunt,
Trina

P.S.—Oh excuse me, dear Sloan. I know I'm such trouble and I don't mean to complain. You know that. It's

just that I worry so. If something goes wrong, what will
become of Arthur?

Sloan ground his teeth. It was vintage Trina, all right, with
her everlasting mantra: "What will become of Arthur?" It
was the unanswerable question, the one that gave her the
power that she had so long wielded.

He could not tell her the truth, of course. If she knew he
was sick, she would carry on and make herself an even greater
martyr.

Sloan shook his head in exasperation. He felt like a man
in an inescapable trap. He would have to reply to Trina, but
choose his words with the utmost care.

SUBJECT: All is Fine, Don't Worry
From: SloanJEnglish@PetroCorp.com
To: TrinaK@SuperNet.com

Dear Trina:
I have arrived, and the situation is under control. To
investigate matters thoroughly, however, will take more
time than I anticipated. I will keep you informed, but
only if you promise to calm yourself.
    Greetings to Arthur.
Yours,
Sloan

He sent the message. It was best to keep things brief with
Trina—he knew this from bitter experience.

There was but one thing to do. Olivia had issued an invitation, and he had accepted it. He must use the situation to
the utmost. Trina's fears were either foolish or they weren't.
He would find out.

He would gird himself against the charms of Darcy Parker.
He would use her only as a means to an end. He would dig

out the truth, the real story of her family, whether she wanted it known or not.

SUBJECT: Everything's Coming Up Roses
From: Olivia@USAserve.com
To: BanditKing@USAserve.com

Sweetest Darling—
I've heard from Darcy, and it's all set!

She's getting the house into shape for company, and she'll pick up Sloan when he's released.

Isn't it exciting? We're really starting to be a *family*.

I always wished Darcy and Emerald had had a big brother—and now they have.

I admit it will take Emerald some time getting used to the idea. But Darcy is so levelheaded that I'm sure there won't be any problems there at all. None whatsoever.

Happy and Full of Faith,
Your Adoring Olivia
P.S.—Going to bed now, and will dream of you, body and soul.

SUBJECT: A Loving Family
From: BanditKing@USAserve.com
To: Olivia@USAserve.com

My dearest bride-to-be—
I'm home now (the run-through went quite well tonight, if I do say so myself).

I know you're in bed, but I can't resist dropping you a note. It is torment to think of your lovely body sleeping apart from mine. I can't wait to have you in my arms all night long.

You're a marvel, Olivia, being so gracious to my errant son. What he did is so unlike him, I still can't quite believe it happened.

I'm deeply pleased that your Darcy is giving him a second chance—most women would not be so understanding.

Ah, dear girl, you are right—we are on our way to becoming a family—a big, *happy* family.

I send you a kiss in your sleep, dear girl. Dream of a future that is serene and without complication.

Yours,

Faithful to eternity,

John

CHAPTER SIX

THE DOOR TO THE HOSPITAL room stood slightly ajar.

Darcy paused before it, heart beating too fast. She raised her hand and rapped smartly on the door frame.

"Come in," said a man's voice. *His* voice.

She eased the door open and entered the room. Sloan English stood by the metal dresser. His suitcase lay before him, open and nearly packed.

He raised his eyes to meet hers, and the greenness of his gaze jolted her. She realized she had never before seen anyone with eyes that color. There was something unsettling in them.

But the smile he gave her was reassuring. His mouth crooked warily, almost shyly, and his expression was abashed.

"We meet again," he said.

"Yes," she said. "We meet again."

She smiled with more confidence then she felt and extended her hand. He took it in a firm grip, shook it. His own hand was cool and strong, and he held hers an instant longer than necessary, perhaps only a heartbeat.

When he released it, they both looked away, as if embarrassed by the intimacy of the touch. Darcy put her hands into the pockets of her sundress with studied casualness.

He laid a folded shirt on top of the other clothing in his suitcase. He closed the lid and snapped the locks shut.

"I keep feeling," he said, "like I can't just walk out that door with you. That I should spend some time groveling at your feet. Rending my garments. Strewing ashes on my head."

"You apologized. I accepted," she said. "No groveling. No rending. No strewing."

"Could I eat a little wormwood, drink some gall as a symbolic gesture?"

"No symbolic gestures required," she said as lightly as she could. "What's over is over."

He stood for a moment, saying nothing.

Darcy stole a look at him. He stared down at the closed suitcase, his lean face solemn, almost haunted. Yet he did not look like a man who had collapsed only the day before yesterday, who had spent two nights in a hospital bed. It was true he was too thin, but his arms were ropy with muscle, his shoulders wide, his chest deep.

He looked up and caught her eyes on him. "You're generous to take this time. It's got to cut into your workday."

She smiled and gave a dismissive shrug. "I work for myself. I can set my own hours."

"A free spirit?"

"I'd like to think so," she said.

In truth, lately she'd had doubts about how free she was. When she'd broken off with her last lover, Claude, his rebuke had been bitter. *"No wonder you like fairy tales, Darcy. You're Sleeping Beauty. God knows I tried to wake you, but I couldn't. Maybe it's not possible."*

He'd accused her of being repressed and afraid of her own feelings. *"You resist your own sexuality,"* he'd said. *"Maybe you haven't really got any."*

A year later, the words still stung, but she tried to push the memory aside. After all, she'd gone to trouble today to seem attractive. She'd worn her prettiest sundress, one she had made out of bright yellow fabric. It was sleeveless, with a scooped neck and full skirt. It was simplicity itself, yet elegant.

She'd gathered her hair into an upsweep so artful that it seemed artless, with dark tendrils curling at her ears and nape. She seldom wore perfume, but for this occasion she had spritzed herself with her best.

She did not want to seduce Sloan English—God forbid. But she wanted him to find her appealing, a person pleasant to look at and talk with, and above all, someone easy to trust.

It was a universal truth, she knew, that men loved to talk about themselves. Brightly she said, "My mother says that you've been all over the world. That you're quite the traveler."

She thought she saw an emotion fleet across his face like a dark cloud. The expression vanished so quickly, she wondered if she'd imagined it.

"I've logged some miles," he said.

She took a deep breath and was about to ask more, to draw him out, but a young male attendant appeared, pushing a wheelchair.

Sloan frowned and the corners of his mouth jerked down in disgust. "Oh, no."

"Sorry," said the attendant. His blond hair had been dyed a fluorescent pink, and he had a rhinestone stud in his nostril. "Hospital policy. You want to split this place, I got to give you the buggy ride to the parking lot."

"I'm not an invalid," Sloan grumbled.

"Do it as a favor to me," said the young man. "I need the fresh air."

"All you have is your suitcase, right?" Darcy asked Sloan. "I can carry it."

"*I'll* carry it," he said emphatically, locking the handle in his grip.

"And that's all you have?" she asked.

"No," Sloan said. "You can take *that*."

He gave an abrupt nod in the direction of the clay vase with its wildflowers. Some of the more delicate blooms were already withering, and others were drooping.

"They're not going to last," she said. "Most of them aren't meant for picking. They fade fast."

"I like them," he said, surprising her. "And you don't want to leave the vase."

"That thing?" she said, more surprised still. "It was just

an experiment. It didn't turn out. Leave it here. They can throw it out—''

''I like it,'' he said. ''If you don't want it, let me have it. Okay?''

Her breath thickened in her chest. She was both disconcerted and touched, without knowing the reason for either.

''Please.'' He said the word seriously, and he kept his gaze fastened on hers. ''I'd be honored if you'd let me have it.''

''Of course,'' she murmured. She moved to the bedside tray, glad to have activity to distract her. Wasn't she supposed to be the one disarming and charming *him?*

The pink-haired attendant watched them with a bored air. He said, ''Hey, buddy, your chariot awaits. You ready?''

Darcy picked up the wildflowers. Behind her, she heard Sloan's grudging voice. ''Ready.''

She wondered how ready she herself was.

''Then,'' said the attendant, ''let the fun begin.''

THE YELLOW DRESS was driving him crazy. It made her look like the goddess of all the yellow flowers nodding in the sunny fields.

It emphasized her narrow waist, then billowed out like a mysterious bloom over her hips, forcing him to think of the body beneath. The neckline was cut just low enough to show him a faint velvety shadow, a maddening hint of cleavage.

She drove with her head held high, and he liked the graceful curve of her neck, the lines of her profile. She'd pinned her hair on top of her head, but delicate strands had slipped out and hung enticingly down the back of her neck and around her ears.

She had the window slightly open on the driver's side, and the breeze tossed her hair into even more fascinating disorder. Sloan forced himself to turn away, to look out his own window. The yellow flowers of the countryside seemed to go on for miles.

''It's beautiful country,'' he said.

''Yes,'' she said. ''And this is the prettiest time of year. If you're feeling better later in the week, I could take you for a tour. Everything's in bloom—it's a wonderful sight.''

He nodded, kept himself from looking at her. "I'd like that. If it's not an imposition."

"It's not," she answered. "I'd go by myself, anyway. When the Hill Country's in bloom, it seems almost like sin not to explore it. So, work always takes a back seat at this time of year."

He stared at the rolling fields of green and gold. For much of his life, work had never taken a back seat to anything. It had obsessed him, consumed him. It came before anything else—and that included relationships.

This woman, who would willingly leave her work for a show of wildflowers, was as unlike him as it was possible to be. He must remember that.

Two days ago, when he'd come so ignominiously to her house, he hadn't seen her car. He'd fantasized her in a little sports car, a white Corvette, perhaps, to set off the exotic darkness of her hair and eyes.

The fact was she didn't drive a car at all. It was a rattling green utility vehicle, pocked with dents and spotted with rust. Its back hatch was filled with things that rattled mysteriously and without ceasing.

Something rolled across the floor at his feet. He picked it up. It was a spool of gold metallic thread, just a few yards left. He balanced it in the palm of his hand. "You're an artist," he said.

"A fabric artist," she said. "At least that's what some people call it. I make things out of cloth."

He nodded to himself, looked at the spool of gold. "I looked for your studio yesterday downtown."

"We lost our lease," she said. "It was a cooperative of craftswomen. But then we didn't have a roof over our heads, so we disbanded—scattered."

He heard the note of regret in her voice and looked at her again. Her chin was up; there seemed no self-pity in her. But he said, "I'm sorry."

She shrugged one nearly bare shoulder. It was fascinatingly smooth. "We parted friends. The painter got married. The silversmith went back to San Antonio. The glassblower moved to Dallas."

"And you moved out to your mother's place."

She threw him a humor-filled glance. "I didn't have much choice. I had an apartment over the studio, and lost that, too, of course. Real estate's high in Austin. I've got my eye on another place down on Sixth Street. But it won't be available till early next year."

"So in the meantime?" he asked.

"I make do," she said, and slipped him a smile that struck him as shy.

"Your mother's lake house," he said. "I saw the For Sale sign. What will you do if it sells?"

She turned her attention back to the road. "Something'll turn up," she said. "It always does."

It seemed a hell of a scattershot way to run either a life or a business, but he said nothing.

They were both silent for a moment. Moodily he rolled the spool of gold thread between forefinger and thumb. He thought of the bizarre circumstances that had brought him and this woman together.

He said, "About my father and your mother—"

But at exactly the same moment, she said, "About my mother and your father—"

They both stopped, laughed self-consciously. She wiped a fluttering strand of hair from her face. "I suppose we should talk about it."

He watched the tendril of hair blow back again, caressing her cheekbone. "I suppose we should."

She inhaled deeply, which did absolutely arresting things to the bosom of the yellow dress. He imagined sliding his hand beneath its yellow strap, cupping the warmth and weight of those rounded breasts.

The thought excited and startled him. He realized he hadn't had a woman since he'd gotten back to the States, almost two months ago. But of all the women for him to want in his bed, she should be the last.

He tightened his yearning fingers into a fist around the spool. "My father's a good man," he said.

She gave a brief nod. "My mother's a good woman," she said. "It's just that this...surprised us. She swore she'd never marry again."

"So did my father," he said.

If ever I say I want another wife, John had told him, *subdue me. Straitjacket me, and put me in a padded cell until I come to my senses.*

Darcy swallowed. "This has happened to them so fast. Too fast. Emerald, my sister, says it's because of the Internet. Things tend to move at warp speed."

"So I've heard," he said.

The flowers in the landscape had changed, become more varied. There were blankets of vibrantly colored bluebonnets, bold red and gold Indian blankets, wine-pink blooming sand-burrs.

The look she gave him was troubled. "Has your father been on the Internet long?"

Sloan laughed in spite of himself. "No. I gave him the computer for Christmas. So we could keep in touch. What about your mother?"

Darcy's expression turned rueful. "The same thing. I gave her one for her birthday in January. She's a mere babe in the woods."

"So's my dad," he said. "At first he hated the thing."

"Mother, too."

"I guess they're faster learners than we thought."

She sighed again. Once more the bustline of the yellow dress moved so enticingly that Sloan swallowed. He looked away, crossed his legs, and wondered if Olivia had this effect on his father.

"Oh," Darcy said with concern. "Are you uncomfortable?"

"Not at all," he lied.

"I don't think I can move the seat back any farther," she apologized. "But we're almost to the house. It won't be much longer."

Thank God, he thought. *Stick to business,* he told himself. And he made himself think of his father, whose misguided sexual urge had brought down so much confusion.

"What concerns me," he said in a tight voice, "is not that our parents find each other attractive. That's not a problem for me."

She glanced at him, her dark eyes wide. "It's not a problem for me, either. I mean, they're adults. Like I wrote you, 'Live and let live.'"

"Exactly," he said. "I'd never interfere—"

"Me, either," she said with an emphatic shake of her head.

"—if it weren't for the how quickly they got serious—"

"Oh, *precisely,*" she agreed.

"—my concern is that they're leaping into a permanent relationship too soon—"

"That's *absolutely* the same reservation I have."

"—I don't want to see either of them hurt—" he persisted.

"No. No. I'd hate for anyone to be hurt," she said. "I mean, she's my mother. I'm *protective* about her."

"Of course," he said, and crossed his legs more tightly. "You should be. I feel the same way about my father—"

"Of course," she echoed. "That's perfectly natural."

She turned off the highway and down the road that led to the lake house. Dogwood trees bloomed on either side of the road, their white blossoms like a living veil of lace.

"I'm glad you can talk about this so rationally," he said. Beneath the surface, his own thoughts were anything but rational. He tensed his jaw and stared at the flowering dogwood.

"I feel the same," she said. "Now my sister, I'm afraid, is going to be emotional. Emerald's not a bad person. But she's got certain insecurities."

"I understand perfectly," he said. "It's the same with my aunt."

"And our parents *are* being hasty," Darcy said. "I'll be the first to admit it. The natural reaction is concern."

"Even alarm," he said.

"Yes, even alarm," she said sadly.

They'd reached the drive. She pulled into the driveway, parked the UV. The mysterious collection of things in the rear gave one last rattle.

She turned to him, her face serious. "Let's promise not to be alarmists," she said, her dark eyes earnest. "That you and I will be sensible about this."

Behind her, he could see the lake sparkling in the noon light. Its twinkling was a bit dazzling; it made her image dance in his eyes as if his fever had come back.

He said, "When I came here, I'm afraid I was hardly sensible."

"You weren't well," she said, as if she were his chief defender.

"You're kind to give me a second chance."

"This isn't about you and me," she said with feeling. "It's about our parents. That's what we have to remember."

"Positively," he said, although at the moment he couldn't for the life of him remember what his father even looked like.

"And no matter what happens, we will be levelheaded and cool. Because somebody has to."

He nodded solemnly, feeling neither levelheaded nor cool. The yellow dress addled his brain more powerfully than any fever. *I'm still tired,* he told himself. *I'm still convalescing. It's just that my libido got well before the rest of me did.*

"Promise?" she asked. She looked up at him with those depthless onyx-black eyes. She leaned toward him. He saw the hint of cleavage deepen, its shadow darken.

She held out her hand to him. It was silkily smooth and its grip firm.

"I promise," he whispered.

She squeezed his hand more tightly and smiled. He gave her a shaky smile in return.

"Come on," she said. "I'll show you around."

She was out of the UV. She reached into the back seat and took out the clay vase of flowers.

Numbly he got out, retrieved his suitcase.

"Come on," she repeated. "You'll love the view."

She led the way up a flagstone path. The breeze rose off the lake. It swirled the yellow skirt, lifting it above her knees, showing him the briefest glimpse of a smooth, lightly tanned thigh.

She was right. Good God, how he loved the view.

FROM THE OUTSIDE, Olivia's lake house looked deceptively modest.

Inside, the soaring cathedral ceilings made it spacious and airy. It was almost luminous with the light that spilled through the tall windows. Sliding glass doors framed the view of Lake Travis and led to the sweep of flagstone patio.

A white brick fireplace stood free and was all that divided living room from dining room. Carpet and walls were off-white, and Darcy herself had chosen the few large antique prints that hung on the walls.

It combined elegance with hominess, yet it had a sense of loneliness about it—the kind that houses get when weeks have passed with no one living in them. The silence of the place seemed like a palpable thing, poised in the air, waiting for something to happen.

This morning, as Darcy had stocked the refrigerator and arranged flowers, this silence had seemed peaceful. Now, with Sloan at her side, it made her inexplicably uneasy.

"Nice place," he said tonelessly.

She stole a glance at him. He might sound blasé, but she sensed his surprise. "It's one of those houses that opens up unexpectedly," she said, trying to sound nonchalant. "It's bigger than it looks from the outside."

"Yes," he said. "Well."

The green eyes seemed to be taking in everything with keen analysis. Did he surmise that Olivia was a rich woman, and was he trying to calculate exactly *how* rich?

Or did he wonder if Olivia, now widowed, could no longer maintain a house in such a style alone? And if she needed another man—such as his father—to support her expensive tastes?

He stared out at the blue-gray lake, the cliffs rising in splendid solitude on the far shore. "If I had a place like this, I don't know that I'd ever sell it," he said. It was a question disguised as a statement.

"She never really wanted a weekend place," Darcy said defensively. "She loves the house in town and says it's plenty to keep up. This is too much. It was my stepfather's idea. My mother isn't the outdoor type."

He arched a dark brow, looked her up and down. "And your stepfather was?"

"No. But he liked to think he was." Darcy moved to the coffee table, set down the vase of wildflowers.

He kept watching her. "Meaning?"

She straightened and rubbed her hands nervously in the folds of her skirt. Sometimes the only way to gain a confidence was to offer one.

She said, "Gus—my stepfather—had visions of himself as…I don't know what. He thought he'd retire here, buy a sailboat and host barbecues on the patio."

"And?" Sloan prodded.

She shrugged. "He could get away from his work maybe one weekend out of the month. He didn't know how to sail a boat or light a grill. When he *was* here, he was always on the phone back to the city."

Yelling, she thought sadly. *He was always on the phone yelling at someone.*

"So he didn't exactly commune with nature?"

She smiled bleakly. "Once in a while he went out on the patio and looked at the lake while he drank scotch. Or he took a nap in the hammock. That was it."

"So what did he do for a living?" Sloan asked casually. He glanced around the room. "Whatever it was, he was successful."

"He was a stockbroker," Darcy said. "Let me show you the kitchen."

She headed toward the kitchen, which had an octagonal breakfast nook with windows on four sides. Sloan strolled after her, looking about.

"The refrigerator's stocked and so is the pantry," she said. "The coffeemaker's in this pull-out cabinet. If you need directions for the microwave, they're in this drawer."

She turned to face him and nodded toward an open door. "There's a bar in the rec room. Help yourself to anything."

He gave her a look of peculiar intensity. He did not smile. It was as if he was asking, *Does "anything" include you?*

She gave a strange, inward shudder. *No, don't even think about it.*

But she realized he was thinking about it. And so was she.

It was ridiculous, she thought, angry with herself. She was here to protect Olivia from sexual foolishness, not to commit it on her own. She crossed her arms, raised her chin slightly.

"What about your father?" she asked, trying to sound friendly. "What does *he* do? I don't think Mama ever told us."

A cloud of uneasiness passed over his face, but was quickly gone. He said, "His main business is real estate."

She cocked her head in interest. "And that's in Florida?"

"Yes. The Keys," he said.

She knew little about the Florida Keys except that Key limes grew there, and, she supposed, alligators.

"Well," she said, "I suppose the real estate business is always brisk in Florida. Has he always done that?"

Sloan shrugged, gave her a one-cornered smile. "He's done other things. Sold insurance. Been in advertising—radio and television."

"Ah," she said as if satisfied. But he said no more, and she could read nothing in his face. She could suddenly think of no more to say.

She turned toward the hallway. "I'll show you your room."

She walked past the master bedroom, conscious of him close behind her.

She paused at the next door, put her hand on the knob.

"This room used to be Emerald's—my sister's," she said.

She swung open the door. Olivia had redone the room in cream and earth tones. A king-size bed stretched its width beneath an antique quilt. Darcy had opened the windows this morning, and the diaphanous curtains fluttered in the breeze. She could smell the spring scents of the garden.

"There's the bath," she said, gesturing toward a door that stood ajar. "You should find everything you need—"

"You're extremely generous," he said in a low voice. He set his suitcase on the luggage caddy.

He looked at the arrangement of flowers on the dresser. His lean fingers caressed a blossom with surprising gentleness. "This is your work. I recognize…the touch." Sloan raised his eyes to hers.

She turned away and shrugged almost irritably. She had vowed to be friendly, to ingratiate herself and disarm him. But flirting with him was another matter, a road she'd never meant to take.

"The laundry is at the end of the hall," she said. "Come outside. I'll show you the pool. And there's a path that leads to the boat dock. There's a little motorboat you can take out if you like. But be careful around the water. Mama'll never forgive me if I let you drown yourself."

She strode down the hall, feeling that her plan was doomed to fail, that it had failed already. She wished she had never agreed to let this man invade the sanctuary of the lake hideaway. She'd been mad.

As she pushed open the back door, she sensed him behind her. His presence pressed against her like a prickling weight.

The pool was a rectangle of brilliant azure water. At its bottom, shimmering like an illusion, was a large mosaic of a cluster of water hyacinths. Gus had wanted a mermaid with large bare breasts, but Olivia would not stand for it.

Gus had prevailed about the fence that surrounded the pool.

Olivia wanted a privacy fence of cedar planks, but for once Gus had gotten the better of her in a decorating decision.

"Privacy from *what?*" he'd railed. "Privacy from *who?* My God, I paid half a million dollars to get us away from goddamn everybody! And for this view—now you want to wall it off?"

Finally Olivia gave him his way, although she thought the chain link fence a horror. Gus did not even want vines planted to beautify it: "Who am I, Tarzan, that I want to look at vines?"

Darcy felt both rueful and sad at the memory of her volatile stepfather.

What would he think if he knew Olivia wanted to marry again? Would he be resentful, jealous, bitter? Was he turning in his grave because Sloan English now stood here on his property, his stronghold?

"Something wrong?" asked Sloan.

She shook her head. "A lot of memories here, that's all."

"Good ones or bad?"

"Both," she said, not wanting to reveal more. "I guess it'll be good when the place is sold, and we all move on."

"You can't leave memories. They go with you, whether you like it or not," he said. He sounded like a man who knew.

"They get dimmer," she said. "And mellower."

"You don't like to look back?" he asked.

"Why?" she challenged. "You can't *go* back. You have to live in the present."

The wind stirred her disarranged hair, blowing it across her face and neck in tickling strands. With one hand she smoothed it back, and with the other held down the fluttering skirt of the yellow dress.

"The present," he echoed in a tone that seemed strangely intimate.

She avoided his gaze and instead scanned the familiar scene, wondering what it looked like to his eyes. Olivia's touch was everywhere.

About the pool were jardinieres spilling with flowers and

glossy, trailing vines. Beyond the pool was the informal garden of wildflowers mixed with tame perennials. Stepping stones of native limestone meandered through the blooms, leading north to the guest cottage where she worked and lived.

To the west was the back gate in the fence. It opened to a path that wound out of sight down through the mesquite trees and loblolly pines to the open water.

"That goes to the lake," she said. "If you want to use the boat, an extra set of keys is there—" she pointed at the statue of a horned toad squatting by a potted cactus "—under the toad."

But Sloan ignored the toad. His eyes traveled to the guest house instead, and he smiled. "How's my friend the bookworm?"

"I have to pack him up and deliver him to the library this afternoon," Darcy said. "Now that you know your way around, I'll leave you alone. I'm sure you'll want to rest, so I'll stay out of your way."

"You said something about a tour through the Hill Country," he reminded her.

"Yes," she said. "Well. We'll have to set that up some time. At the moment, I have to be on my way."

She started to turn to go, but he said, "Darcy?"

Her name held her in place like a charm.

"Yes?" she said reluctantly, looking up at him.

He held out his hand. "Thank you."

She took his hand and shook it firmly. But when she tried to release it, his fingers tightened around hers, warm and strong. He moved imperceptibly nearer.

"I don't deserve any of this," he said. "If your mother's anything like you, then my father's a very lucky man."

Her heart turned a slow cartwheel in her chest. "My mother," she said with feeling, "is a much better person than I am."

She is, Darcy thought dazedly. *She's warmer, braver, more original, more giving. You have no idea what she's been through.*

She said only, "She deserves to be happy."

He bent nearer. "So does my father."

"My mother hasn't had an easy life," she said, raising her face to his.

"Neither has my father," he said.

"It's true she made some wrong choices along the way—" Darcy breathed.

"So did my father," he murmured.

"But who hasn't?" she asked, gazing helplessly up into his eyes.

"We all have," he agreed. "But some of us get second chances."

He raised his free hand and gently stroked a tendril of hair from her eyes. When the breeze blew it free, he stroked it out of the way again and held it in place, his fingertips gentle against her temple. She felt her vein jump beneath his touch.

Don't let him touch you like this, she warned herself. *Move away.* But she did not move away.

He stared down at her, consternation and longing in his eyes. She knew he wanted to kiss her and was waiting for some signal to tell him "yes." Or "no."

He could have bent and taken her lips without any further invitation than her lack of resistance. She knew this. But she knew such an act would be a complex and certain wrong. And yet—

Sloan's nearness had shut out awareness of all else. Dimly, on the outskirts of her consciousness, she heard a foreign sound. It was like the tick-tocking of a clock that grew steadily louder.

Too late she realized it was the slow, clopping sound of hoofbeats.

"Hey!" cried a voice sharp with indignation. "What's this?"

Darcy's head whirled, and her eyes widened when she looked up to see Emerald sitting on an enormous black horse.

Her face was pale with anger, and she stared through the fence in disbelief.

Darcy felt Sloan's muscles stiffen. They both stood as if paralyzed.

"Darcy!" Emerald's voice quaked with emotion. "What are you doing? What *is* this? What's going *on?*"

CHAPTER SEVEN

SLOAN SAW THE expression of guilt flash across Darcy's face. She snatched her hand away from his and took a quick step back from him.

Emerald sat astride the horse looking like the incarnation of outraged justice. Her back was straight, and her cheeks blazed with two patches of angry red.

Sloan looked the girl up and down with cool appraisal. She was dressed almost normally, in jeans and riding boots, but her white shirt had an old-fashioned flair. The sleeves billowed, and it was cinched with a belt of leather and gold chain.

"Your mother insisted I stay here when I got out of the hospital," he said evenly. "Your sister was kind enough to bring me."

"You're staying *here?*" Emerald demanded. "I don't approve of this!"

Darcy's self-control came surging back. After all, Emerald had no right to make a scene. "You don't have to approve," she said. "Mother insisted. It's her house, and he's her guest. It's no concern of yours."

"If my being here is going to cause trouble—" Sloan began.

Darcy interrupted, "My mother *wants* you here. She'd be very upset if you leave—"

"And you!" Emerald flung at Darcy. "You're collaborating with the enemy. You're aiding and abetting him."

"The last thing I want," said Sloan, "is to cause conflict. I'll be perfectly comfortable in a hotel."

"Good," said Emerald with a toss of her head. "The sooner the better."

"Emerald," Darcy retorted, "you're being rude and unreasonable—"

"I'll take my things and go," Sloan said, and turned toward the house.

Darcy's hand shot out and seized him by the elbow. "No, you won't. Mother'd have a fit. Emerald, you will not emotionally bully your way—"

"He's not only on our property—you're making goo-goo eyes at him," Emerald said in reproach. "You're as bad as mother."

"Emerald!" cried Darcy.

"I refuse to be in the middle of this," Sloan said with a shake of his head. He tried to draw away from Darcy, but she refused to release him.

"This is Mama's house," she said stubbornly. "And you're here by her invitation. Emerald has no say in this."

"I have no say in *anything*," Emerald retorted. "I told you I didn't want this. You *know* how I feel—you stabbed me in the back, Darcy."

"That's not fair," Darcy countered.

"I won't be part of this," Emerald said. With an angry movement she pulled at the reins. The horse danced nervously and turned in the direction from which they'd come. "You can call me when *he's* gone," she said over her shoulder. "And when you're ready to apologize."

She kicked the horse's flanks, and he broke into a gallop, Emerald hunched over his neck like a jockey. They disappeared around the curve in the drive.

"Oh, Lord," Darcy moaned. Her hand fell away from Sloan's arm. "I'm *so* sorry." She moved to the lawn chair and dropped to sit on it, her elbows on her knees and her face hidden by her hands.

Sloan stared at her in alarm. Was she crying? He hated it when women cried. It was one of the ways Trina used to manipulate him. Conflict jostled in his chest, and opposing desires tore at him. He wanted to go to her, put his arm around her, draw her near and comfort her. And he wanted to escape this craziness.

Darcy was beautiful and desirable—and she meant nothing but trouble. Her sister was unhinged, and her mother was about to become his stepmother.

Her back shook, as with sobs, but she made no sound.

"Are you crying?" he asked uneasily.

"No," she said in a tone of disgust. "I'm laughing."

"Laughing?" he echoed in disbelief.

"At the absurdity," she said, letting her hands fall away. She sat up straight again, and her pretty face seemed wanly amused. She shook her head ruefully. "I'm sorry," she repeated.

"You're not responsible for your sister's behavior," he said, clenching and unclenching his right fist.

"She can be…difficult."

This seemed a masterpiece of understatement. "I understand. My aunt's the same. She overreacts to things."

Darcy shook her head again and said nothing. She gazed toward the lake with an air of resignation.

"Listen," he said, clenching his fist again. "I'll move into town. It's the best thing for all concerned."

She quickly turned to face him. The dark eyes looked both pleading and full of defiance. "But you *can't*," she protested. "Especially not now—Mama will be mortified."

"She'll understand," he said, hoping he was right.

"She won't," Darcy said with conviction. "For years we've been trying to teach Emerald she can't have her way just by making a fuss. I mean, it's *wrong* to cave in to her wishes."

"It's wrong to set a family against itself," he said, watching how the breeze played with her loosened hair.

"She's a—complicated person. But she can't get her own way just because she pitches a fit. Mama'll be upset twice over. Emerald's got to grow up, dammit."

Her voice gave an emotional catch when she said "dammit,'' and his heart came undone. He went to her and sat down beside her on the lounge. ''Your sister's got problems,'' he said.

''Yes,'' she said unhappily. ''And I don't blame you for wanting to leave. You don't need somebody else's problems. Nobody does.''

''Try me,'' he said. ''Tell me about her.''

She looked at him warily.

''Hey,'' he said, and gave her a one-sided smile. ''It's okay. It's all in the family.''

''I suppose you'll have to tell your father this happened,'' she said. She clasped her hands together and squeezed them between her knees.

He had the urge to trail his fingers over her bare shoulder and down the smooth, clean curve of her arm. ''I'll let your mother handle it,'' he said. ''You'll tell her, won't you?''

She nodded and cast him a searching sidelong look. ''Will you stay?''

''If you'll tell me about Emerald. When I first saw her I thought she was dressed like a knight. Or was that a fever dream?''

She gave him a resigned smile. ''Her life revolves around the Medieval Society. They try to recreate the Middle Ages— or at least their fantasy of it. Emerald didn't like being a damsel or a wench. So she liberated herself.''

Her upper lip had the most fascinating curve, and he imagined tracing it with his tongue. He tried to force himself to concentrate on the conversation instead. ''The horse,'' he said. ''Is that her palfrey or whatever you call it?''

''Her steed,'' Darcy said with another half smile. ''Yes. She boards it at a neighbor's. There's no pasture for a horse here. And my stepfather was allergic to horses. But she'd been losing interest in it. I didn't expect her to show up here today.''

''You and your mother didn't tell her I was here. Why? Because you knew what her reaction would be?''

''Yes. And I suppose that was a tactical error.'' She sighed.

"But with Emerald, sometimes it's easier not to tell her everything."

"She doesn't like the thought of your mother remarrying." He could understand that idea all too well, thanks to Trina.

"Emerald didn't like our stepfather. Her father died when she was four. It was very traumatic for her. He was in a car accident. She was with him. He was killed instantly. She woke up in the hospital terrified, in a lot of pain. They didn't know if she'd walk again."

"I'm sorry."

She shrugged sadly. "There were a lot of medical bills. Then therapist's bills. Because after the accident, Emerald was...different. She became demanding. Shy, but demanding. And Mama met Gus. He was willing to take us all on. Most men wouldn't have."

"But your sister never accepted him?"

"Not really. No."

He studied her solemn profile. "You said 'Emerald's father.' You had different fathers?"

"My father died before I was two," she said. "An aneurysm. It was very unexpected. He was only twenty-nine."

"I'm sorry," he said again. "And Gus?"

"He was sick a long time," she said. "So yes, my mother's been married three times."

And outlived all three husbands, Sloan thought with an ominous twinge. He didn't like the idea of his father being the fourth in a fatal series.

Darcy smoothed her tousled hair. "Emerald's been better these last few years. She's finishing college this spring, and she's going to graduate school in the fall. Last year, she moved out of Mother's house in town and got an apartment on her own. She seemed ready to try her wings."

"That's why your mother decided to get a place in Maine?"

Darcy nodded. "She's always missed the sea. For years she'd dreamed of going back. She thought a summer place would be wonderful."

"Your sister didn't protest?"

"Not a lot. She'll be going away herself. She has her choice of graduate schools, though I can't imagine her going off very far. And she knows Mama's full-time home will always be here."

She frowned slightly. "Or that's what she—we—thought. Until your father came into the picture."

"Your sister feels threatened."

She nodded silently and turned to him again. He realized that their faces were within inches of each other. If he leaned forward…

She said, "What do you suppose their plans are—our parents? If they marry, would your father want her to move to Florida?"

Sloan looked about unhappily. Olivia had four dwellings, counting the guest house, even though the lake property was for sale. The lake house, with its pool and tended gardens and sweeping view, made his father's one-bedroom apartment look like a rat hole.

He shook his head. "My father has land in the Keys. But he doesn't live there. It's not developed. He hangs on to it, waiting for the right deal to come along. He lives in an apartment."

"In Key West?"

"No. The neighboring key. He rents. He's been alone for a long time. His work keeps him busy. His…projects."

She gave him a long, searching look that seemed to curl the edges of his heart. "What kind of projects?" she asked softly.

It was the question he'd been dreading. "It's kind of complicated," he said. "He's got a lot of irons in the fire."

"I told you about Emerald and my family," she said.

"Yes. You did."

"I'd like to know about yours."

A sudden inspiration struck him. "That's complicated, too," he said. "And you said you had to take the bookworm to the library."

Startled, she looked at her watch. "You're right," she cried, "I'm running late." She leaped to her feet.

He rose, too, putting his hands on her bare shoulders. "I'll tell you what you want to know—if you'll have supper with me tonight."

Her dark eyes widened. "You're convalescing. You shouldn't go out."

"We'll have it here," he said. "God knows, there's a mountain of food in there—too much for one man. Join me."

She hesitated. Her flesh felt warm and velvety beneath his fingers. She looked down at the cement.

"Join me," he repeated. "I'm a stranger in a strange land. And we need to talk. This is, after all, about family."

But as he touched her, his thoughts were not of family, not of his parent or hers. They were carnal thoughts laced with a strange tenderness that was foreign to him, yet pleasant.

A less pleasant thought crossed his mind. "That is—" he said, "unless you have other plans. Unless there's someone you're seeing…"

She shook her head. "No. Nobody right now."

Then the men of Austin are hopeless fools to let you run around unclaimed, he thought with feeling. He said, "Then you'll say yes?"

"Yes," she said, but she seemed uneasy that he was touching her. "Just something quick and simple. I'll need to go back to my place early. I…planned the evening to catch up on my paperwork."

He stepped back, reluctantly let his hands fall away from her warmth and softness. "Sure. I understand."

"Yes, fine," she said, but there was still uncertainty in her air. "I'll see you later, then."

"What time?" he asked.

"Around seven," she said. "Is that all right?"

"Perfect," he said, although it seemed an eternity away. She turned, gave him a tentative smile over her shoulder, then headed for her own house. He watched her go, his heart beating as if his fever were back.

Her skirt swung softly about the curves of her hips. That yellow dress really *was* driving him crazy. He loved it on her. He loved even more the idea of taking it off her.

SUBJECT: Has that Poor Boy Arrived?
From: Olivia@USAserve.com
To: DesignByDarcy@USAserve.com

Dear Darcy-Duck—
Has that poor boy arrived at the lake house?

I tried phoning several times, but all I got was that evil answering machine of yours. I *hate* talking with a tape recorder; it never has anything original to say.

At any rate, darling, please do everything in your power to make poor Sloan comfortable.

John says he may seem like an uptight business sort, but his heart's in the right place. He seems cool around women because he had a very traumatic childhood—*not* John's fault, by the way.
Love and hugs, Mama

Darcy looked at her mother's message and sighed in exasperation. "The poor boy" was no boy. He was a man, and in spite of his illness he seemed an extraordinarily virile one.

As for his being "cool toward women," her shoulders still tingled from his touch. He had been, by turns, amiable, flirtatious, kindly and seductive.

She understood: he found her sexually desirable. He wanted her. And she found him bewilderingly exciting and wanted him in return, which was totally insane.

It's the lure of the forbidden, she told herself. To become involved with him would shock Olivia—and hopelessly complicate her already complicated romance. And Emerald, of course, would never forgive her.

Darcy shook her head at her own folly. *Forget about him,* she told herself. *There are plenty of men in Texas—millions.*

And not one of them comes with such a tangle of strings attached.

But as she bundled up the bookworm in layers of tissue, she found Sloan was not easy to forget. She'd vowed to pry out all his family secrets. Instead, he'd gotten hers, and she'd learned almost nothing.

Oh, hell, she muttered, giving the bookworm one more layer of tissue paper. She both anticipated and dreaded seeing the man again tonight. For someone who had just been sick, how did he radiate so much masculine energy? What was he like when he was *well,* for God's sake?

She wrapped the bookworm up in a final cocoon of brown paper and tied him securely with string. Then she threw a wary glance at the computer. Its screen glowed tauntingly. Before leaving for the library, she knew she should write Olivia, but she'd make it short.

SUBJECT: Before This Goes Too Far…
From: DesignByDarcy@USAserve.com
To: Olivia@USAserve.com

Sloan English (the "poor boy") is here, and, frankly, I don't find the situation comfortable.

For starters, we were standing by the pool when Emerald surprised us and threw a major fit. You'll probably hear all about it from her.

Mother, before this goes any farther (and gets even more awkward), would you mind saying if you *really* plan to marry John English?

My main concern—and I'm sure it's Emerald's, too— is your happiness and security.*
Love, D.

*P.S.—I can't emphasize this *too much.*

With a twinge of reluctance, she sent the message. It might not be pleasant or graceful, but at least it was honest. Especially honest was the part that it was not comfortable having Sloan so near.

There were such problems with the situation, she thought, frowning. And so many unanswered questions about John English—and his son. Sloan's sexual attractiveness struck her as dangerous; it dizzied the mind and clouded the judgment. What she needed were facts—hard, cold and dependable.

Her gaze roamed the room and fell on the bookworm, shrouded in his cocoon of paper. Where was he going, of course, but to the library? And in what did the library specialize?

Information.

She smiled with sudden inspiration. She knew Brian MacVey, the new young head of the reference department. Indeed, he acted as if he had a bit of a crush on her.

She rose and picked up the bookworm purposefully. "Come on, buddy," she said. "We've got a mission. And it's right up your caterpillar alley."

In THE GUEST BEDROOM of the main house, Sloan heard Darcy's rattling vehicle pull away. Its sound slowly faded into the distance, until there was silence.

He was alone in Olivia Ferrar's house.

It was a spy's most succulent dream come true. What answers did the place hold? What secrets did it hide? A cursory glance around the room told him little about Olivia, except that she probably had money and she certainly had taste.

But the house also made a powerful statement about hospitality—both hers and Darcy's. Fresh toiletries ranged the bathroom counter; clean towels were folded over the racks; a vase of cut flowers stood next to the sink. A man's expensive Turkish bathrobe, looking freshly laundered, hung on a hook.

In the bedroom, more fresh flowers decorated the dresser. The spicy scent of a mood candle, although unlit, mixed with the flowers' fragrance. On the bedside table were arranged a trio of bestsellers, the latest issue of *Time* magazine, and a crystal dish of wrapped candies.

Laid across a cedar chest were a pair of men's swim trunks and a sand-colored terry-cloth beach jacket with a matching towel. There were even rubber thongs for poolside, a bottle of tanning lotion, and men's sunglasses.

He tried to be cynical and wonder if Olivia always kept such niceties for the overnight male guest. Or had they been the property of the late, unfortunate Gus?

Yet somehow cynicism didn't work in this room. The space seemed pervaded by Darcy's touch, both so artful and artless. It was in the flowers and in other nuances so small that he couldn't articulate them. But he could feel them, and they made him ashamed of himself.

His schemes of espionage put a bad taste in his mouth. A gentleman, he told himself in disgust, does not accept hospitality in order to pry.

Neither did a gentleman go lusting after his potential stepsister. A gentleman took a cold shower.

Instead, he went to the sink, filled a glass, and took a choloroquinine pill and two aspirins. Then, he opened his suitcase and took out the notebook computer.

He'd purposely kept his cell phone switched off, the better to deflect Trina. She did not like e-mail and used it only as a last resort; it confused her, and she did not type well. Her fingers often fumbled, and she would accidentally delete the messages that came to her or erase the ones she tried to send. It didn't stop her, but it slowed her considerably.

He sat down on the bed, switched on the machine and typed in his password. When he pulled up his e-mail, he smiled to himself grimly. Sure enough, there was a message from Trina.

SUBJECT: Why Haven't I Heard From You?
From: TrinaK@SuperNet.com
To: SloanJEnglish@PetroCorp.com

Sloan—Why haven't I heard from you? It's been almost 24 hrs since Ive had a shred of news from you and I can't get thru on your celluloid phone, it is very frustating and you havent even told me where you are staying at, is everything alright?

Have you made contact with that woman's family? I just have no idea what's happening. It is not me myself I worry about, no it is poor Arthur.

Your devouted aunt,

Trina

Sloan thought of Trina's cheerless little house in Tulsa, with its grinding, everlasting sense of genteel poverty. Trina didn't *have* to live that way; he knew this for a fact. But she chose to, because of her morbid fear that if she didn't, she and Arthur would be left penniless.

She would not only be jealous of Olivia's life-style, but sneeringly critical of it. Worse, she would feel threatened by it. She would see Olivia as a gold digger who would lay waste the English family fortune—or what in Trina's mind passed for it.

Sloan gritted his teeth. He did not get the impression that Olivia needed money. Indeed, she seemed far better off than his father. It seemed clear that if anybody in the picture would be accused of gold digging, the likeliest suspect was John.

This was a painful admission, and Sloan leaned back against the headboard, brooding upon it. He thought a long time.

At last, he knew what he should do—the thing he should have done at the beginning of this circus. He sent Trina a short e-mail that told her to be patient, that he was tending to things.

Then he snapped open his cell phone and started making calls.

EMERALD WALKED IN TO the Armadillo Café with her head held high. She wanted to look cool and controlled, but she was nervous. Never in her life had she done anything so boldly seditious. She was relieved that even in daytime the restaurant's lighting was dim.

Before coming here, she had sent her mother an e-mail. It had been emotional and dramatic, but she didn't regret it. She wanted Olivia to know *exactly* how she felt.

Peanut shells crunched beneath her feet, and the smell of beer was coppery on the air. Neon liquor signs glowed in the shadows, and the jukebox sat silent in the afternoon business lull.

Emerald looked around, knowing *he* would already be there. He was. He sat alone in a leatherette booth, underneath a pair of mounted steer horns.

His gaze met hers with naked longing. She smiled stiffly, trying to hide the resentment she still felt against him.

She hadn't seen him for almost three years. Yet a frisson of surprise rippled through her. He had changed.

He was taller now, and he'd lost his horrible baby fat. He'd become almost lanky, and he must have gotten contacts, for his thick-lensed glasses were gone.

"Hello, Henry," she said, drawing to a halt beside his table.

She wore a doublet of green silk, leather breeches, and high boots of soft leather. He had always said he was an absolute sucker for silk and leather. She was hoping that he still was. She crossed her arms and stared down at him with a confidence she didn't feel.

"Emerald," he said almost reverently. He stood. "You look—beautiful. Won't you sit down?" He made a timid gesture toward the empty space beside him.

Her only answer was a regal nod. She sat across from him, not next to him. The power, so far, was hers, and she intended to keep it.

His gaze fell away as if in shame. He had a glass of something dark, and he pushed it aside, a nervous gesture.

"Still drinking Dr. Pepper?" she asked, a falsely polite edge to her voice.

He grinned sheepishly. He was almost three years younger

than she, not old enough to drink beer, and if he tried, even a single glass made him dizzy and giggly. "Yeah," he said.

"So," she said with elaborate casualness, "how are things going?"

"Great," he said, turning the glass in aimless circles. "I'm going back to Stanford in the fall."

"That's good," she said. She'd heard he'd dropped out spring semester because he'd come home to donate a kidney to his young sister, Shelley. The story had been in all the local papers. She'd hated it because it made him seem heroic, when, in truth, he was a toad. After what he had done, he should have to give up both his kidneys, his pancreas, his penis, and his testicles.

But she said, "What you did was very noble, Henry."

He shook his head, wouldn't meet her eyes. "It was family, that's all," he mumbled.

She took a deep breath. "Family," she said. "Then maybe you'll understand why I called you."

Slowly he raised his gaze to hers.

She was unpleasantly shocked to realize that he had actually turned into a rather good-looking young man. He no longer wore braces on his teeth. The skin across his cheekbones skin was slightly pitted from his old acne problem, but the shallow scars seemed to add character to his face.

He said, "You know all you have to do is snap your fingers, and I'd come to you, Emerald. I keep hoping someday to put it right between us."

He looked away from her. He began to twist the glass again, and he swallowed as if something in his throat hurt.

He stared down at the table. "Are you still in the Medieval Society?" he asked.

"Yes," she said brightly.

"Does it still make you happy?" he asked.

"Yes," she said, although these days she was not sure that it did.

"Good," he said with a humble nod. "I want you to be happy."

She leaned toward him, filled with conflicting emotions. He had broken her heart and humiliated her once, this boy, this *child*.

She had encountered him on the Internet when she was eighteen and too shy to deal with men in real life. They had met in a fantasy role-playing game, and she'd been bewitched by his intelligence, his self-deprecating wit, his sweetness. Most impressive, he seemed to be a genius with computers.

For months they'd flirted, and for months he'd lied to her. He said his name was Harrison, not Henry; that he was twenty-two, not fifteen; and that he was a senior at Harvard, not a high school sophomore in the suburbs of Austin.

He'd said he was six feet tall and had sent her a photo that was really of his cousin Weldon, who was very handsome and naturally athletic.

Emerald had been completely smitten. She had not known her conquest was a fat little high school boy with bad skin and a mouth full of metal. The worst and most shameful thing was that she'd had "virtual sex" with him. They wrote each other long, steamy messages of intimate acts they imagined committing with each other, and Emerald still blushed hotly at the memory.

Henry's older brother had found out and had sent Emerald an e-mail telling her the truth. He also sent an unattractive yearbook photo of Henry playing the bassoon in the high school pep band. Emerald had been devastated and had never told the whole truth to anyone.

But if Emerald had been devastated, so had Henry. He hitchhiked from the suburbs on a Friday afternoon to find her on the university campus and apologize.

He had begged forgiveness and cried. It had been terrible— this little fat boy weeping over her.

"I'll always love you, Emerald," he'd sworn. "True love—heart's love—age and appearance has nothing to do with it."

"Yes, it does!" Emerald had cried angrily in return. And she never went back to the fantasy game rooms again. She discovered the Medieval Society, and now she only socialized with men she could actually see. And she had been careful not to have sex with even one of them, no matter how real he was.

Henry sent her e-mails that she never answered. He sent her real letters, beautifully written. She refused to reply. Sometimes he sent her a single rose, an original poem, a book or recording he thought she might like.

But her heart was hardened against him.

Until now.

Now she leaned nearer to him. When she put her hand on his arm, she heard the sharp, helpless intake of his breath.

"Henry," she said as seductively as she could, "once you said there was nothing on earth you wouldn't do for me. Did you mean it?"

His face grew both pained and radiant. "Yes," he breathed. "Oh, yes."

Her grip on his arm tightened. "Are you still an Einstein with computers?"

He swallowed again. "So they say."

"Can you get in somebody's e-mail? Can you find out their secrets?"

He looked into her eyes worshipfully. "For you, I'd do anything," he said. "Anything. Anything in the world."

CHAPTER EIGHT

THE CLOUDS WERE LOW and leaden in Maine, with the wind keening out of the north. Rain threatened, and the sky was already turning dark.

Olivia didn't care. She was in John's strong arms, warm and safe in her bed. His flight had arrived safely, beating the gathering storm.

But the weather had delayed him, and the wait had made them both nervous. Nerves had made them amorous, so it had come to pass that Olivia hadn't opened the wine or set out the canapés or warmed up the clam chowder.

Instead, when she brought him home from the airport, they'd helped each other out of their coats, kissing and nuzzling, and one thing had led to another. They'd left a trail of clothing into the bedroom, which was cozy and dim, its drapes drawn against the fading light.

A small Tiffany lamp glowed on the bedside table, casting jewel-colored glints through the shadows. Olivia sighed with satisfaction and rubbed her cheek against John's chest. It was a good chest, still firm with muscle and sprinkled thickly with salt-and-pepper hair.

"You're really here," she said, and kissed his shoulder.

He smiled as he drew her down to kiss her on the lips. His mustache tickled. She laughed softly in delight.

"What's so funny?" he asked.

She raised herself again to look down at him fondly. He was a big man, tall and wide-shouldered. Although his thick hair was silver, his brows and mustache were still dark. He had a mischievous glint in his green eyes, but his smile was always kind.

"It's odd," she said, "our finding each other. I never intended to fall in love with anybody at this point in my life."

"Neither did I," he said. He lifted her hand and kissed the palm again.

She loved that. No other man had kissed her so often and so affectionately. She took her forefinger and traced his mustache. "I like that cookie duster."

"The better to dust your cookies, my dear," he said, and pulled her close again.

She settled against his bare shoulder, as he played with a strand of her hair that had come loose. She drew the sheets up to more fully cover her naked breasts.

"Going shy on me?" he asked against her ear.

"A little," she breathed. She had been married three times, yet she had never before felt comfortable being naked with a man. She was just learning how.

Sex with Gus had been frequent, but almost brutally swift. His snores had always started as soon as it was over, and she'd covered herself and slipped from his bed as quickly as she could. There had never been foreplay, cuddling, pillow talk…

Thinking of Gus made her sad. It also made her remember her daughters and the e-mails she'd gotten from them today. The messages made her feel lonely for them, yet also unpleasantly guilty.

John sensed the change in her mood immediately. "Olivia? Is something wrong?"

She sighed. "I have to keep telling myself it's all right to be this happy."

"I know," he said. "I do, too."

She nestled more intimately against him. Another man might have answered her with some smooth catchword, tried to give her easy assurance. Not John. He understood her as no other person had ever done.

"It's your girls, isn't it?" He ran his hand up and down her arm.

"Oh, John," she said, turning to him, "you should be a psychic."

It was a private joke, and they laughed together gently. He laid his forehead against hers.

He said, "Did you hear from them?"

Her heart beat faster, and she coiled her arm around his neck. She snuggled against his chest again. "Yes."

"And?"

She paused. She did not want to tell him that having Sloan at the lake house angered Emerald and made Darcy feel "uncomfortable." John would insist that Sloan move out, and Olivia could not stand for such a thing. It was her house, and her daughters should not dictate to her—especially Emerald.

John took her chin between his thumb and forefinger, tilting her face so that she had to meet his eyes. He said, "I can guess. Your girls think we're plunging into this too fast. And they're probably not too happy having Sloan on their hands."

"He's not on their *hands,* darling," Olivia hedged. "They don't have to see him at all. Especially Emerald. Maybe I should have told her he'd be there. But I didn't, and now she's in a snit."

John put his hand to his own forehead as if going into a trance. "Wait—" he said, his eyes fluttering shut. "I'm having a vision. Emerald thinks…he's there to check up on *you.* That he'll be looking under your beds and going through your cabinets and desk drawers."

Olivia's mouth turned into a circle of surprise. "Good grief, you *do* have powers."

He opened his eyes and smiled. "No," he said. "Nothing paranormal. Just an imagination. You're her beautiful mama, and she's protective. She thinks I'm the conniving evil wooer. Now my larcenous family is in your very stronghold, probably trying to crack your safe."

She rose on her elbow again and gave him a smile. "You

really *are* impressive. The Amazing Mr. English, mentalist *extraordinaire.*''

He waggled his dark brows. ''You should see me in my black cape.''

''I prefer you without it,'' she said saucily, and settled down beside him again, hugging him tightly. The sheet had fallen away, and her naked breasts were exposed and pressed against him, but she didn't mind. She liked the feeling. She rubbed her nose affectionately against his shoulder.

''Did I really get it right?'' he asked, sounding pleased with himself. ''About Emerald, I mean?''

She went still in his arms.

''Olivia?'' he said. He had a rich baritone voice, and it could prickle her to her marrowbones.

She said nothing, not wanting to conceal things from him, but not wanting to burden him, either.

He said, ''There's something else, isn't there? What is it?''

She hesitated. ''Well, Emerald said exactly what I'd have expected her to say—except for one thing.''

''Which was?''

Olivia laughed self-consciously. ''She said she thought that your son was 'making a play' for Darcy—and that Darcy liked it.''

John's body tensed. ''She said *what?*''

Olivia ran her fingers over the silky hair of his chest. ''That she thought he was 'making a play' for Darcy,'' she repeated. ''And Darcy liked it.''

''Nonsense,'' John said gruffly. ''Sloan isn't that kind. I mean, he seems to have perfectly normal urges. But he avoids commitment. And he never 'makes a play' for a woman. He's never had to. They're like moths, and he's like a flame. He waits for them to come to him.''

Olivia didn't find this comparison either pleasant or assuring. She said, ''Well, Darcy's hardly susceptible herself. She could have almost any man she wants. She just never wants one—at least, very much.''

They were quiet a moment, holding each other but lost in their own thoughts.

"I actually wish he'd find someone," John said at last. "I worry about him. He's such a lone wolf. And he likes going to dangerous places. After this fever hit, I told him he should think of settling down. He said, 'I've got one word for you—*never.*'"

"He should meet a nice girl," Olivia said. "Have a family."

John sighed. "I'm afraid he's seen what happened to me, and it's made him phobic about marriage."

Olivia pondered this. "Exactly. I feel the same about Darcy. She saw what I went through, and it's made her too independent for her own good."

Again they went quiet. Olivia thought of Darcy, whom she loved. She thought of John, and how much he cared for Sloan. How odd if her daughter and his son would— She pushed away the idea. It was too disconcerting.

"Maybe Emerald's just trying to plant some dark guilt about incest in your mind," John said moodily.

Emerald isn't like that, Olivia almost said, but she bit back the words. Instead, she said, "If Sloan isn't the type and Darcy isn't the type, Em's probably just imagining things, poor child."

"Poor child," John repeated, but he didn't sound convinced.

"After all," Olivia said earnestly, "the point is that they really are worried about us, that we're running into this too fast, that we're pretending it's simple when it's really quite complex."

She paused again. There were, after all, questions she and John had to answer—hard ones. Where they were going to live. Whether he would give up the dream in Key West he'd waited so long to achieve—

"Olivia," John murmured against her hair, "maybe we're doing the opposite. Making it complex when it's really quite simple."

"Simple?" she said dubiously, and started to pull up the sheet to cover herself again.

He held the sheet where it was. He lowered his head and kissed her between her breasts. "Yes," he whispered. "This simple."

And she wanted to believe him, because he made her happy—happier than she had ever been.

She pushed the sheets away so that they were both completely naked, and gave herself up to loving him.

DARCY FERVENTLY HOPED her mother was making decisions with her head, not her hormones. Hormones had suddenly become a deeply troubling issue to Darcy, one she didn't choose to dwell on. She had business to tend.

She had to present the bookworm to the library board, a sort of unofficial preliminary unveiling. She dreaded this, for she hated red tape of every sort, and the library board came festooned with it.

Although Carmelita, the president, had promised a short meeting of the board, in truth, there was no such thing. Darcy answered questions about her work that she'd answered half a dozen times before. Was it really worth what the library had paid for it? Was it appropriate? Was it sturdy? Was it safe? Was it politically correct?

Darcy addressed each issue with all the tact and good sense she could muster. She stayed for the obligatory cookies and punch, then escaped. She was sorry to leave the bookworm, whom she would miss, but glad to be done with officialdom.

Throughout the meeting, she had been haunted by thoughts not only of Olivia, but also of Sloan. He dwelt in the back of her mind, green-eyed and troubling. He was alone now in her mother's house. *Doing what?*

In a short time, she would be with him. The knowledge filled her with clashing feelings and an uncertainty that was foreign to her.

Well, she thought, it was clear that there was one thing she must do. She didn't yet know the truth about John English, so she must find it. Olivia might be horrified at such snooping, but if she wouldn't check out John English herself, Darcy would.

She made her way to the desk of Brian MacVey, the reference librarian. Brian was a tall young man with a rounded face, rounded shoulders, and a rounded stomach that hung over his belt. He wore tiny metal-rimmed glasses, and freckles spattered the bridge of his nose.

Even in warmest weather, Brian wore a tie and a long-sleeved shirt with French cuffs. He always had cuff links that matched his tie clip, and a plastic protector in his pocket to shield it from the threat of a leaking pen. He wore his blond hair cut short and slicked relentlessly in place.

His boyish face brightened when he saw her. "Darcy," he said happily, "I heard you'd be here. That you'd be bringing us the *el fabuloso* worm today. Where is he?"

"He's being inquisitioned by the board," Darcy said. "Listen, Brian, I have a strange question—"

Brian beamed. "Strange questions are my specialty."

Darcy shifted uneasily. "It's a rather delicate matter. I'm not sure—I don't know about the ethics of using a public library to find answers."

Brian's smile died. A worried line appeared between his eyebrows. "Maybe you'd better explain?"

She leaned across the reference desk and lowered her voice confidentially. "It's about a man, Brian. I need to check him out. It can be done on the Internet, right?"

He stole a guilty look at the hint of her cleavage and swallowed. "Right," he said, and then quickly looked away and began to fiddle with the pencils in his pencil holder.

"This man is dating…a friend of mine," Darcy said, trying not to flinch at her own words. "I'm worried about his motives. He may not be what he pretends to be. I don't want…my friend to get hurt."

Brian picked out the longest pencil and put it into the electric sharpener.

It buzzed as it ground the length shorter. He pulled it out, blew away the shavings, then thrust it back in the sharpener.

"Brian," she said, "you're not going to have any pencil left."

He gave a little start, withdrew the pencil and set it back in the holder, considerably shrunken. He folded his hands primly before him, but didn't meet her eyes.

He said, "I can't do such a thing for you. It *wouldn't* be ethical." He paused and his shoulders squirmed in an uneasy shrug. "But I could tell you how it could *be* done…"

"You could?" she said, her heartbeat skipping in excitement.

He turned and stared out at the library's banks of computers. He still did not make eye contact. He was like a man in a spy movie who is giving out information without seeming to be having a real conversation.

"You can do it from here," he said. "But you'll have to give your own e-mail address. And give a credit card number. It's not free, and the library can't pay for it."

"That's fine," she said. "It doesn't matter. Just tell me how."

He kept staring into the mid-distance. He groped for the pencil and stroked it nervously. "There are services—businesses that sell such information. You can contact one. You won't get your answers instantly, but you'll get them."

Darcy could have hugged him. She could feel her hopes rising. "Tell me more," she said.

SLOAN HAD WANDERED AROUND Olivia's house doing his best to be virtuous. But he couldn't help noticing the framed family photos that Olivia had almost everywhere.

There were dozens of Darcy and Emerald growing up. Darcy always looked poised and at the same time mischievously curious. And Emerald—it bothered Sloan to admit it—always looked *vulnerable*. It was as if the camera stripped away her dramatics and exposed an abiding insecurity that touched him, in spite of himself.

Olivia was in some of the photos. Sloan saw that she had always been a beautiful woman: tall and blond, with a cheerful coolness in her smile that was rather mysterious. Was she really happy in these pictures? Or was she a very good actress, so good that she fooled perhaps even herself?

There were no pictures of any of Olivia's late husbands. This, too, Sloan found vaguely disturbing. Did they not count in her life? Had she cast them aside as a black widow spider casts aside the shells of its mates once they are sucked dry?

Or did she have no pictures of these men because remembering them caused her pain? If so, what kind of pain? Grief? Or something more elusive? Was there an unhappy pattern, and would his father fall into it and repeat history?

Sloan was tempted to open Olivia's bedroom door and look into her most private chamber. Perhaps there were other, more telling photos on display. But such an act would be wrong; he kept the door closed.

He glanced at his watch. It was nearly six. Darcy had been gone a long time, it seemed. How long did it take to deliver a damn bookworm?

Restless, he went back to the guest room. He logged on to his computer to reread Darcy's e-mail message to him. Troubled, he realized this action was foreign to his nature. He seldom read mail more than once.

He had new messages, mostly junk mail, but one stood out from the others. It was from his father. Sloan hit the key to bring it to his screen.

SUBJECT: A Father's Prayer
From: BanditKing@USAserve.com
To: SloanJEnglish@PetroCorp.com

Dear Son—I'm at Olivia's in Maine (she's fixing supper even as I write this). She says you have arrived at her lake house. I pray you will prove worthy of her generosity and not abuse her trust.

In other words, don't snoop and don't chase her daughters.

Remember that these people are about to become family.

Conduct yourself accordingly.

Lovingly,

Your Old Man

Sloan winced. His father had made two insulting assumptions: that Sloan would try to get into either (a) Olivia's private business, or (b) her daughters' pants.

This displeasure, however, was garnished with guilt, because, of course, both ideas had crossed his mind. How had the Old Man known?

With chagrin, Sloan realized the answer. The Old Man knew because he had once been a young man, and he and Sloan were blood of each other's blood.

John had said not to snoop. Sloan would not—but he would investigate. That was different, he told himself, very different.

As for his attraction to Darcy, it was simply natural. She was lovely, she was intriguing, and she was forbidden. It was a triumvirate of qualities guaranteed to tempt any man. And he was tempted. But he was also strong enough to resist.

No, Sloan assured himself, it was not his own urges he had to worry about. It was his father's.

It was damn disturbing that John was in Maine with Olivia. The breakneck speed of this romance wasn't slowing in the least. What the devil was John doing, leaving his "business" in Florida?

This time, John had sworn that he'd found his niche. This time, he'd vowed, he was committed to succeed. He had sunk everything into this plan; although it would be hard, ceaseless work, he'd said wild horses could not drag him from it.

But one slender blond widow could.

John had abandoned his pet project and run north like some adolescent Romeo hell-bent on reaching his Juliet. Sloan gritted his teeth and thought, *Jeez, no wonder Trina worries.*

He should have resisted the urge to be sarcastic, but he could not. He pecked out an answer to his father.

SUBJECT: Snooping and Chasing Women
From: SloanJEnglish@PetroCorp.com
To: BanditKing@USAserve.com

Thanks for your advice. Yeah, I'm being a regular James Bond, spying and seducing.
Yours in sexual espionage,
007

As soon as he sent the message, he regretted it. He swore at himself. That was one of the many dangers of e-mail—it was too easy to send in the heat of emotion.

A regular letter had to be written, sealed in an envelope, stamped, borne to a mailbox. It gave you time to think twice, to change your mind—

His musings were interrupted by sounds that put him on alert: tires grinding on the gravel in the drive and the familiar rattle of Darcy's vehicle. She was home. She was here.

His heart kicked savagely in his chest, and his pulses took off in a race he could not control. He went to the window and pulled back the curtain.

She got out of the UV, a bemused look on her lovely face. She had pulled her hair back loosely, and a few tendrils had come free; she put up her hand to smooth them.

She did not cast so much as a glance in his direction. She headed for her own small house, and the wind fluttered the skirt of the yellow dress, making it sway back and forth around her hips like a bell.

My God, he thought. Had his father been right, after all? Was he out to bed this woman?

I can resist her, he told himself. He was so sure of this that he told it to himself a second time. And then a third.

SHE QUICKLY CHANGED out of the yellow dress and into a pair of jeans and a green T-shirt with a batik design of frogs.

She thought it was probably the least erotic T-shirt in Texas, possibly the whole Southwest. It was dangerous to look and feel like a woman around Sloan English. She wanted to seem as sexless as possible.

She pinned her hair into an unadorned knot at the back of her head and glanced at her watch. It was five minutes until she was due to meet him. She wanted to be neither early nor late. And five minutes was just time enough to check her e-mail.

She sat at her desk, licked her dry lips and switched on her computer. There, in her mailbox, was a group of new messages, and among them was one that made her heart beat speed with anxious excitement. She held her breath and summoned it to the screen.

SUBJECT: Confirmation of Investigation
From: InfoTruthInc@Intellinet.com
To: DesignByDarcy@USAserve.com

Dear Ms. Parker:
This is to confirm your request for the investigation of the following individual:
JOHN ENGLISH
   WORK PLACE: KEY WEST, FLORIDA
   E-MAIL ADDRESS: BanditKing@USAserve.com
   Since we must ascertain the subject's social security number before implementing our search, the information will take slightly longer to retrieve.
   You may expect preliminary results within two (2) days.
   Thank you for your patronage.
J. D. Smithee
Research Associate, InfoTruth, Inc.
Your Confidential Source Of The Truth

The blood rose hotly in Darcy's cheeks. It was as if she had suddenly been forced to look at proof she had committed a shameful and underhanded act.

It *wasn't* shameful, she told herself stubbornly. Perhaps John English's finances were sound as a rock, and he himself was the very model of honesty, a man without stain. That would be wonderful.

But, she told herself uneasily, *the facts might say something altogether different.* John English might be a liar and poseur. In his background might lurk debt and bankruptcy, even— horrors!—arrests. What if he had a police record? Darcy imagined a host of unsavory crimes: nonsupport, extortion, bigamy, fraud.

No, no, no, she scolded herself. She was becoming as paranoid as Emerald. With luck, John English's background would be an open book that contained only good deeds and responsible acts.

InfoTruth promised the facts. Until Darcy had those facts, she would act serenely innocent. She would tell Olivia and Emerald nothing until she knew the truth.

And she would certainly not tell Sloan English.

She glanced at her watch. It was seven o'clock, straight up. Time to meet him. He said he would tell her about his family. She would let him, but then she would check his version against InfoTruth's.

Like his father, maybe he was honest. And maybe he wasn't. She would soon know.

EMERALD STOOD BESIDE HENRY as he sat hunched over the computer keyboard in his bedroom. Her arms were tightly crossed, and she fought the impulse to tap her foot nervously.

"How long will this take?" she asked with false calm.

"You can't ever tell," Henry said, peering at the screen and typing.

Emerald glanced around Henry's room. It was a nerd's room, she thought bitterly. Scientific texts crammed the bookcases, and on the wall hung posters of the solar system and the table of elements. The single bed was as neatly made as an army bunk. It had an old bedspread printed with pictures of Buzz Lightyear.

It was in this very room, thought Emerald, that Henry had courted her and seduced her by computer three years ago. He had written her the steamiest descriptions of erotic things he wished to do to her—and she had replied in kind, not knowing he was a little four-eyed adolescent twerp.

Now, ironically, she was in the very bedroom where he'd indulged in such lustful fantasies about her. She cringed. It was here he had read her fantasies about him—or, rather, about the man he'd pretended to be. It was too horrid, too disgusting. She could not bear to remember it.

"What if your parents come home and find me here?" she asked, trying to put him on the defensive. "You'll get in a lot of trouble."

"They're gone for the week," he said, not taking his eyes from the screen. "They took my sister to the Mayo Clinic for her checkup."

"Humph," said Emerald, and shrugged. "Lucky for you. They'd boil you alive if they caught you with a woman in your room."

"No, they wouldn't," Henry said with unsettling confidence. "I'm an adult now. My dad'd give me the safe sex talk. That's about it."

This took Emerald aback. She was trying to avoid admitting that Henry had indeed become an adult. She still wanted to think of him as a hateful little boy, not a grown man nearly six feet tall.

"You have the safest sex possible," she said acidly. "It's over a computer."

He turned and gave her a hurt glance. "I don't do that anymore. I learned my lesson. Aren't you ever going to forgive me?"

She looked into his eyes. They were a startling shade of azure blue, and if they hadn't been *his* eyes, she would have found them remarkably attractive.

"No," she said, crossing her arms even more tightly. "Shut up about that. Tell me what you're doing."

He sighed. "Okay. I just got the USAserve system downloaded. Now I'm going to try to get into your mother's e-mail. I'll need her password. You don't know it?"

"I told you I didn't," Emerald said with aristocratic indifference.

"Okay," Henry said, resignation in his voice. "Most people use a word they won't forget. Like the name of a child or a pet. I already tried your name and your sister's. They don't work. Has she got a cat or dog?"

"She had a dog," said Emerald. "His name was Mr. Right."

Henry tried typing in the name several different ways. "It doesn't work," he said. "What was your stepfather's name?"

"She'd *never* use my stepfather's name," Emerald sniffed. "Or any of her other husbands, either. She was supposed to be through with men."

Henry's blue gaze seemed to ask, *Like you?*

She looked away.

She *did* want to be involved again with a man. But in real life she never found anyone as exciting and compatible as she had once believed Henry to be. Her problem was not simply that Henry had lied to her, but that he had lied so well.

"Look," he said gently, "let's try nicknames. Does your mother have one?"

Emerald shook her head. "She always goes by Olivia. She hates 'Ollie' and 'Livvie.'"

"What about you and your sister?"

Emerald looked at the worn Buzz Lightyear bedspread. It troubled her that Henry had lain there on those childish pictures having lascivious fantasies about her. He had not been much older than a child himself.

"My sister's nickname is Darcy-Duck. Or just Duck. Or sometimes Darce."

Henry typed in various combinations. "I can't get it to work. What about you?"

She glanced around the rest of the room, so scholarly it seemed almost monkish. "Em," she said, and tried to keep the quaver out of her voice. "Sometimes she calls me dearest Em. Or my—my jewel."

The only sound in the room was the light tapping of the keys. Emerald suddenly wished she hadn't phoned Henry, hadn't come here. Too many painful emotions twisted her heart, and among them was guilt for what she was doing— trying to invade her mother's privacy.

She should tell Henry to stop, then leave and keep her vow to never, ever have anything to do with him again.

Henry's voice, disturbingly deep, broke the silence. "Got it!"

Startled, Emerald's eyes flew to him. He was hunched tautly over the keyboard. The light from the screen silvered his face, and his expression was frozen in a mixture of wariness and wonder.

"We're in," he said softly. "You're the password. 'DearestEm.' It's you."

Me, she thought. *I'm Mama's password. She cares so much about me, she used my name. What would she say if she knew what I'm doing?*

Henry turned in his chair to face her. "I've reached her mailbox. We can get in, read everything that she's sent and received for the last week, maybe more."

Emerald stood, muscles tensed. She clenched and unclenched her fists as her emotions swirled more wildly.

Henry studied her face, his own expression worried. "This is serious business, Emerald. Do you want to keep going?"

She didn't answer. She thought of her own humiliation and heartbreak when she'd found the truth about Henry.

"Do you want to keep going?" he repeated.

She swallowed. "Yes," she said.

He looked more troubled than before. "You're sure?"

Unshed tears burned Emerald's eyes. "I don't want—I don't want—" she stammered.

He rose from his chair, took a step toward her. "Em? Are you all right? What is it?"

She held her hand up for him to stop. She willed the tears to go away and her voice to be hard as steel. From between her teeth she said, "I don't want somebody to do to her what you did to me."

Henry looked stricken.

She sat down purposefully in his chair and looked at the screen. She pushed the keys to bring Olivia's e-mail into view. She thought, *I'm doing this for you, Mama. I'm doing it because I love you.*

CHAPTER NINE

THE SCREENED DECK of Olivia's lake house had a table and chairs. Sloan had set the table, and he had set it like a bachelor.

The tablecloth hung crookedly, the place mats didn't match, and the napkins were folded oddly, as if he'd been packing very small pup tents.

It would seem impossible to mismatch Olivia's flatware, but somehow he had done it.

Containers of food from the refrigerator sat unceremoniously on the tabletop, tablespoons stuck in them for serving. In the center he had placed one of Darcy's clay pots of wildflowers and a silver candelabra from the mantelpiece.

"It's—very lovely," Darcy said diplomatically. "You shouldn't have gone to such trouble."

"I don't know much about this stuff." He frowned as he began to light the candles. "So I didn't go to much trouble. I don't know how."

He wore faded, low-slung jeans and a light green sweater, its sleeves pushed up on his lean forearms. The V-neck showed a triangle of bare flesh and a feathery hint of dark hair.

The breeze from the lake snuffed out his match before the candle's wick caught. He turned his back to the wind, bent over the candelabra protectively and struck another flame.

Something fluttered and tightened in Darcy's stomach. The unsteady glow gilded the strong features of his face, highlighting the lines that illness had sharpened, making the hollows beneath his cheekbones seem deeper.

A lock of dark hair hung over his forehead, and the match light reflected in his eyes. His expression was a study in concentration, and his body was taut with graceful purpose.

One by one he lit the candles, then smiled at her. He had a wide mouth, the lower lip straight and full, the upper more narrow but sculpted with evocative curves.

"You changed your clothes. I liked that yellow dress."

She gave a shrug she hoped was casual. "I thought we were going to be informal." She tugged at the hem of the green T-shirt with its batik print. "So I wore frogs."

He looked her up and down, making her skin prickle with awareness of him. "You look good in frogs."

"It's a gift I have," she said. "You should see me in toads."

He smiled again. "Have a seat. I'll pour the wine. Is *pinot grigio* all right?" He pulled one of the white metal chairs out for her.

"It's fine," she said as she sat. At least he knew about wines, she thought. The bottle was chilling in an ice bucket, and he had set out the correct glasses.

He took out the wine and twisted the corkscrew into the cork. "Was the bookworm a success at the library?"

She smiled. "Mostly. When you have a committee, you always have a debate."

Sloan shook his head wryly. He filled her glass, then his own. He raised his. "To your mother's hospitality," he said. "And yours. Which is beyond reproach."

Except I'm having your father checked out by paid investigators, Darcy thought guiltily, but she clinked her glass against his.

HE WAS GLAD she no longer wore that yellow dress that so bedeviled him, but he'd told her the truth, dammit. She *did* look good in frogs. Another woman might have looked like an advertisement for the American Amphibian Society. She didn't. The green T-shirt wasn't tight; in fact, it disguised all but her most obvious curves. Unfortunately, this caused him to imagine, with yearning, what lay beneath.

But he remembered his father's injunction to leave Olivia's daughters alone. He made small talk. He tried to put her at ease, though he did not feel so himself.

"Have another drink," he said, when they had polished off the last of the shrimp salad.

"No." She smiled. "I don't drink much, really."

But he had already refilled her glass. He had not drunk much since his fever had first struck, but he topped off his own glass, as well.

He cleared his throat. "I suppose you know," he said with elaborate casualness, "that your mother and my father are together right now. At her place. In Maine."

He pretended to stare out at the sky darkening over the lake, but he watched her from the corner of his eye. She stiffened in her chair, and her face went wary.

"No," she said. "I didn't."

"Yeah," he said, turning to face her. "They are. I got e-mail from him this afternoon."

She did not seem to know what to say. She took a quick sip of wine. "Well," she murmured. "Their romance seems to be picking up speed, doesn't it?"

"Yes. It does."

The candlelight played over her troubled expression. "I sent her e-mail. I asked her if they were really going to get married. She hasn't answered—yet."

She dropped her gaze and traced an invisible pattern on the tablecloth. She said, "Maybe I shouldn't have asked. She probably thinks I'm interfering. I suppose I am. She's an adult, after all…"

The breeze ruffled her dark hair, and he longed to reach out and smooth it. Instead he said, "You worry about her. I know. I worry about my father, too."

She looked up sharply. "Your father. You said you'd tell me about him. He's a Realtor? In Key West?"

"Yes." He fought the desire to grit his teeth. What he said

was not a lie. But it was not the full truth. He wasn't sure she was ready for that.

She held his gaze across the littered table. "For how long?"

"Key West? He's been there six months."

She blinked in surprise. "That's all? Where was he before that?"

"Marathon, Florida," he said. "Miami. Tampa. Hot Springs. Phoenix. Santa Fe. He's—been here and there."

She was silent for a moment. She took another sip of wine. "Well. As they say, your papa was a rolling stone."

"Yes," he said. He would not disguise that fact.

She spun the stem of her wineglass between her finger and thumb. "This question isn't very subtle, but—does he have trouble settling down?"

He paused. To give himself time, he took a drink of his own wine. It was making the front of his forehead feel heavy, and he wondered if the alcohol was hitting him too hard after a long abstinence.

The moon had risen. It shone on the water, which reflected it, giving the evening sky a peculiar luminosity. Carefully Sloan said, "Once there was a poet who said, 'All my life, my heart has hungered after something I cannot name.' That line makes me think of my father. He's always had—dreams. Life never gave him much of a chance to pursue them."

She put her elbows on the table and leaned her chin on her locked hands. "What do you mean?"

He exhaled harshly. "He grew up in a little town outside Tulsa. His father was a rodeo rider. He sent money home if he had it. Mostly he didn't have it. His mother clerked in a hardware store. She didn't make much, but she managed to raise two kids on it. My father and my aunt."

"Trina." Darcy watched him with disconcerting steadiness.

"Trina," he repeated. He took another drink.

He said, "Sometimes my grandfather came home, worked as a hand on a ranch. Mostly he drifted. Finally he drifted away for good. My grandmother got sick, died. My father was seventeen. Trina was fifteen.''

"I'm sorry," Darcy said. Her eyes seemed larger, more liquid in the candlelight.

"My father had dreams. He had an artistic streak. He wanted to go to college. Instead he dropped out of school, did ranch work himself. He had to take care of himself and Trina, too. She got to finish high school. He didn't.''

He frowned and looked away from Darcy. The frogs on her shirt seemed to dance disconcertingly, and her eyes had grown too mesmerizing.

So he stared out at the moon-dazzled night. Memory had made him both bitter and sentimental. He took another drink to celebrate the phenomenon.

He set his jaw and said, "He sent Trina to junior college for a year while he patched fences and branded calves. But then, when she was nineteen, she got married. He was free— or so he thought.''

"What do you mean?" she asked.

He watched a moth outside, battling to get inside to the flame. The moth made him think of his father.

Sloan narrowed his eyes and finished his wine. "He got his high school credits. He signed up for college. He made it through one semester—straight *A*'s. And then—''

And then he discovered his fatal flaw.

"And then what?" Darcy urged.

"He met a beautiful woman.''

A tall, cool, beautiful blond woman, from a better home than his, whose family had more money than he'd ever dreamed of having.

"He got married?" Darcy asked quietly.

Sloan looked at the silver globe of the moon. "He got married. She was pregnant. He wanted to do 'the honorable thing.' Besides, he loved her. He was crazy for her.''

He heard the contempt in his own voice. *He was crazy for her.* That craziness had ruled and ruined his father's life. Sloan had always vowed it would never do the same to his.

"I was the kid," Sloan said sarcastically. "My aunt always claimed my mother got pregnant on purpose. That she trapped my father into marriage."

"That's a terrible thing to tell a child," Darcy said indignantly.

He shrugged. "It's probably true. He was a handsome guy. Other people said the same—she wanted him any way she could get him. When she got him, she got tired of him. She left."

"So you didn't get to see much of your father while you were growing up?" Darcy asked with sympathy.

He laughed. "I didn't see anything of *her*. She was gone for good."

"You mean she deserted you? Both of you?" Darcy asked in horror.

"That she did," Sloan said. He looked critically at his empty glass. He tried to refill it and was displeased to find the bottle empty.

He hated telling her this story; it seemed to beg for pity, which he despised and did not want. Perhaps he would not have told her so much if it weren't for the wine.

"Maybe I should have some coffee," he said. "You want some?"

"I'm not sure," she said, and she sounded uneasy. "It's getting late."

"Only one cup," he said. He got to his feet. "You wanted to hear about my family. Now's your chance. While I'm in the mood to say it."

Suddenly the air seemed to shimmy in front of him, and the light on the water fractured and bucked. He staggered slightly.

Darcy was at his side, her hand grasping his elbow. She looked up at him earnestly. "Is it your fever again? What's wrong? Are you all right?"

Was it the wine making him so strangely dizzy? He'd drunk little since his illness, and he probably shouldn't have drunk at all. Now a pair of round moons seemed to dance over the water's edge, and the deck swayed under his feet like a boat on a gentle tide.

He put one hand to his forehead. It was cool, but it had begun to throb strangely, and his thought processes had become hazy, disconnected.

"Sloan?" Darcy said, gripping his arm more tightly. "Maybe you should go to bed. You're barely out of the hospital. Go ahead. I'll clean this up." She gave a curt nod toward the table.

My God, she's pretty, he thought, his senses in confusion. The touch of her hand on his flesh sent waves of warmth scurrying through him, and his mind spiraled out of control. His head no longer throbbed, but his groin did; and he hungered to seize her and pull her close to him.

No, he thought. *No. I can't do this.*

"I'm not drunk," he said, and he knew it was the truth. The wine had affected him, certainly, but the truth was more complicated.

"I know you're not," she agreed. "But your resistance is down. Please. Go lie down and rest. You're alarming me."

If she was alarmed, she was resolute, and she didn't give ground. She tried to lead him toward the door. "We'll talk later."

Don't touch me any more, he thought. *If you know what's good for you, don't touch me at all.*

But then, as if by magic, his mind cleared. The two waltzing moons slid together and became one stable moon. The floor beneath his feet grew steady. There was no haze or heaviness in his head.

The heat he felt wasn't fever, but it still burned hotly. "I'm going to be okay," he said. "Let's have some coffee."

She gazed up at him, her beautiful face awash with moonlight and uncertainty. Her hand on his arm grew more tentative.

"I mean it," he said. "I had a fuzzy moment. It happened once or twice after the first fever, too. It lasts a few seconds. It's nothing. I'm fine."

Her eyes searched his. "You're sure?"

He nodded. "I'm certain. But I'd really like that cup of coffee."

His gaze fell to her lips. "Please," he said.

Her hand fell away. "I'll make it. You sit down. All right?"

He gave her a crooked smile of assent. She turned quickly away and hurried through the door. After a moment, he heard her moving in the kitchen, opening drawers, running water.

But he didn't sit down. He stayed standing.

It's not the wine, he thought, looking after her, his pulses kicking crazily. *It's you.*

DARCY SIPPED the hot, black brew and tried not to notice how the candlelight danced on Sloan's chiseled features. He had gone moody on her, quiet. He stared down into his half-empty coffee cup.

She said, "Maybe you shouldn't talk any more. You've had a long day. Some other time—"

"It's okay," he said shortly. "Ask what you want. Let's get it over with."

Darcy was both hesitant and curious. "Your mother was gone," she ventured. "Where did she go?"

"Dallas. To be a model. She was. Not a famous one, but successful enough on a local level. She married a doctor."

"Do you ever—see each other?"

"I have no desire to. Neither does she."

Darcy shook her head at the strangeness of it. Olivia might not seem like a mom-and-apple-pie sort of mother, but she would have fought like a tigress to keep from being separated from her children.

"So your father raised you?"

"No," he said, looking out over the lake. "Trina did. Her marriage didn't work out, either. She was left with a kid, too. My cousin Arthur. She needed money. My father needed a home for me. She took me. He went to the city and sent back money."

He sounded bitter. Darcy chose her words carefully. "This is the aunt who's so...concerned about your father."

"Right." He raised the cup and took another drink, set it down. He seemed to think a moment, then he turned to face her. She couldn't see his eyes in the shifting light.

"Look." He said it with the air of a man who has something unpleasant to announce. "Your mother probably knows all this. But you and your sister may find it easier to understand if I tell you the whole story."

Darcy sat straighter in her chair. A revelation was what she had hoped for, wasn't it?

The line of his mouth skewed sardonically. "My cousin—Arthur—and I are almost the same age. He was born ten days before me."

Darcy, listening intently, nodded.

His expression changed to reveal another emotion—resignation, perhaps. "Arthur," he said, "is *special.* He had lots of health problems. But he's also got schizophrenia. He's had it since childhood."

Darcy felt as if an icy hand had been laid on her. "Schizophrenia? Oh, how terrible. I *am* sorry."

"So am I," he said, with a twist of irony in his voice. "And Trina's made it her life's work to fuss about him. I guess she can't be blamed. He doesn't have to be institutionalized—as long as she's there to take care of him."

Darcy understood. "But she worries. About what happens when she *can't* take care of him?"

"Precisely," Sloan said. "I've set up a trust fund for him. Not big, but it should be adequate. But it doesn't make her feel any more secure. That, unfortunately, is where my father comes in."

Now Darcy was puzzled. "Your father? How?"

"Oh, hell," Sloan said unhappily. "It's money, dammit. It's torn more than one family apart."

"Money?" The word had a sinister and ugly ring.

Sloan drained his coffee, set the cup back sharply on the table. He rose, shoved his hands in the back pockets of his jeans and began to pace the deck restlessly.

"I've done all right in my life. I had breaks my father didn't. He made them possible. He doesn't have to worry about me any longer. But Trina and Arthur are going to be on his conscience his whole life long—she's made sure of that."

"How? And why?"

"When Trina was six months' pregnant, she and Dad were in a car wreck. Dad was driving. Nobody seemed hurt. But afterward, when Arthur turned out the way he did…" His words drifted off.

"She blamed your father?"

"Subtly, of course. And when she took on the responsibility of raising me, she always reminded him that all that made me different from Arthur was luck. I had it all. Arthur had none. And whose fault was that?"

He moved back and forth in front of the moon like a panther trying to find its way out of a cage. Darcy could sense the thwarted energy burning in him as dangerously as his fever had done.

"It preys on your conscience, too," she said quietly. "Or you wouldn't have come here."

He stopped pacing and watched the moth batting futilely at the screen. "Touché," he said. "But that was a temporary lapse. If that damn mosquito hadn't gotten me, I'd still be in Southeast Asia, with my brain cells at a constant, optimum temperature. She couldn't do her hoodoo on me."

Couldn't she? Darcy wondered. But she said nothing.

"About ten years ago," Sloan said, still watching the moth, "when my father went to Florida for the first time, he made a killing in real estate."

He laughed and turned toward her, mockery in his stance. "For the first time in his life, he got lucky. He used some of the money to make investments for Trina—very conservative, very stable. She should always have an income from them. Not huge. But decent.''

Darcy was certain of one thing: he was telling the truth, and the cost in pride was high. *He hates talking about this,* she realized. *He just hates it.*

He cocked one hip and looked up at a wind chime swaying in the shadows. ''Unfortunately, my father didn't play it as safe with the money he set aside for himself. He speculated on more land. He thought it had potential. Maybe it will— someday. Right now, he couldn't give it away.''

He shrugged and gave another soft, derisive laugh. ''Except to Trina. When he bought it, he was as excited as a kid. He told me, 'The money from this? When I'm dead, it'll go to you and Trina.'

''I said, 'I'm taken care of. Give it all to her.' He finally agreed. Unfortunately, he told Trina. If he dies, whatever he has is hers. She's convinced the land's worth a king's ransom. Fat chance. But she likes to think so.''

The breeze rose, making the wind chimes jangle and the candlelight dance more wildly. Darcy could see the bitterness of his smile. ''My dad's land rich, but money poor,'' he said. ''What profits he's made in the meantime have gone into another...venture. But Trina's worried that your mother's caught Dad in her web, and *she'll* get the juicy prize—not Trina.''

Darcy squirmed. She didn't want to ask what the other ''venture'' was. Sloan had told her more than she'd had any right to expect.

She wondered how he'd feel if he knew that she'd hired investigators to dig into these secrets of blood and money. She fought down a strong twinge of guilt.

She said, ''I know it must be hard to talk about this. I'm sorry it's so complex—''

''It's not complex,'' he said with the same jeering edge in

his voice. "It's just about money. Not even money, only the idea of money. This whole uproar is about swampland in Florida."

Darcy pushed her coffee cup, still half full, away. "You don't have to tell me more—"

"I wanted to be honest," he said. He took a step toward her.

"It's—it's very difficult to talk about money," she stammered. "I appreciate your frankness."

She rose to go, but to her bewilderment he had moved closer. He loomed between her and the door.

"I haven't been frank about everything," he said.

I haven't either, she thought. She should escape, give herself time to breathe and think. Here she could neither breathe well nor think clearly. Yet she could not move away from him; she stood as if he had cast a spell on her.

He moved closer still. "Your family background. It gets twisted up, too, doesn't it? Like mine?"

"Yes," she said, her chest so tight it was painful.

"You've never married?" he asked.

"No," she said, watching how the golden light danced on the curves of his mouth.

"Did you ever even get close?" he asked.

She took a deep breath. "I guess I always thought that Mama got married enough for both of us."

He nodded. "I felt the same way about my father."

"Your father—" she managed to say. "How many times has he been married?"

"Three," he said in a low voice. "The same as your mother."

He raised his hand. His fingertips touched her face as lightly as the wing stroke of a moth. He said, "It didn't give me the greatest faith in marriage."

"I know," she said.

"I go my own way. I've never been one for commitment," he said. "I probably never will be."

"Me, either," she said, and swallowed.

"My father told me not to spy on your family," he said, his touch on her cheekbone firmer now. "And not to chase you."

Darcy felt a heady boldness tumbling through her like the most powerful intoxication in the world. "I don't think I'm running," she said.

"No," he said, bending nearer. "You're not. I said I tried to be honest with you."

"Yes," she said helplessly. Her knees felt odd, as if they had turned to blown glass.

"I should be frank about one more thing," he said.

Her heart beat so hard, it jarred her whole body. "Yes?" she whispered.

"I feel a strong attraction between us," he said. "Do you?"

His other hand rose so that he framed her face and tilted it up to his. Desire welled in her, unbidden but undeniable.

"Yes," she said, and she couldn't keep the catch out of her voice. "What are we going to do?"

"This," he said.

His lips descended to hers.

Yearning jolted through her. The touch of his mouth was so satisfying, she could not get enough. She put her arms around his neck, not shyly but eagerly.

He gave a ragged gasp that sucked her breath, and his arms went around her so tightly she gasped in return.

He deepened the kiss, his tongue taking hers in a seductive game that both pleased and maddened. He held her body crushed to his, but she strained to be closer still.

She was dazzled by his agile mouth and the rock-hard leanness of him.

He was amazingly strong, but there seemed to be desperation in his strength, as if it were driven by the most primitive of hungers.

Her own need inflamed and frightened her. His hands were under her green shirt now, moving against the bare flesh of her back. His fingers found the fastener of her bra and undid it with a single, expert move.

He pushed up her shirt, and she knew in another half-minute he would have it off her. She wanted this to happen, yet she was appalled by how wildly she wanted it.

He grasped her hand and guided it to his belt buckle, an invitation to undo it. At the same moment, his other hand groped for the snap of her jeans.

Good grief, Darcy thought in panic, *we're going to be naked and pumping away at each other like a couple of animals—*

She had a sudden vision of Gus. He was wasted and deathly pale, but his eyes flashed with anger. *"For this I worked myself into an early grave?"* he demanded. *"For you to be an easy lay on the floor of my deck?"*

"No!" Darcy exclaimed breathlessly. A chill washed over her like an icy wave.

She tried to push away from Sloan. He held her fast. He bent to take her lips again. She turned her face from him. He kissed her throat instead, and beneath her shirt his hand moved toward her breast.

She wrenched back from the touch so forcefully that he had to let her go. She backed up warily until she was pressed against the wall next to the door inside.

He came toward her, trying to keep her there. She looked up at him and shook her head. "This is going too fast," she said, her heart knocking like a savage drum.

He stopped. His hands at his sides tightened into fists. "You're right," he said. His voice was as breathless as hers. They stared at each other for a long moment. The candlelight danced, phantom-like, over his features, making them more unreadable and enigmatic.

At last he said, "I'm sorry."

"I have to go," she said. She meant it. If he touched her again, her resolve would melt. She would do something she could only regret later.

"Yes," he said. There was an ironic resignation to his tone. "You should."

We're no wiser than our parents, she thought in consternation. *Perhaps we're even more foolish.*

She turned and left and did not look back. She did not dare.

CHAPTER TEN

HENRY HAD ALWAYS THOUGHT Emerald was the most fascinating woman in the world.

She was like a creature from another more intense plane of being, giving herself over to her feelings so bravely and freely that she took away his breath. Henry had been raised not to show his feelings; indeed, to pretend he didn't even have most of them. He had lived within the tight little ship of rational thinking, fearful of what pulsed beneath its fragile hull.

Yet Emerald was a paradox. For all her bravery, she was vulnerable, and for all her freedom, she still seemed trapped by a world too harsh for her sensitive spirit. To him, she had been like a wonderful princess who was imprisoned in a tower and needed a knight to rescue her.

He had been only a boy, but he had been a bright and articulate one, and foolishly he had pretended to be that knight. He loved her. She loved the man he had pretended to be.

It had all come crashing down, of course.

Henry, who previously had been too scornful to pray, had prayed fervently for a second chance. Now it was here. The most fascinating woman in the world was sitting on the edge of his bed.

But it wasn't going as he had hoped. She, who hated to cry, was crying.

In her hand she clutched a sheaf of papers—printouts of the recent letters her mother had sent and received from John English.

Henry sat at his desk, helplessly watching her. Her turbulent emotions had always torn his heart. To see her weeping nearly killed him.

He wanted to rise and go to her, but he knew he didn't dare. "Emerald," he said. "Please—don't."

She had a tissue in her hand. She blew her nose into it mournfully. "I can't *believe* my mother would write such things. I can't believe she'd even *think* such things."

Henry put his clasped hands between his knees and squeezed them. In truth, he did not think the letters between Olivia and John English were so shocking. True, they were a bit erotic, but he and Emerald had once written far more explicit fantasies to each other. Now, of course, was not the time to remind her of that.

"Emerald, it's okay," he said haltingly. "I mean, it's pretty natural. Parents have sex drives, too."

"Well, I don't want *mine* to," Emerald retorted with passion.

"They have to have sex," Henry reasoned. "Otherwise, we wouldn't be here."

"Well, she doesn't have to *enjoy* it," Emerald said bitterly. "I never thought she did. I was the more deceived."

"It's—it's a perfectly normal urge. Nature programs it into us for the survival of the species. Some women don't find the sexual aspect of their being until they're older. There's probably a sound biological reason for this—"

Emerald gave him an angry look, and fresh tears welled in her eyes.

"Emerald," he said desperately, "even my mother likes sex. I know it's hard to believe, but—"

"Your mother?" Emerald said scornfully. "How do you know? Do you have an Oedipus complex on top of everything else?"

She buried her face in her hands. Henry couldn't stand it. He went and sat down beside her, very gingerly. He wanted to put his arm around her and draw her to his chest, but he did not.

"My father used to have these awful talks with me. He used to assure me that sex could be a very satisfying thing between a man and a woman. That it was only reasonable that he and mother enjoy their biological selves as nature intended. To do otherwise would be unhealthy. Can't you look at your mother as if she's just—sort of getting healthier?"

"Henry, be *quiet*." She gave a moan. "And they're together right *now*. Oh, God." Her sobs grew harder.

He ached to take her in his arms, but he sat as stiffly as if he were paralyzed. "Emerald, please," he begged. "What can I say? What can I do? Just tell me."

She cried soundlessly for a full three minutes, while he watched, stricken. He repeated his plea. "Just tell me. What can I say to help? What can I do?"

Her sobs ceased, but she kept her face in her hands. At last, she raised her eyes to his. They were red from crying, and tears streaked her delicate face. Henry's heart fell down and died at her feet.

"John English—" she said with a sniffle. "Find out more about him. I don't trust him. I just don't."

Henry swallowed. She looked like a lovely waif held together only by pride. He was speechless with love and desire. He could only stare at her.

"You got into my mother's e-mail," she said, her voice quavering but grim. "Can you get into his?"

Not that, Henry thought, feeling like a man teetering at the edge of an abyss. *If I do that, where will it end?*

But Emerald, whom he had once betrayed so badly, held him in thrall. He would grant her any wish if only it would gain her forgiveness.

She lifted her head higher. "Could you?" she challenged.

"It'd be a lot harder," he said, his voice tight.

"But you could do it?"

He looked deeply into her sad eyes. "I could try," he said. The abyss seemed to open beneath him like a pit filled with hellish imps, waiting to claim him. He did not care. He loved Emerald too much.

OLIVIA SAT ON THE COUCH, snuggled in the crook of John's arm. He was nursing his after-dinner brandy. She found herself in a pensive mood, thinking of Darcy and Emerald and herself and John.

"I haven't heard any more from either of the girls," she said. "I suppose they're still upset. Maybe I should call or e-mail them. I'm not used to being at odds with them."

He nuzzled her cheek, his breath fragrant with the scent of brandy. "I hate to see them cause you trouble, love."

His statement sent a ripple of unpleasant surprise through Olivia. She did not think of her daughters as troublemakers. Emerald could be difficult, but she was not malevolent, and Darcy was strong and dependable.

Olivia shook her head. "John, it's really *us* causing the trouble. I suppose we seem reckless. But they can't see into our hearts. They don't know the depth of our feeling—they can't believe it."

"How could they?" John asked gruffly. "I wouldn't have believed it myself before it happened."

Olivia gave him an adoring smile. "Exactly. Oh, John, it's still like a miracle to me, finding you."

"And one to me, finding you, my dearest love."

She sighed and looked at the closed drapes. Outside, the wind was howling from the east, sweeping in over the icy-cold sea. She'd forgotten how lonely that sound could be.

"The truth is," she said, "we've been so busy discovering each other, that actually we've made very few concrete plans."

"Plans?" he said.

"Well, yes, you dear, mad, romantic man. Emerald demanded to know where we intended to live if we get married."

John gave a sort of solemn *harrumph*. "There are so many things to consider about that, as you know."

"I do know. And we've talked of this and that—and even of running off and just eloping." She laughed affectionately at him. "Don't you suppose that if we mean it, we ought to make some?"

"Plans, you mean."

"Yes, darling," she said. "That's what I mean."

"Oh, yes," he said, his voice sounding peculiarly stiff. "Certainly. There are things we need to talk about. Plans."

Is something wrong? she thought. But, no, she did not want to believe such a thing. She knew that her finances were in sounder shape than his and that he was somewhat sensitive about it. But not overly so. He was a man unusually secure in himself.

She lowered her voice, almost purred. "I love you, John. I love being with you. To kiss you. To touch you."

"Oh, Olivia," he said with sudden passion, "I love you, too. Desperately. That is the only word for it—*desperately*. And you're right. It's time we did talk about certain things. It's past time."

Again she felt a little frisson of foreboding, as if the sea wind had penetrated the walls of her cozy home and breathed its cold into her soul.

He said, "I'm sixty. Almost old enough to retire. But my money's tied up in land. And the business. I can make this business work, Olivia. I've told you that. I know I can."

"I know it, too," she said fondly. Real estate was how he made his living, but his true love was the project he had been working on for the past six months. For years he had dreamed of such an enterprise.

"But if you really don't want to come to Florida," he said, "I can give it up. I can get a license up here to sell real estate. Or in Texas. Wherever you want, Olivia. I've been a rolling stone. I don't get attached to places."

"Oh, John," she said. "You *love* what you're doing in Key West. I can't ask you to give it up just when it's starting to go really well for you."

He shook his head. "All these years you've wanted to

come back to Maine. And you've still got your home base in Texas. Your children are there.''

Olivia closed her eyes and laid her cheek against his shoulder. It was true she didn't want to relocate away from Emerald and Darcy, at least not on a permanent basis.

Olivia sighed. This was one reason they had so seldom discussed the details of their future. There were hard decisions, and someone had to make a sacrifice.

John's arm tightened around her. ''There's another thing,'' he said, his voice somber. ''I live in a tiny apartment in the Keys. It's all I can afford at this point. I couldn't buy you a house.''

''I don't need a house,'' she said. ''We'll get a condo.''

''I can't afford that, either,'' he said. ''Do you know what property costs down there? And what about this place? *This* is where you want to be.''

''I wanted to come back to Maine,'' she said, nuzzling his shirt, enjoying the warmth of his flesh beneath it. ''And I did come back. But who was it who said, 'You can't go home again'? I don't really belong here any longer, John. I could sell this place and get another condo in Key West.''

John drew back slightly, and she opened her eyes because she sensed a strange tension in his body. He took her chin between his thumb and forefinger and tilted her face. ''Do you mean that? You'd give up this place—for me?''

She smiled. The place was lovely and growing lovelier all the time. But without him, it would seem like an empty shell, beautiful but lifeless.

''I missed the sea,'' she said. ''Key West is on the ocean. The very *same* ocean.''

''Dear girl,'' he said softly, ''you'd lose money. You've sunk so much in this place, getting it the way you want. You can't sell it at this point and get your investment back. Not if you hope to sell it quickly.''

''It doesn't have to sell quickly. The lake house is for sale in Austin. Someone's sure to buy it. We'll use whichever money comes first.''

His face bent nearer to hers. "But if you move to Key West, what about your other house in Austin, the one in the city?"

Olivia's heart sank. She had never been fond of the lake house, but she loved her home in the city. It was a big colonial-looking house sitting on a wooded acre, and she had lavished care on its every room. Darcy and Emerald had grown up there, and it was the center of her happiest memories.

It's only a building, she told herself. *It's the girls that are important, not the house. And it's really too big for just me…*

She swallowed and said, "I—I suppose I could sell it, too. We could always get a condo on Lake Travis, and then when we went back to Austin we'd have a place to stay. And maybe when you decide you want to retire, we could move back to Austin."

She tried to make her smile seem happier than she felt about the prospect. "That way we'd both get what we want— eventually. I mean, if you were willing to come back to Austin with me someday."

He took both her hands in his and kissed first the right, then the left. "I'd go to the ends of the earth with you, Olivia. You know that."

Olivia tried hard to be enthusiastic. "We'll get a big enough place in Key West so the girls can visit any time they want. I mean, Darcy's free to come and go as she likes, and Emerald will have school vacations. And Sloan could visit whenever he liked. *All* of them could come and stay."

John laughed. "My dear, in Key West, a place that big would cost you a million dollars—more."

"I don't care," Olivia said impulsively. "I'd *have* to have a place where my girls could come. Then I could be happy there."

John studied her face, his own serious. "Are you sure of that?"

"Yes," Olivia said. "I am."

But as he bent to kiss her, she thought, *That's not true. I'm not sure at all.* Then his mouth took possession of hers, and desire drove doubt from her mind.

WHEN DARCY'S THOUGHTS were troubled, she found fresh air and the sounds of nature soothing. She would have liked to curl up in a lawn chair on her little patio and stare up at the star-strewn sky.

But the patio was separated from the lake house only by the gardens and the pool. If Sloan came to her, she didn't know if she could resist him again. So she locked herself inside, safe from him and from herself.

Normally she liked the little guest house, but tonight it seemed claustrophobic. She sat at her drawing table, trying to work on her designs. She had been commissioned to make a series of character dolls: the sprites spirits, and fairies of Shakespeare.

Although she'd been excited by the project, tonight it seemed to mock her. She was having particular trouble with the character Puck. Puck was the mischievous elf with the power to make people fall instantly in love. Each time she sketched him, he looked strangely sinister—ears too pointed, eyes too feline, smile too cruel.

Why couldn't she draw him? Was it because she disapproved of him—or because she feared him? What he created was a kind of madness, the sort that had Olivia in its grip.

"You're so repressed," Claude had told her, *"that if your sex drive ever does kick into gear, you'll run off screaming in denial."*

"I will not," she'd countered.

"Yes, you will. You couldn't let yourself fall in love if your immortal soul was at stake. Your imagination's free. But you keep your emotions on such a tight leash, they're strangling."

"They are not."

"You'll never let them run free. You're incapable of it."

She erased, she redrew, she started over again. But try as she might, Puck still looked threatening.

She was grateful when the phone rang, offering a respite.

But almost as soon as she touched the receiver, apprehension stabbed through her. What if it was Sloan? What would she say?

But it was Emerald. "Well," Emerald said frostily, "you're finally home. I called earlier. You were out. Where were you? With that man? I hope not."

To Darcy's disgust, she found herself blushing. "I was out, that's all."

"Where?" demanded Emerald.

Darcy's jaw tightened defensively. "I don't dig into your business, Emerald. I'd appreciate it if you didn't—"

"Do you know where Mama is?" Emerald interrupted in a haughty voice. "She's with that man. He went up to Maine, and they're spending the week together. What do you think of *that* little news bulletin?"

"He and Mama think they're in love. It's natural they spend time together," Darcy hedged. "And it's not a bulletin, I already knew it."

"How?" Emerald challenged. "Did your new boyfriend tell you?"

"He's not my boyfriend."

"Oh, no? You were certainly making goo-goo eyes at him."

"I was not," Darcy said, "making goo-goo eyes."

"I call things the way I see them," Emerald said. "And he was flirting with you. You'd better be careful. He's sort of attractive. In that kind of intense, tubercular way."

"He's *not* tubercular," Darcy snapped. "He had a fever."

"You know what I mean," Emerald said loftily. "That kind of lean, doomed look of a romantic poet."

"He's not a romantic poet, for Pete's sake. He's an oil executive."

"Which proves he's not your kind. He exploits the environment. He's cutting down the rain forest. He's causing oil spills and killing seabirds."

"Lighten up, Emerald," Darcy warned.

"Don't you think it's strange that he isn't even in Mama's

house a day, and he's putting moves on you?'' Emerald asked. "At first I was mad at you, but then I realized how vulnerable you are. Maybe I should come over and chaperone you."

"Chaperone me?" Darcy repeated, appalled. "I'm thirty years old! And I'm *not* vulnerable."

"Your biological clock is starting to tick," said Emerald.

"It most certainly is *not.*" But Darcy turned the picture of the mocking Puck facedown, just to protect herself from such a preposterous accusation.

"Listen," Emerald said, "You *are* vulnerable when you reach that age. I mean, it's traumatic, right? The big three-*O?*"

"Oh, good grief, Emerald," Darcy said in disgust. "I'd hoped you were calling to apologize for going off in such a snit this afternoon. Instead, you're worse. Don't be insulting."

"I don't want you to fall into the same trap as Mama," her sister said righteously. "What do you really know about either of these men? John English or his son? Maybe they work together. Like tag team wrestlers. The world is full of con men. I know. Rose Alice says so, too. I asked her. She's going to give me a book about it."

Darcy sighed. Rose Alice loved accounts of true crime and had a large collection of books on the subject. Gus had once acidly observed, "That woman never met a serial killer she didn't like."

Darcy said, "I think this conversation's gone on long enough."

"I'll come stay with you," Emerald offered. "I don't think you should be alone with him."

"No," Darcy said emphatically.

"Then promise me you'll be careful of this man," Emerald said. "Don't make a fool of yourself. I just don't want either you or Mama getting hurt."

Darcy opened her mouth to reply, but from Emerald's end

of the line she heard a muted male voice say something she couldn't make out.

"I've got to go," Emerald said hurriedly. "Remember, Darce, I only said all this because I love you. 'Bye."

The line went dead. Frowning, Darcy lowered the receiver. Emerald was with a man? Who? She never dated, at least that Darcy knew of. What was she up to?

Darcy shook her head. She thought of her sister's words, *Don't make a fool of yourself.*

She thought of Sloan's mouth on hers, his body crushed against hers, his hands on her bare skin. "My stepbrother," she said to herself miserably. She picked up the disturbing sketches of Puck and dropped them into the wastebasket. Then she put her elbows on the table and her head in her hands.

The phone rang again, startling her so much that her body jerked as if in a spasm. She picked it up on the second ring. "Yes?" she said, hoping it wasn't Emerald again.

"I saw your light was still on," said Sloan.

Her heart wrenched into a runaway beat.

He said, "I owe you an apology. I meant it when I said I was sorry. I was completely out of hand."

But so was I, she thought. *So was I.*

She heard him take a deep breath. "If you'd like me to leave, I'll understand. I can come up with some excuse that won't hurt your mother's feelings."

She found she could make no answer. She clenched the receiver so tightly, her hand felt numb.

He said, "I'll be honest. I'd rather stay here, near you. It scares me that I do, but I do. But if you'd be more comfortable with me gone, I'll go. Do you want me to?"

Yes, she thought with a rush of desperation.

"No," she said softly.

There was a moment of silence between them.

"You're sure?" he finally said.

He's giving me a second chance to back away, she thought. *Take it. For God's sake, take it.*

"I'm sure," she said, feeling breathless.

Another silence descended between them. But it didn't feel awkward; it felt strangely intimate.

He said, "Are you still willing to show me the Hill Country?"

Tell him, "No."

"If you'd like," she said.

"When?" he asked, his voice low.

"Any time," she answered.

"Tomorrow?" he asked.

This is the primrose path to hell, she thought. *It's rash. It's insane.*

But with a rush of liberating recklessness, she said, "I'd love to."

EMERALD SNAPPED OFF her cell phone and stood for a moment on the upstairs landing. Her heart hammered in her chest, and her cheeks flamed. Nobody took her seriously. Not her mother, not Darcy.

Neither of them would listen or act with a grain of sense—it was up to her.

She looked at Henry, who stood in the open doorway of his room. He seemed like a stranger now that he had become handsome. It unsettled her, and so did the way he stared at her.

"What?" she demanded irritably.

He ran his hand through his tousled dark hair. "I've got something for you to look at."

She stalked back to Henry's room. When he sat at his desk, she came to stand beside him, but not too closely. He was doing strange and arcane things to his computer screen, like a young wizard intent on his spells.

"How are you doing?" she asked uneasily. "*What* are you doing?"

"We could guess the way into your mother's mail because you know her so well," he said, his blue eyes steady on the screen. "But this guy's another matter."

Emerald nodded stiffly. She knew next to nothing about John English. But his mail might tell her all kinds of secrets— including dark ones that Olivia didn't suspect.

She said, "You don't have it yet? I thought maybe you had it."

He shook his head, his mouth a straight, hard line.

She said, "How hard is this going to be?"

"Maybe really hard. But I'm going to try the easy way first."

"What do you mean?"

"I can't get into his mail without his password," Henry said. "So I'll just ask him for it. It's an old scam. But maybe it'll work."

"Ask him?" Emerald said in displeased surprise. "You've got to be kidding. He'll never fall for *that*."

"People fall for it all the time," Henry said grimly.

"Only if they don't know their way around the Net," she protested.

"Maybe he doesn't," Henry answered. "We'll see."

He pulled an image to the screen, and Emerald clasped her hands together nervously. She understood now what deception Henry was weaving.

He had forged an official-looking piece of mail to send to John English. It looked like an official notice from USAserve. The message contained a simple lie and a simple request. The lie was that John English had an error in his Internet billing. The request was that he give his password to verify his account.

If English didn't know this scheme, he might innocently reveal his password. Empowered with that password, Emerald could then read all the mail he sent and received. And, if she chose, she could create every sort of mischief.

Henry turned to her. His expression was both serious and apprehensive. "Do you want me to send it to him?"

Emerald tensed. Henry could get into trouble if he were caught—but he wouldn't be caught, he was too clever.

As for the morality of breaking into John English's mail,

she knew it was wrong. But she was frightened for her mother, and now for Darcy, too.

"Yes," she said. "Send it."

He squared his shoulders and hit the key. The message was sent.

"Done," he said. "From here on out, it's a waiting game."

"Is that all you're going to do?" challenged Emerald. "Can't you snoop around on the Internet and find out more about him? I mean, I *have* to have information."

He turned in his chair to face her. "I can try. I'll look all night if you want me to. You—you can stay if you want."

She shifted uncomfortably. She had been with him far too long now.

"It's getting late," she said gruffly. "I'm going. I have a book to pick up from Rose Alice. If you find anything, call me, all right?"

He nodded with a kind of weary resignation. "You know I will. Come on. I'll walk you to the door."

He rose from the chair.

How did he get so tall? Emerald felt a surge of something akin to panic. *How had he changed so much in three short years?*

"I'll let myself out," she said, turning from him and making her way out the door. She ran down the stairs as fast as she could. As she reached the front door, he called to her, an almost desperate note in his voice.

"Emerald!"

She spun around, her hand on the knob, and looked to the top of the stairs. He stood, his body tense and his hands gripping the banister. "Emerald," he said, "think carefully about what you want to do. Innocent people can get hurt—"

"You ought to know," she said bitterly. She opened the door and fled into the night, her pulse drumming.

CHAPTER ELEVEN

SLOAN WATCHED from the front window, as Darcy crossed the flagstones leading to the lake house. The morning air seemed to sparkle around her.

My God, she's a lovely thing, he thought in reluctant wonder.

She wore her dark hair swept back and up in a ponytail that was high, bouncing and pertly sexy. Her clothes were simple—dark boots, jeans and a short-sleeved white shirt, crisply starched.

She carried a white western-style hat, which she swung by her side, and she walked with a sure, graceful stride. Nothing was fancy about her, yet everything seemed elegant.

She had sent him a short e-mail this morning.

You're just out of the hospital, so I'll drive. Pick you up at nine-thirty, okay? D.

He'd written a single word in reply, *Fine.* They'd kept their messages brief, but he sensed that their words were as highly charged as the electric force that carried their messages between the two computers.

He let the curtain fall back into place when Darcy reached the porch. He opened the door with counterfeit aplomb and made his smile blasé. He reassured himself that he was a sophisticated man and an expert in emotional detachment.

But when he saw her standing there, it didn't matter. He felt as if he'd been caught in some molecule-mixing machine that had combined Cary Grant with Beaver Cleaver.

"Hi," she said brightly. "Ready to ride?"

"I don't know," he said carefully. "I'm usually in the driver's seat."

He thought her smile hinted at the same nervousness he felt. But the look she gave him was impudent.

She cocked her head in the direction of her vehicle. "I worried that you're used to a higher-priced model," she said. "Faster. Flashier."

"No." His gaze met and held hers. "Fast and flashy don't interest me the way they used to."

"Then what does?" she asked.

Magic, he wanted to say, then wondered why in hell he'd thought such a damn fool thing. The word had come to him unbidden and seemed inevitably right, although he could not say such a thing.

So he only smiled his most worldly smile. *I am a moron,* he thought. *I have regressed to the age of seven.*

DARCY HAD TRIED TO KEEP the conversation light as she drove out of Austin. But no matter what was said, an erotic undercurrent coursed beneath their words.

Even the scenery seemed to conspire against her. The fields were a crazy quilt of wild blossoms, and she usually observed this season with an artist's eye, appraising and appreciating its beauty. Today she saw spring in all its sexual creativeness; she felt its energy throb in the air.

She stole a sideways glance at Sloan, who seemed to be taking in the countryside. His long frame radiated a leisurely grace that marked a man comfortable with his own body. And yet she sensed the same primal restlessness in him that she felt herself.

Stop it, she scolded herself. *My mother's in love with his father, for crying out loud.*

Just as daunting was the fact that she'd hired a detective agency to check out John English. How could she be attracted to a man at the same time she was furtively trying to pry out his family secrets?

She shifted uneasily. She had always prized honesty, but now she had become two-faced. It gave her a deeply unpleasant feeling.

She had come to hope fervently that the agency would find nothing at all suspicious about John English. Then no one need ever know of her tawdry little experiment in sleuthing.

On the other hand, she thought, what if the agency *did* turn up something unsavory about John English? Such thoughts tamed the spring fancies trying to frisk in her blood.

As if Sloan read her mind, he suddenly spoke. "Have you heard from your mother?"

Darcy quelled a guilty start and shook her head. "No. I suppose I should phone her."

She stole another glance at him. He kept his gaze on the passing scenery, but his expression had turned strangely serious. "I sent my dad an e-mail. He probably won't like it."

A ripple of curiosity stirred in her. "Oh?"

He set his jaw and turned to her. "Yeah. After you left last night, I checked my own e-mail. I had another message from Trina. Very overwrought. Demanding answers."

"I'm sorry," said Darcy. Trina sounded like a truly difficult woman.

"So am I," Sloan said dryly. "Of course, she keeps saying she's worried for Arthur's sake. In a way, I suppose that's true."

"I understand." Darcy nodded. "She sees Mama as a threat."

"Right," he agreed. "Blood is thicker than water, all that good stuff. Except that for Trina, the thickest substance of all is money." He frowned. "I'm starting to see that no matter how much she has, it'll never be enough. And she's scared to death that your mother's going to get Arthur's 'legacy'— that precious swampland."

Darcy felt partly amused, partly defensive. "I sincerely doubt that Mama wants anybody's swampland."

"So do I," said Sloan. "So I told my father if he intends to keep his promise to Trina, he should make a prenuptial agreement stipulating that the land goes to her. Then maybe she'll back off and let him live in peace.''

''Sounds sensible to me. I don't think Mama would object at all.''

''No,'' Sloan said, ''but my father might.''

She blinked in surprise, then gave him a questioning look. His green eyes had trouble in their depths. ''My father,'' he said, ''has been burned by divorce. His last two wives took him for all he had—which, frankly, wasn't much. It was before his famous rise and fall in real estate. Still, in spite of everything, he's stayed a romantic kind of guy. He thinks that prenup agreements are cynical. That they poison trust.''

Once again the cold pall of suspicion fell over her. Did Sloan want her to accept this as a mere ''peculiarity'' in his father? Wasn't such an arrangement—or lack thereof—a danger to her mother's interests?

She stared at the highway worriedly. She was glad to see a familiar side road ahead. It led to a hilltop over a bend of the Perdenales River, a semi-wooded spot where wildflowers usually bloomed in bright profusion.

''Let's take a little detour,'' she said brightly, wishing they didn't have to have this conversation.

''Fine,'' Sloan said, but his serious expression didn't change. ''I don't want to meddle in my father's business. But I will if I have to. He's got to understand that a prenup isn't just to protect his family's interests. It'll protect your mother's, too. He's got to do it for her sake.''

He had thrown her another unexpected curve. She had been busily questioning his motives about Olivia—yet now he seemed to show true concern for her. Darcy darted him an uneasy glance.

His eyes met hers with a gaze of startling intensity. ''I want your mother's security insured,'' he said. ''Not only for her, but also for your peace of mind. And your sister's. I mean that.''

Do you really? She wondered in a storm of confusion. And

she realized she believed him. Almost desperately, she believed him.

JOHN HAD GONE OUT WALKING. It was his habit to walk several miles a day, no matter what the weather. He said these hikes burned off nervous energy, that he became fidgety if he stayed cooped inside.

Olivia had not joined him because it was too cold. The temperature had plunged into the low forties. She had fretted that his jacket wasn't warm enough and that he didn't think he needed a hat.

"I'm hot-blooded," he'd told her with a smile. "You know that."

He'd kissed her goodbye and gone out.

She'd watched him from the window until he'd disappeared, his head bent against the wind. She sighed. He was a restless man and needed activity; she would have to get used to it.

She knew that he was full of creative urges that he had never been able to follow—until the last few years. He'd had too many responsibilities, too many reversals, to follow his own desires. It was important for him to stay in Key West, where he'd finally begun to realize his dreams.

Yet dreams, she knew, were tricky entities. They changed and shifted their shapes. She knew. Oh, yes, she knew. She stared out the window at the now-deserted shore.

For years Olivia had comforted herself with memories of the ocean.

In the troubled years in Texas, the mere thought of the sea had been balm to her. She had thought of coming here as returning to her true home.

Now she no longer had to dream of it; she was back. But she had been unsettled to find it did not comfort her as much as it once had.

Today the outside world had no color in it, and the shore was a strip of stony black, edged with restless scallops of white foam. A cold gray sea stretched out endlessly beneath an equally cold gray sky.

The only sign of life was a lone seagull that dipped against the wind like a solitary pilgrim. It looked powerless and frail against such a vastness of sky and water.

Back in Texas, the sky would be blue. The hills and fields would be quickening with new life, the spring flowers patching them with rainbow brightness.

With a sudden shudder, she realized how homesick she was. This homesickness had never been part of her dream, and she had never imagined how much she would miss Austin and her daughters.

She had told John she would gladly sell this condo and leave Maine. In truth, this was no sacrifice for her. But to go with him permanently to Key West? Sell her longtime home in Austin? See the city only on visits?

In the harsh light of day and without John's exciting presence, these ideas unsettled her. She had never seen Florida; Gus had always refused to go. *"What's Florida got that I want?"* he'd grumble. *"Hurricanes hit it. Alligators eat the dogs and children. If I got to see a palm tree, I'll go to Vegas."*

She would have to be honest and tell John of these second thoughts. She needed to see Florida before she made a decision about leaving Austin. He would understand. Of course he would...

She turned from the window. She had a sudden and irresistible desire to talk to her daughters. She picked up the telephone and dialed Emerald's number. *Emerald,* she thought, *my dear, sweet problem child. Let's talk.*

But she heard five rings, then the *click* of the answering machine. *"Greetings. This is Emerald, but I'm not in the castle right now. Leave a message if thou dost so wish, after the sound of the wizard's beep."*

Olivia smiled. When the *beep* sounded, she said, "Hello, honey, it's Mama. I just called to say I love you."

Then, feeling strangely wistful, she dialed Darcy's number.

There was no answer there, not even by the machine. Disappointed, Olivia hung up.

Emerald, she realized, was probably in class at the university. But where could Darcy be? She usually worked in her studio during the morning. Not that Darcy was a creature of habit, by any means, but still, what if she was in some kind of trouble?

Stop it, Olivia told herself sternly. She was needlessly worrying. After all, Darcy was her dependable daughter, coolheaded to a fault. How could *Darcy* possibly get in trouble?

I THINK I'M IN TROUBLE, fretted Darcy. *I shouldn't have brought him here. It was a tactical error.*

It was too beautiful in this place, and too isolated. It was like being in Eden, and temptation was like perfume in the spring air.

She and Sloan had hiked from the dirt road to a hill overlooking the winding green river. Its course meandered past verdant stretches of trees and low limestone cliffs.

Although the hill's topsoil was sparse, it was rich enough to nourish hardy trees and the country's famous wildflowers. The cacti were in blossom. The prickly pears sported fat yellow boutonnieres, and tall white clusters of flowers flared up from the sword-like leaves of the yucca plants.

"My God," Sloan breathed in wonder. "This is something. It's like the first day of creation."

The thought was close to her own. She said, "I hope the walk wasn't too far for you."

She'd brought a basket with a thermos of cold tea and fruit in case he needed nourishment, and an old quilt in case he needed to sit down and rest. He'd insisted on carrying them both.

She said, "I mean, you've been sick. And we came over a mile."

Now he turned from the river view and looked down at her. "It was easy. Perfect, in fact. The first time I got out of the hospital, I wouldn't pace myself. I was running, lifting weights, trying too much. It backfired.''

''But why would you do such a thing?'' she asked. ''Push yourself so hard?''

His expression grew self-mocking. ''I didn't want to admit I was mortal. It was too frightening. I wanted to believe I'd live forever.''

''And?'' she asked.

''And now I know I won't,'' he said simply. ''I've been thinking about it. Human life doesn't go on forever. A day like this is a gift. It's—precious.''

He said *precious* as if such a word didn't come easily to his lips. He shook his head. ''When you nearly die, it changes the way you think. Or it should. But I didn't want to change.''

He gazed up at the sky with a bemused expression. ''So I had that relapse. It was like Death said, 'All right, you stupid SOB, you don't get it. Let me spell it out again.'''

They had come to a patch of the flowers called Indian blankets, Darcy's favorites. She paused, gazing down at their brilliant scarlets and golds. Sloan stopped, too. For a moment neither of them spoke.

Then he said, ''In the hospital I had a dream. Death was outside my door, dressed all in black. He said I needed to learn to stop and smell the flowers.''

She smiled. ''That wasn't Death. It was Sister Mary Francis.''

He smiled back. ''Same difference. They both have cold hands and a steely stare.''

''She was talking to me,'' Darcy said.

''And you brought flowers to me. They were there when I woke up. And now you've done it the other way around. You've brought me to the flowers. It seems symbolic.''

Darcy gave a self-conscious laugh. ''It's not symbolic. It's only what my mother wanted. To show you a little hospitality, that's all.''

''You've shown more than a little.''

There was an intimacy in his tone that she found profoundly disturbing. It made the center of her stomach flutter. "You worked overseas," she said, changing the subject. "I suppose you'll be going back?"

"Yes," he said.

She began to walk again, and once again he kept pace by her side. "You're in charge of overseas development?"

"The second stage," he said. "First the suits go in and check the potential, do the negotiating. Once it's set, I come in, go into the field, do the rough stuff. Get the physical operation up and running."

"Sounds complicated."

"It is."

"And you've been posted all over?"

"Lately in Southeast Asia. The tropics."

Darcy had been carrying her white Stetson. She put it on, adjusted the brim against the sunshine. *The tropics,* she thought. To her it sounded as exotic as if he'd said he'd been posted on Mars.

"You've been all over the world, haven't you?" she asked.

He nodded wryly. "I've seen more of foreign countries than of my own."

"I think that would be wonderful," she said a bit dreamily. "I've never traveled much. The only other country I've been to is Mexico."

He shrugged one lean shoulder. "Yeah. Sometimes traveling gets old. But you get used to it."

"How long does an assignment last?"

"Six months, a year. Sometimes more. It depends. Then it's on to the next boondock."

She gave him a searching sidelong glance. "But you love it, don't you?"

He laughed as if to himself. "I suppose. It's what I do."

"And that's one of the reasons you pushed yourself so hard? To get back?"

"That's part of it." His brow furrowed critically. "One company exec has hinted about basing me in Tulsa now. Giving me a desk job. Just posting me to Europe and Asia now and then.''

She sensed deep regret in him and felt a tug of sympathy. ''But you'd hate that—wouldn't you?''

''Probably,'' he said, not looking at her. ''I never tried it.''

The sun had risen higher, and Darcy and Sloan had reached a grove of clustering mesquite trees.

''I'll show you something,'' she said. ''Then we should turn back. I don't want to wear you out.''

She followed a wide, dim path into the shade. It was the remains of a dirt lane, thickly overgrown. He followed. The birds that had twittered in the grove went silent at their approach. The only sound was the stiff leaves of the mesquites rattling in the breeze.

Then the trees opened to an even wider, more breathtaking vista of the river. But even more surprising, they revealed a ruin.

A rectangle of scarred cement was set at the highest crest of the land. The jagged remains of two brick walls met in a corner that was blackened by fire. On the opposite side of the slab stood a fireplace, still remarkably intact, although the chimney had crumbled.

Sloan's brow furrowed. ''A house?''

She nodded. ''It burned. About eight years ago. The owner cleaned out the rubble. You can see the trees that were burned. And the new ones that are coming in.''

Around the house stood a few scorched corpses of trees. Young ones sprang from their roots, thrusting up strongly and nodding in the breeze.

''It's beautiful here,'' Sloan said. ''How come nobody built it back?''

''The owner was too heartbroken,'' Darcy said. ''The property's for sale now. My stepfather looked at it when he wanted to build. That's how I know it's here. He decided it was too far from town. But I wish he'd chosen it. I love this spot.''

''It's a world to itself up here,'' Sloan said, his voice low.

She nodded. She could see for miles from this vantage point, and there was no other dwelling in sight. She leaned against an unscarred tree. There was something strangely intimate about such a lonely place. Perhaps, she realized, too intimate.

"Want to rest a minute?" she asked. "Then go back?"

He set down the basket, the quilt. He put his hands into his front pockets, then leaned beside her, disturbingly close.

"I'm not really an invalid, you know," he said. "In fact, I could go much farther."

The words clearly had double meaning. She kept her gaze fixed on the hills beyond the river. "This fever of yours—" she said. "Are you in danger of having relapses all your life?"

"Fewer if I keep my resistance up," he said. "But, yeah. It's in my blood for good. A permanent souvenir."

She tried to choose her words carefully. "And would your relapses always be as bad as the one you just had? Or worse?"

"I was a fool. I didn't want to admit it had come back on me so soon. Stupid, huh?"

She realized he'd avoided giving her a real answer about future attacks.

"It was a rogue virus," he said almost contemptuously. He picked up a pebble and pitched it down the hill. "Something I hadn't been vaccinated for. Couldn't be vaccinated for. Nowadays viruses are proliferating like crazy. Especially in the places I was traveling. This one exec's worried about what happens if I meet another one this tough. Or tougher."

She looked at him in concern. How ironic, she thought, that such a tall and strong-seeming man should be condemned always to carry a microscopic threat in his veins. "But they'll send you back?"

"I've applied for it. If they say no, I'll fight for it."

"What do your doctors say?" she asked.

"What doctors always say—be careful. So okay. I'll be careful."

Which means that you're footloose and in love with it, she thought. *You've warned me before, and you're warning me again.*

Yet somehow she thought she understood. "I'd go, too, I guess. I've always wanted to see the world. And if you love something that much, it's a shame to give it up."

He said, "So what about you? What do you love?"

She shrugged with a carelessness she didn't feel. "My work. I'd never give it up."

"But your work doesn't keep you in Austin. If you wanted to travel, you could."

She shook her head. "There's always been my family. I've stuck around for them. My mother—well, you have to realize she didn't have an easy time of it. My stepfather was a demanding man. Very difficult. And for a while she had her hands full with Emerald, too. I could take up some slack for her there. Emerald's a lot more independent now. I think she's really going away to grad school. Not far away, but away." She paused, frowning. "And sometimes I think..." She let the thought trail off.

Sloan urged her on. "And sometimes you think what?"

"Sometimes," Darcy said pensively, "I wonder if that's why Mama bought that summer place in Maine. To give *us* our freedom. To cut the apron strings to Emerald a little bit. And to let me go my way if I want. That probably doesn't make any sense."

"Yes," he said quietly. "It does. If she's free to go off on her own, then so are you."

"But now this," Darcy said. "This thing between your father and my mother."

"Ah, yes." He sighed. *"That."*

"Emerald's taking it hard. I hope she doesn't backslide into her old ways. I don't know what she's up to. It worries me."

"It sounds like you spend more of your time worrying about your mother and Emerald than you do about yourself."

She looked at him in surprise. "But I'm fine. I've got everything I want. Austin's my home, and I love it. I love my life. What should *I* be worried about?''

''Me,'' he said. ''And we both know it.''

HE HAD BEEN KEEPING HIS hands in his pockets for one reason: so he would not give in to the temptation to touch her. Temptation had grown too strong.

Now, slowly and with deliberation, he put his hands on her shoulders and looked into her face. *Yes?* he asked without speaking. *No? Maybe?*

Her expression looked almost stricken with conflict. She knew they should not do this. So did he.

With his eyes he asked her again, *Yes? No?*

He bent nearer. She didn't resist. Instead, she lifted her face to his, her lips softly parted.

He had to move only inches to kiss her, but it felt like a long, tumbling fall through deep space. When his mouth touched hers, a sort of brilliant darkness closed around him. It jolted both his mind and groin.

He burned with need to press the full length of his body to hers. His hands swept down to her waist, and he hauled her tightly against him, his mouth still clamped possessively on hers. Her arms wrapped around his neck with an eagerness that inflamed him even more.

The hat she wore was getting in the way of his kissing, and he took it off her, let it fall. He greedily laced his fingers in the locks of her ponytail, and somehow the band holding it in place came undone. Her hair came down in a silky cascade.

His lower body strove more urgently for greater nearness to hers. His chest strained against the pliant softness of her breasts, and both his mind and flesh pounded with need for her.

She gasped. Or perhaps he did. He could not tell, did not care. Their mouths moved together so hungrily, it was as if he and she were a creature rent in two struggling to become

whole again. Their tongues tasted each other. His hands began
to move over her back, her hips.

He was dimly conscious of the rushing sound of the river
far below, of the breeze rustling the leaves. But the hammer-
ing of his pulses seemed as loud, and her scent, which was
like wildflowers, filled his senses and drunkenly addled them.

He raised his right hand to her shirtfront, began unfastening
her buttons. This was a nicety that he forced on himself from
some civilized corner of his brain that was still working. He
would have gladly ripped off her clothes and his, too.

But her hand clamped around his wrist. She broke the kiss,
drawing back from him. Beneath his stilled hand, her breast
moved up and down.

She gazed up at him, her face pale except for flushed
cheeks. "Don't," she said. "Not here."

"Why?" he asked. "There's no one here but you and me."

She dodged her head, pulled farther from him still. "I mean
it. This is neither the time nor the place—"

He tried to draw her close again. "It is. I feel it. So do
you."

"No."

"I've known it from the start. So have you."

"No," she repeated sharply, breaking away from his arms.

He wanted her badly. And he knew she wanted him. But
he let her go. She took two steps away, putting a safe distance
between them. "Not here," she said unhappily. "Not now.
It's not—"

"So what do I do? Make an appointment?" He asked it
with more acidity than he'd intended.

"I don't know," she said unhappily. She stepped to the
brow of the cliff and stood in profile to him. She looked out
over the river. "I didn't think you'd—we'd—get so carried
away."

"I'm sorry," he said truthfully. "It's been a while for me."

She studied the horizon and bit her lip. Then she said, "Me,
too."

She looked as if she was going to cry. The thought of her

tears threw cold water on the fire he felt, but not enough to make it die.

"So," he said. "Did you love him?"

She shrugged. "In a way."

"What happened?"

She shrugged again. "He wanted to get married. I didn't."

He leaned against the mesquite tree again. "Why not?"

"I guess I didn't love him enough," she said, and kicked at a pebble.

He crossed his arms and watched her. She stood straighter and put up her chin, but she didn't turn to look at him. The breeze played with her unbound hair, fluttered the cloth of her rumpled shirt.

He sensed the inhibitions in her struggling to keep their hold. He understood such inhibitions all too well.

He said, "When *he* wanted to make love to you, what happened? Did *he* have to make an appointment?"

For a moment he thought she wasn't going to answer. Then he saw the suggestion of a smile playing at the corner of her mouth. She raised her chin a fraction of an inch.

"He didn't have to," she said. "But he did."

"That's what I thought," said Sloan.

He walked up behind her. He put his hands on her upper arms and kissed the back of her neck. She shuddered but didn't move away.

He turned her around and took her in his arms. She didn't resist. When he bent to kiss her, he whispered, "Some things shouldn't be done by assignment. They should just be done."

He lowered his mouth to hers.

CHAPTER TWELVE

"I'VE NEVER BEEN so blasted cold."

John huffed and stamped his feet in the entryway. The freezing wind that swept in from the Atlantic seemed to have burrowed into his bones.

"Florida boy," Olivia teased, putting her warm hands on his icy cheeks. "You're used to sitting under a palm tree, wondering if you've got on enough suntan lotion."

"It's a swell climate here—for emperor penguins."

"You're an emperor who should have had more clothes on. You should see your ears. They're vermilion."

His numb fingers fumbled on the fastenings of his jacket, so she helped him unbutton it, then hung it in the entry closet.

"I need a nice warm woman to get my blood flowing again," he said as piteously as he could. "Do you know where I could find one?"

"No," Olivia said pertly. "I know exactly what you want rubbed and why."

"I'd be glad to rub you, too," he offered hopefully.

"Not with those cold hands." Olivia laughed. "I'll warm you up first with some hot soup and a toasted sandwich."

He sighed in resignation as she moved into her kitchenette. He followed her, chafing his hands for warmth. She opened the cupboard door, took down the bottle of Irish Cream, and filled a liqueur glass. She offered it to him. "Here. Maybe this will start the thawing process."

He took it gratefully. "My dear, the country up here can be beautiful, I'm sure. But today it's grim as the Arctic and twice as cold. Key West is always warm, always full of color, the flowers are always blooming. I truly think you could like it there as much as you like it here. Maybe more.''

Her smile faded. ''I don't mind trading this place for one in Florida. But...'' Her voice trailed off as if she wanted to say more, and a haunted look came into her eyes. This was so unlike her that it alarmed John.

''Olivia,'' he said in concern, ''is something wrong?''

''I've been thinking,'' she said, her face growing even more solemn. ''What we talked about last night—about me selling my house in Austin. John, I shouldn't have said that. At least, not yet. I've never even *seen* Florida. Not the Keys, not any part of it.''

Relief swept through him. Was that her only worry, the dear girl? ''Then come back with me. Look around as long as you want. You'll love it, I know you will.''

''I can't leave here,'' she protested. ''I have workmen coming in, things to oversee. I can't put the place on the market when it's only half finished—it isn't ready at all.''

''But why sink more money into it?'' John asked mildly. ''You won't get it back when you sell it.''

''You said that before,'' Olivia said with a small frown. ''But I don't understand why. The nicer it is, the more it should be worth.''

John felt a glow of masculine superiority. ''But my dear, there's such a thing as over-improvement. Your condo will be the most expensive in the neighborhood, and, thus, the hardest to sell. If you want it to sell quickly so you can buy in the Keys, you'll have to price it low. That's how real estate works.''

Olivia looked neither happy nor convinced. ''It doesn't seem right.''

''I know. But that's the way it is.''

He moved behind her, put his hands on her waist and kissed the back of her neck. ''Just accept it and don't bother your pretty head about it.''

She wheeled around, her eyes blazing with resentment. ''John, I *hate* that phrase. That's what Gus was always saying—'Don't worry your pretty head'—as if I were an idiot. *Please* don't patronize me.''

He had never before seen her angry, and her reaction wounded him. "Olivia, darling, I didn't mean it that way."

"I should hope not," she said, and turned back to slicing the loaf of bread.

"Forgive me, please."

She sighed. "You're forgiven. I'm sorry I snapped at you. I've been brooding about my girls. I miss them already. And, oh, John, it's so difficult to talk about money. I just hate it."

So did he, with all his heart. He had been a fool to try to tell her how to conduct her business.

"This is your condo," he said, patting her arm consolingly. "Finish it any way you like. And as soon as you want to come to Key West, let me know. I know a lovely place, The Banyan, where you can stay."

From over her shoulder she gave him a curious look. "But John, I could just stay with *you.*"

Now instead of the warmth of superiority, he felt the sickening chill of shame. "I've told you," he said, "my place isn't right for guests. It's too small. You—wouldn't be comfortable."

His apartment bordered on squalid. It was an efficiency, old, ill-furnished, with a bathroom that was always putting forth a new crop of mildew. He never cooked in the kitchen because it, too, had mildew, as well as the hardy Florida roaches that would survive atomic attack.

And, dammit, his living quarters led back to the vexing matter of money. His was tied up in land and in his fledgling business. He had assets, but little ready cash.

She seemed to sense his discomfort. "It's all right," she said.

Neither of them spoke. They knew that once again they were poised on the edge of a troublesome subject, and both were eager to avoid it.

"Will it be a few minutes before lunch?" he asked, changing the subject. "Maybe I'll check my e-mail. I haven't done it for a while."

She nodded. "Fine." She didn't look up.

He went back into the living room. He sat down by the coffee table, where his computer lay with its screen folded down.

He looked about the room, which was exquisitely decorated. He knew Olivia was sincere when she said she could leave this place without great regret. It was only a vacation getaway, after all; she had barely lived in it and had formed no real attachment to it.

But now she sounded far less certain about leaving her home in Texas. And if she already missed her daughters, could she really live apart from them for most of the year, and be content? Simply to let him take his crazy gamble?

He knew most people would think he was mad to attempt what he was doing. Since boyhood, he'd had a dream, but never the chance to follow it. Once it had been a large dream. Now it was small and perhaps ridiculous. But it was still his, and before he died, he yearned to make it real.

Olivia understood. Or he thought she did. Yet…

He shrugged away these conflicting thoughts, took another sip of liqueur. He picked up his computer, wondering if Sloan had answered his message. He switched on the machine, typed in his password and checked his mailbox. There was, indeed, e-mail from Sloan; in fact, two messages.

John summoned the first to the screen, then blinked in displeasure.

The short note mocked John's warning to Sloan and made a jeering reference to James Bond. John gritted his teeth; Sloan could be damn sarcastic when he chose.

The next note began with a similarly ironic tone, but its contents quickly turned serious, uncomfortably so.

SUBJECT: About Your Prospects of Untold Wealth
From: SloanJEnglish@PetroCorp.com
To: BanditKing@USAserve.com

Today I've had another overwrought message from Trina. I'm forwarding a copy so you can see for yourself.

Dad, I hate interfering, but I also hate being caught in the middle of this.

If you're going to marry again, and if you intend to keep your old provisions about Trina and Arthur, *let Trina know.*

A prenuptial agreement should satisfy her, and it would seem to serve everyone's best financial interests.

Your fiancée clearly has property about which careful arrangements should be made. Otherwise, she and her daughters may suspect your motives. This, I'm sure, is exactly what you want to avoid.

Yours, Sloan

This message, of course, did not cheer John because it reminded him yet again of money, especially the gibe about his "Prospects of Untold Wealth." Once he had believed his real estate investment would make his fortune. It hadn't; it didn't seem about to—and the thought depressed him.

Even less cheering was the message Sloan had forwarded from Trina.

Sloan—

I've heard nothing from you and I have no idea whats going on. I just hope you aren't aiding and abetting your father in this latest scheme.

I had prayed his womanizing days were done, but it just must be in his blood like a disease.

After that last episode of his, I expected him to stick to the straight and narrow and he has made promises to me that *are matters of honor!* If he breaks his word, poor Arthur is like a shorn lamb with next to nothing to protect him from the wind's cruel blast. Please remember this unfortunate boy is your brother *in all but name!*

Sometimes I fear John will not be happy until he has

put everyone, including himself, in the poor house.
Concerned for Arthur, Trina

John swore in disgust. He would not dignify Trina's ranting
with a reply. She was showing her true colors, and he hoped
at last Sloan could see through her. But at the moment, he
did not have the stomach to answer Sloan, either. He'd discussed money enough for one day.

He sipped the last of his liqueur and pulled up his final
message.

More trouble, he thought glumly. It was a letter from his
Internet server informing him of a billing problem.

We need to verify your screen name and password for
our records. Please fill in the information in the blanks
provided.

John sighed and dutifully filled in the blanks. The message
looked so genuine, he did not doubt for a moment it was real.

"EMERALD, I'VE GOT IT!" Henry's voice was tight with nervousness. "I've got his password—I can get into his mail."

Emerald gripped the receiver so hard that her knuckles
whitened. "Can I get into it from my computer?"

"It's safer to do it from mine. Can you come over? I'm
still alone here."

She drew a deep breath and held it, her heart pounding.
She didn't want to be with him in that room again. But for
Olivia, she would do it. "I'll be there."

She nearly broke the speed limit driving to him. He let her
into the house, which seemed bigger and emptier in the daytime. Henry's father owned a successful video production
company, and the success showed in the house's size. Emerald did her best not to be intimidated.

"You look very...nice," Henry said as he led her upstairs.

"Don't talk like that," she ordered. She didn't think she

looked nice; she probably looked like Robin Hood. She wore black tights, high boots, and a green tunic with a leather belt. It looked medieval without quite being a costume, and it was more boyish than feminine.

Henry, blast him, actually *did* look nice. No, Emerald thought uneasily, to tell the truth, he looked positively handsome.

Once his height had been the same as hers. Now he had shot up at least ten inches taller than she was, and he was broad across the shoulders, slim in the hips. His faded jeans emphasized the length of his legs, and his white T-shirt set off the natural golden cast of his skin.

He had shadows under his eyes, probably from lack of sleep. These shadows made him look older and gave his eyes a rather haunted, poetic appearance. For the first time she noticed what a shapely mouth he had now that his braces were off.

He opened the door of his bedroom for her, followed her inside, then closed the door behind them. She felt uncomfortable at the closeness of the space, the sense of intimacy that the room forced on them.

He, too, seemed ill at ease. He looked her up and down, cleared his throat, but said nothing. He kept clenching and unclenching his hands as if he wasn't sure what to do with them.

The silence between them grew awkward. To break it, Emerald said, "Have you read it—his mail?"

Henry shook his head. "It wouldn't be right. This concerns your family, not mine." On either side of his mouth, deep lines had etched themselves, making him look still older and tireder.

He really hates doing this. But he's doing it for me. She was touched in spite of herself, but she would rather have died than let him know.

"Let's see" was all she said, and she made the words brusque.

He sat at the computer and tapped at the keyboard. She

moved behind him and crossed her arms tensely, watching. The screen showed the USAserve logo and the invitation, ENTER YOUR NAME AND PASSWORD HERE. Henry typed in JOHN ENGLISH.

"Okay," he said. "Here goes." He keyed in a string of letters that appeared on the screen only as asterisks.

"His password," she breathed. "What is it?"

"Blavatski," Henry said.

"What's *that* mean?" Emerald asked, puzzled.

Henry shrugged. "Maybe it means Madame Blavatski. That's all I can figure out."

"Who's Madame Blavatski?"

"A mystic. Some people thought she was a genius. Others thought she was a fraud."

"Maybe that's his real name," she said suspiciously. "Maybe he comes from a long line of frauds and grifters and con artists."

"Maybe he's just mystical," said Henry. "There it is. His mailbox." He turned and looked up at her. His jewel-blue eyes were troubled. "You're sure you want to do this?"

Emerald bit her lip. Breaking into John English's e-mail wasn't exactly illegal—so long as she didn't do it to threaten or harass him or steal from him. It was, however, highly unethical.

"I've got to know for my mother's sake," she said. She stared at the list of John's messages. Most were from her mother, and she had no desire to reread those sickening love notes.

But three of the most recent e-mails were from Sloan English. *He* would know the truth about his father, wouldn't he?

"I want to see those," Emerald said, pointing to Sloan's messages.

With clear reluctance, Henry summoned the first. Emerald frowned as she read it, then a chill gripped her. Her most ghastly fears were confirmed.

"Henry," she said, her voice shaking. "*Look* at this." In disbelief, she read the words again.

SUBJECT: Snooping and Chasing Women
From: SloanJEnglish@PetroCorp
To: BanditKing@USAserve

Thanks for your advice. Yeah, I'm being a regular James
Bond, spying and seducing.
Yours in sexual espionage,
007

"The *varlet*," Emerald breathed. She trembled with shock
and outrage. "The cad. The villain. He ought to be put up
against a wall and shot."

"Well," Henry said uneasily, "it doesn't look too good.
But it's e-mail, maybe he was just kidding around. I mean, it
sounds pretty flippant."

Emerald felt an almost murderous rage. "It's worse than I
thought. Show me the next message."

"Emerald, maybe we shouldn't—"

Her voice was commanding. *"Show me."*

His body tensed, but he obeyed. Again Emerald read, and
again she was appalled. "Oh, my God," she moaned. "He's
telling his father to get Mama to sign a prenuptial agreement!"

Henry gave a grimace of distaste as he studied the screen.
"Well, yeah," he said at last. "But this message sounds a lot
more serious than the other one. I mean, a prenuptial arrangement could work to your mother's advantage if she's careful."

Emerald refused to listen. What did Henry know of such
worldly matters? He might have gotten tall, but he was still
practically a child.

"No," she said stubbornly. "Look at what he says." She
pointed at the screen. "He says a prenup 'would *seem* to serve
everyone's best financial interests.' Not that it would—but
that it would *seem* to."

Henry shrugged as if he didn't want to agree. "It's just a

phrase. It doesn't have to be sinister. We don't want to leap to conclusions.''

But Emerald sensed evil omens and proof of knavery. ''Look what he says next,'' she argued, pointing at the next paragraph.

'''Your fiancée clearly has property about which careful arrangements should be made. Otherwise, she and her daughters may suspect your motives. This, I'm sure, is exactly what you want to avoid.'''

Henry gave another dubious shrug. ''I'm not sure...''

''Henry,'' she said impatiently, ''it's as clear as the nose on your face. The son's looked over Mama's property—he's cased the joint.''

''Emerald, circumstantial evidence would seem—''

''He's saying to make careful arrangements about Mama's property so that she won't get suspicious—and neither will we. This John English is after Mama's money. He *is*. And his son is in it, too—up to his neck.''

''Emerald, I don't know,'' Henry muttered with a worried shake of his head.

''I've talked to Rose Alice about it. She *understands* these things. She says this is just like a famous case in England. Just *exactly*.''

''But—'' Henry said.

''Pull up the next letter,'' Emerald ordered.

He brought the next piece of e-mail to the screen. It was not a message written by Sloan himself, but one he had forwarded from someone named Trina.

Emerald read it with rising horror. ''My God!'' she breathed. Without thinking, she clutched Henry's right shoulder.

...aiding and abetting your father in his latest scheme...I had prayed his womanizing days were done, but it just must be in his blood like a disease... After that last shameful episode... I expected him to stick to the straight and narrow... Sometimes I fear John will not be

happy until he has put everyone, including himself, in
the poor house…

Emerald grasped Henry more convulsively, and her free
hand rose, trembling, to her mouth. "Oh," she gasped. "Oh,
it couldn't be more awful. Poor Mama! Poor Darcy!"

Henry said nothing. He looked at Emerald's hand with
wonder and disbelief, as if a leprechaun had just lighted on
his shoulder.

"Henry, *look*," she begged. "Look what this woman's
saying…he's a 'womanizer.' It's like a 'disease.' He has
'shameful episodes.' He'll lose all Mama's money. He'll put
her in 'the poor house.' Oh, my God!"

With obvious effort, Henry made his gaze return to the
screen. He swallowed. "I wonder who Arthur is," he said in
a slightly cracked voice.

"Isn't it obvious?" Emerald asked. "He's John English's
illegitimate son. She tells Sloan he's 'your brother in everything but name.' This Trina must be some cast-off mistress."

"Well…" Henry said uncertainly. He swallowed again.

Emerald's imagination raced to supply the scenario. "John
English had a son by her. But—but it sounds as if something's wrong with the boy. And that man won't keep his
child-support promises. Oh, he's a *beast!*"

"Now, wait." Henry's eyes turned back to her hand as if
he yearned to touch it. "Sloan English was actually encour-
aging his father to provide for this Trina and Arthur, whoever
they are."

"Sloan English," Emerald said bitterly, "is 'aiding and
abetting' his father. He's romancing my sister, while his father tries to bilk my mother out of everything she's got."

Henry kept gazing raptly at Emerald's hand. His voice was
strained. "You think that this Sloan is trying to distract her,
put her off guard?"

"Exactly!" Tears sprang to her eyes. "My family's in-
fested with gigolos," she wailed.

Henry rose to his feet and gripped her by the upper arms. "Emerald, please—don't," he pleaded.

His concern undid her. She cried harder. "I'm the only one who knows the truth. How can I tell them? They won't ever believe me." She collapsed against his chest weeping. "Why are men so awful? Why can't you ever trust them?"

Awkwardly he wrapped his arms around her. "Emerald," he said, his voice shaking with sincerity, "you can trust me. I swear it."

With painful irony she realized it was *Henry,* of all people, who was holding her and vowing his honesty. A fresh tide of woe swept her. She drew back, looking up at him in teary despair. "You?" she cried. "How can I believe in you, after what you did?"

She tried to wrest away from him, but he held her and stared earnestly into her face. "You can believe me because I owe you," he pleaded. "Honor demands it. I lied to you once, but as God is my witness, I'll never be untrue to you again. I swear it."

The insane thing was that she believed him. She believed the ardor in his eyes and the fervor in his voice. She didn't want to, but she did.

"You're only a boy," she said.

"No," he said quietly. "That boy is gone. I'm a man now."

He raised one hand tentatively and wiped her tears first from one cheek, then the other. "I'll help you," he said.

A new onslaught of tears tried to shake her, but she fought them back. "How?" she demanded, her chin defiantly high. "What can *you* do?"

"Whatever you want," he said.

She knew he wanted to kiss her. With dismay, she realized she wanted him to. And it appalled her.

Her mother and even her sister might be swept away by their sex drives, but she would and could resist stirrings. Above all else, a woman must learn to fight down mere fleshly urges.

Darcy had never before behaved in this way. It felt wonderful.

Yet, at the same time, she did not quite believe what she'd done; it was completely out of character. She should be racked with guilt and gnawed by remorse, but she was neither. Instead, she was strangely happy.

She lay in the crook of Sloan's arm, gazing up through the rustling leaves of the mesquite tree. She and Sloan were sheltered by the ruins of the house's remaining wall. Beneath them lay the crumpled quilt.

They were dressed again, although her blouse was buttoned only halfway, and his shirt was still undone. Her hand rested on the warm, hard flesh of his bare chest, and she felt the beat of his heart beneath her fingers.

It was long past noon. They should have started back for the UV half an hour ago. But they hadn't. She did not want to go back to the real world, and neither did he, she could tell.

So they stayed, quiet in each other's arms, not talking. They didn't seem to need words. From time to time they nuzzled and caressed each other. They kissed. Somewhere a meadowlark sang.

She seemed to fit perfectly against him. Too perfectly, perhaps, but she didn't want to think about that. For once in her life, she didn't want to analyze the past or think about the future; she wanted only to stay in this moment with him, just as they were.

At last he spoke. "This feels so natural, it's unnatural."

She smiled up at him and toyed with his shirt collar. "That's a paradox. It can't be both at once."

He drew her nearer, stroked her cheek with his fingertips. "You know what I mean."

She did. It was as if he and she had been fated to make love. They could not resist the force that had drawn them together; it was not possible.

What he'd said was right. It was so right being with him this way that it seemed extraordinary, almost magical.

"I was hoping this would happen," he said quietly.

She nodded. He'd been prepared, and sex had been safe. But she felt her first twinge of chagrin. "I'm not usually this easy," she said in self-reproach and hid her face against his shoulder.

"I know that," he said. "Hey, look at me. I'm not usually so impulsive, either."

He tilted her face so that her eyes had to meet his. "Do you already have regrets?"

She looked into his eyes, surprised by the depth of feeling she saw in them. Wordlessly, she shook her head. *Something's happening,* she thought in confusion. *Something that never happened before.*

"I know," he said quietly. "This hasn't been just about sex. It's about more. I think we're going to have a... relationship. I want us to. Do you?"

She had a strange sensation, as if she were tumbling. "A relationship," she echoed tonelessly.

"Yes," he said. He put his hand behind her head, lacing his fingers in her hair. "I didn't come here looking for one. But then there was you."

She looked at the nodding bluebonnets at the creek's edge. "You'll be going back to Tulsa soon."

"Tulsa's not so far," he said.

"You'll be leaving the country after that," she said. "If they'll let you."

"I'd be back from time to time," he said. "And you could come see me. You said you'd always wanted to travel."

She shook her head. "Our *parents* have a relationship."

"This isn't about them," he said, bending nearer to her. "It's about you and me."

She smiled rather wanly. "We can't leave them out of it. I mean, it's pretty complicated—"

"No," he said earnestly. "It's not. They're mature adults. So are we. You and I aren't related. We have as much right to be together as they do."

She let her gaze drift guiltily to the leaves overhead. She

had hired an agency to investigate his father, and the knowledge galled her. She no longer doubted Sloan's sincerity. She was half in love with him and sick of her own duplicity. She wanted to tell him the truth. But she did not.

"Maybe we should go" was all she said.

She stood and he stood, too. He drew close to her and started to fasten the rest of the buttons on her blouse. She began to button his shirt.

They paused and looked into each other's eyes. He leaned forward and kissed her again, for a long time.

It seemed so right, she thought. It couldn't be wrong. It couldn't.

CHAPTER THIRTEEN

WHEN THEY REACHED the lake house, Sloan insisted on walking Darcy to her door. She sensed that he was tiring but didn't want to admit it.

She fought the urge to lay her hand against his forehead. "Are you feverish?" she asked softly.

He smiled. "Yes. But not the way you mean."

He took her hand and kissed its palm. The touch of his mouth sent tingles scurrying down her like an electrical charge.

"I want to take you out to supper tonight," he said. "Someplace small and wonderful."

She shook her head. "No. Let's have something simple at my place. We've done enough for your first full day out of the hospital."

We've done way too much, she thought, her face growing hot.

He smiled and touched her burning cheek. His hand was strangely cool. "I don't think we've done enough. Not nearly."

She caught his hand and held it, gazing down at it critically. "You're cold as ice."

"No," he said. "Just the opposite."

"You know what I mean," she said. "Are you having a chill? Is your temperature all right?"

"Yes. Is yours?"

He kissed her under her ear, which indeed made her shiver. "Don't," she said. "You need to rest."

Against her throat he whispered, "Rest with me." He kissed her beneath her other ear.

She drew away. "No," she said sternly. "I mean it. You should *rest*."

He glanced up. The clouds had disappeared, and the sky was a deep, hot blue. "I could use some sun," he said. "Would you lie by the pool with me?"

Her heart hammered unaccountably. "If you promise to take it easy."

He gave her a slow smile. "I'll do it any way you want."

"You really do need to learn the fine art of doing nothing."

"Then teach me," he said.

She thought of the dolls to be made in her studio, the sketches that weren't yet complete. "I might," she said. "But I'll have to crochet some elf pants."

He laughed. "Elf pants?"

"I'm doing a series of dolls," she said. "The new one needs britches."

"What happened to the fine art of doing nothing?" he taunted.

"I've mastered it," she said. "You're the one who's got all the learning to do."

"Okay," he said. "I'll check my e-mail and change. I'll meet you by the pool. Bring your elf pants."

"I need to check a few things, too," she said. They smiled at each other with the secret, knowing smile of two people falling in love.

She tore her gaze from his and made herself turn away. She went into her own house, her heart beating too fast and with a joyous cadence.

All right, she thought, flinging her cowboy hat to the sofa, *I've taken a lover. And he's right. It's nobody's business but his and mine.*

She spun around and moved to the window, lifted the curtain aside. She watched Sloan ascend the porch. Now that he thought there was no one to see, he walked as if battling fatigue, his shoulders slightly hunched.

Her speeding heart slowed painfully. He'd seemed well this morning; he'd seemed fine, and as a lover he'd been virile, strong. It had been easy to forget how ill he'd been.

By temperament he was a man who pushed himself too hard, too soon.

He'd admitted it and had sworn to change. She would have to help. She didn't want him sick again; the thought shook her with frightening force.

She let the curtain fall back into place and looked around the studio-living room. There were half a dozen projects spread about in different stages of creation. *This has been my world for so long,* she thought. *And it's always been enough.*

Before Sloan, she had been happy with her work and her family. Her work, she was certain, would always be a source of joy. But her family was another matter. Lately it seemed impossibly tangled.

She knew she had no messages from them on her answering machine. She had left it switched off. She checked her e-mail. There was nothing from Olivia. Nothing from Emerald.

And there was nothing yet from the agency investigating John English. For this she was profoundly grateful. She had the sudden urge to contact the agency, to tell them to stop their search.

But another part of her mind was wary about halting it. What if there were things that Sloan didn't know about his own father? After all, John English hadn't raised Sloan, and Sloan had been out of the country for most of the past fifteen years.

She wavered. Which was the greater evil, to stop the investigation? Or not to?

She was spared making a decision by the phone's sudden shrilling. She rose gladly from the computer and picked up the receiver. "Hello?"

"Hello, Duck, it's me, Mama. I called earlier, but there was no answer."

"Mama," Darcy said, truly pleased. "It's good to hear your voice."

Olivia hesitated a moment before speaking. "Sweetheart, I thought I should pour oil on the waters. We've all been prickly lately. I'm sorry."

"I'm sorry, too," Darcy said, and meant it. "Emerald and I were taken by surprise. We're concerned about you, that's all."

"I understand," Olivia said. "But don't be. I've found a *wonderful* man. You asked if we were really getting married. The answer is yes—but I don't know when, and I don't have details. We have things to work out. Where we'll live, for instance. I might sell this place, get one in Key West. How would you feel about that?"

The idea unsettled Darcy. After all, Olivia had just bought the Maine condo. Wouldn't she lose money selling it so soon? But she said, as diplomatically as possible, "Whatever makes you happy, Mama."

"I don't suppose Emerald would approve," Olivia said.

That's a huge, raging understatement, Darcy thought. But she said, "She—she'd take it hard at first."

"Yes," Olivia said, sadness in her voice.

"But you can't center your whole life around Emerald," Darcy made herself say. "It wouldn't be good for either of you."

"I know." Olivia sighed. "Well, nothing's settled, anyway. I'm not going to say anything to her yet. It'd just get her upset over something that might never happen."

Olivia paused, then said, "I'm sorry that you're not comfortable that Sloan's staying there. I didn't mean to inconvenience you. Can you learn to live with it—for just a little while?"

Darcy's throat constricted. She sensed that now was not exactly the best moment to tell her mother about herself and Sloan. "Oh, yes, I can live with it," she said. Her own hypocrisy rang in her ears.

Olivia gave a little laugh that sounded self-conscious.

"Emerald was concerned that Sloan was trying to get you to have—you know—a little hanky-panky."

"*Really?*" Darcy tried to sound amused, but the word came out in a guilty squeak.

"Really," Olivia said with a more confident laugh. "But John says Sloan's certainly not the type, and I said *you're* certainly not the type, so I'm not worried."

"Worried?" Darcy echoed.

"You're creative, but you've never been impetuous—at least not *that* way," Olivia said fondly. "You've always seemed very sensible about sex. In this day and age, I can't tell you what comfort that gives to a mother."

Darcy felt a bleak sense of irony.

"Listen," Olivia said, sounding more serious. "I'd like you to call my Realtor and make an appointment. I'd like her to go through the house in town. You can give her the key or go with her. Would you do that, Duck?"

"The Realtor? Why?"

"To give me an estimate on it."

"You're thinking of selling it, *too?*" Darcy asked, truly shocked. For her mother to talk of a second home in Florida was one thing. But selling the house in Austin? That was quite another.

"John and I have only discussed it," Olivia said. "Like I say, nothing's written in stone. John says that at least it would be a good idea to find out the current market value. But again, it's probably better that you don't say anything to Emerald yet."

You love that house. You always said you'd die before you'd part with that house, Darcy thought in consternation.

Once again the ugly gnome of suspicion cast its spell over her. Selling the house couldn't be Olivia's idea; it had to be John English's. And it was one that Darcy neither liked nor trusted.

SLOAN HAD CHECKED his e-mail, but there was nothing of importance except a new message from Trina. He didn't bother to read it. Later, when he had summoned the patience, he would write her that he was through, that he refused to be involved in her drama any longer. He should have done it days ago.

He went into the bedroom, peeled off his clothes and pulled on the swimming trunks. They were a bit baggy, but they'd do.

He regarded himself critically in the full-length mirror. Christ, he was still gaunt. But for the first time since his fever, he felt fully alive again. He thought of Darcy, her soft skin, her clever dark eyes—and her body that fit his like a warm silk glove.

Ahh, he thought, *I'm smitten. This is a woman it's going to be hard to leave.* He didn't doubt for an instant that he would leave her. But she understood that. That in itself was a miracle. She didn't want to cling and own any more than he did.

He clapped a hand against his too-lean stomach. He was on the mend and hungry for everything again—food, drink, freedom, travel, work, a woman. He was famished for the vitality, and Darcy seemed to embody it.

For now, he felt as if he could not get enough of her.

A dark thought passed over his mind like a long, wintry cloud. What if he *couldn't,* in fact, get enough of her? What if he didn't want to leave her? What if he wanted, God forbid, to marry her?

It was an alien thought and felt mortally dangerous.

No, he thought. *Not me. I'm immune to that kind of thing. It'll never get me.*

Of course, he had once thought the same about Malay fever.

DARCY CAME OUT OF THE HOUSE wearing a short patchwork robe over her swimsuit and carrying a straw hat. Sloan was already lying by the pool on a chaise longue.

He was so lean that he looked as if he had been doing hard labor. Yet his body was still an attractive one, and his ranginess gave him the air of a survivor, a man too tough to easily defeat.

He looked at her over the top of his sunglasses. "Isn't this the point at which I ask you, as lasciviously as possible, if I can't help you put on your suntan lotion?"

"Yes," she said. "But I say 'No. Let me help you first. You don't have much of a tan. You'll burn.'"

"It's my hospital pallor," he said. "Does it fill your heart with pity?"

"Nope," she said. "My heart's hard as a rock. Sit up. I'll do your back."

She poured the silky lotion into her palm and began to smooth it on the warm, muscled planes of his back. Stroking over the powerful feel of him gave her a deeply sensual pleasure.

His sigh was lingering. "For a woman with a hard heart, you've got a soft touch."

"I talked to my mother," she said. "I didn't tell her that we were getting on rather better than she planned."

He gave her a sideways glance. "I don't think you exactly need to report to her."

"I'm aware of that. But she told me something. And it worries me. I want to talk to you about it."

His smile died, and he crooked one dark brow. "What worries you?" *Everything,* she thought. *That I trust you, but not your father. That I don't seem to be telling the whole truth to anybody these days. That I enjoy touching you way too much.*

She began to rub the complex sculpture of his shoulders, and took a deep breath. She told him about her mother's idea of selling both the condo in Maine and the house in Austin, of buying in Key West. Did she imagine it, or did his muscles tense almost imperceptibly beneath her fingers?

He whistled softly. "She'd be selling *all* her real estate."

"Yes. She would." Her hands moved to his shoulder blades and stroked rhythmically in circles.

He was silent a long moment. Then he said, "These are

serious decisions,'' he said. "She needs to think hard about them.''

"I know. But I'm not sure how *clearly* she's thinking.''

He turned to her. "Because she's in love, right?''

She dropped her gaze. "Right.''

"Here.'' He picked up a towel and began to wipe her hands, slowly and carefully. "You think my father's advising her in this?''

Her heart took an unpleasant skip. "It sounds like it.''

He sighed and set aside the towel. He put his knuckle beneath her chin and tilted it up. "I love my father. But I've got to tell you he's not the greatest business brain in the world. And he's probably not thinking his clearest either. He's head over heels himself.''

"What worries me most is the house in town,'' Darcy said. "She's always loved it. I know it's too big for just one person, but I'm afraid if she sells it, she may regret it.''

He studied her face solemnly. "You'd regret it, too, wouldn't you?''

She shrugged in frustration. "I never thought about it until now. I've always tried not to be materialistic. I don't want possessions to be the most important thing in my life…''

"And yet?'' He urged her to go on.

"And yet, it's our *home*. Emerald and I grew up there. It's got thousands of memories for me—tens of thousands. I never thought of it *not* being there for us.''

She cast an ironic glance at the lake house. "This place is different. I don't have deep feelings for it. But the town place is something else. It's—I don't know.''

"You already said it,'' he told her. "It's home.''

"You understand?'' she asked hopefully. "You've felt that way about a place?''

He touched her cheek. "No. I haven't. But I think I understand. Did you tell your mother how you felt?''

"No,'' she confessed. "I was too surprised. And then, it didn't seem to be my place to say such things. But I'm *worried*. You know?''

"I know." He paused, then said, "I brought something I wanted you to see." He reached to the patio table and drew a folded sheet of paper from between the pages of a book. He handed it to her. "Open it."

She did. It was the printout of an e-mail message from Sloan to his father. Darcy raised her gaze to him in question. She said, "But I have no right—"

"Please. Just read it."

She smoothed out the page and read.

SUBJECT: About Your Prospects of Untold Wealth
From: SloanJEnglish@PetroCorp.com
To: BanditKing@USAserve.com

Today I've had another overwrought message from Trina. I'm forwarding a copy so you can see for yourself.

Dad, I hate interfering, but I also hate being caught in the middle of this.

If you're going to marry again, and if you intend to keep your old provisions about Trina and Arthur, *let Trina know*.

A prenuptial agreement should satisfy her, and it would seem to serve everyone's best financial interests.

Your fiancée clearly has property about which careful arrangements should be made. Otherwise, she and her daughters may suspect your motives. This, I'm sure, is exactly what you want to avoid.

Yours, Sloan

Darcy's brows drew together in puzzlement. "Why are you showing me this?"

He made a deprecating gesture. "I told you I sent it. I wanted you to see what I said. To show you I'm concerned about your mother's welfare. And about what she—and you—think of my father."

She managed a quivery smile. "This doesn't sound like you. It's so stiff and formal."

"Hell," he said ironically, "what's the right tone for lecturing your own father?"

"Good point," she said.

"I told him I didn't like interfering. I don't. I told him I hate being caught in the middle. I do."

"I don't blame you."

He gave her a self-mocking look. "I intended that to be the last I said to him on the subject."

"I don't blame you for that, either."

He took the paper, refolded it and slid it back into the book. Then he took her hands between his. "It's not going to be that easy. For either of us. You need to tell your mother that she should think carefully, and not to do anything in haste."

Darcy nodded. What he said was true. She must speak to Olivia, even if it did no good.

"And I've got to talk to my father. I don't want to, and he won't want to listen. But I can't stand aside and let him lead her into something that might be a serious mistake."

She stared at him, her heart welling with gratitude.

"Does that make you feel better?" he asked.

"Yes. It does."

He leaned nearer. "Then prove it, dammit," he murmured.

He kissed her. She kissed him back. He untied the belt of the patchwork robe and began to slip it off her shoulders.

At that moment, they heard the crunch of tires on the gravel of the driveway. Startled, Darcy looked up, through the chain-link fence. A car door slammed. A familiar figure stalked toward the gate.

Oh, no, Darcy thought, her spirits sinking. *It's Emerald again.*

WHEN EMERALD DROVE UP, she was aghast. *Oh, no,* she thought. *They're kissing! He's taking her clothes off!*

As soon as the car ground to a halt, she leaped out and strode toward the gate. Darcy sprang back from Sloan English, and they both stared at Emerald. His expression was one of frank irritation, but Emerald didn't care.

She threw open the gate dramatically. Sloan still held the lapels of Darcy's robe, lowered now past her bare shoulders.

"Unhand my sister," Emerald ordered in her most imperial voice.

"I *knew* you were going to say something like that," Sloan said, clearly annoyed. He looked at Darcy. "Do you want to be unhanded?"

She nodded uncertainly. He released the edges of the robe. With a sigh of frustration he turned back toward Emerald. He put one elbow on his knees, rested his chin in his hand, and gave her a measuring gaze.

He was a hard man to ignore, Emerald thought. He was tall, powerfully built, and he radiated displeasure. Besides that, he was nearly naked. But Emerald ignored him, anyway.

She spoke to her sister as if he weren't there. "We have to talk."

Darcy had recovered her aplomb. "I thought you weren't going to speak to me until I apologized."

"This can't wait," Emerald said. "It's about *family.*"

"I think," Sloan said with sarcasm, "that's my cue to exit. I'll leave and let you have some privacy."

Emerald didn't like his tone, which was far too confident for a seducer who'd just been caught nearly flagrante delicto. "I'd hoped when I came," she said with false sweetness, "that I'd find you'd already left—for good."

"Emerald!" Darcy cried in disapproval.

Sloan held up his hand in ironic imitation of a man signaling for peace. "Please," he said as he rose. "I'll be in the house."

"Perhaps you'd like to take a nice cold shower while you're there," suggested Emerald.

Darcy gasped in resentment, but Sloan only smiled at Emerald. He turned and went toward the side doors. He disappeared inside.

Emerald crossed her arms, looking after him with a righteous air.

Darcy stood and knotted the belt on her robe with an angry jerk. "That was unspeakably rude. He's mother's guest."

"I know what he is to mother," Emerald said dryly. "What is he to you?"

"That's my concern, not yours," Darcy shot back. "And you should have called before you came. You don't have any right to barge in on people like that."

"I've driven into this driveway probably five hundred times," Emerald retorted. "I never interrupted a—a *coitus* before."

"*Oh,*" Darcy said, clearly infuriated. "If you can't tell the difference between a kiss and a coitus, you really are medieval."

"One thing leads to another," Emerald said condescendingly. "And I *did* try to call before I came. Nobody answered. You were with *him,* I suppose."

"What if I was?" Darcy challenged. "Why should you care?"

Emerald gave Darcy a long, knowing look. "You'd better be careful about getting involved. You may think you know him—but you don't."

Darcy's mouth crooked disgustedly. "I'm a grown woman and a pretty good judge of character, if I do say so."

"He's no good," Emerald said with conviction. "He and his father are in cahoots. He came here to spy on us—and to seduce you."

Darcy's eyes flashed more dangerously. "That's ridiculous. Why would he want to 'seduce me'?" She put a sarcastic flip on the last words.

"To distract you," Emerald said earnestly. "So you won't see the truth about what's happening with mother. So you won't *want* to see the truth."

"You've been watching too many soap operas," Darcy said in disgust.

"I don't watch soap operas," said Emerald.

"Then you've been reading too many medieval fairy stories. Who's John English? An evil wizard who's cast a magic spell over mother? Who's Sloan? A false knight out to do his bidding?''

Emerald had expected resistance, and she knew she must stand her ground. ''You have to believe me. For your own good and Mama's, too.''

Darcy jammed her fists onto her hips and took a step closer. ''Why should I believe you? You can't go around just—just saying such things about people. Where's your proof?''

Emerald fought the urge to shift uncomfortably. The struggle was moving to shaky ground, as she had feared it would. ''I can't tell you everything. But I have concrete evidence.''

This didn't seem to take Darcy aback in the least. ''Evidence? Show me.''

For the first time, Emerald wavered. ''I—can't,'' she said. ''You just have to take my word for it.''

''*What?*''

Emerald drew herself up proudly. ''You have to take my word for it. I've seen…certain privileged information. It was shocking. Shameful. Shattering. These men are up to no good.''

Darcy scoffed. ''You said you had evidence. Give me one iota.''

Emerald's mind spun. She could not admit that she and Henry had broken into other people's e-mail. The action made her seem as underhanded as the enemy.

But more important—and subtler—was that Henry was her secret weapon. She did not want John English to know she had such power, or he would be forewarned and she would be disarmed. Right now, she had an arsenal of tricks, and she must use them to defend Olivia and protect Darcy from herself.

She chose her words carefully. ''Certain information's come into my possession. For instance, John English has an illegitimate son—and a mistress snapping at his heels for child support.''

Darcy tensed. ''How do you know?''

Emerald dodged the question. "Her name is Trina. The child's name is Arthur."

Darcy laughed in disdain. "That's absurd. Trina's his sister. Arthur is his nephew. Sloan told me all about them. He mentioned his aunt the first time he came here. You heard him, for crying out loud."

It was Emerald's turn to be caught off guard. In truth, she had only guessed at the identities of Trina and Arthur, and she had forgotten Sloan ever mentioning an aunt. She tried to cover her discomfiture.

"Can you prove what he says is true?" she challenged.

"Prove it's not."

Emerald decided to attack on another front. "Sloan told his father to get a prenuptial agreement from Mama. I find that sinister—don't you?"

"No, I don't," Darcy shot back. "He told me about it himself. It's for the protection of everybody concerned. *Including* Mama."

"So he says." Even to Emerald's ears, it sounded like a weak retort.

Like opponents, the two women looked each other up and down, and Emerald felt herself starting to sink beneath the weight of her sister's scorn. She began to plead.

"Darcy, *please* believe me. These men can't be trusted. This prenuptial agreement's part of their plot. It's Sloan English's sneaky way of making sure—"

Darcy stalked to the patio table, snatched up the book, and drew out a folded piece of paper. "It's no plot. There's nothing sneaky about it. He's been completely open. Look at this."

She opened the paper and brandished it at Emerald. "Read this."

It took Emerald several seconds to recognize the message. A numbing chill seized her. *This was one of the very letters Henry had intercepted.*

She put one hand on her stomach, feeling slightly nauseated. *My God,* she thought, in horror. *The man's so brilliant, he's a fiend. He's covered his tracks like a fox. He's written this message so it could be read on two levels. He's made Darcy believe it's completely innocent. I am up against a mind of satanic cunning.*

Darcy smiled almost affectionately. "See, Emerald? You're getting worked up about nothing. He's a wonderful man, really, and he's been very honest."

Emerald could say nothing. Darcy offered her the paper again—a friendlier gesture this time. "Would you feel better if you had this?" she asked. "Go ahead, if it puts your mind at ease. He's not a bad person. Not at all. You'd like him, if you knew him."

Emerald shook her head helplessly. She saw the softness that touched Darcy's face, the glow that lit her eyes. With a sickening lurch, she realized the truth: she was too late. Her sister was in love.

"It's all right," Darcy coaxed. "Take it."

"No," Emerald said. The word came out as a croak, but she swallowed, trying to force her voice to seem normal again. "I can see it for what it is."

"Good," Darcy said. She raised her free hand and put it on Emerald's arm. "You shouldn't get so excited. I'm fine, and Mama's going to be fine. I'm doing all I can to make sure of that. We'll look after her. And Sloan wants to help."

I'll bet he does, Emerald thought with bitterness and desperation. There was no reasoning with Darcy; she was caught in the spell of a master sorcerer, just as Olivia was.

Emerald alone was left to save them. But she was just the person for the job.

CHAPTER FOURTEEN

AFTER EMERALD LEFT, the pool's turquoise waters twinkled just as merrily as before, and the sun itself beamed down just as warm and dazzling. But Darcy's face was shadowed by perplexity.

She paced beside the pool, and Sloan sat in the hammock, rocking gently back and forth. She told him of her sister's change of mood.

"I showed her that e-mail, and she looked like she'd seen a ghost," Darcy said, shaking her head in puzzlement.

He frowned. "Let me get this straight. She warned you that I told my father to get a prenup agreement."

"Yes." She stopped, crossing her arms and staring down moodily at the play of light on the water.

"And you said you knew and showed her that note."

"I shouldn't have. I didn't ask your permission."

He waved aside her misgiving. "Hell, I don't care. If I wanted to keep it secret, I wouldn't have shown you in the first place."

Darcy didn't look convinced. "I'd meant to reassure her. Instead, it was like—like I'd just confirmed her worst suspicions. It was *strange*."

Sloan laughed and stretched out full length in the hammock, putting his hands behind his head. "You probably just ruined her fantasy. She had this elaborate intrigue built up in her mind, and you pulled the props out."

"Maybe." Darcy started to pace again. "She was certainly full of conspiracy theories."

Sloan thought on this a moment and found it sobering.

Every family had its difficult members. His own, after all, had Trina. But he wondered—did John really know what a volatile stepdaughter he was about to acquire? A person like Emerald could put a lot of strain on a new marriage.

"Tell me," Sloan said carefully. "Is she always like this?"

"She's always dramatized things," Darcy said. "She does it mostly when she's upset. And I suppose she never thought Mama would *want* to marry again. This has taken her by surprise."

It's taken us all by surprise, Sloan thought. *But just how much trouble is Emerald going to make over it?*

He said, "She's possessive about your mother. And you."

Darcy shrugged sadly. "There aren't many people she's close to. In her way, she's shy."

Sloan thought she had an odd way of showing shyness, but he refrained from saying so. He kept his voice deliberately casual. "She's probably not going to like my father, no matter what."

Darcy stopped, put her fists on her hips, and gazed up at the sky. "Mama's got a right to her own life. Emerald's got to accept that."

But will she? wondered Sloan. He said, "She's obviously not crazy about me, either. Does that bother you?"

Darcy gave him a philosophical smile. "I wish it were different. But I won't let my sister run my life."

He arched an eyebrow. His instinct told him that Emerald would not allow herself to be ignored. "But what becomes of somebody like her?" he asked. "I mean, you and your mother must worry about her—she's not your average citizen. Your average citizen doesn't go around dressed like she's off to the Crusades. Or threatening to smite people with her sword."

"True. But the Medieval Society's a place where she fits in. She's brilliant—she really is. She's been offered scholarships to all sorts of graduate schools. She'll be a professor."

Sloan's forehead furrowed in doubt. "What would she teach? Smiting? Jousting? Armor making?"

"Don't be sarcastic," Darcy said, but there was no real reproach in her words. "Medieval languages. She's got an enormous gift for languages."

Sloan considered this. Somehow it made sense, and Emerald didn't seem so completely silly, after all. "Where will she go to school?"

Darcy began to stroll along the pool's edge again. "She *could* go anywhere she wants. But she'll probably stay close to Austin. And I guess she wants to make sure that Mama's always here for her."

The breeze changed direction, bringing the perfume of Cherokee roses to his nostrils. He found the scent sweetly erotic.

He said, "Why don't you stop that pacing and come here? Lie down beside me and tell me what we were saying before Emerald interrupted us?"

She stopped, but didn't come to him. "We weren't saying anything. We were, um, kissing."

"How wise of us," he said, "on a day like this." He closed his eyes and imagined making love to her in the full light of the afternoon sun.

But Darcy said nothing in reply. His waking fantasy began to turn into a drowsy dream. He gave himself to it. If he couldn't have her in reality, he would have her in imagination.

At last she spoke. "Sloan, I'm trusting you on instinct. Emerald called you a spy and a seducer. I don't believe that."

"Seduction's not such a bad thing, really," he said sleepily. "If you'll come here, I'll let you have your way with me."

But she didn't come to him. When she spoke, her voice seemed distant, far less real than his deepening dream world. She said, "Emerald made accusations about your father, too. I want to believe there's nothing to them. There aren't any deep family secrets, are there?"

"No," he murmured. "Just shallow ones."

He didn't hear her when she asked him what he meant. The

scent of wildflowers had enfolded him like a drug, and he lay in the sun, dozing.

OLIVIA SET THE TABLE for an early supper and lit the tapers in their matching crystal candlesticks.

John had been quiet all evening. He stared out the window moodily. "It gets dark early up here."

"I suppose it seems so," Olivia said a bit defensively. "It's just that it's been dark all day. There are storms rolling in from the north."

He let the curtain drop. "On the news, they said it might snow. Snow—in May." He shook his head as if the idea was an affront, possibly a crime.

"Supper's ready," Olivia said. "Lobster salad, French bread, baked apples. I thought I'd keep it light."

"It never snows in Key West," John said, coming to the table. "I've been swimming on Christmas Day, many a time."

She'd gone to extra trouble to set the table romantically and in style, had chilled an especially good bottle of wine. He didn't seem to notice.

"I didn't even see the sun set," he told her. "No color, no spectacle—nothing. Every day people gather in Key West to watch the sun go down."

"And I'm sure it always does," Olivia said. "Giving them great cause for civic pride."

He shot her a questioning look, but she smiled innocently.

"Of course it always goes down," he said. "The point is that it does so with style. So much that people come to Mallory Square to celebrate and cheer when it sinks below the sea."

"The sun here is a more independent sort," Olivia said, opening the wine. "It doesn't need public approval to set. It just does it."

His dark eyes looked wounded and resentful. "Blast it, Olivia, that's not what I meant, and you know it."

"I know," she said with a sigh. "But ever since I told you

I wanted to think about Key West, you've been trying to sell it to me. Like you were the Chamber of Commerce.''

She gestured for him to sit. In truth, she was tired of hearing him sing the praises of the Keys so zealously; it had begun to grate on her nerves.

He sat. She filled his glass.

''I'm sorry,'' he said as he unfolded his napkin. ''I just think you could be happy there.''

''We'll see,'' she said noncommittally, and poured her own wine. She sat across from him.

''I'm sorry,'' he said again. He did look contrite.

''To our making the right decisions,'' she said, and clicked her glass to his. ''I want to be sure I'm doing the right thing about the house in Texas. Especially in relation to the girls.''

They each drank a sip. They nibbled at their salads. John buttered a piece of bread. He did not look up when he said, ''I thought your daughter said you should do whatever makes you happy.''

Olivia smiled pensively. ''That's what Darcy said—at first. But when I told her I was thinking about selling the city house, she couldn't keep the dismay out of her voice.''

John frowned. ''Dismay? Why? She doesn't live there.''

''No,'' Olivia admitted. ''Not for ages. And Emerald moved out last year. Still it's—our home. Every square inch has its memories. You know how it is.''

John set aside the bread and looked at her. ''No, my love. I suppose I don't. It's odd. I make my living selling houses. But they're just houses. Getting attached to one of them—it's something that never happened.''

Olivia knew he had been something of a wanderer. She wished she could make him understand the depth and intricacy of her feelings about the house in Austin. ''I think,'' she said, ''that the house where your children grow up is always a special place. Besides that, it's stuffed to the rafters with *things*.''

''Things,'' he said without enthusiasm. ''I've never been a big one for owning things.''

Although he did not say it in a critical way, Olivia felt rebuked. A knot of emotion formed in her throat. "A lot of this has to do with the girls."

Her homes were filled with handsome objects for which she had real affection. But there were troves of other things she loved, as well. Decades of snapshots of the girls, boxes of their schoolwork and Darcy's art projects and Emerald's toys.

John's dark brows drew together in concern. "Yes. The girls. I'm sure they're worried about getting what's rightfully theirs."

She looked at him sharply. "What do you mean?"

He set down his silverware and shook his head. "You're a well-to-do woman. I'm sure your girls are concerned about what happens to your property. They'll need to be assured they get their fair share."

Olivia stared at him, stunned. She felt a profound sense of insult, but he didn't seem to notice.

He spoke without looking at her. "I understand these things. Trina's worried about exactly the same thing. That a marriage will cut into her financial prospects. Sloan suggests that we draw up a prenuptial agreement."

Olivia bristled. Why were her finances suddenly *Sloan's* business? She had never even met the man. "Oh, he does, does he?"

"It's for your own protection. And your girls', as well," John said. He kept forging deeper into the subject like a man determined to slog his way through an extremely unpleasant swamp. "They're like Trina. They'll need to know their inheritance is safe."

"Excuse me," Olivia said, a dangerous note in her voice. "Did you just compare my daughters to your sister?"

"Yes," he said with a resigned nod. "It's the same situation, as I see it."

"My daughters are the least materialistic creatures on this earth," Olivia said passionately. "All Emerald cares for is her Medieval Society and her studies. All Darcy ever thinks about is her art, art, art. Why, she could make *tons* more money if she wanted, but that's not what interests her—''

John made a gesture that was supposed to calm her. It did not. "Now, now," he said. "That just proves my point. If they're that careless about money, you'll want to be sure they're provided for—"

"I didn't say they were *careless* about money. I said it wasn't their be-all and end-all."

"Ahh," John said wearily. "Olivia, you're too innocent about money. It's the one thing that can tear apart an otherwise strong family."

"Not mine," she said with spirit.

"I've seen squabbles over estates," he said. "It's part of my business. And divorces—well, I've seen that, too, how ugly arguments over property can get."

"Divorce?" Olivia demanded. "Why are you talking about divorce? We're not even married yet."

At last his eyes met hers, and she saw an enormous sadness in their depths. "I'm speaking in generalities, my love. I'm talking about abstractions."

"Well, I'm not," she said haughtily. "I'm talking about *my* house and *my* daughters. My girls aren't greedy or needy, and they're not drooling over my property—"

"That's not what I said—"

"It's what you implied."

"Olivia, I'm trying to watch out for you. All your life, you've had someone to see to your financial welfare. You haven't had to worry—"

"What?" she said, truly outraged.

"You don't know what it's like to worry about money—"

"I most certainly have worried about it," she retorted. "I wasn't born to money."

"No," he soothed. "But you married it—"

"My *last* husband had money," she said. "The first two were neither rich nor poor. There I was—a widow with two little girls, one of them a psychological wreck from the accident that killed her father. A rich man offered to take care of us if I married him. What choice did I have?''

"I'm not criticizing your choice, my love."

Olivia shook her finger at him. "And let me tell you something, John English. I was a *good* wife to him. He was a difficult man, but I coped with him. I was faithful, I made him exactly the kind of home he wanted, I stood by him in hard times, I nursed him through his long, last illness—''

"My dear, I'm sure you were a paragon—''

Tears of anger stung her eyes. "All I've said is that I'm not sure I want to give up a home I love and move to Key West—a place I've never even *seen.*''

She got up from the table and threw her napkin down beside her untouched plate. "I'm not hungry."

He stood, his face pained. "I've made a mess of this. Forgive me. These are delicate matters. I'm afraid I don't know how to discuss them."

Olivia turned her back to him so he wouldn't see the tears that she fought back. "No. I'm afraid you don't."

She heard him push his chair back and rise from his seat. She felt him move behind her.

"I don't like the idea of prenuptial agreements," he said. "They seem cynical and self-serving."

"Yes. They do."

"It's as if I say out of one side of my mouth that I promise to love, honor and obey you until death do us part. And out of the other side I say, and if that doesn't work out, legally my ass is covered."

In spite of herself, Olivia laughed.

She felt his strong hands settle on her upper arms, and she did not shake off his touch. She found it comforting, in spite of everything.

"Yet," he said in her ear, "we're not two kids, starting out life with nothing. We come with baggage and responsibilities, you and I."

She said nothing, but she realized the truth of what he said. She set her jaw and waited, hoping he would apologize.

"And there's something I've never said in so many words," he murmured.

She wanted to turn to him, put her hand to his lips, and tell him to say no more. Perhaps too much had been said already; she wasn't sure.

"I want to protect your finances because they're larger than mine—and more liquid. Someday my Florida land will sell, and when it does, we'll all be sitting pretty—you and me, Trina and Arthur. But until then, if you want to live with me in Florida, it's going to have to be on your money."

She flinched at the honesty of his words, and knew how much pride it had cost him to say them.

"And maybe," he said, pressing his cheek against hers, "I'm jealous of Austin. And maybe even jealous of your house. It's the one Gus bought you. I'd feel like a parasite moving into it. I'd rather we had a fresh start. Whether it's in Florida or Texas. Can you understand that?"

She could understand. It deeply saddened her, but she understood.

"Oh, John," she said tiredly. "It seemed so simple at first. We fall in love, and we want to spend the rest of our lives together. Why does it have to be so difficult?"

"Maybe to test us," he said quietly.

He turned her so that she had to face him. She looked up into his eyes and saw the hurt, the stubbornness, the kindness, and above all the love.

He put his arms around her waist. Slowly she raised hers and locked her hands behind his neck. He bent and kissed her.

It's going to be all right. It is. It is, Olivia thought. And she prayed that she wasn't deceiving herself.

ONCE AGAIN, it was the situation that Henry had so often hoped for, the situation for which he would have sold his soul. Emerald was in his room, sitting on his very bed. She looked beautiful and full of passion—and she had said that she needed him.

But like others who have been willing to trade their souls, Henry was finding the bargain wasn't *exactly* as he'd anticipated. Emerald was on his bed, but she didn't want to be in his arms. The passion that animated her was not love for him, but the desire to destroy two men he had never met. And what she needed him for was to do the dirty work.

He was giddy with apprehension. He had John English's password. He could do the man a lot of damage. What was Emerald going to ask of him?

"This is war," she said with fervor.

Henry had always admired Emerald's imagination. He was dazzled by it, for his own was quite ordinary. But this time, he wondered if it had not led her too far afield.

Emerald leaned against the pillow and put the back of her hand to her forehead. It was a dramatic gesture, and she did it very well. "When Darcy showed me that e-mail," she said, "it was as if my life passed before my eyes. I went faint."

"Would you like me to rub your temples?" Henry asked hopefully.

She ignored him. "It wasn't until that moment that I realized what we were up against," she muttered. "These are experienced con men. Darcy's fallen for that man—she'll never listen to me. It's like he's hypnotized her. I mean, when I drove up, they were all over each other, kissing and groping. It was disgusting."

Henry found the idea more exciting than disgusting. He thought of kissing and groping Emerald, and it nearly killed him with desire. But as much as he wanted her, some rational part of him didn't want to follow where her fantasy now led.

"Your sister's an attractive woman," he said. "I mean, it's possible that a man could just *like* her, you know?"

She propped herself up on her elbow and gave him a suspicious look. "How do *you* know she's attractive?"

"She had a show at a gallery on Sixth Street last Christmas," Henry said defensively. "I saw her there."

He didn't admit he had gone to the show expressly in hopes of seeing Emerald. He had been disappointed. "She's very pretty," he said diplomatically. But he didn't think Darcy was nearly as striking as Emerald, whose elfin delicacy had always enchanted him.

Emerald sat up, sighing. "Darcy's pretty, all right. Lots of men have chased after her. But I never saw her act… *infatuated* with one of them. Until now. I think it's too much of a coincidence. Don't you?"

Her eyes met his. Such yearning jolted through him that he didn't know what he thought. "What do you mean?" he hedged.

Her right hand curled into a fist. "First Mama. Then Darcy. Both perfectly happy being single. Now suddenly they both fall head over heels for men in the same family? What are the odds of that?"

Henry swallowed. "I don't think I have sufficient data to calculate that with any degree of accuracy."

Emerald shot him an impatient look. "I don't mean the *exact* odds. I mean, just what do these men have that others don't?"

"Great luck?" asked Henry.

She glared at him.

"Well, maybe great genes, which is nearly the same thing," Henry offered. "I mean, your mother and sister are nice-looking. These men are, too. It doesn't seem altogether far-fetched that—"

"Now how do you know *that?*" Emerald shot at him.

"Know what?" Henry asked, disconcerted.

"What these men look like?" she demanded.

"Oh," Henry said, feeling like the fool that he was sure he was. "I found their picture on the Internet."

"You *what?*" Emerald fairly erupted.

"I—I found John English's Web site," Henry stammered. "The ad for the real estate company where he works, actually. It's got pictures and stuff about the staff and their families."

"What?" Emerald cried. "And you didn't tell me?"

"You were so upset about your sister," Henry said. "I—I was concerned for you. The fact got knocked right out of my head.'' Most facts got knocked from his head when Emerald was around, but he knew he dared not tell her that.

She leaped from the bed and came to his side. She stared at the blank computer screen with almost religious zeal.

''Show me,'' she ordered.

Humbly, Henry turned to the computer and began tapping its keys.

In a way, the Internet was like a vast, disorganized magazine. It contained millions of pictures and ads and information of every sort. It was an Alice-in-Wonderland sort of place, where an unwary person might stumble onto almost anything.

But Henry was not unwary in this Wonderland; he knew his way around quite well. He knew how to search for what he wanted, and he usually found it.

While Emerald had been gone, it had occurred to him that if John English was in real estate, his company almost certainly advertised on the Internet. All Henry had to do was find that site. It had been childishly simple.

The site and its information had seemed both genuine and ordinary to Henry, nothing at all remarkable. He'd made note of it and wandered on, looking for other traces of John English. He'd found none.

''This isn't much,'' he cautioned Emerald. But he could sense her excitement; it seemed to radiate from her in tingling waves.

He brought the site to the screen; it showed a glorious sunset over an impossibly blue ocean, a strip of white beach, palm trees. Large letters spelled out:

WELBER & ASSOCIATES REALTY
Helping You Find Part of Paradise!
Read About the Welber Tradition! View Our Properties!
Meet the Welber Team! Send Us E-Mail!

Henry nodded solemnly and hit another button. A new picture appeared on the screen. Banner letters announced Our

Helpful Professional Staff! There were two rows of individual portraits of smiling Realtors.

"There he is—" Henry pointed to the photo of a man with a full head of wavy gray-white hair. In striking contrast, his brows and mustache were dark. His features were rough-hewn, yet handsome.

"He looks like a playboy," Emerald said with conviction.

Henry was not sure this statement was true; he had always imagined playboys as leering, withered old men who smoked pipes and were surrounded by girls in sexy bunny suits. He said, "There's a whole page on John English. There's one on each salesperson."

"Show me." Emerald's voice was cold.

Henry brought another new page to the screen. It showed two candid snapshots of John English. In one, he stood in a tuxedo before a stage curtain, smiling and holding out his hand as if to introduce someone. "John enjoys working in local theater," read the caption. "Here he serves as Master of Ceremonies at the annual Hospital Fund-raiser."

But the other photo commanded more attention. John and Sloan English were together, photographed from the waist up. John's shirt was unbuttoned, and Sloan wore no shirt at all. Both looked tanned, and their hair was tousled. Obviously they were on a dock or pier of some sort, with the sea twinkling behind them. John proudly held up a silvery fish, and Sloan was toasting the cameraman with a can of cola. "John enjoys fishing on his skiff BANDIT KING II. Here he and his son, Sloan, celebrate the day's catch. Sloan, on vacation, is an executive with PetroCorp."

They were handsome men and obviously comfortable together. The son had his arm around the father's shoulders. Both were smiling. It was a nice enough picture, Henry thought. Nothing sinister about it.

But Emerald's reaction was different. "Look at them," she said from between her teeth. "Posing and preening. It's shameful."

"Well…" Henry muttered, unsure. His mother's family

album was filled with similar pictures of his father, himself
and his brother. Of course, he didn't look as good without
his shirt, and his father had not a hair on his head, but in
essence, the photos struck him as the same sort.

"John English probably picked this picture so he could lure
women to Florida."

"Maybe he did it to show off the fish," Henry suggested
mildly.

Emerald ignored him. In a sarcastic voice, she read the text
about John English: "'Whether you're looking to buy, build,
lease or rent, John will provide you with the kind of professional service you can count on! He specializes in helping
people who are relocating to our beautiful area. He is a boat-
ing enthusiast and an avid fisherman. He is also a board member of the Conch Shell Players Group, active in local stage
productions, and is a member of the Key West Arts Society.
He is co-owner of the soon-to-open Mystic Theater.'''

Emerald stared at the screen in silence for a moment. Then
she said, "Blech! It makes me sick."

"Um, exactly what makes you sick?" Henry asked. The
page still seemed innocuous to him.

"Look at how he builds himself up," Emerald said. "Like
he's the perfect catch. *Business*man. *Sports*man. And artistic,
too. A theater owner, yet. I mean, it's all designed to appeal
to women like my mother. A would-be actor. Blech!"

"I tried to find out more about Mystic Theater," Henry
said. "There was nothing on the Net. Maybe it still hasn't
opened."

"It probably won't ever open," Emerald declared. "It's
probably just a scheme to bilk divorcées and widows out of
their life savings. Look at him, with his shirt hanging open
like that. I wonder if all that hair on his chest is real. He's
probably wearing a chest wig."

Henry did not say that his own father's chest was just as
hairy and that his back was hairier still. He sensed this was
not what Emerald wanted to hear.

"Well," he said, "at least it says that his son's an executive with PetroCorp. That's true."

"Oh, pooh," retorted Emerald. "You can say anything on the Internet. That doesn't make it true. You, of all people, should know that."

Henry was appropriately chastened. He said nothing, but he still had his doubts.

"Besides," Emerald said, "even if he does work for PetroCorp, that doesn't make him a good or honorable man. I mean, look at the two of them—they're both in the business of raping the environment. A Florida Realtor and an oil baron. Out for a good time together, murdering fish and flashing their bodies at susceptible women."

Henry stayed silent. He saw a picture of a handsome father and son. The father seemed to be a real estate agent who might be moderately successful. He could see nothing more ominous than that.

"I've got to stop these men," Emerald said rather grandiosely. "And I'll need your help."

Henry chewed the inside of his cheek nervously. There were many things he could do to the hapless John Sloan. He could create nuisances for the man, or he could commit real crimes against him. What would Emerald ask of him?

"What do you want me to do?" he asked, feeling fated for something dire. He looked up at her.

Catlike, she slitted her eyes. "I want you to *change* these pictures," she said, nodding toward the screen. "I want you to show these men for what they really are. Put it on the Internet for the world to see—along with information that'll make Mama and Darcy think twice."

"Emerald," he said, aghast. "I can't do that. It's libelous. They could fine me, put me in prison—"

She laid her fingertips upon his lips, stopping his objections. She nearly stopped his heart, as well. He felt as if he were falling into a deep pit, yet it was an excruciatingly pleasant and titillating fall.

"Sometimes," she said softly, "one has to do a dishonorable thing to attain an honorable end. Do you understand?"

The touch of her flesh against his mouth was more than Henry could bear.

"I understand," he breathed helplessly. "Oh, yes. Yes. *Yes.*"

CHAPTER FIFTEEN

DARCY LET SLOAN SLEEP. For a time she sat beside him on the longue, crocheting elf pants. It seemed strangely domestic and right.

Don't think that way, she told herself. *Don't begin to use terms like* domestic *and* cozy.

But the sun shone, the water twinkled and lapped, and the breeze was fragrant with the scent of spring flowers. The man in the hammock slept peacefully, as if he belonged there.

Still, uneasiness gnawed at the edge of her mind. She knew that Emerald's accusations were wild, even outrageous. Yet Darcy's own suspicions grew from the same seed—what, in truth, did they *know* about John English? Exactly what *were* his intentions toward Olivia's money? Sloan believed his father was honest—but *was* he?

She rose, put aside her crocheting and went into her house. For a moment she stood before her desk, gazing apprehensively at the computer.

She thought of Sloan, whom she instinctively trusted. She thought of his father, whom she did not. She thought of Olivia selling the house in Austin and all her other property and setting out for an unknown future.

Resolutely, Darcy sat down. She struck the keys that would show her if she had new mail. The screen flashed the message that she did, and her body went rigid with anxiety. She held her breath as she read.

SUBJECT: Preliminary Report—Highly Confidential
From: InfoTruthInc@Intellinet.com
To: DesignByDarcy@USAserve.com

Dear Ms. Parker:
InfoTruth has prepared the following PRELIMINARY
REPORT on the subject in question.
Case Number: 03273126
Subject: English, John James

In cool, clinical language, InfoTruth laid out the bare bones
of John English's life. It listed his birth date, his address and
phone number, his social security number. His present marital
status was "divorced," and his employer was Welber & Associates Realty, Key West.

It named his son and two other "significant relatives," a
sister and nephew.

There was a brief employment history. Before moving to
Key West, John English had sold real estate in Marathon,
Florida, and insurance in Miami. How he had made his living
before this, said InfoTruth, was still "Under Investigation."

At this point the report changed. There was a subheading
Finance, in large black letters. It was followed by a welter of
financial information that Darcy found bewildering. Her own
accounts were so simple that she could keep track of them in
a single notebook.

John English's money situation was far from simple and
seemed full of paradoxes. He did not own a house, and he
had little money in the bank. He had recently gone into debt
to buy part interest in a building in Key West, an abandoned
movie theater. He had gone into even deeper debt by taking
out a loan for "improvements" to this building.

He would seem to be a man in imminent danger of having
his outgo exceed his income. And yet, he had one asset that
seemed, on paper, to be staggeringly large: 21.3 acres of un-
improved property in a place called Big Torch Key, Florida.
Its appraised value made Darcy's heart skip a beat—over four
and a half million dollars!

But who had appraised it at that extraordinary amount?

John English himself? A friendly co-worker? Was the property really worth millions of dollars? Or was it merely, as Sloan had scoffed, "swampland in Florida"?

Darcy cursed her own curiosity. So far, what she had learned was not heartening. More disturbing, the report's end raised a series of unanswered questions.

Bankruptcy History——UNDER INVESTIGATION
Marriage and Divorce History——UNDER INVESTIGATION
Known Police Record——UNDER INVESTIGATION
Civil Court Case Record——UNDER INVESTIGATION
Aliases——UNDER INVESTIGATION

Under investigation—the phrase recurred like an ominous drumbeat. Darcy disliked the words; they seemed a forecast of certain trouble. The report ended with a promise she did not find comforting: "Further information will be forthcoming."

Darcy suppressed a shudder. Did she really want more information? She felt like the fairy-tale character who had opened the bottle and loosed a genie more powerful than she could control.

SLOAN DOZED IN THE HAMMOCK for almost three hours. In his dream he wanted to stay with Darcy, but instead he found himself alone in the oil fields of South Africa. From Africa he somehow drifted to the city of Doho in Qatar, where he looked out across the waters of the Persian Gulf.

He still wanted Darcy, but he could not go to her. He had to cross the Gulf and go on to Afghanistan, following the rumors of new oil fields in the wastes of both Dasht-e Margow and Rigestan.

It was the assignment he had especially wanted, because it was the most difficult, the most challenging. But it was also the most dangerous—and no place for a woman.

It was a vast desert, where no trees grew. The few plants

that could eke out a life had names as harsh as their lives: camel thorn, Russian thistle, spiny restharrow, poison vetch.

It was a land torn by religious and political strife and surrounded by volatile neighbors. Violence always simmered there, ready to boil over like a kettle filled with generations of hot, bad blood. No, he told himself again, it was the destination he'd yearned for, but no place to take a woman.

So in his dream, he went on his solitary way into the dangers of Afghanistan. Then Afghanistan got mixed up with Turkmenistan and Uzbekistan and Kazakhstan and Tajikistan, all the "stan" countries the U.S. oil companies were so ardently trying to court. A man could spend years in the mysterious 'stans. Dozens of years.

The old lure of exotic places caught him. He dreamed of the peaks of the Hindu Kush and the deserts of Karakumy. And yet, no matter how spellbinding the images, he missed something and was haunted by a feeling foreign to him. It was loneliness.

He awoke, vaguely troubled, not quite remembering his dreams. The last wisps quickly vanished. He looked about. There was no sign of Darcy, and the place seemed empty without her.

The sun had started its descent. He glanced at his watch. It was almost six o'clock. He should shower and get ready for dinner. He got out of the hammock and headed toward the lake house.

As he entered he wished, suddenly, that he had a gift to take to Darcy tonight. but he had nothing. When he got back to Tulsa, he would buy her something. A necklace, maybe. Yes—a necklace. A simple diamond pendant on a platinum chain.

No, he corrected as he entered the guest room. Not a diamond. Women tended to attach too much symbolism to diamonds. Although, Darcy was different—

His cell phone, lying on the bureau, rang. He looked at it with mild surprise. For almost a full afternoon he'd forgotten the damn phone. He'd used it last night and hadn't turned it off.

He picked it up, flicked it open. *Please, God,* he prayed. *Don't let it be Trina.*

"Hello?" he said.

"Sloan, it's me," said Tom Caspian.

Sloan frowned. Was Tom calling as a doctor or a friend? "What's up?" he asked. "Am I dying, after all, and you want to break it to me gently?"

"You're too mean to die," said Tom. "When do you see Dr. Nightwine again?"

"Tomorrow," said Sloan. "Why?"

"I want her to call me after your appointment."

"Why?"

"I want to keep track of your progress, that's all," Tom said a bit too glibly. "How're you feeling?"

Sloan thought of his morning with Darcy. "Fine. Great, in fact."

"Glad to hear it," said Tom. "You managing to rest? Not starting out the day with five hundred push-ups and a ten-mile run?"

"I went out and looked at wildflowers this morning," Sloan said wryly. "This afternoon I slept by the swimming pool. It hasn't been the pentathlon."

"Good," said Tom. "I want you to *really* rest this time. Think you can get it right?"

Sloan cocked one dark brow. "What's this about? You're not calling me up just to tell me to take my cod liver oil."

"I don't believe in cod liver oil," said Tom. "Did it do the cod any good? Obviously not. He's deader than a mackerel."

"Is there a point to this conversation?" Sloan asked.

"Yeah, there is a point," said Tom. "I wondered if I should tell you, but thought maybe it'd motivate you, health-care wise." He paused for drama. "I played golf today with Meyer Bidwell."

Sloan's body tensed. Meyer Bidwell was the executive vice

president in charge of overseas project development. He was the one man at PetroCorp who controlled Sloan's future.

Sloan kept his voice cool. "How badly did he beat you?"

"Not *that* bad," Tom said rather testily. "At any rate, your name came up."

Sloan's heart beat faster. "Yeah?"

"Bidwell's very interested in your health. He *wants* you to be healthy."

Sloan didn't allow his tone to change. "Yeah?"

"Yeah. He asked my opinion."

Sloan gritted his teeth. "Look, I know you think I should stay in the States and be so still I grow moss—"

"He asked me a very provocative question, friend. Would you be well enough to go back *if you wanted?*"

"And?" He felt his future hanging in the balance.

"I said *if* you took care of yourself, and *if* you wanted to, and *if* you passed the company's insurance requirements, yeah. I suppose you could go back. If I was in your shoes, I wouldn't. But I'm not you."

Sloan exhaled, feeling half dizzy with relief. "Thanks, Tom."

"He's even talked to Nightwine. She's impressed by your recuperative powers. If she continues to be, you might be traveling soon, buddy. Bidwell *really* doesn't want to replace you. He has big plans for you. Be good, get well, and I think he'll put some plane tickets in your hand."

"Plane tickets to where?" Sloan asked.

"Where would you want to go?" Tom's voice was teasing.

A fragment of Sloan's dream drifted back. He had a waking vision of sand and camel thorn and poison vetch. "One of the 'stans would be challenging," he said carefully.

"That," said Tom, "is a very interesting answer."

SLOAN APPEARED AT HER DOOR at precisely seven o'clock.

The subtle scent of expensive cologne hung around him, yet he looked slightly rumpled, as if he'd inexpertly put his jeans and green linen shirt through the washer and drier, but hadn't bothered with an iron.

Still, he looked handsome to Darcy's eyes. Sun and sleep had obviously agreed with him. He stood on her step with one hand in the front pocket of his jeans, the opposite hip cocked. The posture seemed both boldly careless and boyishly shy.

In his free hand he held a single clover blossom and a leaf. "I hate always coming to you empty-handed," he said.

Her heartbeat speeded pleasurably, a sign she knew was dangerous. "You're not supposed to bring anything. You're our guest."

"If I brought you a bottle of wine, it'd come from your mother's wine cellar," he said. "If I picked you flowers, they'd come from her garden. I would have driven into town to get you something, but I slept so long..."

"It doesn't matter," she said, her throat dry.

"So I looked until I found this growing by the drive," he said, offering her the clover. "I figure no gardener planted it. It just happened. I wish it was a bouquet of orchids."

It was only a four-leaf clover, its stem still joined to that of its white blossom. She took it gently from him, her fingers brushing his. "Maybe you can press it in a book or something," he said. "For luck. And to remember me by."

"I'll do that," she said. She moved to her worktable where the volume of Arthur Rackham prints lay open. She set the clover on the page with the drawing of Puck and his fellow spirits, but she did not close the book.

Sloan moved beside her, put his hands on her upper arms. He bent and kissed her lips, lightly yet lingeringly enough to make her know he wanted more.

"I'm sorry I feel asleep," he murmured. "It was rude."

There was such tenderness in his eyes, it made her catch her breath. "Not at all," she said. "You need rest. How do you feel?"

Something subtle altered his expression. It grew almost solemn. "Like I never had Malay fever. Like it never happened."

"But you felt that way before your relapse," she said. "You still need to take it easy."

He nodded.

She started to pull away, but he held her in place. She did not resist. She said, "You go to the doctor tomorrow?"

He nodded. "Come to town with me? I'll buy you lunch."

"Let me drive," she said. "I know the city. The traffic can be confusing."

"It's a deal," he said, and started to kiss her again.

This time she did draw away. "You shouldn't spend any energy until you replenish your fuel supply," she said. "You're an oil man. You should know that. You've got weight to regain."

He gave her a wicked smile. "I have that lean and hungry look?"

"Yes," she said and thought, *I wish it wasn't so damn becoming.*

THE SUPPER SHE HAD MADE was northern Mexican style, a salad with *chiles estilo sonora* and beef fillets with chipotle sauce. She liked adventurous cooking, and approached it the same way she did an art project, with her sleeves rolled up and her enthusiasm high.

But she knew that this evening she had cooked to lose herself in activity and stop brooding. Now she wondered if she had gotten carried away.

"Maybe I should have picked something blander," she said worriedly. "Your system probably doesn't need to be assaulted by chili peppers."

"My system needs chili peppers," he said. "Probably why I had a relapse. Hadn't gotten the daily minimum requirement of peppers."

She smiled, for he did eat with gusto. When, at last, he pushed his plate away, she poured the spiced coffee and brought out dessert, the delicate turnovers called *coyotas.*

He complimented her; she accepted his compliments. And then the conversation fell off into a silence that wasn't altogether comfortable. There were things she wanted to ask him and had put off until now. He, too, had seemed a bit distracted during supper.

"I've been meaning—" she began.

But he spoke at the same moment. "I need to tell you—"

They both stopped, looked at each other, gave embarrassed smiles.

"You go first," he said. "What were you going to say?"

She took a deep breath. "This afternoon, right before you fell asleep, I asked if your family had any deep secrets. You said no, just shallow ones. What did you mean?"

He'd picked up his third *coyota,* but he set it back on his plate, untasted. "Oh," he said. "That."

"Yes," she said.

He gave a stiff shrug. "I told you my father isn't the world's most efficient businessman. Most of his assets are tied up in the famous Florida swampland."

Darcy nodded, feeling guilty for knowing how much land—21.3 acres, and where—Big Torch Key.

Sloan shook his head. "He thinks it's worth a fortune. Maybe it is, maybe not. One of his buddies appraised it as worth millions of dollars."

Darcy felt another twinge.

"But," Sloan said, "that's only what one of his friends says. Maybe nobody'll buy it—at any price. Unless somebody does, it's just soggy dirt."

"I'm sorry," Darcy said.

"So am I." Sloan's face was hard. "He made sure Trina was relatively secure. But then he plunged everything he had into that land. He had to work hard to get a healthy bank balance again. But he did. Very large, very healthy."

Darcy blinked in surprise. She knew how much money John English had in the bank: less than five thousand dollars. It was hardly an enormous sum for a man his age.

Sloan drained his coffee cup and set it down. He laced his

fingers together and gazed at her over them. "Then he took that hard-earned money and invested it in what most people would think is the biggest damn fool scheme in the world."

Darcy felt an unpleasant chill of apprehension. "Yes?"

He gave a smile with no happiness in it. "He went into a partnership and bought an old movie theater. In downtown Key West. Then he took out a good-size loan to remodel it."

Darcy's mouth had gone dry. She recognized what he was talking about, but she still couldn't understand what John English was doing with a movie theater.

Sloan's smile grew more twisted, and his green gaze held Darcy's wary one. "I told you my father's a romantic," he said. "All his life he's worked to pay the bills, mostly other people's. He's never been able to follow the one dream he's wanted most. He wants to be a professional actor."

He said the word *actor* with a combination of resignation and mockery. He couldn't have surprised Darcy more if he'd said John English wanted to be a trapeze artist.

She knew that her face must show amazement akin to shock. "An actor?" she echoed. She realized there was a slightly strangled note of horror in her voice.

He watched her reaction carefully. "Yes. And a sort of…magician."

"A magician?" she said in even greater disbelief. "Does…does my mother know this?"

"Yes," he said. "I asked him. Excuse me for saying this, but you look like you've just swallowed a frog and it didn't taste very good."

She pushed back from the table and made an embarrassed gesture. "I'm sorry. I just wasn't expecting you to say…*that*."

"Yeah," he said sardonically. "If you think you're having problems with it, you should see Trina. She thinks he should be committed."

Darcy's thoughts tumbled a bit insanely. "He's *always* wanted to be an actor?"

Sloan nodded. "He would have studied it in college if he'd

gotten the chance. He's got a good voice. He's a nice-looking guy. When he worked with the ad agency, he did a lot of commercials. He's been in amateur theater, that kind of thing.''

''And a magician?'' she said weakly.

''He always fooled around with magic, sleight-of-hand. When I was a kid, it fascinated me.''

Darcy looked about her little house rather desperately. She was an artist, and some people would say an eccentric one. Austin was full of artists and craftspeople, and it was famous for its musicians.

But she had never known an actor; the profession struck her as somehow unsavory—men who wore makeup and played at being what they were not. Actors were notoriously vain, footloose and temperamental.

And a magician? Magicians struck her as even more suspect than actors. In her mind's eye, she saw a man who made flourishing gestures and did pointless tricks involving silk scarves, Chinese rings and sawing blondes in half.

Sloan kept watching her. ''His project isn't completely crazy,'' he said. ''On the other hand, it's not the typical thing that a man does in his sunset years, either.''

''What exactly *is* he doing?'' Darcy asked uneasily.

''You've got to understand—it's not as crazy as it sounds.'' Sloan set his jaw and linked his fingers together more tightly. ''He wants to hold séances.''

''HE WANTS TO WHAT?'' Emerald demanded. She sat on the edge of Henry's bed, looking horrified.

Henry knelt before her, holding one of her hands between his. ''He wants to have séances. That's why he bought into the theater in Key West.''

''A *séance?*'' Emerald demanded in dismay. ''Like—like where you contact ghosts and dead people and stuff?''

''Yeah. I guess that's the idea,'' Henry said, gripping her hand in greater consolation. His face was taut with sympathy.

Emerald's free hand flew to her midsection. ''I think I'm

going to be sick," she wailed. "You shouldn't have made me eat."

To her left was a small television tray on which Henry had put a goblet of milk and a crystal plate with a peanut butter and jelly sandwich. She had only sipped at the milk and nibbled the sandwich. Now her stomach roiled in rebellion.

"You had to eat something," Henry reasoned earnestly. "You didn't eat supper last night or anything today."

But Emerald kept her free hand pressed against her stomach as if she were in the throes of poisoning. "This—this *ghost* business—how did you find it out?"

He looked at the floor. "When we looked at the Web pages on real estate in Key West, I saw some telephone numbers. The Chamber of Commerce. The Visitor's Bureau. While you were eating, I phoned. From my father's study. The Visitor's Bureau told me."

"That he's a medium? Some kind of guru or spirit channeler?"

Emerald had a terrible vision of John English: he wore a robe and a turban with some sort of occult jewel. He sat in a darkened room, and before him was a glowing crystal ball. It cast a sinister, almost demonic light on his face.

"I don't know exactly what they're doing," Henry said. "He and two partners bought an old movie house. They're remodeling it. They're going to have some sort of show about local ghost lore and mind reading and—and communication with the beyond, stuff like that. John English is going to be the mentalist or the master of ceremonies or whatever you call him."

"*Fraud* is what I'd call him," Emerald said bitterly. "Isn't that a racket—preying on poor, grief-stricken survivors? Telling them you'll put them in touch with their loved ones?"

"Well, it can be," Henry said. "There's certainly that possibility, but—"

Emerald's chin assumed a militant angle. "It's a particularly heartless racket, in fact. It's despicable. Rose Alice told me all about it. She saw it on *Jerry Springer* and *Oprah* and *America's Most Wanted.*''

Henry looked troubled. ''Emerald, I'll admit that it doesn't sound like the world's most savory business. But the Visitor's Bureau said their information listed it strictly as entertainment, a tourist attraction.''

Emerald gave him a superior look. ''Sure—that's the impression John English and his partners want to create. Entertainment? Ha! That's only their front.''

''We don't know that,'' Henry said. ''We can't verify it. And I didn't tell you this to upset you. I only want to help you get to the truth.''

''The truth keeps getting worse and worse,'' she said unhappily. ''I don't want my mother married to some—some necromancer. If she has to fall in love, why does it have to be with somebody who talks to dead people? Aren't there enough live ones in the world?''

''Emerald, control yourself. Before you do anything, talk to Darcy again. Let her call the Visitor's Bureau and find out for herself. Then the two of you can—''

''I've *told* you,'' Emerald said, her voice shaking. ''It's up to us. Darcy won't listen to me, she's too infatuated. And whatever I told her, that Sloan English would have some slick explanation.''

Henry's brow creased with worry. ''Maybe I should talk to this guy myself. Confront him. Lay it on the line to him, by God.''

Emerald was touched, but unconvinced. She put her hand on his cheek. ''Oh, Henry,'' she breathed, ''what good would it do?''

She could see her words pierced him like a sword. He tensed. ''You don't think I'm man enough?''

His blue eyes, so thickly lashed, looked beautiful and vulnerable and full of idealistic fire. She felt her own nerves grow taut with a strange, deep sympathy for him. ''Oh, no,'' she said with feeling. ''It's not that, at all.''

Again he took her hand. He was breathing hard. ''Emerald," he said, "I have a question to ask you. Maybe you won't want to answer. That's all right. Just tell me."

Her breath suddenly seemed wedged in her throat. "Yes?"

He held her hand more tightly. "After what I—after what I did to you, you didn't come back to the Internet much, did you?"

"No," she said, grieved at the memory. "I didn't trust it."

He hesitated, then said, "But you joined the Medieval Society."

She bit her lip and nodded. The people in the Medieval Society were interested in the same things she was, the same sort of chivalric fantasies of good and evil. But unlike characters on the Internet, they were real people, tangible and solid.

A muscle played in his jaw as he said, "But when you picked a character, you decided to be a knight. A boy, not a girl. Is that my fault? Don't you *like* being a woman anymore? Did I make you hate being female?"

Emerald had to look away because her eyes stung with tears. "No," she said. "That's not the reason I did it."

"Then what is?" he asked.

She stared past him at the glow of the computer screen. Her heart hammered with apprehension, but she wanted to tell him the truth. "When I met you," she said sadly, "I thought you were my knight in shining armor. I thought you were perfect. Until then, I hadn't felt whole. Somehow you made me feel complete."

He said nothing. He bent and kissed her hands, first the right, then the left. There was something humble yet passionate in the gesture, and she knew it was a kind of apology, one that went deeper than words.

She swallowed, then said, "When I found out you'd fooled me, I hated you. I hated myself for being fooled. And I was unhappy that I'd thought I needed someone else to make me whole. So I decided instead of wanting somebody else to be my knight, I'd be my own. I'd learn to be complete in myself."

They were silent for a moment. At last he asked, "And now? Are you complete in yourself?"

"More than I was," she said honestly. "But I didn't want to fall in love again. Not after you."

"There was never anyone for me but you," he said.

"That's different."

"Is it?"

"Yes. It is." She looked at him. He no longer seemed at all like a boy to her. He seemed a man and a strong one, even on his knees. Yet it was hard to forgive him. Hard and probably foolish.

He said, "I meant what I said about Sloan English. I'll go to him. Make him talk to me, man to man."

"It won't do any good. If he can fool Darcy, he's a very fast talker. Too fast."

She drew her hand away, rose and walked to the computer. She touched it sadly. "Men like that make a woman believe almost anything. I know. I just never thought Darcy would make such a mistake."

SLOAN'S STORY WAS convincing, Darcy had to admit. Very convincing.

She had poured the after-dinner wine, and now he gazed at her over the rim of his wineglass. "Think of it," he said. "Can you imagine *your* life without imagination?"

"Of course not," she said. "That's a paradox."

"But it's also true. If you hadn't been able to use your creativity, what would your life have been like?"

Darcy found the question difficult, perhaps impossible. She glanced around her studio. Without this work, her life would seem unspeakably empty. "You mean, how would it have been if I had to spend my life doing a job I didn't like? Like your father has?"

"That's what I mean."

"I'd hate it," she said with conviction. "I'd feel stifled and incomplete." She paused. "But if I *had* to do it, to support my family—"

"Yes?"

"—then they'd come first," she finished. She frowned self-critically. "Your father did the honorable thing. Maybe that's why I never had a family of my own. I stayed free. To follow *my* dreams."

"I did the same thing," he said.

"Our dreams—yours and mine—are poles apart," she said. "You're a corporate man in a corporate world, where the bottom line is profit. Oil is big business. This—" she made a gesture that took in all the overspilling projects of her studio "—is as far from big business as it gets."

He finished his wine and rose, his face meditative. He strolled to a bulletin board where a collection of sketches was tacked haphazardly. He touched the corner of a drawing of a fakir sitting on a flying rug. Darcy had never considered the design a success; she had never gone beyond the sketch stage.

But Sloan was obviously drawn to it. "This is who I wanted to be," he said, tapping the fakir's windblown robes. "The man on the magic carpet. To go every place, see everything. PetroCorp was the carpet—the means, not the end."

"But it flew you first class," Darcy pointed out. "And made you rich in the bargain. You didn't have just vagabond dreams. There has to be more to it than just seeing the world."

He stared at the pattern in the carpet. "Oh, yeah," he said softly. "I wanted to be rich—of course. And free. Not like my old man. My life was going to be as different as possible."

"And the dream," Darcy asked, her heart beating strangely fast. "Has it been enough for you?"

"So far." He gave her a level look. "How about yours?"

She glanced away, her feelings mixed and confusing. "I love my mother. But I wanted the same thing as you—a completely different kind of life. She married young, then was left alone with huge responsibilities. To give Emerald and me the best, she made a—a marriage of convenience."

Darcy's face burned. She knew that in a sense Olivia had

sold herself for her children's sake. Darcy had trained herself to need neither marriage nor anyone's money but her own.

"That doesn't answer the question," Sloan said. "You're different. You're your own woman. Does it make you happy?"

"I've got the life I want," she said, not quite sure it was true.

"Ah," he said. "We're two of a kind, aren't we?"

She turned to face him. She gave him a smile that was careful and controlled. "I suppose we are."

He touched the corner of the drawing again. "And our parents—they deserve to be happy."

"Yes," she said. "They do." She spun her wineglass, still half full, back and forth without lifting it. "Maybe we should call them and tell them that."

A sardonic smile touched one corner of his mouth. "Maybe they'd prefer it if we didn't interrupt them. After all, this is their week of romance."

Darcy grimaced slightly at the thought. "I'm sorry. I just haven't got used to the idea yet."

"Yeah," he said. "I try to picture it, but I can't. A little Freudian censor in my head tells me that I shouldn't dwell on my father's sex life. It's unseemly."

"So," she said, "I guess we'd better not think about it."

"Right," he said. He was silent a moment, then said, "I'll think about you, instead."

He moved behind her chair. His hands settled on her shoulders, his touch sure and charged with sensuality. He bent and kissed the back of her neck in a way that made her stomach feel as if it were filled with drunken hummingbirds.

He drew her to her feet and away from the table. He put his arms around her, pulled her close. "I want to make love to you," he said, his voice somewhere between a purr and a growl.

"I want it, too," she said. She raised her lips to his.

But he did not kiss her, although he leaned nearer. "There's something else I have to tell you."

The hummingbirds spun a bit more crazily, their flight now touched with apprehension. "Yes?" she said, looking into his eyes.

"I got a call this afternoon. There's word that if I get a clean bill of health they want to send me to Afghanistan. For at least a year. Maybe longer."

She blinked in stunned surprise. Afghanistan sounded as far away as the moon. She forced her voice to stay steady. "And you'll go?"

"Yes," he said. "It's what I do. It's who I am."

She made herself smile and nod, but a knot of pain choked her throat.

"I understand," she said. "How soon would they send you?"

"In six weeks, if possible. If the doctor here gives me clearance, I need to get back to Tulsa for more medical tests. As soon as I pass, I start making arrangements to leave."

A sickening sense of loss surged through her.

"I'll see you all I can before I leave," he promised, his face taut. "We can spend every weekend together—if you will. Will you?"

"Yes," she said, knowing the decision wasn't wise.

He touched her face gently. "I'm sorry. It doesn't give us much time."

"Then let's make it count," she breathed, raising her lips to his. "Every minute of it."

CHAPTER SIXTEEN

HIS KISS WAS FIERCE and hungry, almost desperate, and she kissed him back the same way.

His lips moved along her jawline, down to the throbbing pulse in her throat. "I don't want you to regret this," he said, his breath warm against her skin. "To wish that it—that we'd—never happened."

"I don't regret it," she whispered. "I couldn't."

He leaned back slightly, took her face between his hands. Her hair had come undone, and he laced his fingers through the silken tumble of it. "I want to make every moment of it good for you."

Her heartbeats crowded on one another, making her breathless. "It is good."

"I want to be a miser of time with you. Stretch every second to the breaking point. Make it last."

He dipped his head and put his mouth to hers in a kiss so long and seductive that reason flew off, reeling. Only sensation was left. A crazy abandon burned in her veins, a need to possess and be possessed. His questing hands began to move over her body.

His breath, his tongue, tasted of wine. "Tell me what you want," he said against her mouth. "Exactly what and how."

His touching made her ache for more. "I want—I want to go into the bedroom."

"Do you want me to carry you?"

"No," she said. "I want to lead you there."

"Then take me."

She stared up at his face. His eyes had darkened with desire, and hunger tensed his features. But he gave her a lazy smile. "I'm in your power."

It was true, she realized; he was. Just as she was in his. She took two steps backward, as if testing the power of her own magic. She held out her hand to him, palm up. He took it.

"This way," she said, and moved down the hall to the bedroom door. A small light was on beside the bed. She stopped, staring at it as if mesmerized. His hand was still around hers, possessive and strong.

"The light," he said. "Do you want it off? Or on?"

"On," she murmured.

"Good," he said. He looked her up and down in a way that made her shudder in anticipation. "Then what?"

"I want you to kiss me again."

"How?" he teased.

"Like the world will end if you don't do it right."

"That's a big order."

"I think you're up to it."

"Then come here."

He pulled her into his arms, and his mouth swept down to claim hers.

His intensity shook through her with tremors of fresh pleasure and need.

She locked one arm around his neck, straining to press closer to him still. Her other hand ran over his chest, savoring the feel of the muscles bunched and lively beneath his shirt.

She began to undo the buttons, but her fingers were atypically unsteady.

"Help me," she whispered against his lips. "I want to touch you."

He groaned and moved back from her just enough to tear the shirt open unceremoniously. His hand gripped hers and brought it against his bare chest. He wrestled his way out of the garment, letting it fall to the floor.

Her fingers skimmed the hard, warm flesh, tangled in the

silky mat of chest hair, stroked the nipples until they hardened like pebbles. Her breasts swelled and throbbed in response.

"Do you want me to touch you the same way?" he asked from between gritted teeth.

"Yes."

Immediately his hands were on the tiny buttons of her blouse, fumbling desperately with their intricacies. "My God," he panted, "am I going to have to tear it off you?"

"Yes," she said, seeking his lips again. "Do." A liberating rush of recklessness swept her as she felt and heard the fabric split. She fought her way free of the shirt's hampering cover. His fingers, impatient, undid her bra and stripped it away.

He lowered his mouth and took her breast, making her gasp with pleasure and even greater desire. His lips and tongue made love to first one nipple, then the other, and she threw back her head, close to losing all restraint.

They struggled out of their remaining clothes. He looked her up and down for a long moment. "You're so beautiful," he breathed. "Too beautiful. If I keep looking…"

His words trailed off, and he held her body as tightly as he could against his. His mouth seemed to devour hers, his flesh trying to forge itself into one with hers.

Her hands wanted to touch him everywhere at once. The skin of his back was warm and smooth beneath her fingers. His hips were tight with driving muscle, and he thrust his pelvis against hers with primitive rhythm.

"I want to take you to bed," he said against her mouth.

"Yes."

He lowered her to the bed, so that his body covered hers. His hands moved down to cradle her bottom. "I have to have you. Now," he said between clenched teeth. "I can't help it."

"Then take me," she gasped. It was half plea, half command. Everywhere he touched her ached with pleasure and wanting, and her body throbbed like a song.

Effortlessly, he raised her hips, and she clasped her legs about him. He entered her with a groan of exultation, and they clung together like two people tossed in a tempest, pounded by its force, rocking with its waves.

She drowned in the joy of it, and when the tide of fulfillment surged over her, she cried out his name.

Afterward, she lay in his arms unable to sleep. She was haunted by the ardor of their lovemaking. She knew why it had been so intense, so bittersweet. They were starting to say goodbye.

OLIVIA WOKE EARLY. Drowsy and affectionate, she nuzzled John's warm shoulder. He did not respond. He only sighed and hugged his pillow instead of her.

Sleepyhead, she thought. *You don't know what you're missing.*

She tried to drift back into slumber herself, but now she was restless. Memories of the night before came back, niggling and unpleasant. She and John had come close to quarreling.

She was uncertain about Key West, about selling her beloved house in Austin, about so many things. She was sure of only two things: she loved John, and she loved her daughters.

She thought of the girls. She hadn't been frank with Emerald. She must remedy that soon. She was being cowardly, trying to avoid the inevitable scenes.

But first she and John had to reach an agreement about their future. Olivia wanted everything thought completely through, *considered.* When she was on firm ground, then she would take on Emerald.

Darcy would help. Darcy, bless her, was being more than understanding. She was even managing to put up with John's son. The thought should have eased Olivia's mind, but, strangely, it did not. She was more awake than before.

She might as well get up. She slipped from bed as quietly as she could. Then she stood a moment, staring down at John. The night-light silvered the edge of his big form, glimmered on his thick hair.

Once again an amorous urge tugged at her, and she wished he'd waken. She gave in to temptation, bent, and softly brushed her lips against his cheek. He did not so much as stir.

She sighed and shrugged into her silk robe. She went softly into the kitchen to make coffee. It was still dark outside, and no light peeped through the blinds. She didn't turn on the television or radio. She loved the early morning silence.

But while the coffee brewed, she decided to check her e-mail. Maybe there would be a note from one of the girls. She went into the spare bedroom, sat down at the computer.

She smiled when she saw that she had a new message and that it was from Emerald. Eagerly she summoned it to the screen. Her smiled withered and died.

SUBJECT: Mama, Please Be Careful!
From: MaidOfOrleans@USAserve.com
To: Olivia@USAserve.com

Dear Mama—Please be very careful! Things are not always what they seem. Please look at the attached.
   Truly and deeply concerned, Emerald
   CLICK HERE TO SEE:
    HTTP://FUN_BACHELORS_WANT_LOVE.COM

Olivia felt a sense of foreboding. *Fun bachelors? Who want love?* What did this mean? What was Emerald up to now?

There was a picture beside the words CLICK HERE TO SEE. The picture showed a magic lamp.

Olivia knew that if she clicked on the magic lamp, it would transport her to another part of the Internet. She did not know how this worked, only that it happened.

Sometimes John had sent her similar messages. "Here's something I thought you'd enjoy seeing." Or "I thought you might be interested in this."

Olivia would click the symbol and be whisked off to a Web

site—*abracadabra!* The new site would show her something interesting, perhaps about wine or food or decorating.

But Olivia had no idea what a site called Fun Bachelors would be like. It sounded rather risqué. Why did Emerald want her to see it? Fighting another wave of uneasiness, Olivia clicked on the symbol.

Instantly the screen changed, and she blinked in confused surprise.

A red banner across the top of the screen announced, THE FUN BACHELOR PAGES! DOZENS OF FUN BACHE-LORS! A yellow banner at the bottom blared, LOADS OF HUNKY GUYS WHO LOVE LADIES!

And in the middle of the screen was a photograph with a familiar face. The face was John's.

Olivia's hand flew to her mouth in shock. "My God," she breathed.

John stood with another man, whom she recognized as Sloan. She had seen him in photographs before. But never like this. Sloan was bare-chested and raising a beer to the camera in a toast. John had one arm around his son and the other around a blond woman of about forty. She was pressed against him suggestively.

The blonde had huge breasts and a tiny bikini. She held a bottle of champagne. John's grinning face was clearly marked with her lip prints.

John and the woman and Sloan were surrounded by people obviously having some wild sort of gathering. It looked al-most—but not quite—like an orgy.

Over the picture was a label: Bachelor 38—John English! He's looking for your love!!!

Olivia's nose wrinkled in horror. Beneath the disgusting picture was a message, just as disgusting. She read it with growing hurt and anger.

"Hi! I'm John English. I'm from Key West where we party hearty!

"But even a party animal gets lonely. Could you be the one who tames me and makes me your willing love slave?

"I am a well-to-do Realtor with a million-dollar-a-year business and my own boat.

"I'm also an accomplished actor and gifted psychic. I sense that you want to get to meet a fun guy who has a deep, sensitive side—and knows how to pamper a lady!

"This is a picture of me at the famous Halloween celebration in Key West! I'm with my son, Sloan, a wealthy oil executive. He's a bachelor, too. Any mother-daughter combos out there looking for lots of expert love?

"Send e-mail to me in care of this Web site. I answer all my mail—especially if it's naughty!

"P.S.—We don't know who the blonde is, she just wanted in our picture!"

Good Lord, Olivia thought in dismay. *What is this filth? He's in some sort of damn Lonely Hearts Club?*

Tears of outrage pricked her eyes. *This can't be real,* she thought. Yet there it was, right in front of her, glowing in full color from her screen. It *was* John's picture, and she *did* recognize Sloan.

She was so repelled that she actually felt faint. How could he have done such a thing? He sounded like a shallow, vain, lying fool who was trolling for women even more shallow and foolish than himself.

And who had he caught but her? She grew more nauseated. Was this what he was *really* like?

"It can't be," she whispered fiercely. "It can't."

Where had Emerald found this hellish thing, this abomination? And how? There was only one way to find out. Olivia forgot how early it was. She stalked to the living room, snatched up her cell phone and dialed Emerald's number.

The phone rang. It rang again. Olivia felt like a caged animal. She paced back to the computer to look again at the image on her screen. It was abhorrent to her. It made her want to gag.

At last Emerald answered, sounding dazed with sleep. "Hello? Hello?"

It took Olivia a moment to find her voice. When she spoke, her words shook with emotion. "Emerald? It's Mama."

"I was sleeping," Emerald said in a complaining tone.

"Emerald, I just got your—got your message. This thing about John—where did you find it? Is it real?"

There was a long pause. When Emerald spoke, she no longer sounded sleepy. "Oh," she said. "You got it."

"The question," Olivia said from between her teeth, "is where *you* got it. And how."

Another pause. "It's on the Internet."

"It's real? It's genuine?"

"It's on the Internet," Emerald repeated.

"But how did you find it? Is it some sort of hideous...joke?"

Again Emerald hesitated. "There are these things called 'search engines,'" she said. "If you want to find out something, you type the name into the search engine. It searches the Internet for you."

"You found this with a—search engine?"

In a small voice, Emerald said, "It's easy. Anybody could find it."

Anybody could find it, Olivia thought, her mind reeling. Oh, heavens, it was there for the whole world to see. "Emerald, you put John's name into this—this search thing..."

"Um," said Emerald. "That's how you do it."

"And it found this ghastly page?"

"It's on the Internet," Emerald said for the third time.

Olivia raked a hand through her hair in distress. "And this horrid Fun Bachelors is a site where men are looking for women?"

"That's exactly what it is," Emerald said, sounding surer of herself. "It's like a dating service. They pay to put their pictures on. They want women to get in touch with them."

"It's a real site?"

"Yes," said Emerald. "Absolutely."

For once in her life Olivia was speechless. That John could ever do such a cheap and tasteless thing revolted her. The whole time they had been together, he had still been hunting for other women? It was humiliating.

"Mama," said Emerald, "are you all right?"

"I'm—stunned," Olivia managed to say.

"I didn't send it to hurt you," Emerald said. "But it's easy to get fooled by someone you meet on the Internet. You know what they say—'When in doubt, check him out.' I sent Darcy a copy, too. So she'd know what's going on."

Olivia leaned against the wall, her temples beating so hard that her head ached. She squeezed shut her eyes. Had she ever really checked out anything about John? No. She had been too infatuated.

Emerald said, "I'm sorry you're upset, Mama. But maybe you should slow things down with this man. Isn't it better to wonder about him *now* than after you're married?"

Olivia kept her eyes shut and rubbed her fingertips against her throbbing head. "I—I'm going to have to talk to him about this. That's all. We'll have to talk."

"Mama?"

"Yes?" *Dear God,* she thought. *Have I been a complete and utter fool?*

"What if he denies it?" asked Emerald, sounding uneasy.

"I don't know," Olivia said. She suddenly felt infinitely weary. "But I guess I'm going to find out."

EMERALD HUNG UP THE telephone, her stomach twisting with guilt.

Technically she hadn't lied to Olivia.

There *was* a site called Fun Bachelors Want Love. Henry had found several such "lonely hearts" sites for men. Emerald chose Fun Bachelors because it was the sleaziest. Most of the men advertising themselves sounded like losers or liars or both.

And John English's picture *was* on it—Henry had put it there.

Henry had copied the photo from the real estate site. He'd doctored it at his father's studio, adding the party in the background, the beer in Sloan's hand, the blonde, and the lipstick on John's face. Emerald herself had written the damning "self-description," trying to make John sound as fatuous as possible.

When Emerald had talked to her mother, no lie had actually passed her lips. Yet she had committed a monstrous falsehood, and she knew it. She had created a slander against John English, and Olivia, believing it, had been devastated.

Emerald hadn't meant to hurt her mother. Still, she felt she must slow Olivia's mad plunge into marriage. Who knew how bad a rascal John English might be?

A troublesome thought crossed her mind. *Suppose he wasn't a rascal at all?* Henry was always asking, what if she was wrong? It was maddening.

But what if she *was* wrong? Suppose she had misinterpreted everything, and John English was actually a good man—her mother's chance to be happily married, at last. And Emerald had ruined that chance?

No, she thought stubbornly. There was too much evidence against him. She had to protect her mother by whatever means possible. And Darcy, too. She had sent Darcy a message much like the one she'd sent Olivia.

But for the first time, she began to understand Henry. He had told colossal lies on the Internet. Now she was doing the same thing, for the same reason. She loved someone too much *not* to lie.

The knowledge was bitter, and it was humbling.

JOHN DREAMED PLEASANT DREAMS of the Gulf of Mexico. He and Olivia were in his little boat, the Bandit King. The sea was smooth and blue as turquoise, the air tingled with freshness, and a wedding ring glinted on Olivia's hand.

She reached out and touched his shoulder. She spoke his name. But something began to go wrong with the dream. Neither her tone nor her touch was loving—

Her hand gripped his shoulder, hard. She shook him. "John? Wake up. *Now.* We have to talk."

John struggled out of his dreams like a man fighting his way out of watery depths. "What?" he muttered, disoriented. "What?"

"Please get out of bed," Olivia said, and her voice was icy as the Maine wind. "It's important. I want to show you something."

He raised himself slightly and cast a drowsy glance at the window. Only blackness showed between the blinds. "It's night," he groaned. He shut his eyes, clutched his pillow more tightly and tried to sink back into the lulling tide of sleep.

But Olivia shook his shoulder even harder. *Annoyingly* hard, in fact.

"John," she said grimly, "I asked you to please get out of my bed. Right now. This instant. We need to talk."

"About what?" he grumbled. "Nobody's up at this time of night."

"It's not night. It's after six a.m. And *I'm* up." She jerked the covers off him unceremoniously.

"What is this?" He frowned and opened his eyes. She stalked to the doorway, switched on the overhead light. It was blinding, and John recoiled, shielding his eyes. "Olivia, in the name of all that's holy—"

"In the name of all that's holy, get out of that bed. Come in and look at my computer."

"Your computer?" he said resentfully. "For God's sake, why?"

"I can't explain. You have to see it," she snapped.

He forced himself to sit up. He yawned. "This had better be good."

"You're telling me," she retorted. She tossed her head, turned and stamped down the hall.

What's the hell's wrong with her? John wondered. He had never seen her like this, and it was upsetting. But he heaved himself up from the bed and groped for his robe. The floor was cold, and he couldn't find his slippers.

He shivered and plodded down the hall barefoot. He entered the other bedroom. Olivia stood beside the computer, her arms crossed. She was glaring at him as if he had done something unforgivable. He had no idea what was wrong with her.

Until he looked more closely at the computer. All traces of sleepiness fled. He stared at the screen in astonishment. "My God, what's *that?*"

"I was hoping you'd tell me."

He put his hands on the back of the desk chair and bent closer to the computer. There was a picture of him with Sloan that looked both familiar and horrifyingly unfamiliar. "Good Lord, it looks like we're at an orgy."

"Yes," Olivia said from between clenched teeth. "It does."

John squinted, unable to believe his eyes. "Who's that blonde?"

"Why ask me? You're the one with her lipstick on your face."

"I never saw her before in my life," he declared. "She doesn't even look real. She looks like she's made out of silicone."

"Really? It didn't seem to bother you at the time."

"What *is* this idiocy?" he demanded in rising anger. "Who are all those people? What is this—John English! He's looking for your love? What? *What?*"

"It's your picture. Your description," she said in that icy way. "There for the world to see."

John read the description with equal parts disbelief and rage. "This is garbage!" he practically roared. "I never saw this picture before! I never wrote these words. My God, it makes me sound like a fool."

"Yes," Olivia said, folding her arms more tightly across her chest. "You've got that right."

"What is this nonsense? Fun Bachelors Want Love? What sort of moron would put his picture here?"

"That," said Olivia, "is precisely what I'm trying to find out."

"Surely you don't think that I—that I—" he sputtered, then he swore.

"I don't know where this monstrosity came from," he said. "It's some kind of...trick."

"Then who would play it?"

"I don't know, but if I ever find him, I'll sue him for libel and defamation of character. *After* I crack his head open. How did you find this travesty?"

"Emerald found it with a caboose," Olivia said. "She sent it in a clicky thing."

"She what?" he said in fresh disbelief.

"A search caboose." Olivia was pale with anger, but her chin quivered as if she were going to cry. "She put it in the mail, and I clicked it. And there it is, in all its glory."

John's nostrils flared. Olivia was not being rational, and she obviously didn't understand what was happening. "It's a search engine, Olivia. Not a caboose."

"Whatever," she said with an impatient shrug. "I hardly think this is the time to correct *me*."

"You want me to *defend* myself?" he asked indignantly. "I've already told you this is not my doing. What sort of man do you think I am?"

"That's what I'm trying to find out."

Tears sparkled in her eyes. They devastated him as much as her suspicion insulted him. "My love," he said. He held his hands out, palms up in supplication. "I would never do something like this. You *know* me."

"Do I?" she said with a catch in her voice.

"Of course you do," he said. "And I recognize this picture—it's been tampered with, faked. It's one of the photos from my page at the realty company's Web site. I sent it to you in an e-mail once. You've seen it."

"No, I haven't," Olivia said. "I could never get it to come out of the clicky thing."

John sighed in frustration. "It's not a 'clicky thing.' It's called an attachment, my dear. You attach it to an e-mail and—"

She gave a small, angry shake of her head. "John, I don't want a computer lesson," she said. "I just want the truth."

"I'll show you the real picture," he said tiredly. "Let me pull up the company's Web site."

"Don't you dare 'accidentally' delete that Fun Bachelor's page, John. It won't do you any good. Emerald can find it again."

He resented the implication that he would destroy evidence, and he resented Emerald. "She had no business putting my name in a search engine in the first place."

"It's a free country," said Olivia.

He let the remark pass. She was hurt and angry, and he supposed he couldn't blame her; this hoax was nasty and meant to cast him in the worst possible light. She would see the truth when he showed her the real picture. He tapped the computer's buttons.

But to his amazement, the picture was gone. His whole *page* was gone from the Welber Realty site. "Hell's bells!" he cried. "Somebody's stolen it—stolen it, by God!"

"How convenient," said Olivia.

"Convenient?" he countered. "I'm appalled. What is this, a conspiracy? I'm telling you the real picture was here, and now it's gone."

Olivia looked skeptical.

He stared at her. "You don't believe me? Can't you see how upset I am by all this—this tripe?"

"Well, John," she said with chilling quiet. "You're acting upset. But then you're *supposed to be* an actor—aren't you?"

He didn't like her tone, which seemed belittling and sarcastic. "Olivia, someone's playing an extremely mean-spirited joke, and you're behaving like you *want* to believe it."

She flounced to the window and opened the blinds. The day was dawning, gray and joyless. She stared out at it, her back to him. "Emerald said you'd probably deny it."

Emerald again, he thought with another surge of anger.

And at that moment he knew the ugly truth, and it came down to Emerald.

He tried to stay calm, to lead into it carefully. He knew how difficult it would be. He said, ''You have to trust me. Some person is—somebody's trying to undermine my reputation.''

She kept gazing at the dreary sky. ''That's hard to believe, John. Why would anybody do such a thing?''

Her coldness both hurt and offended him. ''To make me look bad in your eyes. I guess they succeeded. I thought you had more faith in me.''

She turned and gazed at him dubiously. ''Ah. You want me to believe *you're* the victim here.''

''We both are, dammit,'' he said. ''Can't you see, Olivia? There's somebody who doesn't want us together, and she's gone to all this—''

Her eyebrow arched militantly. ''Who? Who would do such a thing?''

Oh, hell, he thought in disgust, couldn't she see? It was all too clear to him. She didn't want to face facts; he would have to force her to do so. ''Who found that page in the first place?'' he demanded.

''Emerald.''

''Who sent it to you?''

''Emerald.''

''Who said I'd deny everything.''

''Emerald. But *surely* you're not suggesting—''

''I'm suggesting exactly that,'' he said, crossing his arms. ''She put up a false page and wiped out my real one. She wanted to come between us, so she did a low, vicious thing—''

''Don't you *dare* talk about my daughter like that.'' Olivia's eyes flashed dangerously. ''She's not capable of such a thing.''

''You told me once that she was into computers,'' John argued.

''She—she played little pretend games, that's all,'' Olivia

said hotly. "She wasn't some sort of whiz who could do all those things. And she is *not* low and vicious. I resent that deeply. You owe me an apology, John."

"I beg to differ," he returned. "You don't want to face the truth about your own flesh and blood. You'd rather believe lies about me."

"My flesh and blood? What about yours? If someone's telling lies, what about that money-hungry sister of yours?"

He was shocked at her suggestion. "Trina? Trina's barely mastered e-mail. She's a technophobe. She could never do such a thing. And neither could Arthur. It would be impossible."

"She could *get* it done," Olivia said, narrowing her eyes. "There are people out there who do all sorts of sabotage by computer. She could hire one. They called them wankers or whackers or whack-offs or—something."

John clenched his teeth. "Hackers, Olivia. They're called hackers and crackers. The difference between them is—"

"Don't change the subject," Olivia said. "We're talking about your sister. We both know she doesn't want you to get married again. She's scared to death she'll lose her hold on what little money you have."

He felt his cheeks redden as if she'd slapped him. "I have property. A good deal of property. Suddenly that's not enough for you?"

"Well," Olivia said with a jerk of her chin, "it *would* be nice if it wasn't a swamp and a spook house."

"That," said John, his head beginning to throb wildly, "was unkind, Olivia."

"So were your remarks about Emerald," she flung back.

But John was still smarting from Olivia's words about his property. "I suppose Emerald doesn't think I'm good enough for you or rich enough for her. She thinks I'm going to gouge her out of her inheritance. She's unstable and jealous and she'll stop at nothing—"

He had to duck. Olivia had flung a silver hairbrush at his head.

AN HOUR LATER, Emerald's phone rang again.

It was her mother. Olivia's voice was cool and controlled. "Well, you were right. And it's over. He's gone for good. I nearly made a terrible mistake. You saved me. But I'm just...humiliated."

"He's gone?" Emerald asked anxiously. "What...what did he say?"

"I don't want to talk about it," said Olivia. "I can't."

Emerald sat at her desk chair, wrapped in a quilt that Darcy had made her. She had been unable to sleep since Olivia's first call. She felt small and hollow and slightly sick to her stomach.

Her mother's voice was clipped, almost brittle. "I thought he loved me. Isn't that a hoot? As if for *once* with a man, I'd finally got it right. How stupid of me. Well, there's no fool like an old fool. I'm sorry if I embarrassed you. Forgive me, won't you?"

Emerald was stricken by the pain she heard beneath Olivia's words. "Mama, there's nothing to forgive. I—I just hope you're better off. I sincerely do."

There was a moment of silence so long that it pressed down on Emerald's body like a killing weight. "Mama?" she said. "Are you all right?"

"I'll be fine," Olivia said stiffly. "Thank you for—for all you've done."

To Emerald's horror, Olivia began to cry uncontrollably. Never before had she known her mother to break down and weep. "Mama!"

"It's all right," Olivia said between sobs. "Later. We'll talk later." She made a little choking sound. She broke down again.

But she managed at last to say, "I love you, honey. Thanks again. Don't worry. I just *sound* sad. I'm glad to know the truth. Here's a kiss."

Emerald heard the kiss, then the *click* of the receiver. She sat, dumbstruck, the receiver still in her hand.

She began to shiver. She tried to pull Darcy's quilt around

her, but it didn't help. Shudders kept tearing through her. *What have I done?* she thought. *What have I done?*

She cowered in the chair, trying not to cry, trying not to shake. The receiver slipped from her hands and fell to the floor. She could only stare at it as if it were a gun she'd used to mortally wound someone.

I can't do this to her, she thought desperately. *I'll fix it somehow.*

But she knew she could not fix it alone. She forced herself to pick up the phone again. With trembling fingers, she called Henry.

CHAPTER SEVENTEEN

WHEN DARCY TRIED to slip from bed, Sloan was still asleep, but his arm tightened reflexively around her. Gently she freed herself. She threw her robe over her shoulders and gazed down at him for a moment.

From between the blinds, the morning's new sunshine streaked the room with slender bars of gold. They fell across Sloan's lean body, making him seem striped like a tiger.

She smiled. Sleeping, he did indeed remind her of a big jungle cat, all the coiled strength lying at lazy, graceful ease. She resisted the desire to stroke him.

She took a long, sensuous shower. She felt happier in her body than she had ever imagined she could. Sloan had taught her that. As she dried her tingling skin with a fluffy towel, she wanted to purr like a big cat herself.

She dressed in fresh jeans and one of her batik shirts, then went into the kitchen. She would make him a big breakfast, Texas style—steak, eggs, biscuits and gravy. There would be cheese grits and strong black coffee.

She wanted to keep busy and not think about his going away. While he was here, she wanted to live entirely in the moment.

She was measuring the ingredients for biscuits, when the phone rang. She pounced on it, not wanting the sound to waken Sloan.

"Darcy, it's Mama," said Olivia.

Darcy stiffened in alarm. Olivia sounded terrible. Her voice was shaky and thick with tears. "Mama, what's wrong?"

"I'm coming home. John and I just broke up. I never want to see that damn man again. I never want to hear his name."

Shock struck Darcy like a fist. The damn man's son was naked and sleeping in her bed. "You broke up?"

"It's *over*," Olivia said emphatically. She made a sound as if blowing her nose. "Well, there's no use crying over spilt milk. I made a fool of myself, but I didn't marry him. Now *that* would have been a disaster."

"But Mama, what happened? You were so in love."

"Love is for idiots," Olivia said. "Only knotheads fall in love. Stay single. If some man comes chasing after you, run like hell. Or be like Rose Alice. Grab a weapon and aim for his head."

"John's gone? Where is he?"

"Probably sitting in the airport waiting to go back to his precious swamp. I don't know, and I don't care."

"I take it," Darcy said dryly, "that you had words."

"Indeed," Olivia said. "We had words and words and words."

"About what?"

"About everything," Olivia said with a melancholy sigh. "It started when Emerald found his picture on the Internet. He and that son of his, acting like a couple of overage playboys."

"Sloan?" Darcy asked in disbelief.

"Yes. Have you checked your e-mail this morning?"

"No." Darcy hesitated. "Why?"

"Because Emerald sent you the same thing. It's this awful site about 'fun bachelors' advertising for women. It's enough to make you wretch."

Darcy frowned. "John English was advertising for women?"

"He denied it. Then he had the gall to accuse Emerald of faking the whole thing. I said, 'You leave *my* family out of this.' One thing led to another. The scales dropped from my eyes, and I saw him as he was. I'm coming home. I don't even want to be on the same ocean as he is."

Darcy took a deep breath and held it nervously. "Mama, do you realize Sloan English is still here? That you invited him?"

"Oh, bugs and rats," Olivia said in disgust. "I forgot."

"We can't ask him to leave," Darcy said. "It would be rude."

"If John has a decent bone in his body—a highly questionable premise—he'll tell Sloan to leave. That man had no business intruding on you in the first place. You should have let Rose Alice whack him."

"Mama, you're upset," Darcy reasoned. "Sloan's a very nice man—"

"He goes to orgies," Olivia said.

"Orgies?" Darcy echoed.

"Go look at the picture."

"What picture?"

"The picture Emerald found with the search train."

"*What?*"

"She sent it to us both. I keep telling myself it could have been worse. It *could* have been—the man could have been an ax murderer."

"Let me get this straight. Emerald found a compromising picture on the Internet—"

"*Compromising* is a polite way of putting it. I prefer *damning.*"

"But John says he doesn't know anything about it—"

"Oh, he was very indignant," Olivia scoffed. "But he was acting. He's been acting all along. And I, like a fool, fell for it."

"He blamed Emerald?"

"He said she's eccentric. He can't insult *my* family."

But she is *eccentric,* Darcy thought rather wildly.

Sloan appeared in the doorway, naked except for a towel knotted around his waist. His hair was tousled, his jaw shadowed by his unshaven beard. He gave her a slow, suggestive smile.

"It's all too gruesome," Olivia said. "I'll tell you when I

get home. No. I won't. I don't ever want to talk about it again.''

Sloan leaned against the door frame, lazily crossing his arms. He studied her face and raised an eyebrow.

Darcy's mind spun like a whirligig. ''But,'' she said to Olivia, ''when will you be here—exactly?''

''As soon as I can. Tonight, if possible. I'll phone and let you know. I have some things to arrange about the condo. Then I'm out of here.''

''The condo,'' Darcy said. ''Will you keep it, after all?''

''No,'' Olivia practically spat. ''*He's* been in it. I'm putting it back on the market. It's been an expensive mistake. But I missed making a worse one by marrying *that man.*''

Darcy winced at the rancor in her tone.

''I'm coming back where I belong,'' said Olivia. ''And I never want to have anything to do with that man again. If anyone even mentions his name, I'll scream.''

But I'm in love with his son, Darcy wanted to cry out. She bit her lip.

''I'll be in touch soon, love,'' Olivia said. ''I have a thousand things to do. And you don't have to tell Emerald he blamed *her.* She knows it's over. She doesn't have to know any more. Oh, I *hate* talking about this.''

''But—''

'''Bye, Duck. I love you.'' Olivia hung up.

Numbly, Darcy put the receiver back in its cradle. She looked across the kitchen at Sloan. ''Our parents had a fight,'' she said. ''They've broken up.''

He came to her, putting his hands on her shoulders. ''A fight? About what?''

Haltingly, she told him the story.

When she was finished, he gripped her shoulders more tightly. His mouth twisted scornfully. ''I never heard of a 'Fun Bachelors' site. I think somebody's pulling a fast one. Let's check your e-mail.''

She nodded reluctantly.

Sloan looked at the screen in disbelief. There he was, and so was his father, smack in the middle of—what? It wasn't an orgy. But it certainly seemed like a hell of a wild party.

"What is this garbage?" he demanded from between his teeth. "What a crock of—"

He glanced at Darcy. She stared at the screen, her pretty face pale. "Oh," she said, shaking her head. "Oh, *no*. Poor Mama."

"Good Lord," Sloan said impatiently, "you can't *believe* this claptrap. My dad couldn't write anything like this. And this picture's a fake, a forgery. I can prove it."

She said nothing, but her dark eyes seemed to beseech him to prove it.

"Dammit," he said, "this is the same picture that's on my dad's real estate page. But it's been doctored. I'll show you."

Angrily he tapped at the keys to bring up John's page. But it was gone—vanished completely. "What the hell," Sloan said. "Where is it? Has somebody *highjacked* it? What's going on?"

She stared at him, disappointment in her expression. It was as if he had failed her, and she feared she could no longer trust him. It gave him a sick feeling in the pit of his stomach.

"I *can* prove it," he insisted. "I carry that same picture in my wallet."

He slapped his hip to claim his wallet, but realized he was still wearing only a towel. He swore. "I have to get my pants. Wait. Don't go anywhere."

"Why would I go anywhere?" she asked defensively. "I live here."

Good point, he thought. He strode to the bedroom, chagrined that he hadn't dressed. He'd wakened full of amorous yearnings and had hoped clothes wouldn't be necessary.

He extracted his wallet from his pocket, then yanked on his jeans. He didn't bother with shirt or shoes. When he went back to the main room, Darcy had brought the incriminating picture back to the screen, and she stood studying it with unhappy fascination.

"Look," he said, flipping open the wallet and riffling through the credit cards and IDs. He showed a photo that was a miniature version of the one on the screen.

Except there was no roistering crowd, no print of lipstick on John's cheek. There were only a dock, boats and the sea. Sloan held a can of cola, not a beer, and instead of a woman, John held a fish.

Darcy looked from the photo to the screen and back again in bewilderment. "Where's the party?"

"It obviously came out of another picture. Somebody grafted my father and me into a different background."

"The blonde?" she asked dubiously.

"There wasn't any blonde. It was a mackerel."

She raised her eyes to his. "Somebody made a composite picture? How?"

Sloan shook his head. "I don't know. Computer graphics or something. They can do anything with that stuff."

Darcy turned back to the screen, her face pale. "But why? Who would do such a thing to your father? And you?"

Sloan didn't answer. Emerald had sent the picture. Emerald claimed to have found it. And Emerald, in all probability, had created it and the lying text that went with it.

"Mama believes it," Darcy murmured, looking more pained than before. "I have to call her and tell her the truth."

"We don't know the whole truth yet," he said. "I want my father's version of this. And there's somebody else we need to talk to."

She was silent for a moment. She swallowed. "You mean Emerald, don't you?"

Sloan rested his hand on the back of her neck. He caressed her as he might caress someone who had been physically hurt and was in need of comfort. "I'm sorry," he said.

BACK AT THE LAKE HOUSE, Sloan found a message on his cell phone.

"Don't try to get in touch with me," John's recorded voice said. "I'm traveling. I suggest that if you're still in Olivia's house, you get out. That woman and I are through. *Kaput.* Finished. Don't even ask about it."

In his father's tone, Sloan heard both the false bravado and the true distress. He swore under his breath and checked his e-mail. There was a second message from John. He was more expansive in print than by phone.

Dear Son—

I'm sitting in an airport in Portland, waiting for a flight back to Florida. I'm a free man again. It was a narrow escape.

Someone libeled me on the Internet. I am the victim of lies, and so, I'm sorry to say, are you. Olivia believes them and won't listen to reason.

If you want a laugh, go to the Web site below. I know who's behind this outrage. It's Olivia's viper of a daughter, that nutcase who thinks she's a knight. I'm going to sue the iron pants off that kid.

Please get out of Olivia's house and remove yourself from the situation entirely. Make an old man happy and don't stir up this matter any more. God knows, enough people have meddled in my affairs, and this is the last goddamn straw.

John closed with the address of the Fun Bachelors Web site and a P.S.

There are federal statutes against what that kid pulled. She's a little terrorist, and she will *not* get away with defaming my character. I've already called my lawyer.

Exasperation seized Sloan. John was a passionate man, and one of the things he was passionate about was his good name.

If he said he meant to prosecute Emerald, he might very well do it.

If he did, Olivia, of course, would never forgive him.

Sloan's head began to ache. His father loved Emerald's mother. He himself was half in love with Emerald's sister. Yet Emerald didn't seem to want anybody loved except herself.

Sloan could understand John's anger. His own fingers itched to close around Emerald's throat, but he tried to fight down the feeling; it only made things worse. Darcy would want to defend her, but what the kid had done was, in truth, indefensible.

Still, mostly for Darcy's sake, he tried to phone his father, to reason with him. Nobody answered.

Sloan sighed and sat down at his computer. He would send his father a written message. He hit the key that let him compose a reply to John, then stared at the empty screen, not knowing what to say.

Suddenly, his cell phone rang; he had forgotten to turn the damn thing off. He picked it up. "Yes?"

"Sloan, it's me," said a quivering feminine voice. "Trina."

Oh, hell, Sloan thought bleakly.

"I got your note," she said. "The one about not interfering with John's decision any more. I think you're right."

Now what's she up to?

She took a breathy little pause. "Sloan, I've been checking around, asking people. A woman at my church has a cousin who lives in Austin, and that cousin knows somebody who actually knows Olivia Ferrar—her housekeeper, Rose Alice. And the cousin says Olivia Ferrar is rich—actually *rich*. That this Rose Alice brags on her. That she has lots of money and five or six houses."

A sickening disgust, cold as death, began to creep through him. "What are you getting at, Trina?"

His aunt made another of her small gasping sounds. "Well, maybe if she's family, she'd be interested in helping Arthur.

I think we should *welcome* her to the family. I'd like her to meet Arthur. Don't you think she should meet Arthur and me?''

Sloan swore to himself. *Would she never change? Never?*

''There's not going to be any marriage,'' he said stonily. ''They broke up. They're through with each other.''

A strange satisfaction filled him as he spoke. He was suddenly glad to be able to tell her this; it would thwart her.

Trina began to cry. ''But Sloan, she was going to be *family*. She was going to be my *sister*. That's what *sister-in-law* means, by law she'd really *be* my sister. You can't let them break up. You've got to do something—''

''I can't do anything,'' he said shortly. ''I have to go. I'll call you when I get to Tulsa.''

He hung up the phone, turned it off and sat at the desk, staring at the vase of wildflowers on the dresser. A sense of hopelessness overtook him in a drowning tide, and he swore again more vehemently.

Nothing in this sorry plight was going to work out. Nothing *could* work out. Both families were poisoned from within as if by venomous snakes. First it had been Trina and her jealousy, then Emerald, and now Trina again.

One of the most powerful reasons he'd left the States so long ago was to escape Trina and her suffocating claims and needs. *Get away, get away, get far away,* all his instincts had warned. He loved his father, but his father had always been in Trina's grasp. The clinging of family, he thought with growing fatalism. What had it ever meant but trouble? When was a man free except when he was alone?

His father's words echoed in his mind…. *Remove yourself from the situation entirely…don't stir up this matter any more. God knows, enough people have meddled…this is the last goddamn straw.*

John was right, it was the last goddamn straw. Things were too broken to be mended; they were too sickly and twisted to be cured.

Sloan shut off the computer. Suddenly all he wanted was

to escape to the deserts of Afghanistan, where he was far from anything resembling tangled emotional bonds.

HENRY HAD SAID THAT EMERALD sounded so distraught he was coming to her right away.

She had told him no. She didn't want him to come until he had put everything back the way it had been before. He could do it, she knew he could. After all—he was Henry.

When his car pulled up in the driveway of her apartment, she nearly went faint with gratitude. She met him at the door, flinging it open and throwing her arms around his neck.

He was so tall that she had to stand on tiptoe to look into his eyes. "Henry," she said, half drunk with joyous hope, "did you fix it?"

Henry swallowed and put his hands on her waist. "Well, um, almost."

Her fledgling hope fell to earth. "What do you mean, 'almost'?"

"Um," Henry said, and swallowed again, "can I come in?"

"Yes, yes." She took him by the hand and drew him inside. She led him to the couch and made him sit down. She sat beside him, still clutching his hand imploringly.

"Tell me," she begged. "Did you take John English's picture off the Bachelors' Web site?"

Henry nodded. "It's gone. For good."

Her heart fluttered again in hope. She knew that in a way it must have hurt Henry to destroy the page he had worked so hard to create. But it was a Frankenstein's monster that never should have been created at all.

She squeezed his hand harder. "And the real estate page? Did you put the old picture back?"

"Yes," Henry said. "It's exactly the way it was."

"Thank heaven," Emerald said. The false picture had been on the Internet fewer than six hours. Perhaps damage could be kept to a minimum. Hope positively flapped its wings.

"And the mail I sent to Darcy," Emerald persisted. "You got it back?"

A muscle twitched in Henry's jaw. "I can't do that, Emerald. Once it's sent, it can't be unsent. I'm sorry."

"Oooh," moaned Emerald, dropping his hand. She put her elbows on her knees and hid her face in her hands. She hadn't wanted Darcy to see the doctored photo, the lying text. It would only compound Emerald's sins, which were already considerable.

Henry touched her shoulder tentatively. "I'm sorry. I thought you'd know that."

"I guess I did," she said in despair. She kept her face covered. "I just hoped that you—that somehow you could do it."

"I couldn't. I'm sorry."

Emerald could not speak. Her throat was choked with regret.

Henry patted her shoulder again. "It wouldn't do any good, anyway. Your mother's already seen it. The real damage has been done."

Don't remind me, Emerald thought. "What am I going to do?" she pleaded. "Mama sounded heartbroken. Maybe I've ruined her one chance at happiness—forever. What if he's really a *good* man?"

She began to whimper. Henry took her into his arms. He held her tightly. "We'll think of something. I promise. Shh. Don't cry. Please."

She clung to him and wept. "Henry? Do you think I'm a bad person?"

"No. I'd never think that."

"I didn't mean to harm Mama. I only wanted to help her."

"Nobody knows that better than I do," he said against her hair.

"I lied. And maybe did a terrible wrong. An unforgivable wrong."

"I know how that feels, too."

She nestled against him, feeling grateful that there was one person in the world who understood and would give her comfort. For a long time they held each other in silence.

"Emerald?" he said at last.

"What?" she said.

"You're wearing a nightgown."

What difference does that make? she thought. She burrowed more deeply against his shoulder. "So?"

"I guess I thought you slept in armor, or something," he said, yearning in his voice.

"I should sleep in sackcloth and ashes. I should mortify my flesh. I should do penance for a thousand years."

"Emerald, I—" he said.

The phone rang, and Emerald's body snapped to terrified attention. Her arms tightened around Henry's neck.

"Emerald, I—" he began again.

Again the phone rang. It sounded like the crack of doom. *Trouble,* she thought fatalistically. *I set it in motion, and now it's come back on me like a curse.*

"Emerald, I—" he tried for the third time.

For the third time, the shrill of the telephone interrupted him. Emerald drew away from him. "I've got to face the music," she said.

Feeling like a woman going to her own execution, she rose and went to the phone.

"Hello," Emerald answered in a wary voice.

"EMERALD, I'M GLAD you're home." Darcy frowned, concentrating on what she must say. "There's a little matter we need to discuss."

"Oh?" said Emerald, clearly feigning innocence.

"I know you talked to Mama. She told me so. She's very upset."

"Um," said Emerald. "Well…"

"You sent us both that picture from the Fun Bachelors' site. That picture of John and Sloan English."

"Oh," Emerald said. "That."

"Yes, *that.*" Darcy put her hand on her hip. "Emerald,

that photo's a *fake*. Don't argue with me. I've seen the real one. Sloan carries a copy in his wallet.''

Emerald's only answer was silence, but Darcy felt the guilt pulsing through it in thick, fast waves. She pressed harder. "Em? Did you hear me? The picture's a forgery. Sloan says the whole page was a forgery. That his father would never say such things.''

"Oh," Emerald said in a strange little voice. "Well, it's the Internet. Glitches happen. If you looked for that photo now, it's probably gone. Just a little mistake.''

Darcy drew a deep breath for patience. "It was more than a little mistake. John English's real Web page disappeared. Somebody took it.''

"Sometimes it's like the Internet sort of burps," Emerald said. "Or hiccoughs. I'll bet that site's back now. No harm done.''

Darcy blinked in resentful anger. "Give me a straight answer. You stole that page, and faked the other one—didn't you? Don't you *dare* lie.''

"I just wanted Mama to slow down," Emerald said in a high, wavering voice. "I wanted her to stop and think, that's all. You, too. I mean, what do we really *know* about these men?''

Sick anger swarmed through Darcy. "So since you didn't know anything, you *made it up?* Good grief, Emerald! Mama loved this man, and you slandered him—that's *criminal.*''

"I was afraid *he* might be criminal. I was only trying to protect Mama—and you.''

"When I need your protection, I'll ask for it," Darcy retorted. "And I told you, *I* was checking out John English. Well, I've got word from a professional investigator. There are no skeletons in John's closet—not one.''

And that, Darcy thought joylessly, was the most darkly ironic thing of all. The complete report had just come from InfoTruth; it had been in the same batch of new mail as Emerald's lying message.

John English's past was spotless; his record was clean.

There was no reason to doubt his motives or mistrust his feelings for Olivia. Emerald had harbored uncharitable suspicions about him, and so had Darcy.

The man was innocent. They had both wronged him.

CHAPTER EIGHTEEN

SLOAN CAME BACK to the guest house; he looked as grim as Darcy felt.

At first neither of them spoke. She could tell by his face he was troubled, and she truly dreaded telling him the truth about Emerald.

She went to the counter and busied herself with pouring a cup of coffee. She pushed it toward him and forced herself to try to sound calm. "My sister confessed. She did it."

She kept her head down, but sensed that Sloan moved close beside her. He settled his hand on her shoulder, the classic gesture of a man about to deliver bad news. "My father's threatening to take her to court."

"To court?" Darcy wheeled to face him, her eyes widening. "He wouldn't do that—would he?"

"She hurt him. He wants to strike back. It's human nature."

"But Mama would never forgive him. They'd *never* get back together."

He let his hand fall away. "Maybe they won't. Things may be broken beyond fixing."

"But they can't be. They just *can't.*"

She looked at him imploringly, but his face stayed hard as granite. "A great deal of damage has been done," he said. "It can't be undone."

"But it's only a misunderstanding. It's—"

"No," he said. "It's more than a misunderstanding. It's malice. What your sister did was malicious."

"No. No, not really. If they know the truth—"

"The truth won't set them free. It'll only make things worse."

She didn't understand what he meant. She raised her eyebrows questioningly.

He said, "People say Romeo and Juliet were star-crossed, but they were under a more powerful curse than stars—family."

He uttered the word *family* with such bitterness that she winced.

"Darcy, face it," he said. "Family has a hold over both of them. Trina and Emerald are important forces in their lives. They've both interfered beyond toleration. This relationship can't stand up under the strain."

"But Emerald knows she's wrong. Her motive wasn't really vicious."

"Of course not. Her intentions were actually good. Which means nothing except they've been great for paving the road to hell."

"B-but she's put everything back the way it was," Darcy stammered. "There's no trace that she changed anything. I checked—it's true. You can look yourself."

She threw a hand out, gesturing toward the desk. He glanced dismissively at the computer and shook his head.

"Everything's back to normal," she pleaded.

"No. My father's not back to normal. He's been libeled and made to look like a fool. She tampered with his business, his livelihood."

Darcy struggled to downplay his charges. "She didn't mean to do anything to his business—"

"He's a real estate agent. She erased his ad. She put up a page that could damage his credibility with his employers and with potential customers."

"I'm sure she didn't think of that when—"

"Dammit, she didn't think at all," Sloan said in disgust. "And what about our parents' relationship? Can she put *that* back the way it was?"

"Maybe if she tells them exactly what she told me and—and she apologizes—"

"Apologizes?" he scoffed. "Does she think she can smooth everything over just by saying 'I'm sorry'?"

"It's a start. Then they could—they could—"

"Face it. Emerald got what she wanted. She broke them up. Who knows? Maybe it's for the best."

"That they break up?" Darcy asked in disbelief.

He shrugged. "Maybe it wasn't meant to last. Better that they split now than after they marry. Their whole affair's been pretty headlong."

So has ours, thought Darcy, her heart suddenly pinching.

But Olivia and John's affair was different; they had made serious commitments to each other, and Darcy could not remember Olivia seeming happier. She said, "Our parents could patch things up. What we have to do is—"

"For God's sake," he said with a burst of impatience, "don't meddle with them. People have meddled enough."

His sudden passion, verging on anger, surprised her. "But—"

He pressed his forefinger against her lips, and his voice was full of warning. "No. Emerald should tell your mother the truth. After that, let her and Dad work it out for themselves. Promise me. *Promise.*"

She could not promise, so she said nothing. She turned her face away to escape his touch.

His voice became more kindly, although gruffness still edged it. "Look. I've always had my doubts about their relationship. So have you. So has everybody else."

His words, simple as they were, made yet another chasm of trouble yawn before her. She glanced at him warily.

"Admit it," he said. "You do, don't you? Have doubts?"

"I—I *did.*" Her throat went tight. "I had serious doubts. I didn't trust him. But not anymore. I know your father's a good man. I believe in him. And I believe my mother should give him another chance."

Sloan gave her a strange look. His eyes seemed to grow

greener, more feline. "You *know* my father's a good man? You didn't trust him before, but now you've had a change of heart? Why?"

She took a deep breath. She had hesitated on the brink of truth long enough. With a dizzy feeling, she stepped into whatever its abyss held.

"I had him investigated," she said. "I wanted to be sure about him, for my mother's sake."

Sloan's face went blank. For a long moment, he said nothing.

"The complete report came just this morning," she said nervously. She began to fiddle with the coffeepot again so that she wouldn't have to look at him. "I— Perhaps I shouldn't have done it. But I had to know. And I realized I had to tell you."

She raised her eyes and saw that his expression was still unreadable. He said, "You had him investigated? That's— very ironic."

"Ironic?" she echoed. "Why?"

"Because I did the same thing with your mother."

"You hired an investigator? When?"

"As soon as my fever broke, my head cleared, and the hospital set me free."

"You mean you did it after you got *here?*"

"I should have done it before I ever came. If I'd been in my right mind I would have. I should have done it *instead* of coming here."

She was both stunned and hurt. "The whole time you were making love to me, you were having my mother *investigated?*"

He frowned. "You were doing the same."

"But that's different," she countered. "You were her guest, living in her house, eating her food—and you put *detectives* on her?"

He gave a mirthless laugh. "I wanted to know the truth. Same as you."

"But you can look around you and see the truth," Darcy

answered with rising indignation. "She's no gold digger. And she's been extraordinarily generous—"

"Things aren't always what they seem. You know that. So do I."

A sudden coolness swept through her blood. "No. They aren't, are they? So tell me—did my mother pass muster? Did she meet your rigorous standards?"

"Absolutely. And then some."

"I'm so glad," she said, turning from him in resentment. "Now your father can know that he's walked out on the best."

He came behind her and gripped her shoulders. "Don't be a hypocrite, Darcy. It's not your style."

The cold that had settled over her was suddenly laced with heat. She rebelled against it, stiffening herself against his touch. She said, "Neither of us told the whole truth. It seems we're both hypocrites, aren't we?"

"No. We're the cautious ones. Our parents seemed to throw caution to the wind. We had reason to ask questions."

"But it made liars out of us," she said. "And I don't think we've been so cautious, either. We rushed into something as crazily as our parents did."

"Yes," he said. "We did. Do you regret it?"

She ducked her head. "I don't know. It didn't seem wrong. And yet—it doesn't seem right, either."

He brought his mouth close to her ear. "Once you said it did. Now you've changed your mind. Why?"

"We had to hide it from the people we loved most."

His hands tensed on her, went deadly still. "You mean family?"

"Yes," she said. "Family."

She sensed him draw back from her, and knew instinctively that he was pulling back in psychological distance, as well. He said, "And you don't suppose now is the time to tell them what's happened between us."

She closed her eyes. "No. I don't suppose it is."

"Which means we go on hiding it?" he asked.

"Why make a complex situation even more complex?" she asked miserably. "Besides, you're going away soon. It's not as if this is something...permanent. Something they have to accept for the rest of their lives. They never have to know it happened at all."

"More lies, Darcy?" he asked softly.

"No. Not lies. Just discretion." A sense of inevitability flooded over her. "We were consenting adults. What we did in private was nobody's concern. We had a lovely time, but it became too...awkward."

His fingers tightened on her almost painfully. "You're talking in the past tense."

She shrugged. "I guess I am."

He sighed harshly. "I never should have come here."

She felt stung. But she said, "No. It was a mistake."

He kissed her neck. "But I'm glad I did. How much poorer my life would have been if I hadn't had this time with you. I'll always cherish it. Really. I will."

She sucked her breath in between gritted teeth. "That's very sweet. It truly is. And it sounds like an exit line."

He was silent for a moment. But she felt volumes of conversation, unspoken, passing between them. There were a hundred reasons why their affair was not meant to last. They both knew all of them by heart.

She smiled sadly. "It probably would be easier if you left now. My mother's coming soon and—well, you know."

"I know. I'm the last person she'll want to see. It would be strained. You're right. I should go. But I'll be in touch."

No, you won't. All this family business between us has gotten too messy. You're a man who doesn't like entanglements.

She said, "Right. Drop me an e-mail sometime."

"I'll do that."

"Let me know the doctor's report." She paused. "I hope you get to go to Afghanistan."

"Thank you."

He gave her a lingering kiss on the side of the throat. She

almost melted and turned to him, wanting him more than she wanted her pride. But she didn't weaken.

"*Arrivederci*, Darcy," he breathed.

She said nothing. She let him go.

EMERALD NEARED THE LAKE HOUSE just in time to see Sloan English hurl his overnight bag into the back seat of his BMW, then wrench open the door on the driver's side.

When he saw her car, his face clouded with an anger so intense it seemed thunderous. Every line of his body was taut with displeasure, and she knew she was the cause.

He gave her a bitter smile and raised his hand in a curt greeting that was more contemptuous than any words he might have said.

Then he got in the car, gunned the engine and drove off with a grinding of wheels and a cloud of gravel dust. Emerald's heart rattled fearfully in her chest, but at the same time she felt as if a great weight had been lifted from her.

It was cowardly, she knew, but his leaving almost dizzied her with gladness. His anger scared her. Unlike Darcy's or her mother's displeasure, his was untempered by love.

It was going to be hard enough to face Darcy. She didn't even want to think about her mother.

Henry had wanted to come with her, to "protect" her, he said. Emerald had forbidden it. He might look like a man, but he was only a child, and she would not let a mere boy shield her.

Besides, how could Henry protect her when she felt it her duty to protect *him*? They had committed a crime, but Henry would not be involved if it hadn't been for her. On his own, he would not have lifted a finger against John English.

She was older, she had unfair power over him, and she had used him shamelessly, dragging him into a dirty mess that could ruin his reputation if the truth came out. It must never be known. The blame was hers, and she must face it.

She hadn't told this to Henry, of course. She had dismissed

his offer of help as if it were an insult to her. She had told him she didn't want him along; he would only be a nuisance.

But she never felt as alone in her life as when she approached the door of the guest house. Her knees felt as insubstantial as bubbles beneath her, and she was slightly sick to her stomach. She set her jaw, raised her hand and knocked.

The door swung open almost immediately. Darcy's eyes glistened strangely, as if she'd been crying, and her cheeks were flushed dark pink. "Well, well," she said in a scornful voice. "Look who's here. The spirit of chivalry."

Emerald cringed. She had exhibited none of the knightly virtues lately.

The least she could do was pretend to be brave in the face of punishment.

She raised her chin and said, "I saw Sloan English leaving. He threw a suitcase in the car. Is he gone for good?"

"You'll be delighted to hear that the answer is *yes*," Darcy said icily. "But don't congratulate yourself too much. He was going on his way anyhow. You just speeded the process."

Darcy stood tall and she acted proud, but she was obviously hurt, and Emerald knew it was her fault. "I'm sorry," she said.

"Practice that phrase," said Darcy. "You're going to be using it a lot."

She opened the door wider. "Come in," she said, but there was scorn in the invitation. "I want you to see the report on John English. He's about as villainous as a teddy bear."

Emerald stepped inside like a prisoner first setting foot into her cell on Death Row. Darcy led her to the computer. "Sit," she said. "Make yourself comfortable. Would you like something to drink while you read? Coffee? Tea? Truth serum?"

Strychnine, Emerald thought fatalistically. But she shook her head and sat down before the screen. She had willfully and heedlessly done wrong. It was time to start paying the price.

EMERALD HAD A REVELATION. It is easy to act recklessly when you are puffed up with righteousness. When you believe all truth and goodness are on your side, it is simple to commit evil. But it is indeed bitter to admit you have been a fool and that you have hurt innocent people, including those you love most deeply.

Tears blurred her vision. She turned from the screen, trying to scrub them away, but new ones rose to take their place.

"Well?" Darcy demanded, her voice hard.

"He seems like a—a nice man," Emerald said, her voice choked. "How was I to know?"

"For starters, you might have checked," Darcy retorted sarcastically.

Emerald held her head up, but her chin quivered. "This whole thing about the séances sounds suspicious, though. You've *got* to admit that. I mean, séances? Talking to dead people?"

"You could have checked that, too." Darcy crossed her arms tightly. "He didn't plan to hold real séances. Just put on a performance. Ghost tours and séance shows are done in lots of places with colorful pasts—New Orleans, Salem, Charleston—even Honolulu. It's a business, Emerald. Not a scam, just entertainment. A legitimate business."

"But how was I to *know?*" Emerald repeated piteously.

"Next time, try asking," Darcy said with acid. "As a knight you're not exactly Sir Parsival the Saintly. You're more like Don Quixote, tilting at windmills because you imagine they're giants. Except windmills don't have feelings. And Mama and John English do."

Emerald stifled a sob. "We'll just tell her the truth. We'll fix it."

"What if it can't be fixed? They're not even speaking."

The import of these words tolled in Emerald's mind: *Mama's miserable because of me. Mama's lost the love of her life because of me. An innocent man has been libeled and betrayed because of me.*

The guilt was too much to bear, and her thoughts scrambled madly to escape it. "We'll make them speak to each other," she said desperately. "Call Mama and tell her I've run away from home. Call John English and tell him Mama's distraught that I'm gone, and only he can comfort her. Then when they're together again, I'll reappear and apologize, and everything will be fine again—"

"Stop it—just stop it!" Darcy's expression was one of absolute disgust. "Won't you ever learn? No more lies."

Emerald's mind darted in another direction. "All right, then we tell the truth. We were both worried about this man. I thought the worst and acted to save her. You were more…scientific. You had him investigated. Your investigation proves my fears were unfounded. It also shows Mama that he's a perfectly nice man. There's just been a little mix-up, that's all."

Darcy threw her arms out in exasperation. "You just don't get it, do you? This has stopped being about the stupid lies you told. Now it's about *you*. John English is talking about taking you to court."

Emerald felt dizzy. She imagined herself in court, wearing chains. She imagined herself imprisoned in a dark, damp cell in a tower, with only rats and spiders for companions.

"He—he wouldn't do that," she said. "I'll apologize."

"This may be a long way past apologies."

"I'll grovel. I'll flail myself. I'll eat dirt."

"Stop being dramatic. You vandalized this man's Web site and tried to make him an object of ridicule. You libeled him and alienated Mama's affection. He could throw the book at you. And frankly, he has every right."

Emerald's thoughts went into panicky overdrive. She had done all these things that were, indeed, punishable by law. She thought of poor Henry—he had helped her commit these acts, and yet she could not shift even a fraction of the blame to him. Like John English, he was her victim.

"Then he'll take me to court," she said in bleak resignation. "If I plead guilty, do you think he'd make up with Mama?"

"Oh, *Em*." Darcy looked as if she were about to cry.

"Don't you see? If you go through that, Mama will never make up with *him*. It's an impasse. Either he forgives you for the unforgivable, or Mama can't forgive him. It's a vicious circle."

And I'm at the center of it, thought Emerald hopelessly.

She looked away from Darcy, no longer able to face her. Darcy had made no more mention of her own romance, but Emerald knew she had brought that tumbling down in ruin, too.

Darcy's phone rang, but Emerald was so perplexed she hardly noticed. It barely registered on her consciousness when her sister swore under her breath and marched over to snatch up the receiver.

The outside world had ceased to impress itself on Emerald's mind. She was aware only of a growing sense of doom. *There's no way to fix this,* she thought in despair. *And nobody on earth who can put it right.*

Emerald did not listen to Darcy's end of the conversation. All she heard was the roiling of her own guilty thoughts.

But when Darcy hung up, her face was pale. She was so pale that the fact struck even through Emerald's obsession with her own plight. She wondered if her sister was going to faint.

"Who was that?" Emerald asked. She had a brief, mad hope that it had been the president, granting her a pardon.

Darcy's mouth gave a strange twitch. It might have been a failed smile, or it might have been the kind of quiver that was prelude to a sob.

"It was Sloan English," she said. "He wants to come here tonight to see you."

Emerald looked at her blankly.

"His father will be with him," Darcy said. "They both want to talk to you."

OLIVIA'S FLIGHT WAS A MAD, jerry-rigged, seemingly illogical affair, a wild hopscotching from one airport to the next. It was because of weather. Torrents of spring rain kept her marooned in Chicago for hours. A tornado watch kept her stranded in Dallas for still more hours.

The flight was delayed so long that she called Darcy and told her not to wait up for her. "It'll be after midnight. I'll take a cab to the house in town," she said. "It'll be easier on all of us."

Oddly, Darcy didn't try to change her mind.

Olivia was relieved. She was far too tired and disheartened to face talking to her daughters. In the morning, perhaps, she would have the strength to put on at least a show of resilience and a false air of *toujours gai*.

Although she had sorely missed her girls in Maine, the process of getting back to them was so wearying, she needed to be alone. This was ironic, and she was tired of ironies. She wanted only to rest.

When she got off the plane in Austin, she expected no one to meet her and was glad of it. She was surprised when a tall man in his mid-thirties made his way purposefully toward her. He was a lean, handsome man with dark hair and eyes as green as a cat's.

Just as he touched her arm, recognition shot through her. *Sloan. Sloan English. John's son. But what is he doing here?*

"Mrs. Ferrar?" The timbre of his baritone voice gave her another jolt. It was so like John's voice, it might have been John speaking to her.

Her eyes widened, and her lips parted, but no words came to her. She was too stunned.

"I'm Sloan English," he said. "I know you weren't expecting anyone to pick you up. I know you're tired. But I was in town, and I came for you. To take you home if you'll let me. And to give you a message."

Olivia blinked in confusion. Adrenaline had turned her fatigue to sheer alertness. "A message?" she demanded. "From Darcy? Is something wrong? What message?"

"It's not from Darcy, ma'am," he said. "It's from my father. He's here. He'd like to see you."

So many emotions cascaded through her that she could not

identify them. Beneath them all was a current of alarm, a fear of feeling still more hurt and disappointed if she dared to hope.

"John?" she said warily. "What's he doing here? What's he want?"

"It takes some explaining," said Sloan. "But it started with an e-mail he got. He was halfway back to Florida, on a layover in Atlanta, when he got it."

Olivia could only stare at him. "An e-mail?"

"Yes, ma'am," he said. "From someone named Henry."

DARCY'S TELEPHONE RANG. Emerald, sitting on the couch, winced as if someone had pinched her, very hard. She looked at Darcy with fearful eyes.

It was late; they both had been nervously waiting, and they both knew that the ringing phone meant matters were about to come to a head.

It rang again.

Darcy rose to answer it, anxiety swimming through her system like an electric charge. *Now,* she thought. *Whatever is going to happen will happen now.*

"Hello?" she said, her throat raw.

"Darcy? It's Sloan. Your mother's here. We're coming there, if it's still all right. You're sure it's not too late?"

She swallowed. "No. It's not too late." *Let's get it over with,* she thought. *I won't be able to rest until it's done.*

Neither would Emerald, obviously. She looked as dismal as if she were about to be led to the executioner's block.

"Mama—my mother—" she said. "She agreed to talk to him?"

"They're talking right now. Over in the gate area. I'm on a pay phone. Just to give them some privacy."

"They didn't clash?"

"Let's just say they were happy to see each other," Sloan said dryly.

Darcy gave a weak sigh of relief. "That's good. Isn't it?"

"We'll see," he said, his voice even more sardonic. "For

a man who wasn't going to meddle, I seem to have gotten back into the thick of it."

"Soon you'll be out of it again," she said.

"Good old peaceful Afghanistan," he said. "Grenades, rebels, tanks, fanatics. Droughts, locusts and drug runners. But no Emerald."

She grimaced slightly. She could gleefully throttle Emerald herself, but it still hurt to hear someone else condemn her.

He said, "I should warn you. Someone else will be coming. Besides your mother and my father and me."

"Someone else?" she asked automatically. She was too nervous for real puzzlement to register. "Who?"

"It's better that I don't say. And don't warn Emerald. Don't tell her anything except we're on our way."

"All right," she agreed. But suddenly she didn't want him to hang up. This would probably be her last private link to him tonight. Perhaps for much, much longer.

"Sloan, Dr. Nightwine— What did she tell you? Did she give you a clean bill of health?"

"Pretty much," he said.

"What does that mean? Is she worried about anything?"

"Not really. She said I'll have these relapses from time to time. I just need to catch them in time. I knew that before. It's no big deal."

It's no big deal, she thought in alarm. *You might have died, but it's no big deal.* But he wasn't a man who tolerated alarm. "You just need to be…vigilant, then?"

"That's about it. Here come the parental units. We'll see you soon."

She heard the *click* of his hanging up. Slowly she put the receiver of her own phone back in place. She turned to Emerald. "They're on their way," she said. "And you're lucky. They're talking again."

"They're talking about what they're going to do to me. It probably involves b-b-b-boiling oil." Emerald began to sob again.

"You should get off so easy," she said. But in the end she

went to her sister, sat beside her, and put her arm around her. "There, there," she said gruffly.

"Maybe Mama and John English will get back together," Emerald wailed against her shoulder. "But what about you and Sloan? I came between you, too. Didn't I?"

Darcy held her more tightly. "It's all right. He and I—it was never meant to be. It was going to end, anyway."

Emerald would not be consoled. "You're just saying that," she said and wept.

No, Darcy thought in grief and resignation. *It's true.*

CHAPTER NINETEEN

A CAR, ITS HEADLIGHTS OFF, waited at the end of the drive of the lake house. It was a black vintage MG, just as the kid had described.

Sloan stopped and rolled down the window. "Are you Henry?"

"Yessir," said the kid. He had a surprisingly deep voice. In the darkness, Sloan could see nothing of his face but a pale, shadowy blur.

"Okay," Sloan said. "Follow us."

"Yessir."

The MG's lights flicked on, its motor started. Sloan headed down the long, twisting road that led to Darcy. In his rearview mirror, he saw the MG creeping behind him. He could also see his own back seat, where his father was kissing Olivia Ferrar's neck. It gave him an odd, surreal feeling.

This morning he had left Darcy, thinking it would be wisest never to come back, never to travel this road again. Now, less than twelve hours later, he was on it again, going back to her.

No, not back to her. They would not be alone; they would pretend they had never been lovers; they, who were not made for hypocrisy, would play out another hypocritical charade.

In the meantime, in the back seat was the woman who was probably going to be his stepmother, and his father was seriously nuzzling her. Trailing them, like a duckling following his elders, was the mysterious kid named Henry. Sloan still wasn't sure how in hell Henry fit into the picture.

The two houses came into view, the large one and the small. As Sloan pulled up between them, his heartbeat took a series of tricky skips. He was glad Dr. Nightwine's stethoscope wasn't pressed to his chest.

He got out of the car, and helped out Olivia Ferrar.

The kid parked and got out, too. He came and solemnly introduced himself. "I'm Henry Weaver," he said. "Thank you for letting me come. I—I'll try to explain more once we're inside."

Olivia drew herself up and gave him a cool look. "There's a lot to explain, young man."

"There, there," John said, putting his arm around her. "All's well that ends well."

"It hasn't ended yet," Olivia said tartly.

Darcy swung the door open, and a beam of golden light fell across the darkness. "Mama!" she cried. She ran to Olivia and threw herself into her mother's arms. They hugged each other hard and kissed cheeks. For some reason, this display of pure affection gave Sloan another episode of skittish heartbeats.

Then Olivia was introducing John to Darcy, and John was being charming, and Henry was hovering at the edge of the group like a nervous wraith.

But Sloan's consciousness was riveted on Darcy. She was wearing the yellow dress.

"Hello," she said to him, almost shyly.

"Hi," he said. *Congratulations, you eloquent SOB,* he told himself.

Somehow they all made it inside. Sitting in the center of the couch, looking wan and frightened, was Emerald.

When she saw Olivia, tears sprang into her eyes, her shoulders hunched, and she bowed her head in shame. She reminded Sloan of a dog waiting to be beaten. He felt almost sorry for her.

Olivia went to Emerald, took her chin in her hand, and raised her tearful face. She kissed her on the cheek. "Hello, Em," she said. She nodded toward John. "This is my friend John. I understand you have something to say to us."

Emerald met John's eyes and immediately burst into tears. "I'm sorry, I'm so *sorry-y-y*..." she wailed.

Oh, lord, Sloan thought unhappily, *now she's going to be hysterical.*

But somehow Emerald pulled herself together. She looked at John again. "I—I did a t-terrible thing to you," she said. "Can you forgive me?"

John gave her a long, level gaze. "If I don't, I lose the woman I love. And that would make me a damn fool, wouldn't it?"

Sloan almost smiled. Forgiveness as a tool of survival and enlightened self-interest; he'd never quite thought of it that way.

"I've died a thousand deaths since I did it," Emerald said wretchedly.

"I've died a few myself," said John. "None of them easy."

"I tried to excuse myself by saying I did it because I loved Mama," Emerald sniffled. "But there's no excuse. Love shouldn't be...devious."

"Indeed," said John. "It shouldn't."

"It shouldn't be self-righteous and high-handed." She clutched a tissue and wiped at her nose.

"No," John said. "I found that out the hard way."

"It shouldn't be possessive," Emerald said, looking up to Olivia.

Olivia smoothed the girl's short hair. "No," she said softly. "It shouldn't."

"We were lucky, young lady," John said gruffly. "*You* were lucky. You have a loyal friend."

Emerald tried to blink back her tears. She looked puzzled, almost dazed.

John gripped Henry by the elbow and pushed him forward. "This young man had the courage to e-mail me and tell me the truth of what happened. Or most of the truth. I was sitting in the airport in Atlanta, checking my e-mail out of boredom and despair. What he wrote hit me like a thunderbolt. He's the reason I'm here.''

Emerald stared at Henry as if she had never before seen him. He was a tall, handsome boy, Sloan saw, with very blue eyes and slight scarring on the skin over his cheekbones. But Emerald hadn't even noticed him until now.

Henry looked crestfallen, even wounded unto death. Sloan thought, *You poor shmuck. You're in love with her, aren't you? And she didn't even notice you were here.*

"Henry," Emerald said in a bewildered voice. "Why are you here? I told you I didn't want you to come."

"I had to come," he said, and swallowed. "To apologize to everyone. Especially you."

"Henry, go *away*," she ordered, fresh tears springing to her eyes. "You'll just get in *trouble*."

"Let him speak," said Olivia, her hand on Emerald's shoulder. "If he's in trouble, I'm afraid you got him there."

"No, ma'am," Henry said humbly. "I got myself there."

He took a step forward so that he stood directly before Emerald. He said, "Emerald, I let you do things that weren't right. I knew they weren't right, but I didn't stop you. Instead, I helped you do them, every step of the way. That was cowardly of me. Because of it, people got hurt. And *you* got hurt. I'll regret the pain I caused everyone—especially you—for the rest of my life."

Emerald stared at him with parted lips, her face disbelieving and pale.

Henry, in contrast, looked self-conscious, his cheeks flushed bright red. He turned to the others.

"She couldn't have done what she did to you without me," he said. "Alone, she couldn't have done any of it. I'm responsible. Me. I was willing to commit any kind of wrong, and I committed it."

He paused, and his expression grew more pained. "I thought maybe I could make her love me." He gazed down sadly at Emerald. "But she's right. Love's no excuse for doing wrong. The truth is, I didn't really act out of love. Love should have made me stop her. I acted out of...selfishness. Because I wanted her. I sacrificed my honor out of that self-ishness. But what's worse is that I sacrificed hers.''

He cleared his throat and looked about the room uneasily. ''I've wronged her and her family and their loved ones. I apologize to you all and hope someday you can forgive me.''

He paused and stared at Emerald again. ''But I apologize to you the most. I had a second chance to be your knight. But I failed you again. I'm—sorry.''

Tears glistened in his eyes. ''I'm sorry,'' he repeated. ''So sorry. I'll go now. Emerald, I would give you—give you the living heart out of my body if it could make up for my letting this happen to you. Don't ever blame yourself. You're a good person. Nobody knows that better than I do.''

He turned and, with a strange, lonely dignity, walked out the door.

No one in the room spoke.

Sloan's eyes met Darcy's. He looked at her, and it was as if his heart stumbled and rolled down a long hill and got lost in some place completely new and unexpected. He could not stop staring at her because he thought, *I'll be damned. I love you, don't I? Is it that simple? Has it been that simple all along?*

''My goodness, Emerald,'' Olivia said, putting her hand to her chest. ''How long have you been friends with *that* young man?''

''He means it,'' Emerald said in a rattling, breathless voice. ''He *means* it. He really would give me the living heart out of his body—he's already given away one kidney.''

John and Olivia exchanged puzzled looks.

''Henry!'' cried Emerald. ''Don't go! Henry!'' She bounded from the couch and raced after him into the night. ''Henry! Henry!'' The door slammed shut behind her.

''My God,'' said John, staring after her. ''Should you go after her?''

''I think not,'' said Olivia. ''I think she's about to have a significant moment.''

"He's sort of…extraordinary," said Darcy, staring at the shut door.

What does he see in Emerald? Sloan wondered. But then he thought of what the boy had said, and he knew. When Henry looked at Emerald, what he saw was his chosen destiny.

Sloan gazed at Darcy and saw his own.

He had escaped his everlasting running from Trina and the past. It was like being freed from an evil spell. He realized he could have a life that wasn't predicated on never getting strongly attached to another human being. It stunned him, yet he felt both liberated and at peace.

"I could use a drink," said John.

"I believe I could use one myself," said Olivia. She headed toward the liquor cabinet. She set out four sherry glasses and began to pour. John hovered near, trying to help.

Sloan tried to give a shrug that seemed casual. "What do you think?" he asked Darcy. "The kid and Emerald. Does he get to be her knight in shining armor? Or not?"

Her mouth curved in the gentlest of smiles. "I think he's definitely knight material. Absolutely."

Olivia handed Sloan a glass of sherry, and John gave one to Darcy.

"To your mother," he said, raising his drink. "Thank God, we came to our senses."

"We're going to have a longer courtship," said Olivia. "A little less mad and impulsive this time. I'm taking a trip to Key West." She lifted her own glass. "To John. And the sacred virtue of forgiveness."

The two touched glasses and drank. But then Olivia looked at Sloan in mock disapproval. "What? You won't drink to our future?"

Sloan's own future suddenly seemed a thing of certainties reversed and expectations turned on their heads. But he said, "Of course. To your future." He raised his glass to touch theirs.

Darcy hesitated only a second to join in. "And to yours," she said to him brightly. "In Afghanistan."

He looked at her across the rim of his glass. My God, but she was beautiful. She was brave and bright and funny and sweet and beautiful.

"I'm going to have to rethink Afghanistan," he said.

"Really?" she said dubiously.

"Really," he said.

"I'll drink to that," she said.

IT WAS SPRING AGAIN, and the Texas Hill Country was in bloom. Wild roses clambered up the fences, violets blossomed along the creeks, and the bluebonnets blanketed the fields so thickly, it was as if they were turning the earth into a second sky.

The Hill Country was celebrating spring, and at its heart, the city of Austin celebrated, too. It was the time of the yearly Old Pecan Street festival.

Olivia would go to the festival later. Now she sat at her little mahogany desk, trying to write. It would be one of the last times she would use this little office, she thought with nostalgia. Out in the yard stood the sign that said Sold. She and John had a house in Key West now, and were buying a condo in Austin for when they returned to visit.

Both girls would soon be living far from Texas. Their lives were elsewhere, and they knew hers was, too, and there was no real reason to regret the sale of the house. Emerald had gone to Stanford to be with Henry. Darcy and Sloan would be going to Belgium after they were married. He had opted for a less strenuous job in a less exotic climate, a less dangerous place. He wanted, he said, a safe place to raise a family.

Olivia was grateful and knew that Darcy was, too. John, too, was relieved, although he didn't like talking about it. "I think a man gets to cheat death just so many times," he'd admittted once. "Sloan was pushing his luck. He'd had enough travel for a dozen men. It's time to settle down."

Now John sat on the velvet settee in the office, practicing a complicated card trick. Olivia nibbled her pen thoughtfully, then laid it down and turned to him.

"Darling, how do we say this? 'Darcy Ann Parker of Austin and Sloan J. English of Tulsa, Oklahoma, plan to marry at 2 p.m., June 17, at the Umlauf Sculpture Gardens.

"'The bride is the daughter of John and Olivia English of Key West, Florida. The groom is the son of John and Olivia English of Key West, Florida—' John, it just doesn't *sound* right, does it?"

"My love, you're correct. It gives the wrong impression."

"Well, what should I do?" she asked.

"Leave out his parentage," John said.

"But I'm sure it's supposed to go *in*," Olivia argued.

"Say he was found in the hills and suckled by wolves," suggested John.

"That also gives a wrong impression," said Olivia. "You're no help at all. And are you sure we have to invite Trina?"

"Unfortunately, yes," he said. "She loves weddings."

"Yes," Olivia observed. "They give her an excuse to cry all she wants."

"She hasn't cried much since I sold the land. She's set for life now. Even she has to admit it."

John had put half his money in trust for his sister and nephew, and it should easily provide for their needs, even if Arthur lived to the age of a hundred and thirty. John had used the other half of the real estate money to buy their home in Key West and pay off his debts. He was well-pleased with how his investment had turned out.

"I knew that land would pay off someday," he said.

"It was perfectly lovely land," Olivia said. "I'm surprised it didn't sell sooner. It really wasn't so very swampy."

"Absolutely. It was only swampy here and there. Drat, where'd that ace go? My hands have lost their cunning."

Olivia got up from the desk and threw herself down beside

him on the couch. She wound her arms around his neck. "Your hands are still *wonderfully* cunning. I should know."

"Indeed, you should, my love." He looked at Olivia with desire; then a concerned expression crossed his face. "Are we alone here? Or are Darcy and Sloan lurking around somewhere?"

"We're alone," Olivia said, cuddling closer to him. "They went out to visit a hill or a meadow or a river or something."

"Why would anybody visit a meadow?" he teased. "When they could stay in a nice house with a nice bed with a nice bouncy mattress?"

"It's the season for wildflowers," Olivia said pertly. "Aren't you interested in wildflowers?"

"Not at all," said John. "Those kids don't know what they're missing. Shall we go upstairs, Mrs. English?"

"Let's," she agreed.

IT WAS BEAUTIFUL AND ISOLATED in this place. It was like being in Eden, and temptation was in the fragrant spring air like perfume.

The cacti were in blossom. The prickly pears sported fat yellow boutonnieres, and tall white clusters of flowers flared up from the sword-like leaves of the yucca plants.

Darcy and Sloan had hiked from the dirt road to the hill overlooking the green Perdenales River. Now Sloan lay on the quilt beside Darcy in the shade of the mesquite trees. He looked into her eyes. "That was something," he said, touching her face. "You always make it seem like the first day of creation."

"So do you," she said fondly. She brushed his dark hair back from his brow. "I love this place. I love coming back here with you."

They lay in silence for a while. Then she stretched and sighed luxuriously and sat up. A look of regret crossed her face, and she reached for her blouse.

"We should go back. Mama and your father will be wondering what's become of us."

His hand, warm and strong, clamped around her wrist. "I think your mama and my father can amuse themselves just fine," he said. "Why don't you come back here."

The blouse fell from her fingers. She let him draw her down to him again.

"Got to stop and smell the flowers," he said.

She lost herself in his kiss. Around them, the flowers nodded, as if in approval.

HARLEQUIN®
SUPERROMANCE®

You are now entering

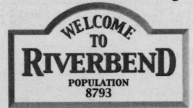

WELCOME TO
RIVERBEND
POPULATION
8793

Riverbend…the kind of place where everyone knows
your name—and your business. Riverbend…home of
the River Rats—a group of small-town sons and
daughters who've been friends since high school.

The Rats are all grown up now. Living their lives and
learning that some days are good and some days
aren't—and that you can get through anything
as long as you have your friends.

Starting in July 2000, Harlequin Superromance brings
you Riverbend—six books about the River Rats and
the Midwest town they live in.

BIRTHRIGHT by **Judith Arnold** (July 2000)
THAT SUMMER THING by **Pamela Bauer** (August 2000)
HOMECOMING by **Laura Abbot** (September 2000)
LAST-MINUTE MARRIAGE by **Marisa Carroll** (October 2000)
A CHRISTMAS LEGACY by **Kathryn Shay** (November 2000)

Available wherever Harlequin books are sold.

HARLEQUIN®
Makes any time special ™

Romance is just one click away!

love scopes

➢ Find out all about your guy in the Men of the Zodiac area.

➢ Get your daily horoscope.

➢ Take a look at our Passionscopes, Lovescopes, Birthday Scopes and more!

join Heart-to-Heart, our interactive community

➢ Talk with Harlequin authors!

➢ Meet other readers and chat with other members.

➢ Join the discussion forums and post messages on our message boards.

romantic ideas

➢ Get scrumptious meal ideas in the Romantic Recipes area!

➢ Check out the Daily Love Dose to get romantic ideas and suggestions.

Visit us online at

www.eHarlequin.com

on Women.com Networks

HARLEQUIN®
SUPERROMANCE

COMING NEXT MONTH

#936 BORN IN A SMALL TOWN • Debbie Macomber, Judith Bowen and Janice Kay Johnson

Here's what small-town dreams are made of! This is a special 3-in-1 collection featuring *New York Times* bestselling author **Debbie Macomber**'s latest Midnight Sons title, *Midnight Sons and Daughters*. There's also a new Men of Glory title from Judith Bowen—*The Glory Girl*—and *Promise Me Picket Fences*—a return to Elk Springs, Oregon, by Janice Kay Johnson.

#937 HOMECOMING • Laura Abbot

Tom Baines, one of Riverbend's favorite sons, has come home to recuperate. After the year he's had, he needs the peace and quiet. More important, he wants to reestablish a relationship with his estranged children. But he never expects to meet Lynn Kendall, a woman unlike any he's ever met. Living in Riverbend might just have its advantages!

Riverbend, Indiana: Home of the River Rats—a group of men and women who've been friends since high school. These are their stories.

#938 MATT'S FAMILY • Lynnette Kent
The Brennan Brothers

Kristen had known the Brennan boys forever. She'd loved Luke as a friend, but she'd been *in love* with soldier Matt Brennan for as long as she could remember. Then Matt was reported missing, presumed dead. Luke persuaded the young, scared and pregnant Kristen to marry him. Slowly they turned their marriage of convenience into a real one. A second baby was born. Then five years later Matt Brennan—the man she'd never stopped loving—came home.... By the author of *Luke's Daughters*.

#939 SNOW BABY • Brenda Novak
9 Months Later

Two strangers spend a snowy night together. Chantel Miller falls for Dillon Broderick, the man who helped and comforted her during the blizzard—and then she discovers that her estranged sister, Stacy, is in love with him. The sister whose affection she's trying to regain... It's a painful coincidence that becomes devastating when Chantel discovers she's pregnant.

#940 THE NEWCOMER • Margot Dalton
Crystal Creek

Is the town of Crystal Creek for sale? Read *The Newcomer* to find out what happens when an eccentric movie star sends Maggie Embree to put in an offer on her behalf. Maggie runs into stiff opposition from the mayor of the town. Now she has to choose between her loyalty to her boss—the woman who helped raise her—and the man she's beginning to fall in love with.

#941 THE CATTLEMAN'S BRIDE • Joan Kilby

If Sarah Templestowe finds the wide-open spaces of central Australia unsettling when she arrives from Seattle, wait until she meets Luke Sampson! He's part owner of the isolated cattle station her father recently willed to her. Laconic and self-reliant, the quintessential outback hero, he's been managing the station for ten years, and he's about to turn Sarah's world even more upside down than her trip Down Under already has.